John Guille Millais

The life and letters of Sir John Everett Millais, president of the Royal Academy

Vol. I

John Guille Millais

The life and letters of Sir John Everett Millais, president of the Royal Academy
Vol. I

ISBN/EAN: 9783337022143

Printed in Europe, USA, Canada, Australia, Japan

Cover: Foto ©Raphael Reischuk / pixelio.de

More available books at **www.hansebooks.com**

The Life and Letters

of

Sir John Everett Millais

The

Life and Letters

of

Sir John Everett Millais

PRESIDENT OF THE ROYAL ACADEMY

BY HIS SON

JOHN GUILLE MILLAIS

AUTHOR OF

"A BREATH FROM THE VELDT," AND "BRITISH DEER AND THEIR HORNS"

WITH 316 ILLUSTRATIONS

VOL. I.

NEW YORK

FREDERICK A. STOKES COMPANY

MDCCCXCIX

𝔘𝔫𝔦𝔳𝔢𝔯𝔰𝔦𝔱𝔶 𝔓𝔯𝔢𝔰𝔰
JOHN WILSON AND SON, CAMBRIDGE, U. S. A

PREFACE

THE task of selecting from such a vast mass of material as has been kindly placed at my disposal by friends and relatives has been no easy one, and I venture to hope that, so far as I may have exceeded my duty as a biographer, the interest of the extraneous matter may, in some measure at least, atone for its admission.

I cannot adequately thank the many friends who have so generously helped me with contributions, or in allowing me the free use of their pictures for these pages. To Messrs. Graves and Son, Thomas Agnew, Arthur Tooth and Sons, Thomas McLean and Sons, and the Fine Art Society my special thanks are due for liberty to avail myself of their copyrights; but most of all am I indebted to my father-in-law, Mr. P. G. Skipwith, for his invaluable assistance in preparing this work for the press.

JOHN GUILLE MILLAIS.

MELWOOD, HORSHAM,
July, 1899.

CONTENTS

CHAPTER I

CONTENTS

CONTENTS

CONTENTS

CHAPTER XII
1865–1880

LIST OF ILLUSTRATIONS

PHOTOGRAVURES

ILLUSTRATIONS

LIST OF ILLUSTRATIONS

THE LIFE AND LETTERS

OF

SIR JOHN EVERETT MILLAIS

CHAPTER I

The birth of Millais — His parents — Early days in St. Heliers — A mother who educates and helps him — School a failure — The Lemprieres — First efforts in Art — The family move to Dinan — The Drum-major's portrait — Return to St. Heliers — Millais goes to London with his mother — Sir Martin Shee's advice — Millais enters Mr. Sass' School, and gains the silver medal of the Society of Arts — His love of fishing — Original amusement — He enters the Royal Academy — Early successes — Anecdotes of the poet Rogers — William Wordsworth — Oxford's attempt on the Queen's life — Millais as an Academy student — General Arthur Lempriere on Millais as a boy — Poem on students' life — Sergeant Thomas — First visit to Oxford — Mr. Wyatt — Mr. Drury — "Cymon and Iphigenia" — "Grandfather and Child."

IT was at Southampton on the 8th of June, 1829, that the late Sir J. E. Millais made his first appearance in the world as the youngest son of Mr. John William Millais, the descendant of an old Norman family resident in Jersey, where for many years he held a commission in the Island Militia. There, according to local tradition, John William Millais and his ancestors had been settled ever since the time of the Conquest. He was a man of fine presence and undeniable talent, being not only a very fair artist but an excellent musician, with command of four or five different instruments. But with all his gifts he was a man of no ambition save where his children were concerned, and desired nothing more than the life he led as a quiet country gentleman. My uncle, William Millais, describes him as a typical old troubadour, who won all hearts by his good looks and charming manners, and was known in his younger days as the handsomest man in the island.

1 — 1

When quite a young man he chanced to meet an English-woman of gentle birth and great natural wit and cleverness, whose maiden name was Evamy, but who was then the widow of a Mr. Hodgkinson; and, falling in love with each other at first sight, they soon afterwards married.

Mrs. Hodgkinson had two sons by her first husband — Henry, who lived a quiet life, and recently left to the nation two of my father's best works; and Clement, who greatly distinguished himself as an explorer in the wilds of Australia. In the old days Clement was the principal A.D.C. of Sir Thomas Mitchell, and himself discovered several gold-fields in Northern Australia.

My grandparents, John William and Emily Mary Millais, at first settled at " Le Quaihouse," just out of St. Heliers, where their

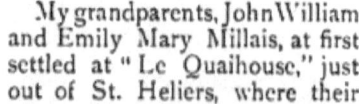

CAPTAIN EDWARD MILLAIS, 1760
(MILLAIS' GRANDFATHER)
From a miniature

daughter Emily Mary was born; but later on they removed to Southampton, where my uncle William Henry and afterwards my father, were added to the family. They presently, however, returned to Jersey, where, at the age of four years, my father's inborn love of Natural History — a love that lasted his lifetime — found means of development. At St. Heliers some choice sand-eels offered an easy capture. The rocks too abounded with novelties in the shape of " slow, sly things with circumspective eyes "; and at the pier-head no end of little fish were waiting to be caught. Here, then, was Elysium to the young naturalist. To one or other of these places he sped away whenever he could escape from parental control, regardless of the admonitions of his mother, whose anxiety on these occasions was hardly compensated by the treasures of the beach with which he stocked all the baths and basins of the household, or by the advance in learning he displayed in naming correctly everything in his collection.

There too, at St. Heliers, his taste for drawing began to show itself. Encouraged by his mother, who quickly discerned the boy's special gift, he devoted much of his time to sketching, and was never more happy than when his pencil was thus engaged. Birds and butterflies proved a great attraction, but it mattered little to him what was the object so long as he could express it on paper. Draw he must, and did at every spare moment.

In his maternal grandfather, John Evamy — a dear old man whom he greatly admired, mainly because of his skill as a fisherman — he found a delightful companion; and one

JOHN WILLIAM MILLAIS (Millais' Father)
In fancy dress.   Circ. 1870

of his earliest sketches, done in pencil at eight years of age, gives an excellent idea of this old gentleman engrossed in his favourite pursuit.

But Millais' truest and most helpful friend was his mother, whose love and foresight did so much to advance his aims and ambition, putting him in the right path from the very outset. She herself undertook the greater part of his education, and, being more gifted than most women, grounded him in history, poetry, literature, etc., knowledge of costume and armour, all of which was of the greatest use to him in his career; indeed, my father used often to say to us in after years, " I owe everything to my mother."

One attempt was made to send him to school, but it ended in miserable failure. Throughout his life restrictions of any sort were hateful to him — what he would not do for love he would not do at all — so when, after two days at school, the master tried to thrash him for disobedience, the boy turned and bit his hand severely — a misdemeanour for which he was

JOHN EVAMY (MILLAIS' MATERNAL UNCLE)
Drawn from life at the age of eight

immediately expelled. A happy day this for him, for his mother then resumed her work of tuition, and her method of teaching, in opposition to that of the old dry-as-dust schools, led the child to love his lessons instead of hating them.

My uncle William made an excellent water-colour portrait of his mother, which I am enabled to give here. The reader will see at a glance her strong resemblance to her boy John Everett, presenting the same clever, determined mouth, and

MARY MILLAIS (Millais' Mother)

From a water-colour by William Millais, executed about the year 1869

the same observant eyes. Nor did the resemblance end here,
for she had also the same great love of painting and music.

Others beside his mother very soon began to see that little
John Everett possessed real genius, not mere ordinary talent;
and one of his uncles was so much impressed with this idea
that he used frequently to say to his children, "Mark my
words, that boy will be a very great man some day, if he
lives."

My father never forgot the good friends of his early days
in Jersey, but cherished a lasting affection and regard for
them. Amongst those most anxious to help in the early
cultivation of his talent was a charming family named
Lempriere, then resident in the island. Philip Raoul
Lempriere, the head of the house and Seigneur of Roselle
Manor, was a man whose personality made itself felt by
everyone with whom he came into contact, his strikingly
handsome appearance being enhanced by the dignity and
kindliness of his manner; and the same might be said in
degree of every member of his family. To know them
intimately was an education in itself; and, happily for my
father, they took a great fancy to him, making him ever
welcome at the house. There, then, he spent much of his
time, and, as I have heard him say, learned unconsciously
to appreciate the beauties of Nature and Art. General
Lempriere, one of the grandsons of the Seigneur, I may
add, figures as "the Huguenot" in the famous picture of
that name, painted in 1852.

Roselle, in a word, proved an endless source of interest
and amusement to the juvenile artist. He could fish when
he liked in ponds well stocked with perch and tench, and in
the park was a fine herd of fallow deer, in which he took
great delight. A drawing of his — perhaps his best at that
date — represents the tragic end of one of those beautiful
creatures that he happened to witness. The circumstance
impressed him deeply and, as he often remarked in after
life, aroused in him the spirit of the chase, even in those
early days and amidst such calm surroundings.

My father's cousin, Miss Benest — a wonderful old lady
of eighty — writes: "When he was only four he was continually at work with pencil and paper, and generally lay
on the floor covering sheets with all sorts of figures."
She also mentions, as significant of the frank and open
mind and the zeal for truth that he retained to the end of

his days, that "when he did anything on a larger scale he used to come to my father, throwing his arms round his neck in his affectionate manner, saying, ' Uncle, *you* do not always praise me as the others do; *you show me the faults.*'"

His brother William was exceedingly clever, but without

SHAKESPEARIAN CHARACTER
Original drawing by Millais at the age of 7½ years

the same application and industry. As a young man he possessed a remarkably fine tenor voice, and a good tenor being as rare in those days as it is now, Mario, after hearing him sing, urged him strongly to go on the stage, saying he would make his fortune. But this was far from his idea of a happy life. He had no ambition to walk the boards, but sang because he loved it, and painted for the same reason, becoming ultimately well known as a water-colour landscape artist. His unselfish admiration for my father knew no bounds; he was always helping and taking care of his younger and more delicate brother, and did much by his cheery optimism and consummate tact to alleviate the hard knocks and petty worries that assailed the young painter whilst struggling to make a name.

In 1835 the family removed to Dinan, in Brittany, where a new interest awaited the budding artist, then in his seventh

HOGARTHIAN CHARACTERS IN A WITNESS-BOX
Original study of expression
The writing on the drawing is that of the artist's mother

year. The poetry of the place, as expressed in its fine mediæval architecture and interpreted by a loving mother, took a great hold upon his imagination, setting his pencil to work at once; but joy of joys to the juvenile mind were the gorgeous uniforms of the French officers stationed in the neighbourhood. Of this period William Millais sends me some interesting notes. He says: " I well remember the time we spent together at Dinan, where our parents resided for two years. We were little boys and quite inseparable, he six years old and I two years his senior. Our greatest delight was to watch the entry of regiments as they passed

through the town to and from Brest, and these occasions
were of frequent occurrence. The roll-call generally took
place in the Place aux Chaines, and each soldier on being
disbanded was presented with a loaf of black bread, which
he stuck on the point of his bayonet and then shouldered
his rifle. We usually sat under the *tilleuls* of the Place
du Guesclin, on a bench overlooking the soldiers and away
from the crowd. On one occasion we noticed an enormous
tambour-majeur, literally burnished with gold trappings, wearing a tall bear-skin and flourishing a huge gold-headed cane,

MÉLÉE IN A BANQUETING-HALL.   1838

to the delight of a lot of little *gamins*. Jack at once produced his sketch-book and pencil, and proceeded to jot down
the giant into his book. Whilst this was going on we were
not aware that two officers were silently creeping towards us,
and we were quite awed when they suddenly uttered loud
ejaculations of astonishment at what they had seen, for they
had evidently been witnesses of the last touch made upon
the drum-major. They patted the little artist on the back,
gave him some money, and asked me where we lived. Our
house was only a stone's-throw off, so we took them up into
the drawing-room, and they talked for some time with my
father and mother, urging them most seriously to send the
child at once to Paris, to be educated in the Arts.

" The officers took the sketch back to barracks with them, and showed it in the mess to their brothers in arms. None of them could believe that it was the work of a boy of six, so bets were taken all round ; and one of them went to fetch little Millais, to prove their words. In fear and trembling he came, and soon showed that he really had done the drawing by making, then and there, a still more excellent sketch — of the colonel smoking a cigar. Those who lost had to give the others a dinner."

SCENE FROM "PEVERIL OF THE PEAK." 1841
This is the most elaborate work of Millais' early years

Leaving Dinan in 1837, the family again went back to St. Heliers for two or three years, where Millais received his first instructions in art from a Mr. Bessel, the best drawing-master in the island. Art was not taught then as it is now, so the boy's originality was curbed for the while by having to copy Julien's life-sized heads. In a very short time, however, the drawing-master told his parents that he could teach their boy nothing more ; the spontaneity of his work was so marked that it was a sin to restrain it, and that they ought to take him at once to London and give him the very best tuition to be had there. To this excellent counsel was added that of the Lemprieres and Sir Hillgrove-Turner, then governor of the island. Next year, therefore, they started for London armed with an introduction to Sir Martin Archer Shee, P. R. A., and coaching from Southampton they fell in with Mr. Paxton (afterwards Sir Joseph Paxton), of whom William Millais writes: "During the journey Mr. Paxton fell asleep, and Jack at once went for him and got him into his book. Just as he had finished the sketch Paxton awoke, and, seeing what had been done, was so astonished that he entered into conversation with my mother, which resulted in a letter of introduction to the President of the Society of Arts, Adelphi, where my brother afterwards went."

Their first visit in London was naturally to Sir Martin Archer Shee, and this is what they heard from him the moment they explained the object of their call: "Better make him a chimney-sweep than an artist!" But Sir Martin had not then seen the boy's drawings. When these were produced he opened his eyes in astonishment, and could hardly believe that they were the production of so childish a hand. At last his doubts were set at rest by little Millais sitting down and drawing the Fight of Hector and Achilles; and then with equal emphasis he recalled his first remark, and declared that it was the plain duty of the parents to fit the boy for the vocation for which Nature had evidently intended him.

That settled the matter. To the lad's great delight leave was obtained for him to sketch in the British Museum, where for several hours a day he diligently drew from the cast; and in the winter of 1838–39 a vacancy was found for him in the best Art Academy of the time — a preparatory school at Bloomsbury, kept by an old gentleman named Henry Sass, a portrait painter of repute, but whose works had failed to catch the fancy of the public. Several of Millais' school-fellows there are still living, and remember him as a small, delicate-looking boy, with a holland blouse and belt and a turn-down collar. Here he was in his element, drawing and painting most of the day, and spending all the time he could spare in outdoor pursuits.

At Mr. Sass', as at most of the schools of that day, a good deal of bullying went on, and one of the students (a big, hulking, lazy fellow, whose name I suppress for reasons which will presently appear) took a special delight in making the boy's life a burden to him. This state of things reached a climax when, at the age of nine, young Millais gained the silver medal of the Society of Arts, for which this youth had also competed. The day following the presentation Millais turned up as usual at Mr. Sass', and after the morning's work was over, H. (the bully), with the help of two other small boys whom he had compelled to remain, hung him head

PORTRAIT OF AN OLD GENTLEMAN
Drawn at the age of nine

downwards out of the window, tying his legs up to the iron of the window-guards with scarfs and strings. There he hung over the street in a position which shortly made him unconscious, and the end might have been fatal had not some passers-by, seeing the position of the child, rung the

door-bell and secured his immediate release. Almost immediately after this H. left the school — possibly to avoid expul-
sion — and failing as an artist, but being strong and of good
physique, he became a professional model, and, curiously
enough, in after years sat to my father for several of his
pictures. Eventually, however, he took to drink and came
to a miserable end, leaving a wife and several children absolutely destitute.

Of the occasion on which Millais received his first medal,
William Millais, who was present, says: " I shall never
forget the Prize-day at the Society of Arts when my brother
had won the silver medal for a large drawing of ' The Battle
of Bannockburn.' He was then between nine and ten years
of age, and the dress the little fellow wore is vividly before
me as I write. He had on a white plaid tunic, with black
belt and buckle; short white frilled trousers, showing bare
legs, with white socks and patent leather shoes; a large white
frilled collar, a bright necktie, and his hair in golden curls.

" When the Secretary, Mr. Cocking, called out '*Mr.* John
Everett Millais,' the little lad walked up unseen by his
Royal Highness the Duke of Sussex, who was giving the
prizes, and stood at his raised desk. After a time the Duke
observed that ' the gentleman was a long time coming up,'
to which the Secretary replied, ' He is here, your Royal
Highness.' The Duke then stood up and saw the boy, and,
giving him his stool to stand upon, the pretty little golden
head appeared above the desk.

" Unfortunately the Duke, being weak as to his eyesight,
could make nothing of the drawing when it was held up to
him, in spite of trying various glasses; but he was assured
that it was a marvellous performance. He patted my
brother's head and wished him every success in his profession, at the same time kindly begging him to remember that
if at any time he could be of service to him he must not
hesitate to write and say so. It so happened that Jack did
avail himself of this kind offer. We had been in the habit
of fishing every year in the Serpentine and Round Pond by
means of tickets given to us by Sir Frederick Pollock, then
Chief Baron; but a day came when this permission was
withheld from everyone, and then my brother wrote to the
Duke's private Secretary, and we were again allowed to fish
there.

" In those days the Round Pond at Kensington was a

MILLAIS, BY JOHN PHILLIP, R.A. 1841

favourite resort of ours. It was not then, as we see it now, arranged in a circle, and tricked out with all the finery of a London lake. The shores were fringed with flags and rushes, and here and there were little bays with water-lilies. There was plenty of honest English mud too, in which the juvenile angler could wade to his heart's content, and had to do so in order to get his line clear of the surrounding reeds. We used to tramp to and from the neighbourhood of Bedford Square, buying our fresh bait at the ' Golden Perch,' in Oxford Street, on the way. We were keen sportsmen,

HUNTING SCENE. 1841

and probably the pleasure we took in it was not lessened by the envy of other little boys to whom the privilege was denied. As the result of these expeditions many fine carp, perch, and roach were captured — at least they appeared so to us in those early days."

My uncle goes on to tell of their home life and the amusements in which he and his brother indulged. They were fond of " playing at National Galleries."

" In 1838-39 we were living in Charlotte Street, Fitzroy Square. I went to a private tutor in the neighbourhood, but my brother never went to school at all. He was very delicate as a child, and was still being entirely educated by my mother, who was an exceptionally clever woman and a great reader.

" We were both of us mad upon Art, and we knew every picture in the National Gallery by heart. In our leisure moments we resolved to start a National Gallery of our own, and we worked daily upon pictures for it. I generally undertook the landscape department, and coined no end of Hoppners, Ruysdaels, Turners, etc., whilst the Titians, Rubens, Paul Veroneses, Correggios and Rembrandts fell to my brother's share. I made all the frames out of tinsel off crackers, and we varnished our specimens to give them the appearance of works in oil.

" The pictures varied in size from a visiting-card to a large envelope. We took off the lid of a large deal box, and prepared the three sides to receive our precious works. There was a dado, a carpet, and seats, and to imitate the real Gallery a curtain ran across the opening.

" What joy it was to us when we thought we had done something wonderful! I remember how we gloated over our Cuyp; a Rembrandt too was my brother's masterpiece, and the use of burnt lucifer matches in the darker parts was most effective, and certainly original. When anyone called to see us it was our greatest pride to exhibit our National Gallery."

At the age of ten Millais was admitted a student of the Royal Academy, the youngest student who ever found entrance within its walls, and during his six years there he carried off in turn every honour the Academy had to bestow. At thirteen he won a medal for a drawing from the antique, at fourteen he began to paint, and at seventeen, after taking the " gold medal " for an oil painting called " The Benjamites Seizing their Brides," he contributed to the annual exhibition a canvas which was placed by a French critic on a level with the best historical work of the year. It was the picture of " Pizarro Seizing the Inca of Peru," and was exhibited some few years ago in the galleries at South Kensington, where it attracted marked attention as the production of so young an artist.*

At the Academy, where he was well treated and became a general favourite, they nicknamed him " The Child," a name that stuck to him for the rest of his life at the Garrick Club. He worked unceasingly, and was universally recognised as a

---

* William Millais says: "James Wallack, the celebrated comedian, whose portrait Sir Charles Eastlake, p.r.a., painted in ' The Brigand,' and who afterwards married my sister, was the model for ' Pizarro.' My father was the priest, and also sat for other figures in the picture."

youthful genius from whom great things were to be expected; but, as the smallest and youngest member of the community, he had to "fag," for all that, and was generally told off to fetch pies and stout for his fellow-students whilst they were at work.*

When he received the gold medal of the Royal Academy many famous men took notice of him, and notably Rogers, the poet, whose brilliant breakfast-parties are now matters of

LOVE SCENE. Water-colour. 1840

history. All the literary lions of the day were to be met there, and at that time things were very different from what they are now. Young men listened respectfully, as they were taught to do, when older and wiser men held forth. Rogers, I have heard my father say, would speak learnedly on some subject for perhaps five minutes, and then, after a pause, would say: " Now, Mr. Macaulay, kindly favour us with

---

* " I was told off," said Millais, " by the other students to obtain their lunch for them. I had to collect 40 or 50 pence from my companions, and go with that hoard to a neighbouring baker's and purchase the same number of buns. It generally happened that I got a bun myself by way of ' commission.' "

your opinion of the subject," whereupon Macaulay would
square up and "orate." While he was talking Rogers, who
was a confirmed invalid, would gradually slip down into his
chair, his servant having to pull him up by the collar
when he wished to speak again. He was extremely kind,
though pompous in manner, and with little or no sense of
humour. If a stranger arrived he would say to his servant,
" Thomas, bring down that volume of *my celebrated poems.*"

He took an almost parental interest in Millais, though
occasionally treating him with a severity that bordered on
the comic. My father hated sugar in his tea, and on more
than one occasion openly expressed his dislike. " Thomas,"
the poet would say, "put three lumps of sugar in Mr.
Millais' tea; he *ought* to like sugar. He is too thin."

Rogers had an MS. missal of great value, of which he
was vastly proud. One day little Millais picked it up to
show it to a young lady. " Boy," roared Rogers from the
other end of the room, almost suffocating himself as he
slipped down into his chair, "can't you speak about a book
without fingering it? How dare you touch my missal !"

One day a poor-looking man, apparently a country clergyman, dressed in a shabby tail-coat, came to thank Rogers for
hospitality before leaving town. As the departing guest
vanished through the door, after shaking hands with the
little artist, the poet turned to Millais, who was standing
near, and said in solemn tones, " Boy, do you know who that
was? Some day you will be proud to say that you once met
William Wordsworth."

In 1895 Mr. Gladstone and my father were the only survivors of these famous parties. A singular circumstance
was that though my mother, who was then a young girl, used
frequently to breakfast at Rogers' house, yet she and my
father never met there.

Referring to these early days, William Millais says: " We
were brought up as very loyal subjects, and our chief delight
was to go to Buckingham Palace to see the Queen and the
Prince Consort start off up Constitution Hill for their daily
drive. On one memorable occasion, when we were the only
people on the footpath, and had just taken off our caps as
the Royal carriage passed, feeling proudly happy that her
Majesty had actually bowed to us, a sudden explosion was
heard, and then another. My father, who had seen what had
caused them, immediately rushed away from us and seized

a man who was just inside the railings of the park, and held
him till some of the mounted escort came to his assistance.
This man was Oxford, who had fired at the Queen, and afterwards proved to be a lunatic. Of course we went immediately to examine the wall, and there saw the marks of the
two bullets, which in a few days, with the aid of sticks and
umbrellas, had multiplied considerably."

As a boy Millais was extremely delicate, and only by slow
degrees and constant attention to the laws of health did he
build up the robust constitution it was his privilege to enjoy
in the later years of his life. It was part of his creed — a
creed he lost no opportunity for impressing upon younger or
less experienced artists — that good health is the first necessity for a man who would distinguish himself in any walk of
life, and that that can only be had by periodical holidays, in
which all thought of business affairs is resolutely cast aside.
To him the breezy uplands of the North, where with rod and
gun he could indulge his love of open-air pursuits, offered the
greatest attraction. Every year, therefore, as soon as he
could afford it, he took a shooting or a fishing in Scotland,
and (except on rare occasions) in the first week of August off
he went for a three months' holiday, no matter how important
the work then in hand, or how tempting any commission that
would interfere with his plan. One instance of this I well
remember. Towards the close of a season of exceptionally
hard work he got a letter from an American millionaire offering him a small fortune if he would cross the Atlantic in
August and paint the writer, his wife, and three children life-
size on one canvas. But he declined at once, remarking
privately that the subjects were not interesting enough to
induce him to give up his holiday.

But to trace his history as a sportsman I must go back to
the days of his pupilage, when during the summer holidays
he and my uncle William (himself an expert fisherman) often
started at daybreak and walked all the way to Hornsey and
back for a day's fishing in the New River. Cricket too was
a great delight, and though the latitude of Gower Street did
not lend itself to progress in the art, they practised after a
fashion, played when they could, and assiduously studied the
game at Lord's every Saturday in the season. That was in
the days when the top-hat affliction permeated even the
cricket field, as shown in a sheet of my father's sketches
made on the ground about this time. Lillywhite is seen

there in all his glory as the first cricketer of the day, his amazing head-gear possibly adding to the awe and admiration with which he was regarded by young and aspiring players.

A letter from William Millais is perhaps worth quoting as showing the straits to which he and his brother were put in their determination to master "England's game," and how they encountered and overcame them. He says: " We used to have fictitious matches under the studio in Gower Street,

SKETCHES MADE AT LORD'S, 1843
With portraits of the famous cricketers, Lillywhite and Minns

where there was a sort of small fives-court, by the light of a feeble gas-burner. We imitated the style of the great bowlers and batters of that day. If the ball hit certain parts of the wall it was a catch, and certain other parts denoted a number of runs. We kept a perfect score, and alternately batted and bowled. These matches used to last three or four days; it was great fun. Our cricket enthusiasm took us to Lord's two or three times a week, and we knew the style of every player."

THE BENJAMITES SEIZING THEIR BRIDES. 1840

On this period of Millais' life an old fellow-student is good
enough to send me the following note: "The Sir John E.
Millais of Presidential days was a very different person from
the lad of thirteen whom, in the autumn of 1843, I encountered

CUPID CROWNED WITH FLOWERS. 1841
Millais' first picture in oils

at the Royal Academy, when, with a host of probationers (that
is, students of the Academy on trial), I entered the Antique
School, and was greeted with shouts of 'Hallo! Millais;
here is another fellow in a collar.' These cries came from
the older students assembled and drawing from the statues,
busts, and what not. Their occasion was myself, then just

upon fifteen years old, who it was my mother's pleasure should wear on the shoulders of his short jacket a white falling collar some four inches wide. It so happened that Millais' mother had a similar fancy, and that being younger and much smaller than I his collar had a goffered edging, which, with his boyish features, light, long, and curling hair, made him appear even younger than he was. Upon the cries ceasing, there arose from the semicircle of students a lightly and elegantly-made youngster wearing such a collar as I have described, a jacket gathered at the waist with a cloth belt, and its clasp in front. With an assured air he crossed the room to where I was standing among the arrivals. He walked round me, inspected me from head to foot, turned on his heel without a word, stepped back to his seat, and went on with his drawing. It so happened that the ever-diligent Millais, though much further advanced in the Academy, and a student in the Life and Painting, condescended from time to time to work among the tyros from the Antique, such as I was. At that time he was exceedingly like the portrait which was painted of him about the date in question, by (I think) Sir E. Landseer;* but there was more 'devil' and less sentiment in the expression of his features. After being inspected, I settled to my work, and forgot all about that ordeal till I found Millais, who was then not more than five feet two inches tall, standing at my side, and, with an air of infinite superiority, looking at my drawing, which he greeted in an undertone as 'Not at all bad.' With such humility as became me I asked his advice about it, and he frankly gave me some good counsel. I ought to have said that, long before this, I had heard of his extraordinary technical skill in drawing and painting, and I reverenced him as the winner of that silver medal which (the first of his Academical honours) had fallen to his lot not long before; but he being a pupil in Sass's school and I a student in the British Museum, or 'Museumite,' so called, I had not come across the P. R. A. to-be.

"Abounding in animal spirits and not without a playful impishness, being very light and small even for his age, Millais was the lively comrade — I had almost said plaything — of the bigger and older students, some of whom had, even in 1843–44, reached full manhood. One of the latter was 'Jack Harris,' a burly and robust personage, a leader in all

* The painter was John Phillip, R.A.

the feats of strength which then obtained in the schools, and
the same who sat to Millais in 1848–49 for his exact portrait
as the elder brother who kicks the dog in the picture of
' Isabella ' now at Liverpool.   Profoundly contrasted as in
every respect their characters were, Millais and ' Jack Harris '
were comrades and playfellows of the closest order at the
Academy.   For example, I remember how, because some

MARY HODGKINSON
Wife of the artist's half-brother.   Circ. 1843

workmen had left a tall ladder against the wall of the school,
nothing would do but on one occasion Harris must carry
Millais, clinging round his neck, to the top of this ladder.
It so happened that just at the moment the door of the room
slowly opened, while no less a person than the keeper entered
and took up his duties by teaching the student nearest the
entrance.   Discipline and respect for Mr. George Jones [the
master at that time] forbade Harris to come down the ladder,

and his safety forbade Millais from letting go his hold.
Doubtless the keeper saw the dilemma, for, without noticing
the culprits, he hastened his progress round the room and
left it as soon as might be, but not before Millais was tired
of his lofty position."

The following lines (discovered amongst my father's
papers) afford an amusing insight into the ways and doings
of Academy students at that period. The writer's name
unfortunately does not appear.

Mr. Jones, it must be observed, delighted in aping the
appearance of the Duke of Wellington as far as he possibly
could.*

> " Remember you the Antique School,
> And eke the Academic Stool,
> Under the tutorship and rule
>   Of dear old Jones,
> Our aged military keeper
> And medal-distribution weeper,
> For whom respect could not be deeper
>   In human bones ;

> " Whose great ambition was to look
> As near as might be like ' the Dook,'
> With somewhat less of nasal hook,
>   And doubtless brains ;
> Who, I imagine, still delights
> To try and look the ghost, o' nights,
> Of him who fought a hundred fights —
>   The Duke's remains ?

> .   .   .   .

> " But to return — to go on talking
> Of those young days when we were walking
> Towards the never-ending chalking
>   From casts, or life —
> Days of charcoal stumps, and crumbs,
> ' Double Elephant,' and ' Plumbs,'
> Within the sound of barrack drums
>   And shrilly fifes ;

* " I may say of Mr. Jones that he was chiefly known as a painter of military
pictures, and in dress and person he so much resembled the great Duke of
Wellington that, to his extreme delight, he was often mistaken for that hero, and
saluted accordingly. On this coming to the ears of the Duke, he said, ' Dear
me ! Mistaken for me, is he ? That's strange, for no one ever mistakes me
for Mr. Jones.' "

My Autobiography and Reminiscences, by W. P. FRITH, R.A.

"Now in the circle gathered round
To hear the learned youth expound
Anatomy, the most profound —
        Our Private Green ;
Now in the Library's retreat,
Upon a fine morocco seat,
And in a comfortable heat,
        A gent, I ween ;

"Tracing armour, and trunk hose,
Legs in tights, with pointed toes ;
Meyrick, Bonner, with *set chose*,
        To *parleyvoo* ;
Studying now and then a print,
An old Sir Joshua Mezzotint,
Or portrait which affords a hint
        Of something new.

"In silence let us gently sneak
Towards the door devoid of creak,
Which leads us back to that Antique,
        Where youth still plods.
For now, behold, the gas is lit,
And nigh a hundred brows are knit,
Where miserable heathens sit,
        Before their gods.

"There from the Premier Charley Fox —
That party with the greasy locks,
Who vainly calls on long-tongued Knox
        To hold his jawings —
Every back is archly bending,
For the Silver Prize contending,
This the latest night for sending
        In the drawings.

"Another minute — give them ten —
To cut these from the boards ; and then,
'Past eight o'clock, please, gentlemen,'
        Shouts little Bob.
And in the Folio (very cheap !)
The work of months is in a heap,
Not worth the wages of a sweep
        For one small job.

"But now to times a little later,
When first we drew upstairs from Natur',
When we were passing that equator
        Of days scholastic ;
When we were nightly stew'd or fried
With bald-pates glistening by our side,
And felt ourselves, with conscious pride,
        Beyond the Plastic.

HATFIELD HOUSE. 1844

"We saw the graceful Wild recline
  Exclaiming, 'Oh ! by George, how fine,'
  And with the thumb describe a line
      In aerial wave —
  The right and proper thing to do,
  It mattered not whate'er we drew —
  Her, or the sad Cymmon Meudoo,
      As captive slave.

      .   .   .   .   .

"Enough ! I feel I'm going astray
  From dear old Mrs. Grundy's way ;
  And what her followers may say
      I take to heart.
  Yet, should these lines provoke a smile —
  A moment of the day beguile —
  I 'll maybe send you, in this style,
      A second part."

With so much work to do the little artist had hardly time
to make any new acquaintances outside of those whom he
met daily at the Academy; nevertheless he managed to
occasionally see his two Jersey friends, Arthur and Harry
Lempriere, for they were at school at Brighton, and frequently visited London during their holidays. To Arthur —
now Major-General Arthur Lempriere — I am indebted for
the following note of his recollections of Millais as a boy: —

" I remember Sir J. E. Millais when I was quite a small boy at school at Brighton, where he used to write to me and my brother Harry most beautiful letters, all illustrated and the words in different coloured inks. One of those letters began 'My little dears'; but instead of writing the word 'dears,' a number of deer were drawn, and so on through the whole of a Christmas story, in which he introduced coloured drawings of coaches and horses, travellers, games, etc.*

VIEW FROM MILLAIS' FORMER HOME, NEAR St. HELIERS, JERSEY
Water-colour, executed during a visit in 1844

" We always called him ' Johnny,' and he constantly spent the holidays with us at our home at Ewell, Surrey. My father and mother and all our family were very fond of him, as well as he of us.

" He seemed always, when indoors, to have a pen, pencil, or brush in his hand, rattling off some amusing caricature or other drawing. He was very active and strong, and blessed with a most pleasing, good-tempered, and gentlemanly manner. During the many years I knew him I never once recollect his losing his temper or saying an unkind

* This letter, illustrated with little water-colours, was exhibited in the Millais Exhibition, 1898.

SKETCHES OF ARMOUR

John Everett Millais Del.

COVER OF MILLAIS' BOOK ON ARMOUR. 1845.

word to anyone, and we all really looked upon him quite as a brother.

"I have heard my father say that my uncle, Mr. Philip Lempriere, of Royal Jersey, gave Sir J. E. Millais his first colour-box.

"It was in 1847 that I remember his drawing all the Lempriere family at Ewell standing round a table in the

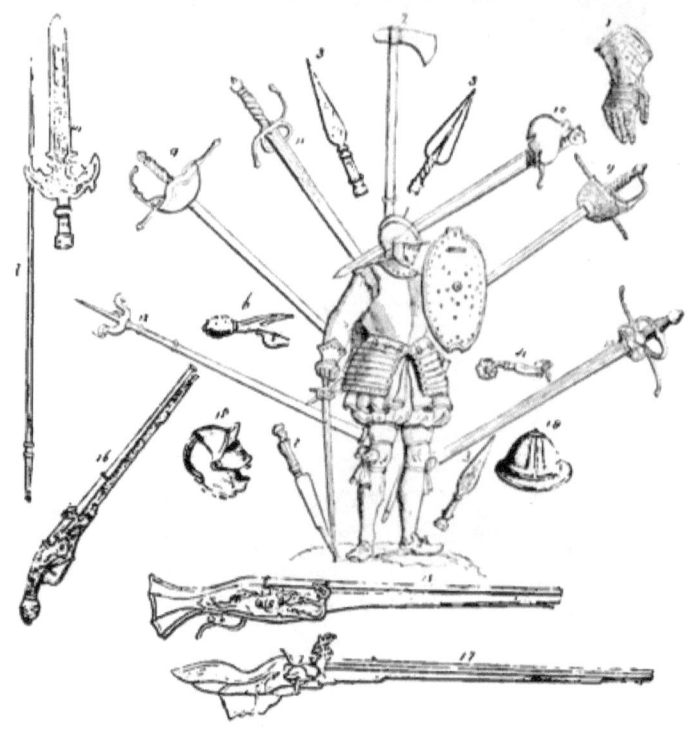

A PAGE FROM MILLAIS' BOOK OF ARMOUR. 1844

drawing-room, and watching eagerly a Twelfth-cake being cut by my eldest sister. It was all so cleverly grouped, and included my father and mother, my five brothers, seven sisters, myself, and himself. It was a picture we all greatly valued, as, in addition to the clever grouping, the likenesses were so excellent.

"Millais' power of observation, even when a boy, was marvellous. After walking out with him and meeting people he would come home and draw an exact likeness of almost anyone he happened to have met. He was also well up in the anatomy of a horse, and knew exactly where every vein and bone should be, and was very fond of drawing them."

In 1845 Millais happened to become acquainted with a certain Serjeant Thomas, a retired lawyer given to trading

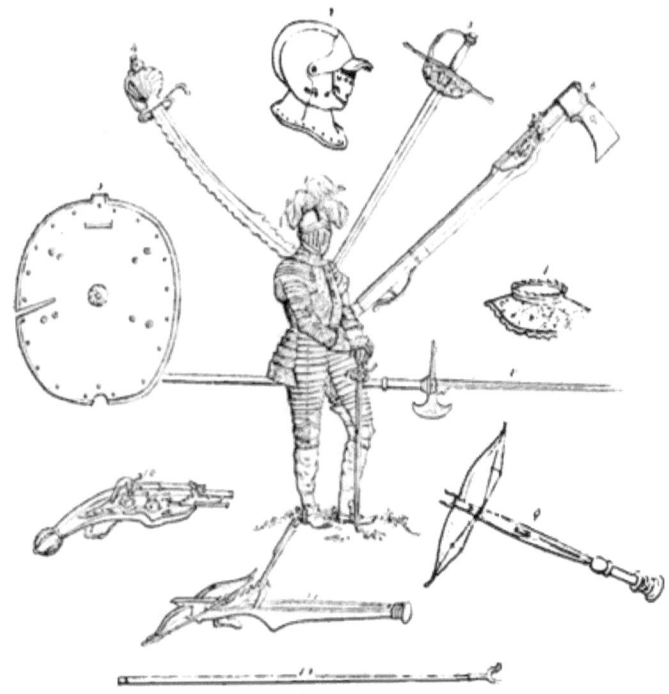

A LEAF FROM MILLAIS' BOOK OF ARMOUR. 1844

in works of art. Recognising his genius, and knowing that he was very poor, Thomas offered him £100 a year to come to his house every Saturday and paint small pictures or backgrounds as might be required. The terms seemed fair enough, and in the end a contract was drawn up by the lawyer and duly signed, binding Millais to serve in this way for two years. Little did he know or think of the galling yoke that was now hung upon his neck. Thomas, who as a picture-dealer got about cent. per cent. profit out of his

1—3

work, worried him beyond measure by his constant inter-
ference, his restrictive rules, and his general insolence of
manner. At last — long before the two years were over —
things came to a crisis. One Saturday morning — not quite
for the first time — Millais came to his work some ten minutes
late, when Thomas attacked him furiously, winding up a
long harangue with a personal remark that stung him to the
quick. He had just arranged his palette with fresh oil-
colours, and in a moment it was sent flying at his employer's
head. Happily for the head it was a bad shot; the palette
struck against the wall, and then slowly descended to the
floor. A violent slamming of the door announced Millais'
departure and his determination never to enter the house
again. They made it up, however, later on. Thomas
agreed to increase the pay to £150 a year, and for a short
time longer Millais continued his work. Finally, however,
he gave it up, though offered far higher terms as an inducement to stay.

Some forty years passed away, and one Sunday morning,
after a long walk with Mr. Henry Wells, R.A., Millais
accompanied him to his studio in Stratford Place. Noticing
a peculiar expression in his face, Mr. Wells said, "What
are you looking at? You seem to know the place."
"Know it!" said Millais, after a long pause, "I should
think I do. Why, this is the very room in which Serjeant
Thomas sweated me, and over there (pointing to one end
of the studio) I still seem to see the palette I threw at his
head, with the paint-mark it left on the wall paper as it
slid slowly down to the floor."

One of the most interesting relics of this period is the
first cheque that the young artist received. It is for £5
("Pay to Master Millais for a sketch"), and signed by
Serjeant Ralph Thomas, dated February 28th, 1846. The
recipient seems to have been so delighted with this sudden
acquisition of wealth that, instead of cashing the cheque
at once, he sat down and made a sketch of himself in his
painting dress on the back of it. It is now in the possession
of Mr. Standen, the owner of "Cymon and Iphigenia."

It was in the summer of 1846 that Millais first travelled
down to Oxford, where he stayed with his half-brother,
Henry Hodgkinson, who lived in that town. One of the
people whose acquaintance he made there was a dealer in
works of art named Wyatt — a remarkable man in many

ways, and one of nature's gentlemen. He took an immediate fancy to " Johnny Millais," and between the years
1846 and 1849 the young artist made frequent visits to
Oxford as his guest.

In a wing of his house was a certain room that Millais used
to occupy, and on the glass window may still be seen two
designs he made in oils, one representing " The Queen of

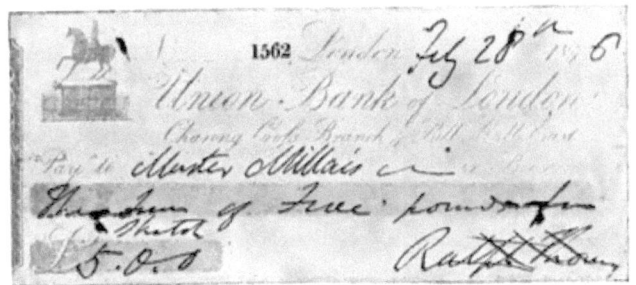

A PHOTOGRAPH OF THE FIRST CHEQUE RECEIVED BY MILLAIS
The young artist was so delighted at receiving this reward that he at once sat down and
made the above sketch of himself on the back of the cheque

Beauty," and the other " The Victorious Knight." At this
period it seems he had quite a mania for drawing; even at
the dinner table he could not remain idle. When no one
was looking he would take out a pencil and begin making
sketches on whatever was nearest to his hand. " Take a
piece of paper, Johnny," Mr. Wyatt would say, " take a
piece of paper. We cannot have the tablecloth spoiled."
" Johnny " was accordingly handed paper to relieve his
superfluous energy, and the number of sketches done at
table, and now in the possession of Mr. Standen (who

married Mr. Wyatt's granddaughter), bears witness to his
ceaseless industry.

Here, too, in 1846 he made the acquaintance of Mr.
Drury, of Shotover, a quaint, benevolent old gentleman,
who loved the fine arts and everything connected with them.
He made a great pet of the young artist, and insisted on
his accompanying him wherever he went in his pony-cart,

MARY MILLAIS (AFTERWARDS MRS. WALLACK). *Circ.* 1844

for being a huge man and a martyr to gout he could not
move without his "trap." Nothing could exceed his kindness to Millais. He gave him a gun, and allowed him
to shoot over his property and to make the place his home
whenever he cared to come. There are several sketches by
Millais of old Mr. Drury and himself taking their toddles
together — done just in a few lines, but (I am told by those
who saw them at the time) highly characteristic.

William Millais tells us something of Mr. Drury and

his peculiar ways. He says, " My brother often went to stay at Shotover Park, and on one occasion I was invited there too for a fortnight. There was no one with Mr. Drury in the huge mansion except his niece, and we boys had the run of the place to our hearts' content, fishing and shooting wherever we liked.

" It is not easy to forget my first impressions there. I

TITLE-PAGE OF A BOOK OF POEMS. 1845

was informed by a stately old butler that 'Master Millais was engaged just then with the master.' I entered a darkened room, where the old invalid could just be seen sitting up in bed with a tallow dip in one hand and a square of glass in the other. He was moving the flame of the candle all over the under side of the greased surface of the glass, which was gradually becoming black with smoke; on this sheet of glass my brother had drawn figures of angels in all positions. I had evidently entered at the supreme moment, for our host, catching sight of me, cried out, '.Ah, ah! we 've got it; you are just in time to see the New Jerusalem.' Upon examination, there really was a certain fascination about the appearance of this extraordinary 'Kalotype,' as he called it, but which might more appropriately have been called a 'tallow-type.'

"The dear old man was under the morbid impression that all his relatives wished him dead, so as to inherit his fortune, and for this reason he made a large 'Kalotype' of the subject, which was most ghastly. I cannot describe it exactly, but remember that a coffin occupied the centre of the picture, whilst a regular scrimmage was going on all round. This design was carried out by my brother under his directions. I shall never forget Mr. Drury's kindness to us boys. He completely spoilt us. I used to sing a great deal, and he expressed the greatest delight at listening whilst I accompanied myself on the organ in the large hall, where the gruesome 'Kalotype' occupied a conspicuous place."

In 1847, competition being invited for cartoons for the decoration of Westminster Hall, Millais sent in a huge canvas which he called "The Widow's Mite." Except "Pizarro," it was the only picture that he ever executed on conventional lines, the figures in shadow being piled and grouped up to the culminating point, where Christ stands against a blaze of light, and addressing Himself to St. John, calls his attention to the woman's act of unselfishness. It was, however, voted "intellectually deficient, lacking the true note of grandeur when Millais was left to himself." This big canvas, which monopolised all the available space in his studio and occupied the young artist the greater part of the year, had as competitors the works of older and stronger men of the day — G. F. Watts, Cope, Armitage, Sir John Tenniel, and others; and I am told by a distinguished artist that "because she [the widow] holds by the hand a little nude child, it set the critics somewhat against the work, as displaying such 'bad taste.'" For some years it was exhibited in the Pantheon in Oxford Street. Ten feet seven by fourteen feet three was not quite the thing for the "show parlours" of the day, so it was cut up and sold in bits. Mr. Spielmann says that one of these sections is now at Tynemouth and the other in the United States, but I have since heard that it was distributed in still smaller pieces.

PIZARRO SEIZING THE INCA OF PERU. 1845

First exhibited picture painted by Millais, executed at the age of 16

" Cymon and Iphigenia " (painted in 1847) was purchased by Mr. Wyatt in 1848, and the dealer was so pleased with it that he asked Millais to come down in the following year and paint a portrait of himself and his grandchild. This was accordingly done, and the portrait is now in the possession of Mr. James Wyatt.[*]

The picture, " Grandfather and Child," is interesting as showing the artist's transition from the technique of " Cymon " of the previous year to the more distinctly Pre-Raphaelite

MR. DRURY AND MILLAIS TAKE THE AIR. 1848.

and technically correct " Woodman's Daughter." A critic says of it: "The infinite patience and imitative skill in draughtmanship, the brilliancy of execution, and the power of reproducing the brightness of sunlight, have manifestly been acquired before the lesson had been learned of harmonious effect and of subordinating the parts to the whole. This portrait of Mr. Wyatt, the print and picture dealer and frame-maker of Oxford, who died in 1853, is unflinchingly true and as matter-of-fact, despite its character, as the flowers in the room and in the garden, or the family china in the

* An excellent copy of this work, now in the possession of Mr. Standen, was made in 1850 by William Millais. Millais also painted Mrs. Wyatt and her child, and (in 1877) Mr. James Wyatt.

case behind him.   It has all been set down with pitiless and remorseless solicitude.   The quaint little Dutch doll-like child has received the painter's most earnest attention, and the head of Mr. Wyatt has been stippled up as carefully as that of Mr. Combe, at Oxford."

Mr. Spielmann's account of the " Cymon " is not quite correct, either as to its subject or its history.   As to its subject, it is certainly not a " riotous dance," and its actual history is as follows:

In the spring of 1852, when it was still in Mr. Wyatt's possession, Millais saw it and suggested some improvements, which the owner willingly allowed him to carry out.   He took it back, therefore, to Gower Street, and having (as he says in a letter) " repainted the sky and touched up the grass and foliage, draperies and effects," he returned it to Mr. Wyatt in the following December.   For its subsequent history I am indebted to a letter from Mr. Standen, the present owner, who says: " When Mr. Wyatt died, in 1853,

STUDY OF AN ACTOR
Executed in Sadler's Wells Theatre, 1845

the best of his pictures and effects were sold at Christie's on July 4th, 1853, your father's picture of ' Cymon ' figuring largely in the catalogue.   Mr. George Wyatt, the second son, bought it for himself, and gave 350 guineas for it. The picture was then taken to Newport, Isle of Wight, where he lived, and it remained there unseen till he died, in 1892.   He left it to me by his will, together with many other interesting works."

CHAPTER II

PRE-RAPHAELITISM: ITS MEANING AND ITS HISTORY

First meeting of Hunt and Millais — The pedantry of Art — Hunt admitted to the R.A. — They work together in Millais' studio — Reciprocal relief — The birth of Pre-Raphaelitism — The name chosen — The meeting of Hunt and D. G. Rossetti — First gathering of the Brotherhood — The so-called influence of Rossetti — Millais explains — The critics at sea — D. G. Rossetti — Ruskin — Max Nordau — The aims of Pre-Raphaelitism — Cyclographic Club — Madox Brown — " The Germ " — Millais' story.

IN this chapter I propose to devote myself exclusively to the history and progress of the Pre-Raphaelite movement, with which Millais was so intimately connected in the early years of his life. Those therefore who are not interested in this subject will do well to pass on at once to Chapter III.

In the art history of this century probably no movement has created so great a sensation as that which is commonly known as Pre-Raphaelitism. For years it was on everybody's tongue and in every newspaper of the day, and after the excitement it occasioned had died out numerous pens were engaged in tracing its history according to their lights; but to this day the actual facts are known but to very few. I have them from the best possible authority — the originators themselves, my father and Mr. Holman Hunt.

How these two men first came together was graphically described to me in a long talk I had with Mr. Hunt shortly after my father's death. He said, " The first time I saw Millais was at the prize-giving at the R.A. in 1838. There was much speculation amongst the students as to who would gain the gold medal for a series of drawings from the antique, and it was generally considered that a man, thirty years of age, named Fox, would be the successful competitor. All voices were hushed when Mr. Jones mounted the steps and read out the name of

43

John Everett Millais.   Immense cheering followed, and
little Millais was lifted up at the back of the auditorium
and carried on the shoulders of the students to the
receiving desk.   Fox, who only got the third prize,
refused to get up when his name was called; but the

CHILDHOOD.   1845

YOUTH.   1845

students would not allow this: they made him go up and
receive his medal."

Later on Mr. Holman Hunt, who, though he had worked
very hard, had failed to get into the Royal Academy, was
drawing one day in the East Room by himself.   "Suddenly,"
said he, "the doors opened, and a curly-headed lad came
in and began skipping about the room; by-and-by he

danced round until he was behind me, looked at my
drawing for a minute, and then skipped off again. About
a week later I found the same boy drawing from a cast in
another room, and returned the compliment by staring at
his drawing. Millais, who of course it was, turned round

MANHOOD. 1845

AGE. 1845

suddenly and said, 'Oh, I say, you're the chap that was
working in No. 12 the other day. You ought to be in the
Academy.'

"This led to a long talk, during which Millais said that
he was much struck by the drawing which he had seen
me working at, and that there was not the least doubt that
if a drawing or two like that were shown for probationer-

ship, I should be admitted at once. When I asked what he thought was the best way of doing the drawings, he replied, ' Oh, I always do mine in line and stump, although it is n't conventional.' "

After this the two boys fell into a discussion on the conventionality and pedantry of art as displayed in the paintings of the day, and it was evident that in both their minds had sprung up a sense of dissatisfaction and the idea of rejecting what they considered to be false and stunted.

A year went by. Mr. Hunt was admitted to the Royal Academy, and then had frequent opportunities for talking to his friend Millais. One evening, some two years later, it came out in the course of conversation that while Millais was painting the " Pizarro," already referred to, Mr. Hunt was engaged at home on a picture for exhibition at the British Institution — a notable incident as marking the first occasion on which either artist painted a picture for exhibition.

Another year passed, and the young artists were in the full swing of their work, Mr. Hunt painting hard at his " Porphyro," and Millais at " Cymon and Iphigenia," a picture in which he seems to have been much influenced by Etty, the only man of the old school whom he really admired. After one of their many talks on originality in art, or rather the absence of it at that time, Millais said to Mr. Hunt, " It is quite impossible to get out pictures done in time for the Royal Academy, unless we sit up and work all night in the last week. Let us paint together in my studio, and then we can encourage each other and talk over our ambitions." This was agreed upon, and from that time the two boys began to study side by side. How tremendously in earnest they were may be gathered from the fact that it was no uncommon thing for them to work on far into the night, sometimes even till four or five in the morning ; this, too, night after night till the sending-in day.

There are always some parts of a picture that an artist hates doing. After a month or two Millais got quite sick of painting the draperies of the girls in his picture; so one evening he turned to his companion and said, "If you will do some of these beastly draperies for me, I 'll paint a head or two in your picture for you "— an offer that was at once accepted. In this way they relieved each other upon occasion, and it is curious to notice how alike their work was in those days ; so much so, that when Hunt examined

"CYMON AND IPHIGENIA." 1847

By Permission of James Standen

the picture in the Millais Exhibition of 1898 he could not distinguish the parts he had painted.

It was from these evening *séances*, and the confidence engendered by the free interchange of thought, that sprang the determination of these youths to leave the beaten track of art and strike out a new line for themselves. Raphael, the idol of the art world, they dared to think, was not altogether free from imperfections. His Cartoons showed this, and his " Transfiguration " still further betrayed the falsity of his methods. They must go back to earlier times for examples of sound and satisfactory work, and, rejecting the teaching of the day that blindly followed in his footsteps, must take Nature as their only guide. They would go to her, and her alone, for inspiration ; and, hoping that others would be tempted to join in their crusade against conventionality, they selected as their distinctive title the term " Pre-Raphaelites."

" Each for the joy of the working, and each in his separate star,
  Shall draw the Thing as he sees It for the God of Things as They Are."

" It was in the beginning of the year 1848," says Mr. Holman Hunt, " that your father and I determined to adopt a style of absolute independence as to art-dogma and convention : this *we* called ' Pre-Raphaelitism.' D. G. Rossetti was already my pupil, and it seemed certain that he also, *in time*, would work on the same principles. He had declared his intention of doing so, and there was beginning to be some talk of other artists joining us, although in fact some were only in the most primitive stages of art, such as William Rossetti, who was not even a student.

" Meanwhile, D. G. Rossetti, himself a beginner, had not got over the habit (acquired from Madox Brown) of calling our art ' Early Christian ' ; so one day, in my studio, some time after our first meeting, I protested, saying that the term would confuse us with the German Quattro Centists. I went on to convince him that our real name was ' Pre-Raphaelites,' a name which we had already so far revealed in frequent argument that we had been taunted as holding opinions abominable enough to deserve burning at the stake. He thereupon, with a pet scheme of an extended co-operation still in mind, amended my previous suggestion by adding to our title of ' Pre-Raphaelite ' the word ' Brotherhood.' "

I — 4

Hunt, it should be explained, first met Rossetti in the Royal Academy schools, where as fellow-students they occasionally talked together. Rossetti, however, was an intermittent attendant rather than a methodical student, and presently, wearying of the work, he gave it up and took to literature, hoping to make a living by his pen. Here again he was disappointed. His poems, charming as many of them were, did not meet with the wide acceptance he had hoped for, and in a fit of despondency he came to Hunt and begged him to take him into his studio. But Holman Hunt could not do this — he was far too busy working for a livelihood, with little time to spare for the indulgence of his own taste as an artist; but he laid down a plan of work to be followed by Rossetti in his own home, and promised to visit him there and give him all the help he could.

Not satisfied with this, Rossetti betook himself to Madox Brown, whose style of painting he admired, and who, he hoped, would teach him the technicalities of his art, while allowing him free play in all his fancies. Madox Brown, however, had been through the mill himself, and knew there was no short cut to success. So, much to the disgust of Rossetti, he set him to paint studies of still-life, such as pots, jugs, etc. By-and-by this became intolerable to a man of Rossetti's temperament, so he once more returned to Hunt, and begged him to take compassion on him; and at last, moved by his appeal, Hunt consented.

These are Hunt's words on the subject: "When D. G. Rossetti came to me he talked about his hopes and ideals, or rather his despair, at ever being able to paint. I, however, encouraged him, and told him of the compact that Millais and I had made, and the confidence others had in our system. Rossetti was a man who enthusiastically took up an idea, and he went about disseminating our programme as one to be carried out by numbers. He offered himself first, as he knew that Millais had admired his pen-and-ink drawings. He then suggested as converts Collinson, his own brother William, who intended to take up art, and Woolner, the sculptor. Stephens should also be tried, and it struck him that others who had never done anything yet to prove their fitness for art reformation, or even for art at all, were to be taken on trust. Your father then invited us all to spend the evening in his studio, where he showed us engravings from the Campo Santo, and other

somewhat archaic designs. These being admired much by
the new candidates, we agreed that it might be safe to accept
the additional four members on probation; but, in fact, it
really never came to anything."

The first meeting, at which terms of co-operation were
seriously discussed, was held on a certain night in 1848,
at Millais' home in Gower Street, where the young artist
exhibited, as examples of sound work,
some volumes of engravings from the
frescoes of Benozzo Gozzoli, Orcagna,
and others now in the Campo Santo
at Pisa.

"Now, look here," said Millais,
speaking for himself and Hunt, who
were both jealous of others joining
them without a distinct understanding
of their object, "this is what the
Pre-Raphaelite clique should follow."
The idea was eagerly taken up, and
then, or shortly afterwards, William
Rossetti, Woolner, F. G. Stephens
(now an Art critic), and James Collinson joined the Brotherhood — the
P.-R. B., as it was now called.

Arthur Hughes, Frederic Sandys,
Nöel Paton, Charles Collins, and
Walter Deverell also sympathised
with their aims, and were more or
less working on the same lines.
Coventry Patmore, the poet, although
in close association with many of the
Brotherhood, was not himself a member, as the association was strictly
limited to working artists.

PENCIL DESIGN FOR
PRE-RAPHAELITE ETCHING
Intended for *The Germ.* 1849

Writing on this subject in the
Contemporary Review of May, 1880,
Mr. Holman Hunt says: "Outside of the enrolled body
[the P.-R. B.] were several artists of real calibre and enthusiasm, who were working diligently with our views
guiding them. W. H. Deverell, Charles Collins, and
Arthur Hughes may be named. It was a question whether
any of them should be elected. It was already evident
that to have authority to put the mystic monogram upon

their paintings could confer no benefit on men striving to earn a position. We ourselves even determined for a time to discontinue the floating of this red rag before the eyes of infuriated John Bull, and we decided it was better to let our converts be known only by their works, and so nominally Pre-Raphaelitism ceased to be. We agreed to resume the open profession of it later, but the time had not yet come. I often read in print that I am now the only Pre-Raphaelite; yet I can't use the distinguishing letters, for I have no Brotherhood."

And now perhaps I may as well give my father's version of the matter as gathered from his own lips in 1896, the year when he was elected as President of the Royal Academy. At that time the papers, of course, had much to say about his art life; and, finding that some of them referred pointedly to D. G. Rossetti's influence on the style and character of his work, I asked him to tell me exactly what were his relations with Rossetti, and how far these comments were correct.

"I doubt very much," he said, "whether any man ever gets the credit of being quite square and above-board about his life and work. The public are like sheep. They follow each other in admiring what they don't understand [*Omne ignotum pro magnifico*], and rarely take a man at what he is worth. If you affect a mysterious air, and are clever enough to conceal your ignorance, you stand a fair chance of being taken for a wiser man than you are; but if you talk frankly and freely of yourself and your work, as you know I do, the odds are that any silly rumour you may fail to contradict will be accepted as true. That is just what has happened to me. The papers are good enough to speak of me as a typical English artist; but because in my early days I saw a good deal of Rossetti — the mysterious and un-English Rossetti — they assume that my Pre-Raphaelite impulses in pursuit of light and truth were due to him. All nonsense! My pictures would have been exactly the same if I had never seen or heard of Rossetti. I liked him very much when we first met, believing him to be (as perhaps he was) sincere in his desire to further our aims — Hunt's and mine — but I always liked his brother William much better. D. G. Rossetti, you must understand, was a queer fellow, and impossible as a boon companion — so dogmatic and so irritable when opposed. His aims and

GRANDFATHER AND CHILD

By permission of James H. Yott

ideals in art were also widely different from ours, and it was
not long before he drifted away from us to follow his own
peculiar fancies. What they were may be seen from his
subsequent works. They were highly imaginative and
original, and not without elements of beauty, but they were
not Nature. At last, when he presented for our admiration
the young women which have since become the type of
Rossettianism, the public opened their eyes in amazement.
'And this,' they said, 'is Pre-Raphaelitism!' It was nothing
of the sort. The Pre-Raphaelites had but one idea — to
present on canvas what they saw in Nature; and such
productions as these were absolutely foreign to the spirit
of their work.

"The only one of my pictures that I can think of as
showing what is called the influence of Rossetti is the
'Isabella,' in which some of the vestments were worked
out in accordance with a book of mediæval costumes which
he was kind enough to lend me. It was Hunt — not Rossetti
— whom I habitually consulted in case of doubt. He was
my intimate friend and companion; and though, at the time
I am speaking of, all my religious subjects were chosen and
composed by myself, I was always glad to hear what he
had to say about them, and not infrequently to act upon
his suggestions. We were working together then, and
constantly criticised each other's pictures."

The friendly intercourse between Millais and D. G.
Rossetti lasted but four years, from 1848 to 1852. From
1852 to 1854 they met occasionally, but after that they rarely
came into contact, and in 1856 even these casual meetings came to an end. One reads then with a smile such
observations as this in Mr. Spielmann's *Millais and his
Works* (1898): — "This is no time to examine the principles
and the bearings of this oft-discussed mission of eclectics;
but it may at least be pointed out how clear a proof of what
can be done by co-operation, even in art, are the achievements of the school. Millais' great pictures of that period
— in many qualities really great — are certainly the com-
bination of the influence of others' powers besides his own.
His is the wonderful execution, the brilliant drawing; but
Dante Rossetti's perfervid imagination was on one side
of him, and Holman Hunt's powerful intellect and resolution
were on the other; while, perhaps, the analytical mind
of Mr. William Rossetti and the literary outlook of Mr.

F. G. Stephens were not without influence upon his work.
In a few short years these supports were withdrawn from
Millais' art, in which we find the execution still, *but where—
at least in the same degree — the intellect or the imagination?*"
The "supports," as Mr. Spielmann calls them, never existed; and as to "intellect" and "imagination," is there nothing of these in "Ferdinand lured by Ariel," "Mariana," "The
Blind Girl," "L'Enfant du Regiment," or "The Woodman's
Daughter," with none of which had Rossetti any concern?
Indeed, as to the three last-named pictures, I think I am
right in saying that Rossetti never saw them until they were
hung on the Academy walls. The "Huguenot," too, and
the "Ophelia" were seen but once by him when the
paintings were in process, and that was at Worcester Park
Farm, when he and Madox Brown called and expressed their
approval. And now I leave it to my readers to say whether
the "Isabella" (the only pure mediæval subject) surpasses
in point of design, execution, or sentiment such of Millais'
later works as "The Rescue," "The Order of Release,"
"The Proscribed Royalist," or fifty others that could be
named. My father hated humbug; and if Rossetti had
been the guiding spirit of his works, as certain critics
represent, he would have been the first to acknowledge it.*
It was the poetry of Nature that appealed to him — the love,
hope, sweetness, and purity that he found there — and it was
the passionate desire to express what he felt so deeply that
spurred him on from the beginning to the end of his art life.
The distinguishing characteristics of Pre-Raphaelite
workers are well set forth by Mr. Kennedy in a recent
article in that excellent magazine *The Artist.* He says,
"The three chief members of the Pre-Raphaelite Brotherhood — Rossetti, Millais, and Holman Hunt — were men of
personalities and endowments that were striking in the
extreme — born makers of epochs, men who, whatever the
vocation that they had elected to follow, would undoubtedly
have left shaping traces of their individualities upon it.
"And, to set themselves to work in triple harness, they
were a trio of a singular diversity of aims and of gifts; one
may add of destinies. Quite extraordinary was the dis-
similarity between the kinds of success attained by each of
them. Millais trod swiftly and straightly the path of popular

* It is a significant fact that in my father's letters of this period (1849-1853),
the name of D. G. Rossetti is hardly ever mentioned.

approbation and academic honours, culminating finally in
the highest dignity that the Royal Academy has to bestow.
Rossetti and Holman Hunt, after the first, held themselves
completely aloof from the Academy and all its works.
Alike in this, how different were their fames in all else.
During the larger portion of his working life Rossetti's
achievements in painting were absolutely undreamed of by
the larger public, were accessible only sparsely and with
difficulty to his admirers even outside of a limited circle of
patrons and private friends. To a good many, I fancy,
Mr. Swinburne's Notes upon the Academy of 1865, describing, amongst others, Sandys' 'Medea' and Rossetti's
'Lilith,' contained the first intimation that Rossetti the
poet was also Rossetti the painter. Holman Hunt, upon
the other hand, had at one time a popular vogue at least
as great as that of Millais, and his painted work excited
emotions and enthusiasms of a more decided intensity.
Those whose memories can be made to extend back to
the period when 'The Finding of our Saviour in the
Temple' was being exhibited in the provinces, will recall
the vividness of the impression that it made upon the
religious public of its day. . . . They found in Holman
Hunt's paintings something of a revelation. Its obvious
sincerity, its intensity of conviction, its determined realisation of the scene in every minutest detail of its setting,
affected profoundly all who were capable of being deeply
stirred by the subject depicted.

" Millais was gifted with a sense of sight of crystalline clear-
ness to which Nature made a perpetual and brilliant appeal;
he had a hand that, even in childhood, was singularly skilful
to record the impressions of the eye. And his hand had
been severely trained, first by the prescribed academic
methods, and later by the minutely elaborate labour of his
Pre-Raphaelite work, until it set down facts almost with the
facility with which the eye perceived them. What, then,
was Millais the Pre-Raphaelite doing in that particular
galère? How came this straightforward depictor of what
he saw before him to link himself with idealists and
dreamers of dreams? It was probably the earnestness and
the devotion to the nature of the movement that attracted
the youthful Millais, and also the scope that its conscientious
minuteness of finish afforded him for the display of his even
then astonishing technical powers."

As to Rossetti, the fact is he was never a Pre-Raphaelite
at heart. Himself a man of great originality, and a free-
thinker in matters of Art, he was captivated by the independent spirit of the Brotherhood, and readily cast in his lot
with them. But it was only for a time. By degrees their
methods palled upon his taste, and not caring any longer to
uphold them before the public, he broke away from his old
associates, determined to follow the peculiar bent of his
genius, which taught him *not* to go to Nature for his inspira-
tions, but to follow rather the flights of his own fancy. His
subsequent career is sufficient evidence of that. Only two

PRE-RAPHAELITE SKETCH. 1850
Probably the artist's first idea of " Apple Blossoms "

years after he first joined the Brotherhood, Mr. Hunt, who
taught him all the technique he ever knew, got him to come
down to Knole to paint a background straight from Nature
whilst he overlooked and helped him. After two days, however, Rossetti was heartily sick of Nature, and bolted back to
London and its artificial life.

In course of time the instruction he had received from
Hunt began to bear fruit — one sees this in his picture called
"The Girlhood of the Virgin " — and with further practice
his art improved rapidly, and continued to do so as years
went on.

The great mistake that nearly all the critics make is in
confounding Rossetti's later work, which is imaginative,
sincere, and entirely of his own conception, with his Pre-

DESIGN OF A PICTURE OF "THE CANTERBURY PILGRIMS." 1850

Raphaelite work, of which he really did very little. They call his pictures such as "La bella mano," "Proserpine," "Venus Verticordia," "Dante and Beatrice," Pre-Raphaelite, which they are not in the very least. They belong to an entirely different school, which he himself founded, and which has since had such able exponents as Mr. Strudwick and Sir Edward Burne-Jones.

A common mistake that critics make is in assuming that the Pre-Raphaelite movement owed its origin to Mr. Ruskin. Amongst other writers on the subject is Max Nordau, and his statements are for the most part entirely wrong. He attributes the origin of the Brotherhood to the teachings of Ruskin, but Holman Hunt and Millais were Pre-Raphaelites before Ruskin ever wrote a line on the subject. At the Academy one of Mr. Ruskin's admirers lent Hunt a copy of *Modern Painters*, and Hunt read it with enthusiasm, as partially embodying his own preconceived ideal of art. Millais, however, when asked to read the work, resolutely refused to do so, saying he had his own ideas, and, convinced of their absolute soundness, he should carry them out regardless of what any man might say. He would look neither to the right nor to the left, but pursue unflinchingly the course he had marked out for himself. And so he did.

Besides what my father has told me over and over again, I have it from Mr. Holman Hunt, his life-long friend, that he was never for a moment influenced by Ruskin's teachings. Mr. Ruskin, it is true, held Millais up as the shining light of the Pre-Raphaelites, and explained his pictures to the multitude according to his own ideas; but that of course proves no more than that he admired my father's work, and approved what he believed to be the object of his aim.

Probably no artist in England ever read less on art or on his own doings than did Millais. On rare occasions criticisms were forced upon his notice, and he read them; but faith in himself and his own opinions was his only guide in determining what was good or bad in a picture, whether his own or that of another artist. When his work was done he banished all thought of it as far as possible, and when by chance his friend Dr. Urquhart, of Perth, called his attention to Max Nordau's statement that Ruskin was the originator and moving spirit of the Pre-Raphaelites in their early days, he indignantly denied it; and, after reading the passages the next day, he wrote to Mrs. Urquhart a letter in which he gave a rough history of Pre-Raphaelitism, and characterised Nordau's remarks as "twaddling rubbish 'on a subject of which he knows absolutely nothing."

Mr. Ruskin held that Art should be a great moral teacher, with religion as its basis and mainspring; but Millais, while agreeing with much of that critic's writings,* was never quite at one with him on this point. He certainly held that Art should have a great and abiding purpose, giving all its strength to the beautifying or ennoblement of whatever subject it touched, either sacred or secular; but though himself at heart a truly religious man, he could not harp on one string alone, nor would his impulsive originality, absolutely untrammelled by the opinions of others, allow him to paint pictures in which he had no heart at the dictation of any man, however eminent.

Holman Hunt, too, painted his religious pictures on the Ruskin lines really as the outcome of the high ideals he had set up for himself from the outset. "Truth and the free field of unadulterated Nature" was the motto of these originators. As Pope says, they "looked through Nature up to Nature's God," being sincere in their art, and resolutely determined to pursue it to its highest ends.

In saying this I by no means lose sight of the fact that the Pre-Raphaelites one and all owed much to Mr. Ruskin for his championship of their cause when he came to the knowledge of what they were striving to achieve. With an eloquence to which probably no equal can be found in the annals of art criticism, he explained to an unsympathetic public the aim and objects of the Brotherhood, and it goes without saying that they were highly gratified by his championship. When too, later on, he turned round and abused some of Millais' best works as heartily as he had praised some others, the circumstance was regarded by Millais amongst others as merely one of the inconsistencies into which genius is apt to fall. No one ever doubted the sincerity of his motive. He expressed only what he believed to be right, and in so far as he was wrong he helped rather than injured the painter's fame.

Before the Brotherhood was formally constituted, another association, called "The Cyclographic Club," came into existence, its object being to establish and circulate amongst

* Millais knew nothing of Ruskin's writings until 1851, when a letter of his appeared in the *Times*.

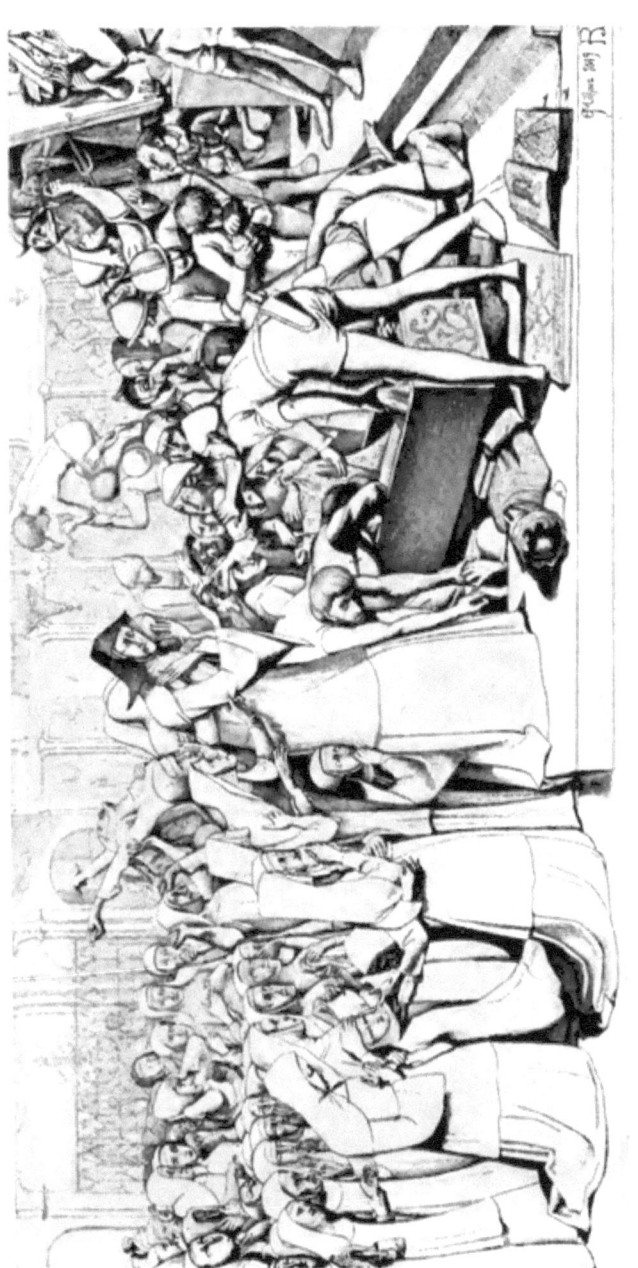

THE DISENTOMBMENT OF QUEEN MATILDA. 1849

Pre-Raphaelite Drawing

By permission of Mrs. Brocklehurst

the members a kind of portfolio of art and criticism. Each
member had to contribute once a month a black-and-white
drawing, on the back of which the other members were
to write critiques. This club, if it may be so called, was
founded by N. E. Green, Burchell, and Deverell, and was
afterwards joined by Millais, Hunt, Rossetti, and Arthur
Hughes. In a contribution to *The Letters of D. G. Rossetti
to William Allingham* Mr. Hughes says, "Millais, who was
the only man amongst us who had any money, provided
a nice green portfolio with a lock in which to keep the
drawings. Millais did his drawing, and one or two others
did theirs. Then the 'Folio' came to Rossetti, where it

PRE-RAPHAELITE DRAWING FOR HIS "GERM." (Not used)

stuck for ever. It never reached me. According to his
wont, he (Rossetti) had at first been most enthusiastic over
the scheme, *and had so infected Millais with his enthusiasm*
that he had at once ordered the case." *

On this subject Mr. Hughes sends me the following note :
" In connection with the circulating folio for designs, a few
members of the Brotherhood met one evening at Rossetti's
rooms at Chatham Place † — Rossetti, Deverell, and myself —

---

* Mr. Holman Hunt says his "influence" is purely imaginary. Millais had the
"enthusiasm" for designs in pen-and-ink, and liked to see what others did.
Some of the drawings were in colour. He adds, "I don't think we ever had
any meeting, and after about four peregrinations we (Millais, Hunt, and Rossetti)
seceded, because the contributions were so poor and the portfolio never arrived."

† This, I think, is a mistake, as Rossetti did not go to Chatham Place till
1853, when the Cyclographic Club had ceased to exist. Perhaps Mr. Hughes was
thinking of the club which Lady Waterford and E. V. B. tried to organise.

and one other, perhaps, but I cannot remember. When
Millais came in he asked if the folio had arrived from him.
Yes, there it was. Then if Madox Brown had agreed to
join, and Rossetti told him that he resisted all persuasion,
and would not. 'What a peevish old chap he is!' cried
Millais. A little later he noticed that Deverell was smoking
a cigarette, and earnestly exhorted him to give it up.
'Don't, Deverell, don't take to smoking; it is frightfully
injurious, it palls the faculties.' He himself succumbed
later on!"

The Brotherhood, it may be mentioned, neither smoked,
drank, nor swore, and that at a period when, as Thackeray
has shown us, all Bohemia was saturated with tobacco,
spirits, and quaint oaths. Millais, however, after attaining
his "artistic puberty," as he called it, came to regard the
pipe of peace as a friend and consoler when (as he sometimes was) well-nigh distraught with his work.

Out of the seven Pre-Raphaelite Brothers five were good
men with their pens, and the Brotherhood being eager to
defend the position they had taken up, were only too glad
when, in 1849, it was proposed to start a magazine in support
of their common creed. In the autumn of that year they met
together in Mr. Hunt's room, in Cleveland Street, to arrange
preliminaries with a view to early publication, when various
plans and names for the magazine were discussed, and at
last, on the suggestion of Mr. William Cave Thomas, it was
decided to call it *The Germ*.

Arrangements were then made with a publisher, pens and
pencils were set agoing, and in 1849 the first number of the
periodical appeared in print. Millais' share in this seems
to have been limited to two or three illustrations, which
are now in my possession. He took, however, a great
interest in the work, and subsequently wrote a complete
story for publication; but, alas! before the time for this
arrived the magazine came to an end for lack of funds to
keep it alive.

Only four numbers ever appeared, and these are now so
scarce that at a recent sale by auction a complete set
fetched £100. I give here an illustration that was done
by Millais for one of Rossetti's stories in this paper, but it
was never published.

In the *Idler* of March, 1898, Mr. Ernest Radford has
some interesting notes on *The Germ* — "the respiratory

organ of the Brethren," * as he humorously calls it. It
was edited, he tells us, by Mr. W. M. Rossetti, and printed
by a Mr. G. F. Tupper, on whose suggestion the title
was changed in the third number to the more commonplace one of *Art and Poetry;* and, besides many valuable
illustrations, it comprised contributions in prose and poetry
by the Rossettis (Christina and her two brothers), Madox
Brown, F. G. Stephens, Coventry Patmore, Thomas
Woolner, and various smaller lights. Millais, he says,
" who never practised an art without mastering it . . .
etched one plate in illustration of a poem by Rossetti, which

DRAWING IN PENCIL

Intended to illustrate a story by D. G. Rossetti in the fifth number of *The Germ*. This
drawing Millais afterwards etched, and a few copies of the plate are in existence

was to have graced the fifth number," but both etching and
poem have disappeared. The drawing for the etching is,
I fancy, amongst those in my possession.

He also wrote a story for the paper, which would have
appeared in the fifth number had the periodical survived
so long. The following is a brief outline of the tale: A
knight is in love with the daughter of a king who lived in
a moated castle. His affection is returned but the king
swears to kill him if he attempts to see his lady-love. The
lovers sigh for each other, but there is no opportunity for
meeting till the winter comes and the moat is frozen over.

---

* It was not of the " Brethren " only, others who were in sympathy with
them also took part in the publication.

The knight then passes over the ice, and, scaling the walls of the castle, carries off the lady. As they rush across the ice sounds of alarm are heard within, and at that moment the surface gives way, and they are seen no more in life. The old king is inconsolable. Years pass by, and the moat is drained; the skeletons of the two lovers are then found locked in each other's arms, the water-worn muslin of the lady's dress still clinging to the points of the knight's armour.

It seems from a letter of Rossetti's to W. B. Scott that, after the Cyclographic Club and *The Germ* had come to an end, Millais tried to found amongst the Pre-Raphaelite Brothers and their allies a sketching club, which would also include two ladies, namely, the beautiful Marchioness of Waterford and the Honourable Mrs. Boyle (then known as E. V. B.), both these ladies being promising artists, above the rank of amateurs; but this scheme also fell through.

CHAPTER III

MILLAIS' first big work in which he threw down the gauntlet to the critics, marking his picture with the hated P. R. B. signature, was " Lorenzo and Isabella," the subject being taken from Keats' paraphrase of Boccaccio's story : —

> " Fair Isabel, poor simple Isabel !
> Lorenzo, a young palmer in Love's eye.
> They could not in the self-same mansion dwell
> Without some stir of heart, some malady ;
> They could not sit at meals but feel how well
> It soothed each to be the other by ;
> They could not, sure, beneath the same roof sleep,
> But to each other dream and nightly weep."

All the figures were painted from the artist's own friends and relations. Mrs. Hodgkinson (wife of Millais' half-brother) sat for Isabella ; Millais' father, shorn of his beard, sat for the man wiping his lips with a napkin ; William Rossetti sat for Lorenzo ; Mr. Hugh Fen is paring an apple ; and D. G. Rossetti is seen at the end of the table drinking from a long glass ; whilst the brother, spitefully kicking the dog, in the foreground, was Mr. Wright, an architect ; and a student named Harris. Mr. F. G. Stephens is supposed to have sat for the head which appears between the watching brother and his wineglass ; and a student

named Plass stood for the serving-man.   Poor Walter
Deverell is also there.

Millais planned this work as late as November, 1848, and
carried it on, as Mr. Holman Hunt says, " at a pace beyond
all calculation," producing in the end " the most wonderful
picture in the world for a lad of twenty."

DANTE GABRIEL ROSSETTI
Study for " Lorenzo and Isabella."   1848

And now let us see what the critics had to say about it.
Fraser's Magazine of July, 1849, was, to say the least,
encouraging ; witness the following critique : — " Among the
multitude of minor pictures at the Academy, nearly all of
which, we are bound to say, exhibit more than an average
degree of excellence, one stands out distinguished from the
rest.   It is the work of a young artist named Millais, whose

"LORENZO AND ISABELLA." 1848

By permission of the Corporation of Liverpool

name we do not remember to have seen before. The subject
is taken from Keats' quaint, charming and pathetic poem,
'Isabella.' The whole family are seated at a table ; Lorenzo
is speaking with timid adoration to Isabella, the consciousness of dependency and of the contempt in which he is held by
her brothers being stamped on his countenance. The figures
of the brothers, especially of him who sits nearest to the
front, are drawn and coloured with remarkable power. The
attitude of this brother, as his leg is stretched out to kick
Isabella's dog, is vigorous and original. The colour of the
picture is very delicate and beautiful. Like Mr. [Ford
Madox] Brown, however, this young artist, although ex-
hibiting unquestionable genius, is evidently enslaved by
preference for a false style. There is too much mannerism
in the picture ; but the talent of the artist will, we doubt not,
break through it."

And Mr. Stephens was still more complimentary. In the
Grosvenor Gallery catalogue of the year 1886 he wrote : —
"Every detail, tint, surface texture, and substance, all the
flesh, all the minutiæ of the accessories were offered to the
exquisitely keen sight, indefatigable fingers, unchangeable
skill, and indomitable patience of one of the most energetic
of painters. Such tenacity and technical powers were never,
since the German followers of Dürer adopted Italian principles of working, exercised on a single picture. Van Eyck
did not study details of 'the life' more unflinchingly than
Millais in this case. The flesh of some of the heads, except
so far as the face of 'Ferdinand' and some parts of Holman
Hunt's contemporaneous 'Rienzi,' were concerned, remained
beyond comparison in finish and solidity until Millais painted
the hands in 'The Return of the Dove to the Ark.' "

But the critics were not all of this mind ; there was considerable diversity of opinion amongst them. Some were
simply silent ; but of those who noticed the work at all
the majority spoke of it in terms of qualified approval,
regarding it rather as a tentative departure from the
beaten track of Art than as the fruit of long and earnest
conviction.

By the general public it was looked upon as a prime joke,
only surpassing in absurdity Mr. Holman Hunt's "Rienzi,"
which was exhibited at the same time, and was equally beyond their comprehension. With a plentiful lack of wit, they
greeted it with loud laughter or supercilious smiles, and in

some instances even the proud Press descended to insults
of the most personal kind. This, however, only stiffened
Millais' resolution to proceed on his own lines, and to defend
against all comers the principles on which the Brotherhood
was founded. The picture was bought of the artist by three
combined amateur dealers, who sold it to Mr. Windus, of
Tottenham. After remaining with him some ten or twelve
years Gambart bought it, and again sold it to Woolner, R. A.
It is now in the possession of the Corporation of Liverpool.

In the following year was exhibited the picture commonly
known as " Christ in the Home of His Parents," but with no
other title than the following quotation from Zechariah xiii. 6 :
" And one shall say unto Him, What are these wounds in
Thine hands? Then He shall answer, Those with which I
was wounded in the house of My friends." It was painted
on precisely the same principle as was that which had called
forth the derision of the multitude, and as both Rossetti and
Mr. Hunt exhibited at the same time important pictures of
the same school, there could no longer be any doubt as to the
serious meaning of the movement. Then, with one accord,
their opponents fell upon Millais as the prime mover in the
rebellion against established precedent. In the words of a
latter-day critic, " Men who knew nothing of Art reviled
Millais because he was not of the art, artistic. Dilettanti
who could not draw a finger-tip scolded one of the most
accomplished draughtsmen of the age because he delineated
what he saw. Cognoscenti who could not paint rebuked
the most brilliant gold medal student of the Royal Academy
on account of his technical proceedings. Critics of the most
rigid views belaboured and shrieked at an original genius,
whose struggles and whose efforts they could not understand.
Intolerant and tyrannical commentators condemned the youth
of twenty because he dared to think for himself ; and, to sum
up the burden of the chorus of shame and false judgment,
there was hardly a whisper of faith or hope, or even of
charity — nay, not a sound of the commonest and poorest
courtesy — vouchsafed to the painter of ' The Carpenter's
Shop,' as, in utter scorn, this picture was originally and
contumeliously called."

What the Academy thought of it may be gathered from
the words of the late F. B. Barwell : " I well remember
Mulready, R. A., alluding to the picture some two years after
its exhibition. He said that it had few admirers inside the

Royal Academy Council, and that he himself and Maclise alone supported its claims to a favourable consideration."

The picture itself, devotional and symbolic in intent, is too well known to need any description. The child Christ is seen in His father's workshop with blood flowing from His hand, the result of a recent wound, while His mother waits upon Him with loving sympathy. That is the main subject. And now let us see how it was treated by the Press.

Blackwood's Magazine dealt with it in this wise: "We can hardly imagine anything more ugly, graceless, and unpleasant than Mr. Millais' picture of 'Christ in the Carpenter's Shop.' Such a collection of splay feet, puffed joints, and misshapen limbs was assuredly never before made within so small a compass. We have great difficulty in believing a report that this unpleasing and atrociously affected picture has found a purchaser at a high price. Another specimen from the same brush inspires rather laughter than disgust."

That was pretty strong; but, not to be left behind in the race to accomplish the painter's ruin, a leading literary journal, whose Art critic, by the way, was a Royal Academician, delivered itself in the following terms: "Mr. Millais in his picture without a name (518), which represents a holy family in the interior of a carpenter's shop, has been most successful in the least dignified features of his presentment, and in giving to the higher forms, characters, and meanings a circumstantial art-language from which we recoil with loathing and disgust. There are many to whom his work will seem a pictorial blasphemy. Great imaginative talents have here been perverted to the use of an eccentricity both lamentable and revolting."

Another critic, bent on displaying his wit at the expense of the artist, said: "Mr. Millais' picture looks as if it had passed through a mangle." And even Charles Dickens, who in later years was a firm friend of Millais and a great admirer of his works, denounced the picture in a leading article in *Household Words* as "mean, odious, revolting, and repulsive."

But perhaps the most unreasonable notice of all was the following, which appeared in the *Times:* "Mr. Millais' principal picture is, to speak plainly, revolting. The attempt to associate the holy family with the meanest details of a carpenter's shop, with no conceivable omission of misery, of dirt, of even disease, all finished with the same loathsome minuteness, is disgusting; and with a surprising power of imitation, this picture serves to show how far mere imitation may fall short, by dryness and conceit, of all dignity and truth."

From these extracts it is easy to see what criticism was a generation ago. As Mr. Walter Armstrong says, " Not the faintest attempt is made to divine the artist's standpoint, and to look at the theme from his side. The writer does not accept the Pre-Raphaelite idea even provisionally, and as a means of testing the efficiency of the work it leads to. He merely lays down its creations upon his own procrustean bed, and condemns them *en bloc* because they cannot be made to fit. And this article in the *Times* is a fair example

ORIGINAL DESIGN FOR "CHRIST IN THE HOUSE OF HIS PARENTS"
(Four figures only)

of the general welcome the picture met with. . . . Such criticism is mere scolding. When an artist of ability denies and contemns your canvas, to call him names is to confess their futility."

In an interesting note on this picture Mr. Edward Benest (Millais' cousin) says, " During the three years I was working in London I was a frequent visitor to the Gower Street house. . . . From the intellectual point of view this picture may be said to be the outcome of the combined brains of the Millais family. Every little portion of the whole canvas was discussed, considered, and settled upon by the father, mother, and Johnnie (the artist) before a touch was placed on the canvas, although sketches had been made. Of course, coming frequently, I used to criticise too ; and if I suggested any alteration, Johnnie used to say in his determined way, 'No, Ned; that has been all settled by us, and I shan't alter it.'

" Everything in that house was characteristic of the great devotion of all to the young artist; and yet he was in no way spoilt. Whilst he was at work his father and mother sat beside him most of the time, the mother constantly reading to him on every imaginable subject that interested

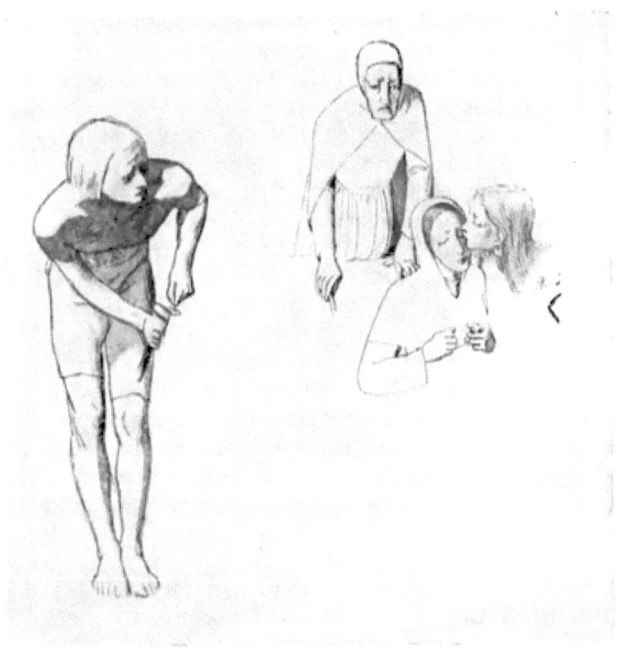

SKETCH FOR "CHRIST IN THE HOUSE OF HIS PARENTS"

the boy, or stopping to discuss matters with him. The boy himself, whilst working joined freely and cleverly in any conversation that was going on; and once when I asked him how he could possibly paint and talk at the same time, and throw such energy into both, he said, tapping his forehead, 'Oh, that's all right. I have painted every touch in my head, as it were, long ago, and have now only to transfer it to canvas. The father—a perfect optimist—when unable to help in any other way, would occupy

himself by pointing all Johnnie's pencils or playing whole
operas on the flute. This instrument he played almost as
well as any professional.

"The principal point of discussion with regard to the
'Carpenter's Shop' related to the head of the Virgin Mary.
At first, as his sketches show, she was represented as being
kissed by the child Christ; but this idea was presently
altered to the present position of the figures, and the mother
is now shown embracing her Son. These two figures were
constantly painted and repainted in various attitudes, and
finished only a short time before the picture was exhibited.
The figure, too, of St. John carrying a bowl of water was
inserted at the last moment."

The picture, when finished (not before), was sold for £150
to a dealer named Farrer, whose confidence in the young
artist was amusingly displayed by pasting on the back of
it all the adverse criticisms that appeared.

The models for this picture were as follows: the Virgin
Mary, Mrs. Henry Hodgkinson, the Christ, Nöel Hum-
phreys (son of an architect), John the Baptist, Edwin Everett,
(an adopted child of the Mr. Everett who married Millais'
aunt), and the apprentice H. St. Ledger. In painting it,
Millais was so determined to be accurate in every detail,
that he used to take the canvas down to a carpenter's shop
and paint the interior direct from what he saw there. The
figure of Joseph he took from the carpenter himself, saying
that it was "the only way to get the development of the
muscles right"; but the head was painted from Millais'
father. His great difficulty was with the sheep, for there
were no flocks within miles of Gower Street. At last, only
a few days before the picture had to be sent in to the Royal
Academy, he went to a neighbouring butcher's, where he
bought two sheep's heads with the wool on, and from these
he painted the flock.

There is a good story about these Pre-Raphaelite days
that I am tempted to introduce here in contrast with the
graver portion of this chapter. Gold-digging is hardly an
adventure in which I should have expected my father to
engage; but the papers, of course, must be right, and in
1886 one of them (an Edinburgh evening journal) announced
that at a certain period in the fifties Millais was travelling
in Australia in company with Woolner, the sculptor, and the
present Prime Minister of England, and for some time

"CHRIST IN THE HOUSE OF HIS PARENTS." 1849

By permission of F. Birt

worked with his own hands in the Bendigo gold-diggings. None of us at home had even heard of this before; but there it was in print, and presently every tit-bitty paper in the country repeated the tale with all the rhetorical adornment at the command of the writer. "The frenzied energy of gold-seekers" was one of the phrases that specially pleased us, and we never failed to throw it at my father's head whenever he was in a bit of a hurry.

And still the tale goes on. Quite recently the familiar old story appeared again in an Australian paper, the writer observing that no biography of the deceased artist would be complete without an account of his experiences in the southern goldfields. It seems a pity to prick this pretty bubble; but as a matter of fact my father was never in the goldfields, and through the fifties he was hard at work at home. It was Woolner alone who went in search of the elusive nugget, but presently returned to his art work in England, richer rather in experience than in solid gold.

Of one of the evening meetings in Woolner's absence Mr. Arthur Hughes obliges me with the following note:—
"While Woolner was in Australia his Pre-Raphaelite Brothers agreed to draw one another and send the drawings out to him; and one day, when two or three of them were about this at Millais' house, Alexander Munro, the sculptor, chanced to call. Millais, having finished his Pre-Raphaelite Brotherhood subject, got Munro to sit, and drew him, and afterwards accompanied him to the door with the drawing in his hand, to which Munro was making some critical objection that Millais did not agree with. There happened to be passing at the time a couple of rough bricklayers, fresh from their work — short pipes and all. To them Millais suddenly reached out from the doorstep and seized one, to his great surprise, and there and then constituted them judges to decide upon the merits of the likeness, while Munro, rather disconcerted, had to stand in the street with his hat off for identification. A most amusing scene!"

Mr. F. G. Stephens tells us something further about these portraits and the final Pre-Raphaelite Brotherhood meetings. He writes: "It was in the Gower Street studio that in 1853 the variously described meeting of the Pre-Raphaelite Brotherhood then in London occurred in order that the artists present might send as souvenirs to Woolner, then

1—6

in Australia, their portraits, each drawn by another.   Millais
fell to me to be drawn, and to him I fell as his subject.
Unhappily for me, I was so ill at that time that it was with
the greatest difficulty I could drag myself to Gower Street;
more than that, it was but the day before the entire ruin
of my family, then long impending and long struggled
against in vain, was consummated.   I was utterly unable
to continue the sketch I began.   I gave it up, and Mr.
Holman Hunt, who had had D. G. Rossetti for his *vis-à-vis*
and sitter, took my place and drew Millais' head.   The
head which Millais drew of me is now in my possession,
the gift of Woolner, to whom it was, with the others, sent
to Sydney, whence he brought the whole of the portraits
back to England.   My portrait, which by the way is a
good deal out of drawing, attests painfully enough the state
of health and sore trouble in which I then was.   This
meeting was one of the latest "functions" of the Pre-
Raphaelite Brotherhood in its original state.   Collinson had
seceded, and Woolner emigrated to the "diggings" in
search of the gold he did not find.   Up to that time the
old affectionate conditions still existed among the Brothers,
but their end was near.   Millais was shooting on ahead; Mr.
Holman Hunt was surely, though slowly, following his path
towards fortune; D. G. Rossetti had retired within himself,
and made no sign before the world; W. M. Rossetti was
rising in Her Majesty's service; and I was being continuedly
drawn towards that literary work which brought me bread.
None of the six had, however, departed from the essentials
of the Pre-Raphaelite faith which was in him."

"Ferdinand lured by Ariel," painted in 1849, was another
important picture that warred with the prevailing sentiment
of the day, its high finish in every detail and the distinctly
original treatment of the subject tending only to kindle anew
the animosity of the critics against Millais and the principles
he represented.   Even the dealer for whom it was painted
as a commission for £100 refused to take it, and when,
later on, it was exhibited at the Academy (now the National
Gallery), it was ignominiously placed low down in a corner
of one of the long rooms.

This shameless breach of contract on the part of the
dealer was a bitter disappointment to the young artist,
for he could ill afford to keep his pictures long in hand.
His parents, never well off, had given up everything for

"Jack," and determined that he should lack for nothing that could in anywise tend to his advancement, and for the last four years — ever since he was sixteen years of age — he had striven hard to requite their kindness, supplying, as he did from the profits of his work, the greater part of the household expenses at Gower Street. To eke out his precarious income he often went to theatres, where he could earn small sums by making sketches of the actors and actresses; but as he seldom got more than a couple of sovereigns for a finished portrait, this loss of £100 was a matter of no small moment to his family as well as himself.

But now another chance for the sale of "Ferdinand" presented itself. Mr. Frankum, an appreciative friend, brought to the studio a stranger who admired it greatly, and made so many encouraging remarks that Millais felt sure he would buy it. To his disappointment, however, no offer was made. The visitors went away, and he dolefully took up the picture to put it back in its accustomed place, when, to his joy and amazement, he found underneath it a cheque for £150! It was Mr. Richard Ellison, of Sudbrook Holme, Lincolnshire, a well-known connoisseur, whom Mr. Frankum had brought with him, and he had quietly slipped in this cheque unperceived by the artist. The picture has since been successively in the hands of Mr. Wyatt, of Oxford, Mr. Woolner, R.A. (who made quite a little fortune by buying and selling the Pre-Raphaelite pictures), and Mr. A. C. Allen, and is now in the possession of Mr. Henry Makins. From one of his letters to Mr. Wyatt (December, 1850) it seems that Millais made some slight alterations in, or additions to, the work after it had been sold to Mr. Ellison, for he took it again down to Oxford and worked once more upon the background, leaving it to dry the while in the possession of his friend Mr. Wyatt.

As to its merits, I need only quote the opinion of Mr. Stephens, who sat for "Ferdinand." In a recent notice of the work he says: "Although the face is a marvel of finish, and unchangeable in its technique, it was begun and completed in one sitting. Having made a very careful drawing in pencil on the previous day, and transferred it to the picture, Millais, almost without stopping to exchange a word with his sitter, worked for about five hours, put down his brushes, and never touched the face again. In execution it is exhaustive and faultless. Six-and-thirty years have not harmed it."

In a letter to me Mr. Stephens gives some further details about the picture and his sitting for it. He says: " My intimacy with Millais, of course, took a new form with this brotherly agreement [of the Pre-Raphaelite Brotherhood], and it was probably in consequence of this that I sat to him for the head of the Prince in the little picture of ' Ferdinand lured by Ariel,' which, being painted in 1849–50, was at the Academy in 1850, and is the leading example of Pre-Raphaelitism.

FIRST SKETCH FOR
"FERDINAND LURED BY ARIEL." 1850.

"According to Millais, each Brother worked according to his own lights and the general views of the Brotherhood at that time. Such being the case, I may describe the manner of the artist in this particular instance. In the summer and autumn of 1849 he executed the whole of that wonderful background, the delightful figures of the elves and Ariel, and he sketched in the Prince himself. The whole was done upon a pure white ground, so as to obtain the greatest brilliancy of the pigments. Later on my turn came, and in one lengthy sitting Millais drew my most un-Ferdinand-like features with a pencil upon white paper, making, as it was, a most exquisite drawing of the highest finish and exact fidelity. In these respects nothing could surpass this jewel of its kind. Something like it, but softer and not quite so sculpturesque, exists in the similar study Millais

"FERDINAND LURED BY ARIEL." 1849

By permission of Mr. Henry Makins

made in pencil for the head of Ophelia, which I saw not long ago, and which Sir W. Bowman lent to the Grosvenor Gallery in 1888.

"My portrait was completely modelled in all respects of form and light and shade, so as to be a perfect study for the head thereafter to be painted. The day after it was executed Millais repeated the study in a less finished manner upon the panel, and on the day following that I went again to the studio in Gower Street, where 'Isabella' and similar pictures were painted. From ten o'clock to nearly five the sitting continued without a stop, and with scarcely a word between the painter and his model. The clicking of his brushes when they were shifted in his palette, the sliding of his foot upon the easel, and an occasional sigh marked the hours, while, strained to the utmost, Millais worked this extraordinary fine face. At last he said, ' There, old fellow, it is done!' Thus it remains as perfectly pure and as brilliant as then — fifty years ago — and it now remains unchanged. For me, still leaning on a stick and in the required posture, I had become quite unable to move, rise upright, or stir a limb till, much as if I were a stiffened lay-figure, Millais lifted me up and carried me bodily to the dining-room, where some dinner and wine put me on my feet again. Later the till then unpainted parts of the figure of Ferdinand were added from the model and a lay-figure.

"It was in the Gower Street studio that Millais was wont, when time did not allow of outdoor exercises, to perform surprising feats of agility and strength. He had, since we first met at Trafalgar Square, so greatly developed in tallness, bulk, and manliness that no one was surprised at his progress in these respects. He was great in leaping, and I well re-member how in the studio he was wont to clear my arm outstretched from the shoulder — that is, about five feet from the ground — at one spring. The studio measures nineteen feet six inches by twenty feet, thus giving him not more than fourteen feet run. Many similar feats attested the strength and energy of the artist."

And now I must introduce two old friends of my father, whose kindness and generosity to him in his younger days made a deep and lasting impression upon his life. In 1848, when he first became acquainted with them, Mr. Thomas Combe was the Superintendent of the Clarendon Press at Oxford — a man of the most cultivated tastes, and highly

respected and beloved by every member of the University
with whom he came into contact — and his wife was a very
counterpart of himself.   Millais was staying at Oxford at
the time, engaged in painting the picture of Mr. Wyatt and
his granddaughter referred to in an earlier portion of this
chapter, and the Combes, who were among the first to
recognise and encourage the efforts of the Pre-Raphaelite
School, took him under their wing, treating him with almost
parental consideration.   In 1849 he returned to Oxford, and
stayed with them while painting Mr. Combe's portrait, and
from that time they became familiar friends, to whom it was
always a pleasure to write.

The following letters, kindly placed at my disposal by
Mrs. Combe, serve to illustrate his life at this period.
Mr. Combe, it must be understood, Millais commonly
referred to as " The Early Christian"; Mrs. Combe he
addressed as "Mrs. Pat."

To Mrs. Combe.

" 17 Hanover Terrace, Regent's Park.
" *November 13th,* 1850.

" My dear Mrs. Pat, — Our departure was so velocitous
that I had no time or spirits to express my thanks to you
before leaving for your immense kindness and endurance
of all whimsicalities attached to my nature.   I scribble
this at Collins' house, being totally incapable of remaining
at my own residence after the night's rest and morning's
'heavy blow' of breakfast.   The Clarendonian visit, the
Bottleyonian privations, and Oxonian martyrdoms have
wrought in us (Collins and myself) such a similar feeling
that it is quite impracticable to separate.   I had to go
through the exceedingly difficult task of performing the
dramatic traveller's return to his home — embracing fero-
ciously and otherwise exulting in the restoration to the
bosom of my family.   I say I had to 'perform' this part,
because the detestation I hold London in surpasses all
expression, and prevents the possibility of my being pleased
to return to anybody at such a place.   Mind, I am not
abusing the society, but the filth of the metropolis.

"Now for a catalogue of words to express my thanks
to you and Mr. Combe.   I have not got Johnson's dictionary

near me, so I am at a loss. Your kindness has defeated the
possibility of ever adequately thanking you, so I will conclude with rendering my mother's grateful acknowledgments.

" Remember me to all my friends, and believe me,

" Yours most sincerely,
" JOHN E. MILLAIS."

Note. — The " Bottleyonian privations " refer to the hard
fare on which Millais and Charles Collins subsisted at the
cottage of Mrs. King, at Botley, whilst the former was
painting " The Woodman's Daughter." Mrs. Combe's
motherly kindness to the two young artists is thus referred
to by Dr. Birkbeck Hill in his book on the Rossetti letters : —
" I have heard Mrs. Combe relate a story how Millais and
Collins, when very young men, once lodged in a cottage
nearly opposite the entrance of Lord Abingdon's park close
to Oxford. She learnt from them that they got but poor
fare, so soon afterwards she drove over in her carriage, and
left for them a large meat-pie. Millais, she added, one day
said to Mr. Combe, ' People had better buy my pictures
now, when I am working for fame, than a few years later,
when I shall be married and working for a wife and children.'
It was in these later years that old Linnell exclaimed to him,
' Ah, Mr. Millais, you have left your first love, you have left
your first love ! ' "

To the same.

"83 GOWER STREET, BEDFORD SQUARE,
" *December 2nd,* 1850.

" MY DEAR MRS. PAT, — First I thank you most intensely
for the Church Service. The night of its arrival I read
the marriage ceremony for the first time in my life, and
shall look upon every espoused man with awe.

" I am delighted to hear that you are likely to visit
Mrs. Collins during the 1851 Exhibition, as you will meet
with a most welcome reception from that lady, who is all
lovingkindness.

" My parents are likely to be out of town at that time.
My mother, not having left London for some years, prefers
visiting friends in Jersey and in familiar localities in France
to remaining in the metropolis during the tumult and excite-

ment of 1851. I hope, however, on another occasion you will have the opportunity of knowing them, in case they should be gone before you are here.

"Every Sunday since I left Oxford Collins and I have spent together, attending Wells Street Church. I think you will admit (when in town) that the service there is better performed than any other you have ever attended. We met there yesterday morning a University man of our acquaintance who admitted its superiority over Oxford or Cambridge. I am ashamed to say that late hours at night and ditto in the morning are creeping again on us. Now and then I make a desperate resolution to plunge out of bed when called, which ends in passively lying down again. A late breakfast (I won't mention the hour) and my lay-figure [artist's dummy] stares at me in reproving astonishment as I enter my study. During all this time I am so powerlessly cold that I am like a moving automaton. The first impulse is to sit by my stove, which emits a delicious, genial, unwholesome, feverish heat, and the natural course of things brings on total incapacity to work and absolute laziness. In spite of this I manage to paint three hairs on the woodman's little girl's head or two freckles on her face; and so lags the day till dark, by which time the room is so hot, and the glue in the furniture therein so softened by the warmth, that the chairs and tables are in peril of falling to pieces before my face. . . . But I, like the rest of the furniture, am in too delicate a state to be moved when the call for dinner awakens the last effort but one in removing my body to the table, where the last effort of all is required to eat.

"This revives just strength enough to walk to Hanover Terrace in a night so cold that horses should wear great-coats. Upon arriving there I embrace Collins, and *vice versâ*; Mrs. Collins makes the tea, and we drink it; we then adjourn upstairs to his room and converse till about twelve, when we say good-night, and again poor wretched 'Malay' [he was always called 'Mr. Malay' wherever he went] risks his life in the London Polar voyage, meeting no human beings but metropolitan policemen, to whom he has an obscure intention of giving a feast of tea and thicker bread and butter than that given by Mr. Hales, of Oxford, in acknowledgment of his high esteem of their services. At one o'clock in the morning it is too severely cold for anything to be out but a lamp-post, and I am one of that body. [An occult reference to his slimness.]

" Respecting my promised visit at Christmas, if nothing happens to prevent me I shall certainly be with you then. Shall probably come the night before, and leave the night after.

" I have entirely settled my composition of ' The Flood,' and shall commence it this week. I have also commenced the child's head in the wood scene.

" I have, as usual, plenty of invitations out, all of which I have declined, caring no more for such amusements. It is useless to tell you that I am miserable, as this letter gives you my everyday life.

" Remember me to Mr. Combe most sincerely, and to all about you, and believe me to remain,
                    " Ever your affectionate friend,
                              " JOHN EVERETT MILLAIS."

In these days he frequently referred to and made fun of his extreme slimness, as to which William Millais writes : " My brother, up to the age of twenty-four, was very slight in figure, and his height of six feet tended to exaggerate the tenuity of his appearance. He took pleasure in weighing himself, and was delighted with any increase of weight. I remember when he went to Winchelsea in 1854 to paint the background for the ' Blind Girl, ' whilst waiting for a fly at the railway station we were weighed. I just turned twelve stone, and when my brother went into the scales the porter was quite dumbfoundered when three stone had to be abstracted before the proper balance was arrived at. ' Ah ! you may well look, my man,' said my brother ; ' I ought to be going about in a menagerie as a specimen of a living paper-knife.' We all know how that state of things was altered in after years ; he might have gone back to his menagerie as a specimen of fine manly vigour and physique."

To Mr. Combe.

"83 GOWER STREET, BEDFORD SQUARE,
" *December* 16*th*, 1850.

" DEAR EARLY CHRISTIAN, — I was extremely surprised and delighted at your letter. The kind wish therein that I might stay a little while at Christmas I am afraid can never be realised, as I can only come and go for that day. My family, as you may imagine, were a little astonished on hearing my intention to leave them at that time. They are, however, reconciled now, and I shall (all things permitting) be with you. I have settled down to London life again for the present, and the quiet, pleasant time at Oxford seems like a

PENCIL DESIGN FOR "THE WOODMAN'S DAUGHTER." 1848

dream. I wish the thought of it would take that form instead of keeping me awake almost every night up to three and four o'clock in the morning, at which time the most depressing of all circumstances happens — the performance of 'the Waits.' To hear a bad band play bad music in an empty street at night is the greatest trial I know. I should not like to visit Dr. Leigh's asylum as a patient, so shall endeavour to forget all bygone enjoyments, together with present and future miseries that keep me from sleep.

"You will perhaps wonder what these ailments can be. I will enumerate them. First, a certainty of passing an unusually turbulent life (which I do not like); secondly, the inevitable enemies I shall create if fully successful; thirdly, the knowledge of the immense application required to complete my works for the coming exhibition, which I feel inadequate to perform. I think I shall adopt the motto 'In cœlo quies,' and go over to Cardinal Wiseman, as all the metropolitan High Church clergymen are sending in their resignations. To-morrow (Sunday) Collins and myself are going to dine with a University man whose brother has just seceded, and afterwards to hear the Cardinal's second discourse. My brother went last Sunday, but could not hear a word, as it was so crowded he could not get near enough. The Cardinal preaches in his mitre and full vestments, so there will be a great display of pomp as well as knowledge. . . . .

"And now, my dear Mr. Combe, I must end this 'heavy blow' letter with most affectionate remembrances and earnest assurances to Mrs. Pat that I do not mean to turn Roman Catholic just yet. Also remember me kindly to the Vicar,

"And believe me to remain,

"Yours most affectionately,

"JOHN EVERETT MALAY."

After his Christmas visit he wrote

To Mrs. Combe.

"83 GOWER STREET, BEDFORD SQUARE,
"*December 30th*, 1850.

"MY DEAR MRS. COMBE, — The last return was more hurried than the first. I found my portmanteau, when at the station, unstrapped and undirected. We, however, got over those difficulties, and arrived safely. I recollect now that we did not say a farewell word to Mr. Hackman; also forgot to ask you and Mr. Combe to give a small portion of your hair for the rings, there being a place for that purpose. Pray send some for both.

"It is needless to say our relatives are somewhat surprised at your kind presents. They are universally admired. I am deep in the mystery of purchasing velvets and silk draperies for my pictures [' Mariana ' and ' The Woodman's Daughter ']. The shopman simpers with astonishment at the request coming from a male biped. I begin to long for these toil-some three months to pass over; I am sure, except on Sundays, never to go out in the daylight again for that time.

" I have seen Charley Collins every night since, and see him again to-night. We go to a dancing party to-morrow ; at least it is his desire, not mine. The days draw in so early now that it is insanity to stay up late at night, and get up at eleven or twelve the next morning. I wish you were here to read to me. None of my family will do that. [In those days he liked being read to whilst at his work, his mother having done so for years.]

" Get the Early Christian, in his idle moments, to design the monastery and draw up the rules . . . and believe me always

" Your affectionate friend,

" JOHN EVERETT MILLAIS."

To the same.

" 83 GOWER STREET,

" *January* 15*th*, 1851.

" MY DEAR MRS. PAT, — I have been so much engaged since I received your letter that I had no time to write to you. . . . I saw Carlo last night, who has been very lucky in pursuading a very beautiful young lady to sit for the head of ' The Nun.' She was at his house when I called, and I also endeavoured to obtain a sitting, but was unfortunate, as she leaves London next Saturday.

" I have progressed a little with both my pictures, and completed a very small picture of a bridesmaid who is passing the wedding-cake through the ring nine times.* I have not yet commenced ' The Flood, ' but shall do so this week for certain.

" Believe me, wishing a happy new year to both of you,

" Yours most affectionately,

" JOHN EVERETT MILLAIS."

* " The Bridesmaid," now in the Fitzwilliam Museum, Cambridge.

DESIGN FOR "THE DELUGE." *Circ. 1890*

The following letter is characteristic as showing Millais' careful regard to details. The materials asked for were for use in painting " The Woodman's Daughter."

To Mr. Combe.

"83 GOWER STREET,
"*January 28th*, 1851.

" MY DEAR MR. COMBE, — You have doubtless wondered at not hearing from me, but want of subject must be my excuse.

" I have got a little commission for you to execute for me. You recollect the lodge at the entrance of Lord Abingdon's house, where I used to leave my picture of the Wood ['The Woodman's Daughter']. Well, in the first cottage there is a little girl named Esther; would you ask the mother to let you have a pair of her old walking-boots? I require them sent on to me, as I wish to paint them in the wood. I do not care how old they are; they are, of course, no use without having been worn. Will you please supply the child with money to purchase a new pair? I shall settle with you when I see you in the spring. If you should see a country-child with a bright lilac pinafore on, lay strong hands on the same, and send it with the boots. It must be long, that is, covering the whole underdress from the neck. I do not wish it new, but clean, with some little pattern — pink spots, or anything of that kind. If you have not time for this task, do not scruple to tell me so.

" 'The Flood' subject I have given up for this year, and have substituted a smaller composition a little larger than the Wood. The subject is quite new and, I think, fortunate; it is the dove returning to the Ark with the olive-branch. I shall have three figures — Noah praying, with the olive-branch in his hand, and the dove in the breast of a young girl who is looking at Noah. The other figure will be kissing the bird's breast. The background will be very novel, as I shall paint several birds and animals one of which now forms the prey to the other.

" It is quite impossible to explain one's intentions in a letter; so do not raise objections in your mind till you see it

I — 7

finished. I have a horrible influenza, which, however, has not deterred me from the usual 'heavy blow' walks with Fra Carlo. . . . I thought I had forgotten something — *the shields* — which you most kindly offered to do for me. I was not joking when I hinted to you that I should like to have them. If you are in earnest I shall be only too glad to hang them round my room, for I like them so much better than any paper, that when I have a house of my own you shall see every room decorated in that way. . . .

> " Yours devotedly,
>
> " JOHN EVERETT MILLAIS."

" The Flood " subject (a subject altogether different from that of another picture called " A Flood," painted by the artist in 1870) was never completed as an oil picture, although he made a finished drawing of it, which is now in my possession, having been given to me by my mother.

As will be seen from his letter to Mr. Combe, " The Return of the Dove to the Ark " (otherwise known as " The Daughters of Noah," or " The Wives of the Sons of Noah ") had the first place in his mind, and eventually he painted it at the house in Gower Street. It represents two girls (supposed to be inmates of the Ark) clad in simple garments of green and white, and caressing the dove. The picture was shown in the Academy of 1851, along with " The Woodman's Daughter " and " Mariana," and was next exhibited in Paris in 1855 with " The Order of Release " and " Ophelia," when, says Mr. Stephens, " the three works attracted much attention and sharp discussion, which greatly extended Millais' reputation." It was again shown in the International Exhibition of 1862, as were also " Apple Blossoms," " The Order of Release," and " The Vale of Rest "; and by Mr. Combe's will it has now become the property of the University of Oxford.

On this subject my uncle, William Millais, writes: " The unbiased critic must be constrained to admit that if there is one thing to criticise in the paintings in these days of his glorious youth, it is the inelegance of one or two of the figures. The girls in ' The Return of the Dove ' and ' Mariana ' are the two most noticeable examples, and I have heard the artist admit as much himself. The head of the little girl in ' The Woodman's Daughter,' which was altered after many years much for the worse, was in its original state distinctly charming, although rustic. It was only at the instance of the owner, his half-brother Henry Hodgkinson, that he at last consented to repaint (and spoil) to a considerable extent the whole picture for a slight inaccuracy in the drawing of one head and the arm and boots of the girl. It was a very great misfortune, for the work of the two periods has not 'blended' as they have done so successfully in 'Sir Isumbras.'"

Millais' life in 1851, his hopes and ambitions, the pictures he painted, what was said of them and what became of them, are perhaps best related by himself in the following letters:—

To Mrs. Combe.

"83 GOWER STREET, BEDFORD SQUARE,
"*February 10th*, 1851.

"MY DEAR MRS. PAT,—The brevity with which my troublesome request was executed astonished me, and I return you all the thanks due to so kind an attention. The pinafore will do beautifully, as also the boots. The 'Lyra Innocentium' I brought from Oxford at Christmas-time. I have given Collins the one directed for him. To-night I commence for the first time this year evening work which lasts till twelve, and which will continue for the next few months. I am now progressing rapidly; the 'Mariana' is nearly completed, and, as I expected, the gentleman to whom I promised the first refusal has purchased it. The Wood scene is likewise far advanced, and I hope to commence the Noah the latter part of this week.

"I have had lately an order to paint St. George and the Dragon for next year. It is a curious subject, but I like it much, as it is the badge of this country.

"I see Charley every night, and we dine alternate Sundays at each other's houses. To-night he comes to cheer me in my solitude. I give up all invitations, and scarcely ever see anybody. Have still got my cold, and do not expect that tenacious friend will take any notice of the lozenge warnings. ...There is at this moment such a dreadful fog that I cannot see to paint, so I devote this leisure hour to you. Remember me affectionately to the Early Christian, and believe me most affectionately yours,   JOHN EVERETT MILLAIS."

To Mr. Combe.

"83 GOWER STREET,
"*April 1st*, 1851.

" MY DEAR MR. COMBE, — I am sure you will never have cause to regret purchasing ' The Dove.' It is considered the best picture of the three by all the artists, and is preferred for the subject as well. It will be highly finished to the corners, and I shall design (when it returns from the Academy) a frame suitable to the subject — olive leaves, and a dove at each corner holding the branch in its mouth.

" I have designed a frame for Charles' painting of ' Lilies,' which, I expect, will be acknowledged to be the best frame in England. To get ' The Dove ' as good as possible, I shall have a frame made to my own design.

" With regard to your remark on the payment, rest assured that when it suits you it suits me. If you had not got the picture a gentleman from Birmingham had decided on having it. One of the connoisseurs has made an offer to Mr. Farrer for the ' Mariana,' which he has declined, being determined to keep my paintings. This from such a dealer as Farrer, the first judge of art in England, proves the investment on such pictures to be pretty safe.

" As soon as the pictures get into the Academy I shall be at leisure to give an account to Mrs. Pat of my later struggles.

" Believe me, very sincerely yours,
" JOHN EVERETT MILLAIS."

To the same.

"83 GOWER STREET,
"*April 15th*, 1851.

" MY DEAR MR. COMBE, — You must be prepared to see an immense literary assault on my works ; but I fancy some papers will give me all the credit the others withhold. To tell you the truth, artists know not what course to follow — whether to acknowledge the truth of our style, or to stand out against it. Many of the most important have already (before me) admitted themselves in the wrong — men whose reputation would suffer at the mention of their names!

" I would not ask anything for the copyright, as the engraving will cost nearly five hundred pounds. That in itself is a great risk, particularly as it is the first I shall have engraved. I shall not permit it to be published unless perfectly satisfied with the capabilities of the etcher. It is to be done entirely in line, without mezzotint. I am myself confident of its success; but it is natural that men without the slightest knowledge should be a little shy of giving money for the copyright.*

" It was very unfortunate that Charley [Collins] could not complete the second picture for the Exhibition. I tried all the encouraging persuasions in my power; but he was beaten by a silk dress which he had not yet finished. I have ordered another canvas to begin again next week, intending to take a holiday when the warmth comes. Such a quantity of loathsome foreigners stroll about the principal streets that they incline one to take up a residence in Sweden, outside of the fumes of their tobacco. I expect all respectable families will leave London after the first month of the Exhibition, it will be so crowded with the lowest rabble of all the countries in Europe.

" Say all the kind things from me you, as a husband, may think fit to deliver to Mrs. Pat, and believe me,

" Ever yours affectionately,

"JOHN EVERETT MILLAIS."

To the same.

" 83 GOWER STREET,

" *May 9th*, 1851.

" MY DEAR MR. COMBE, — I received the shields this morning, and hasten to thank you most heartily. I hope to see them ranged round my studio next week. No doubt you have seen the violent abuse of my pictures in the *Times*, which I believe has sold itself to destroy us. That, however, is quite an absurd mistake of theirs, for, in spite of their denouncing my pictures as unworthy to hang on any walls, the famous critic, Mr. Ruskin, has written offering to purchase your picture of ' The Return of the Dove to the Ark.' I received his letter this morning. and have this

---

* The picture (" The Dove ") was never engraved, the woodcut only appearing.

evening made him aware of the previous sale. I have
had more than one application for it, and you could, I have
little doubt, sell it for as much again as I shall ask you.

" There are few papers that speak favourably of me, as
they principally follow the *Times*. For once in a way that
great leader of public opinion will be slightly out in its con-
jectures. There are articles in the *Spectator* and *Daily News*
as great in praise as the others are in abuse.

" Where are you, in London or Oxford? Mrs. Pat's letter
did not specify the locality. Remember me affectionately to
her, and believe me,

" Ever sincerely yours,

"JOHN EVERETT MILLAIS."

To the same.

" 83 GOWER STREET,

" *May* 10*th*, 1851.

" MY DEAR MR. COMBE, — I think if your friend admires
Charley's sketch he would be particularly charmed with the
picture, and would never regret its purchase, as a work so
elaborately studied would always (after the present panic)
command its price, £150.

" Most men look back upon their early paintings — for
which they have received but poor remuneration — as the
principal instruments of their after wealth. For one great
instance, see Wilkie's ' Blind Fiddler,' sold for £20, now
worth more than £1000! Early works are also generally
the standard specimens of artists, as great success blunts
enthusiasm, and little by little men get into carelessness,
which is construed by idiotic critics into a nobler handling.
Putting aside the good work of purchasing from those
who require encouragement, such patrons will be respected
afterwards as wise and useful men amongst knavish fools,
who should be destroyed in their revolting attempts to crush
us — attempts so obviously malicious as to prove our rapid
ascendancy. It is no credit to a man to purchase from those
who are opulent and acknowledged by the world, so your
friend has an opportunity for becoming one of the first-named
wise patrons who shall, if we live, be extolled as having
assisted in our (I hope) final success.

" Hunt will, I think, sell his ; there is a man about it,

and it is a very fine picture. My somewhat showmanlike
recommendation of Collins' 'Nun' is a pure matter of
conscience, and I hope it will prove not altogether faulty.
                "Very sincerely yours,
                            "JOHN E. MILLAIS.
Hunt wants £300 for his picture."

To Mrs. Combe.

"83 GOWER STREET,
                "28*th*, 1851.

"MY DEAR MRS. COMBE, — I feel it a duty to render you
my most heartfelt thanks for the noble appreciation of my
dear friend Collins' work and character. I include character,
for I cannot help believing, from the evident good feeling
evinced in your letter, that you have thought more of the
beneficial results the purchase may occasion him than of
your personal gratification at possessing the picture.

"You are not mistaken in thus believing him worthy
of your kindest interests, for there are few so devotedly
directed to the one thought of some day (through the
medium of his art) turning the minds of men to good
reflections and so heightening the profession as one of
unworldly usefulness to mankind.

" *This is our great object in painting*, for the thought
of simply pleasing the senses would drive us to other pursuits requiring less of that unceasing attention so necessary
to the completion of a perfect work.

"I shall endeavour in the picture I have in contemplation
—'For as in the Days that were Before the Flood,' etc.,
etc. — to affect those who may look on it with the awful
uncertainty of life and the necessity of always being prepared for death. My intention is to lay the scene at
the marriage feast. The bride, elated by her happiness,
will be playfully showing her wedding-ring to a young girl,
who will be in the act of plighting her troth to a man wholly
engrossed in his love, the parents of each uniting in con-
gratulation at the consummation of their own and their
children's happiness. A drunkard will be railing boisterously
at another, less intoxicated, for his cowardice in being somewhat appalled at the view the open window presents — flats
of glistening water, revealing but the summits of mountains

and crests of poplars.   The rain will be beating in the face
of the terrified attendant who is holding out the shutter,
wall-stained and running down with the wet, but slightly
as yet inundating the floor.   There will also be the glutton
quietly indulging in his weakness, unheeding the sagacity
of his grateful dog, who, thrusting his head under his hands
to attract attention, instinctively feels the coming ruin.   Then
a woman (typical of worldly vanity) apparelled in sumptuous

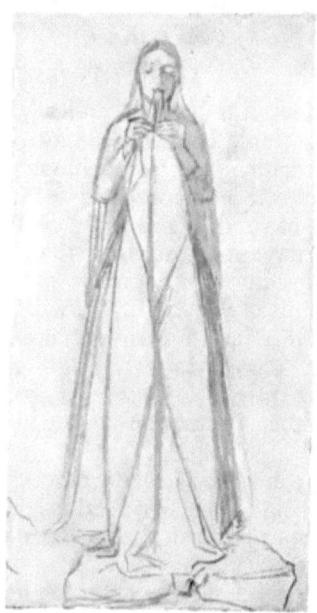

attire, witholding her robes
from the contamination of his
dripping hide.   In short, all
deaf to the prophecy of the
Deluge which is swelling before
their eyes — all but one figure in
their midst, who, upright with
closed eyes, prays for mercy for
those around her, a patient example of belief standing with,
but far from, them placidly
awaiting God's will.

"I hope, by this great contrast, to excite a reflection on
the probable way in which
sinners would meet the coming
death — all on shore hurrying
from height to height as the
sea increases; the wretched self-
congratulations of the bachelor
who, having but himself to
save, believes in the prospect

SKETCH FOR "MARIANA." 1850   of escape; the awful feelings of
the husband who sees his wife
and children looking in his face for support, and presently
disappearing one by one in the pitiless flood as he miserably
thinks of his folly in not having taught them to look to God
for help in times of trouble; the rich man who, with his boat
laden with wealth and provisions, sinks in sight of his fellow-
creatures with their last curse on his head for his selfishness;
the strong man's strength failing gradually as he clings to
some fragment floating away on the waste of water; and
other great sufferers miserably perishing in their sins.

"I have enlarged on this subject and the feelings that
I hope will arise from the picture, as I know you will be

interested in it. One great encouragement to me is the
certainty of its having this one advantage over a sermon,
that it will be all at once put before the spectator without that
trouble of realisation often lost in the effort of reading or
listening.

" My pleasure in having indirectly assisted two friends in
the disposal of their pictures is enhanced by the assurance
that you estimate their merits. It is with extreme pleasure

SKETCHES FOR "MARIANA" AND "THE RETURN OF THE DOVE." 1850

that I received that letter from Mr. Combe in which he
approves of his picture of ' The Return of the Dove to the
Ark,' universally acknowledged to be my best work, parts of
which I feel incapable of surpassing. When you come to
town I will show you many letters from strangers desirous of
purchasing it, which is the best proof of its value in their eyes.
The price I have fixed on my picture is a hundred and fifty
guineas; and I hope some day you will let me paint you, as
a companion, ' The Dove's First Flight,' which would make
a beautiful pendant.   Ever yours affectionately,
                            " JOHN EVERETT MILLAIS."

"Mariana in the Moated Grange" was exhibited this year with the following quotation from Tennyson's well-known poem : —

> "She only said, 'My life is dreary —
> He cometh not,' she said :
> She said, 'I am aweary, aweary —
> I would that I were dead.'"

The picture represents Mariana rising to her full height and bending backwards, with half-closed eyes. She is weary of all things, including the embroidery-frame which stands before her. Her dress of deep rich blue contrasts with the red-orange colour of the seat beside which she stands. In the front of the figure is a window of stained glass, through which may be seen a sunlit garden beyond ; and in contrast with this is seen, on the right of the picture, an oratory, in the dark shadow of which a lamp is burning.

Spielmann's observations on this work are not quite easy to understand. He says the subject is a "Rossettian one, without the Rossettian emotion." * If so, the lack of emotion must be due rather to the poet than to the painter, for, referring to this picture in the *Magazine of Art* of September, 1896, he speaks of Millais' "artistic expression being more keenly sensitive to the highest forms of written poetry than any other painter of his eminence who ever appeared in England." He thinks, too, that the colour is too strong and gay to be quite in harmony with the subject, though immediately afterwards he quotes the particular lines which Millais sought to illustrate : —

> ". . . But most she loathed the hour
> When the thick-moated sunbeam lay
> Athwart the chambers, and the day
> Was sloping towards his Western bower."

The sun, then, was shining in all its splendour, and though poor Mariana loathed the sight, the objects it illuminated were none the less brilliant in colour. And so they appear in the picture. The shadows, too, are there in happy contrast, and every object is seen in its true atmosphere, without any clashing of values.

In the *Times* of May 13th, 1851, Ruskin noticed the picture in his characteristic manner. He was glad to see that Millais' "Lady in blue is heartily tired of painted

* The critic, too, seems to forget that all Rossetti's emotional subjects were painted years later.

"MARIANA." 1851

By permission of Mr. Henry Makins

windows and idolatrous toilet-table," but maintained generally
that since the days of Albert Dürer no studies of draperies
and details, nothing so earnest and complete, had been
achieved in art — a judgment which, says Spielmann, "as
regards execution, will hardly be reversed to-day." With
delightful inconsequence, Ruskin afterwards added that, had
Millais "painted Mariana at work in an unmoated grange,
instead of idle in a moated one, it had been more to the
purpose, whether of art or life."

The picture was sold to Mr. Farrer, the dealer, for one
hundred and fifty pounds, and after passing successively
through the hands of Mr. B. Windus and Mr. J. M.
Dunlop, it now rests with Mr. Henry Makins, who also
owns "Ferdinand" and "For the Squire."

During the execution of this work Millais came down
one day and found that things were at a standstill owing
to the want of a model to paint from. He naturally disliked
being stopped in his work in this way, and the only thing
he could think of was to sketch in the mouse that

> "Behind the mouldering wainscot shrieked
> Or from the crevice peer'd about."

But where was the mouse to paint from? Millais' father,
who had just come in, thought of scouring the country in
search of one, but at that moment an obliging mouse ran
across the floor and hid behind a portfolio. Quick as
lightning Millais gave the portfolio a kick, and on removing
it the poor mouse was found quite dead in the best possible
position for drawing it.*

The window in the background of "Mariana" was taken
from one in Merton Chapel, Oxford. The ceiling of the
chapel was being painted, and scaffolding was of course put
up, and this Millais made use of whilst working. The scene
outside was painted in the Combes' garden, just outside their
windows.

Of all the pictures ever painted, there is probably none
more truly Pre-Raphaelite in character than one I have
already mentioned — "The Woodman's Daughter." It was
painted in 1850 in a wood near Oxford, and was exhibited
in 1851. Every blade of grass, every leaf and branch, and

---

* A similar incident, in which the wished-for model actually appeared at the
very moment when its presence was most desired, occurred some years later, when
a collie dog suddenly turned up to serve as a model in "Blow, blow, thou Winter
Wind."

every shadow that they cast in the sunny wood is presented here with unflinching realism and infinite delicacy of detail. Yet the figures are in no way swamped by their surroundings, every accessory taking its proper place, in subordination to the figures and the tale they have to tell. The contrast between the boy — the personification of aristocratic refinement — and the untutored child of nature is very striking, as was no doubt intended by Mr. Coventry Patmore, whose poem, " The Tale of Poor Maud," daughter of Gerald the woodman, the picture was intended to illustrate.

> " Her tale is this : In the sweet age,
>   When Heaven's our side the lark,
> She used to go with Gerald where
>   He work'd from morn to dark,
> For months, to thin the crowded groves
>   Of the ancient manor park.

> " She went with him to think she help'd :
>   And whilst he hack'd and saw'd
> The rich Squire's son, a young boy then,
>   Whole mornings, as if awed,
> Stood silent by, and gazed in turn
>   At Gerald and on Maud.

> " And sometimes, in a sullen tone,
>   He 'd offer fruits, and she
> Received them always with an air
>   So unreserved and free,
> That shame-faced distance soon became
>   Familiarity."

William Millais contributes the following note on this painting : —

" I think, perhaps, the most beautiful background ever painted by my brother is to be found in his picture of ' The Woodman's Daughter ' — a copse of young oaks standing in a tangle of bracken and untrodden underwood, every plant graceful in its virgin splendour.

" Notice the exquisitely tender greys in the bark of the young oak in the foreground, against which the brilliantly clothed lordling is leaning. Every touch in the fretwork tracery all about it has been caressed by a true lover of his art, for in these his glorious early days one can see that not an iota was slurred over, but that every beauty in nature met with its due appreciation at his hands.

" Eye cannot follow the mysterious interlacing of all the wonderful green things that spring up all about, where every kind of woodgrowth seems to be striving to get the upper hand and to reach the sunlight first, where every leaf and tendril stands out in bold relief.

"This background was painted near Oxford, in a most secluded spot, and yet my brother had a daily visitor — 'a noble lord of high degree' — who used to watch him work for a minute or two, make one remark, 'Well, you are getting on; you've plenty of room yet,' and then silently disappear. After a time these visits ceased, and upon their renewal my brother had in the interim almost finished the background. The visitor, on seeing his work, exclaimed, 'Why, after all, you've not got it in!' My brother asked what it was. 'Why, Oxford, of course! You should have put it in.' Millais, who had his back to the town, explained that although Art could do wonders, it had never yet been able to paint all round the compass."

To be near his work on this picture Millais stayed in the cottage of a Mrs. King, at Bottley, Lord Abingdon's park, where he was joined by his friend Charles Collins.

Mr. Arthur Hughes writes: "F. G. Stephens has described to me how he was with Millais in the country when painting 'The Woodman's Daughter' (the subject from Coventry Patmore), and how Millais was painting a small feather dropped from a bird in the immediate foreground; how he stamped and cursed over it, and then scraped it out, and swore he would get it right — and did.

"The strawberries which appear in the picture, as presented by the young aristocrat, were bought in Covent Garden in March. 'I had to pay five-and-sixpence for the four — a vast sum for me in those days, but necessary' — I have heard him say, 'and Charlie Collins and I ate them afterwards with a thankful heart.'"

It was in this year (1851) that Ruskin took up arms in defence of the Pre-Raphaelite Brotherhood, and no more earnest or more eloquent advocate could they have desired. In the first volume of *Modern Painters* he insisted that "that only is a complete picture which has both the general wholeness and effect of Nature and the inexhaustible perfection of Nature's details"; and, pointing to "the admirable, though strange pictures of Mr. Millais and Mr. Holman Hunt" as examples of progress in this direction, he added, "they are endeavouring to paint, with the highest possible degree of completion, what they see in Nature, without reference to conventional or established rules; but by no means to imitate the style of any past epoch. Their works are, in finish of drawing and in splendour of colour, the best in the Royal Academy, and I have great hope that they may become the foundation of a more earnest and able school of Art than we have seen for centuries."

Here was a heavy blow to the Philistines of the Press; for at this time Ruskin was all but universally accepted as the final authority in matters of Art. But a heavier yet was in store for them. In an addendum to one of his published *Lectures on Architecture and Painting* — lectures delivered at Edinburgh in November, 1853 — he declared that "the very faithfulness of the Pre-Raphaelites arises from the redundance of their imaginative power. Not only can all the members of the [Pre-Raphaelite] School compose a thousand times better than the men who pretend to look down upon them, but I question whether even the greatest men of old times possessed more exhaustless invention than either Millais or Rossetti. . . . As I was copying this sentence a pamphlet was put into my hand, written by a clergyman, denouncing, 'Woe, woe, woe, to exceedingly young men of stubborn instincts calling themselves Pre-Raphaelites.' I thank God that the Pre-Raphaelites are young, and that strength is still with them, and life, with all the war of it, still in front of them. Yet Everett Millais. in this year, is of the exact age at which Raphael painted the 'Disputa,' his greatest work; Rossetti and Hunt are both of them older still; nor is there one member so young as Giotto when he was chosen from among the painters to decorate the Vatican of Italy. But Italy, in her great period, knew her great men, and did not despise their youth. It is reserved for England to insult the strength of her noblest children, to wither their warm enthusiasm early into the bitterness of patient battle, and to leave to those whom she should have cherished and aided no hope but in resolution, no refuge but in disdain."

Thus spoke the oracle in 1853, nor (as will presently appear) was his zeal abated in 1855, when "The Rescue" was exhibited, or in 1856, when "Peace Concluded" appeared on the Academy walls. But, strange to say, after that period works of Millais, executed with equal care and with the same fastidious regard for details (the lovely "Vale of Rest" and "Sir Isumbras" for instance), were condemned by him in unmeasured terms.

THE WOODMAN'S DAUGHTER. 1849

"OPHELIA" and "The Huguenot," both of which Millais painted during the autumn and winter of 1851, are so familiar in every English home that I need not attempt to describe them here. The tragic end of "Hamlet's" unhappy love had long been in his mind as a subject he should like to paint; and now while the idea was strong upon him he determined to illustrate on canvas the lines in which she is presented as floating down the stream singing her last song : —

> "There on the pendent boughs her coronet of weeds
> Clamb'ring to hang, an envious sliver broke ;
> When down the weedy trophies and herself
> Fell in the weeping brook.   Her clothes spread wide,
> And, mermaid-like, awhile they bore her up ;
> Which time she chanted snatches of old tunes,
> As one incapable of her own distress,
> Or like a creature native and indued
> Unto that element ; but long it could not be,
> Till that her garments, heavy with their drink,
> Pull'd the poor wretch from her melodious lay
> To muddy death." *

Near Kingston, and close to the home of his friends the Lemprières, is a sweet little river called the Ewell, which flows into the Thames. Here, under some willows by the side of a hayfield, the artist found a spot that was in every

---

* *Hamlet*, act iv.

way suitable for the background of his picture, in the month of July, when the river flowers and water-weeds were in full bloom. Having selected his site, the next thing was to obtain lodgings within easy distance, and these he secured in a cottage near Kingston, with his friend Holman Hunt as a companion. They were not there very long, however, for presently came into the neighbourhood two other members of the Pre-Raphaelite fraternity, bent on working together; and, uniting with them, the two moved into Worcester Park Farm, where an old garden wall happily served as a background for the "Huguenot," at which Millais could now work alternately with the "Ophelia."

It was a jolly bachelor party that now assembled in the farmhouse — Holman Hunt, Charlie Collins, William and John Millais — all determined to work in earnest; Holman Hunt on his famous "Light of the World" and "The Hireling Shepherd," Charlie Collins at a background, William Millais on water-colour landscapes, and my father on the backgrounds for the two pictures he had then in hand.

From ten in the morning till dark the artists saw little of each other, but when the evenings "brought all things home" they assembled to talk deeply on Art, drink strong tea, and discuss and criticise each other's pictures.

Fortunately a record of these interesting days is preserved to us in Millais' letters to Mr. and Mrs. Combe, and his diary — the only one he ever kept — which was written at this time, and retained by my uncle William, who has kindly placed it at my disposal. Here are some of his letters — the first of which I would commend to the attention of Max Nordau, referring as it does to Ruskin, whom Millais met for the first time in the summer of this year. It was written from the cottage near Kingston before Millais and Hunt removed to Worcester Park Farm.

To Mrs. Combe.

"SURBITON HILL, KINGSTON,

"*July 2nd*, 1851.

"MY DEAR MRS. COMBE, — I have dined and taken breakfast with Ruskin, and we are such good friends that he wishes me to accompany him to Switzerland this summer. . . . We are as yet singularly at variance in our opinions upon Art.

"OPHELIA." 1852

By permission of H. Graves and Son

One of our differences is about Turner. He believes that I shall be converted on further acquaintance with his works, and I that he will gradually slacken in his admiration.

"You will see that I am writing this from Kingston, where I am stopping, it being near to a river that I am painting for 'Ophelia.' We get up (Hunt is with me) at six in the morning, and are at work by eight, returning home at seven in the evening. The lodgings we have are somewhat better than Mistress King's at Botley, but are, of course, horribly uncomfortable. We have had for dinner chops and suite of peas, potatoes, and gooseberry tart four days running. We spoke not about it, believing in the certainty of some change taking place; but in private we protest against the adage that 'you can never have too much of a good thing.' The countryfolk here are a shade more civil than those of Oxfordshire, but similarly given to that wondering stare, as though we were as strange a sight as the hippopotamus.*

"My martyrdom is more trying than any I have hitherto experienced. The flies of Surrey are more muscular, and have a still greater propensity for probing human flesh. Our first difficulty was . . . to acquire rooms. Those we now have are nearly four miles from Hunt's spot and two from mine, so we arrive jaded and slightly above that temperature necessary to make a cool commencement. I sit tailor-fashion under an umbrella throwing a shadow scarcely larger than a halfpenny for eleven hours, with a child's mug within reach to satisfy my thirst from the running stream beside me. I am threatened with a notice to appear before a magistrate for trespassing in a field and destroying the hay; likewise by the admission of a bull in the same field after the said hay be cut; am also in danger of being blown by the wind into the water, and becoming intimate with the feelings of Ophelia when that lady sank to muddy death, together with the (less likely) total disappearance, through the voracity of the flies. There are two swans who not a little add to my misery by persisting in watching me from the exact spot I wish to paint, occasionally destroying every water-weed within their

---

* It was in this year, 1850, that the first specimen of the hippopotamus was seen in London. Millais seems to have been of the same opinion as Lord Macaulay, who says: "I have seen the hippopotamus, both asleep and awake; and I can assure you that, awake or asleep, he is the ugliest of the works of God."

DESIGN FOR A PICTURE OF "ROMEO AND JULIET." 1852

reach. My sudden perilous evolutions on the extreme bank,
to persuade them to evacuate their position, have the effect
of entirely deranging my temper, my picture, brushes, and
palette; but, on the other hand, they cause those birds to
look most benignly upon me with an expression that seems
to advocate greater patience. Certainly the painting of a
picture under such circumstances would be a greater punishment to a murderer than hanging.

"I have read the *Sheepfolds*, but cannot give an opinion

upon it yet.   I feel it very lonely here.   Please write before my next.

"My love to the Early Christian and remembrances to friends.

"Very affectionately yours,
"JOHN EVERETT MILLAIS."

THE LAST SCENE, "ROMEO AND JULIET."   1848

To Mrs. Combe.

"SURBITON HILL, KINGSTON,
"*July*, 1851.

"MY DEAR MRS. PAT,—I have taken such an aversion to sheep, from so frequently having mutton chops for dinner, that I feel my very feet revolt at the proximity of woollen socks.   Your letter received to-day was so entertaining that I (reading and eating alternately) nearly forgot what I was devouring.   This statement will, I hope, induce Mr. Combe to write to me as a relish to the inevitable chops.   The steaks of Surrey are tougher than Brussels carpets, so they are out of the question.

"We are getting on very soberly, but have some suspicions that the sudden decrease of our bread and butter is occasioned by the C—— family (under momentary aberration) mistaking our fresh butter for their briny.   To ascertain the truth, we intend bringing our artistic capacity to bear upon the eatables in question by taking a careful

drawing of their outline. Upon their reappearance we shall
refer to the portraits, and thereby discover whether the steel
of Sheffield has shaven their features. [This they did and
made sketches of the butter.] Hunt is writing beside me
the description of (his) your picture. He has read Ruskin's
pamphlet, and with me is anxious to read Dyce's reply,
which I thank you for ordering. In the field where I am
painting there is hay-making going on; so at times I am
surrounded by women and men, the latter of which remark
that mine is a tedious job, that theirs is very warm work,
that it thundered somewhere yesterday, that it is likely we
shall have rain, and that they *feel thirsty, very thirsty.* An
uneasiness immediately comes over me; my fingers tingle
to bestow a British coin upon the honest yeomen to get rid
of them; but no, I shall not indulge the scoundrels after
their rude and greedy applications. Finding hints move me
not, they boldly ask for money for a drop of drink. In the
attitude of Napoleon commanding his troops over the Alps,
I desire them to behold the river, the which I drink. Then
comes a shout of what some writers would call honest
country laughter, and I, coarse brutality. Almost every
morning Hunt and I give money to children; so all the
mothers send their offspring (amounting by appearance to
twelve each) in the line of our road; and in rank and file
they stand curtsying with flattened palms ready to receive
the copper donation. This I like; but men with arms larger
round than my body hinting at money disgust me so much
that I shall paint some day (I hope) a picture laudatory
of Free Trade.

"Good-night to yourself and Mr. Combe; and believe
that I shall ever remain

" Most faithfully yours,

" JOHN EVERETT MILLAIS."

To Mrs. Combe.

" KINGSTON,
" *July 28th,* 1851.

" MY DEAR MRS. COMBE, — Many thanks for Dyce's answer,
which I received yesterday, and as yet have read but little,
and that little imperfectly understand.

" In answer to your botanical inquiries, the flowering rush

grows most luxuriantly along the banks of the river here, and I shall paint it in the picture ['Ophelia']. The other plant named I am not sufficiently learned in flowers to know. There is the dog-rose, river-daisy, forget-me-not, and a kind of soft, straw-coloured blossom (with the word 'sweet' in its name) also growing on the bank; I think it is called meadow-sweet.

"I am nightly working my brains for a subject. Some incident to illustrate patience I have a desire to paint. When I catch one I shall write you the description.

"I enclose Hunt's key to the missionary picture, with apologies from him for not having sooner prepared it. Begging you to receive his thanks for your kind invitation, believe me, with affectionate regards to Mr. Combe,

"Most truly yours,
"JOHN EVERETT MILLAIS."

To Mrs. Combe.

"WORCESTER PARK FARM, NEAR CHEAM, SURREY.
"*September,* 1851.

"MY DEAR MRS. COMBE, — You will see by the direction that we have changed our spot, and much for the better. Nothing can exceed the comfort of this new place. Little to write about except mishaps that have occurred to me.

"I have broken the nail of the left-hand little finger off at the root; the accident happened in catching a ball at cricket. I thought at first the bone was broken, so I moved off at once to a doctor, who cut something, and said I should lose the nail. I have been also bedridden three days from a bilious attack, from which, through many drugs, I am recovered.

"We all three live together as happily as ancient monastic brethren. Charley [Collins] has immensely altered, scarcely indulging in an observation. I believe he inwardly thinks that carefulness of himself is better for his soul. Outwardly it goes far to destroy his society, which now, when it happens that I am alone with him, is intolerably unsympathetic. I wish you could see this farm, situated on one of the highest hills in this county. In front of the house there is one of the finest avenues of elm trees I ever saw.

"We live almost entirely on the produce of the farm,

which supplies every necessary. Collins scarcely ever eats pastry; he abstains, I fancy, on religious principles.

"Remember me affectionately to the mother who pampers him, and believe me

"Most affectionately yours,

"JOHN MILLAIS."

To Mr. Combe.

"WORCESTER PARK FARM,
"*October* 15*th*, 1851.

"MY DEAR MR. COMBE, — You must have felt sometimes quite incapable of answering a letter. Such has been my state. I have made two fruitless attempts, and shudder for the end of this. Hunt and self are both delighted by your letter, detecting in it a serious intent to behold us plant the artistic umbrella on the sands of Asia. He has read one of the travels you sent us, *The Camp and the Caravan*, and considers the obstacles as trifling and easy to be overcome by three determined men, two of whom will have the aspect of ferocity, being bearded like the pard. Hunt can testify to the fertility of my upper lip, which augers well for the under soil. It therefore (under a tropical sun) may arrive at a Druidical excellence.

"Two of the children belonging to the house have come in and will not be turned out. I play with them till dinner and resume work again afterwards. The weather to-day has prevented my painting out of doors, so I comfortably painted from some flowers in the dining-room. Hunt walked to his spot, but returned disconsolate and wet through. Collins worked in his shed and looked most miserable; he is at this moment cleaning his palette. Hunt is smoking a vulgar pipe. He will have the better of us in the Holy Land, as a hookah goes with the costume. I like not the prospect of scorpions and snakes, with which I foresee we shall get closely intimate. Painting on the river's bank (Nile or Jordan) as I have done here will be next to throwing oneself into the alligators' jaws, so all water-sketching is put aside. Forgive this nonsensible scribble. I am only capable of writing my very kindest remembrances to Mrs. Pat, in which Charley and Hunt join.

"Most faithfully yours,

"JOHN EVERETT MILLAIS."

At this time Millais had serious thoughts of going to the East with Hunt, but eventually gave up the idea.

And now commences the diary, written closely and carefully on sheets of notepaper. The style savours somewhat of the conversation of Mr. Jingle; but, as in that gentleman's short and pithy sentences, the substance is clear.

EXTRACTS FROM DIARY.

I am advised by Coventry Patmore to keep a diary. Commence one forthwith. — To-day, *October 16th,* 1851, worked on my picture ['The Huguenot']; painted nasturtiums; saw a stoat run into a hole in the garden wall; went up to it and endeavoured to lure the little beast out by mimicking a rat's or mouse's squeak — not particular which. Succeeded, to my astonishment. He came half out of the hole and looked in my face, within easy reach.

"Lavinia (little daughter of landlady) I allowed to sit behind me on the box border and watch me paint, on promise of keeping excessively quiet; she complained that her seat struck very cold. In the adjoining orchard, boy and family knocking down apples; youngest sister but one screaming. Mother remarked, 'I wish you were in Heaven, my child; you are always crying'; and a little voice behind me chimed in, 'Heaven! where God lives?' and (turning to me) 'You can't see God.' Eldest sister, Fanny, came and looked on too. Told me her mother says, about a quarter to six, 'There's Long-limbs (J. E. M.) whistling for his dinner; be quick and get it ready.' Played with children *en masse* in the parlour before their bedtime. Hunt just come in. . . . Sat up till past twelve and discovered first-rate story for my present picture.

"*October 17th.* — Beautiful morning: frost on the barn roofs and the green before the houses. Played with the children after breakfast, and began painting about nine. Baby screaming — commenced about ten o'clock. Exhibition of devilish passion, from which it more particularly occurred to me that we are born in sin. Family crying continually, with slight intermission to recover strength. Lavinia beaten and put under the garden clothes-pole for being naughty, to stay there until more composed. Perceiving that to be an uncertain period, I kissed her wet eyes and released her from her position and sat her by me. Quite dumb for some

time; suddenly tremendously talkative.   These are some of
her observations: 'We have n't killed little Betsy (the pig)
yet; she means to have little pigs herself.   Ann (the
servant) says she is going to be your servant, and me your
cook, when you get married.'   Upon asking her whether
she could cook, she answered, 'Not like the cooks do.'   At
five gave up painting.   Bitter cold.   Children screaming
again."

"*October* 18*th*. — Fine sunny morning. Ate grapes. Little
Fanny worked at a doll's calico petticoat on a chair beside
me.   Driven in by drizzling weather, I work in the parlour;
Fanny, my companion, rather troublesome.   Coaxed her out.
Roars of laughter outside the window — F. flattening her
nose against the pane.   Mrs. Stapleton called, with married
son and daughter, and admired my pictures ecstatically.
Collins gone; went home after dinner.   Sat with Hunt in
the evening; pelted at a candle outside with little white
balls that grow on a shrub.   Composed design of 'Repentant
Sinner laying his head in Christ's bosom.' *

"*October* 19*th* (*Sunday*). — Expected Rossetti, who never
came.   Governor [his father] spent the day with us, saw
Hunt's picture and mine, and was delighted with them.
Went to church.   Capital sermon.   Poor Mr. Lewis felt
very gloomy all the day; supposed it to be the weather,
that being dull and drizzling. . . . Found two servants
of Captain Shepherd — both very pretty — one of whom I
thought of getting to sit for my picture.   Traversing the
same road home, entered into conversation with them.   Both
perfectly willing to sit, and evidently expecting it to be an
affair of a moment — one suggesting a pencil-scratch from
which the two heads in our pictures could be painted!   Bade
them good-night, feeling certain they will come to the farm
to-morrow for eggs or cream.   Went out to meet Collins,
but found we were too early, so came home and had tea.
I (too tired to go out again) sit down and write this, whilst
Hunt sets out once more with a large horn-lantern.   Despair
of ever gaining my right position, owing to hearing this day
that the Committee of Judgment of the Great Exhibition
have awarded a bronze medal in approbation of the most
sickening horror ever produced, 'The Greek Slave.'   Collins
returned with his hair cut as close as a man in a House of
Correction.

* This sketch, now in my possession, was never transferred to canvas.

"*October* 20*th.* — Finished flowers after breakfast, after which went out to bottom of garden and commenced brick wall. Received letter from James Michael — complimentary, as containing a prediction that I shall be the greatest painter England ever produced. Felt languid all day. Finished work about five and went out to see Charley. Walked on afterwards to meet Hunt, and waited for him. In opening the gate entering the farm, met the two girls. Spoke further with one on the matter of sitting.

"*October* 21*st.* — Painted from the wall and got on a great deal. Bees' nest in the planks at the side of the house, laid open by the removal of one of them for the purpose of smoking the inmates at night and getting the honey. Was induced by the carpenter to go up on the ladder to see what he called a curiosity. Did so, and got stung on the chin. . . . I walked on to meet Hunt with Collins. Met him, with two Tuppers, who dined with us off hare. All afterwards saw the burning of the bees, and tasted the honey. . . . Read songs in the *Princess*. Have greater (if possible) veneration for Tennyson.

"*October* 22*nd.* — Worked in the warren opposite the wall, and got on well, though teased, while painting, by little Fanny, who persisted in what she called 'tittling' me. . . . Hunt proposed painting 'for a lark,' the door of a cupboard beside the fireplace. Mentioned it to the landlady, who gave permission, with the assurance that if she did not approve of it she should scrub it out. Completed it jointly about two o'clock in the morning. . . .

"*October* 23*rd.* — Our landlady's marriage anniversary. Was asked by her some days back for the loan of our apartments to celebrate the event. 'If we were not too high they would be glad to see us.'

"Painted on the wall; the day very dull. A few trees shedding leaves behind me, spiders determinedly spinning webs between my nose and chin. . . . Joined the farmers and their wives. Two of them spoke about cattle and the new reaping-machine, complaining, between times, about the state of affairs. Supped with them; derived some knowledge of carving a chicken from watching one do so. Went to bed rather late, and read *In Memoriam*, which produced a refining melancholy. Landlady pleased with painting on cupboard."

Of this painting, by the way, my uncle, William Millais,

has another and somewhat different tale to tell.   He says:—
"Our landlady, Mrs. B., held artists to be of little account,
and my brother exasperated her to a degree on one occasion.
The day had been a soaking wet one.   None of us had gone
out, and we were at our wits' end to know what to do.   Jack,
at Hunt's suggestion, thought it would be a good joke to
paint on one of the cupboard doors.   There were two — one
on either side of the fireplace.   Mrs. B. had gone to market.
On coming into the room on her return, and seeing what had
been done — a picture painted on the cupboard door — she
was furious; the door had only lately been 'so beautifully
grained and varnished.'   Hunt in vain tried to appease her.
She bounced out of the room, saying she would make them
pay for it.

"It happened on the following day that the Vicar and
a lady called upon the young painters; and on being shown
into the sitting-room, Mrs. B. apologised for the 'horrid mess'
(as she called it) on the cupboard door.   They inquired who
had done it, and on being told that Mr. Millais was the cul-
prit, the lady said she would give Mrs. B. in exchange for the
door the lovely Indian shawl she had on; so when the
painters came in from their work, Mrs. B. came up cringingly
to my brother and said the only thing he could do was to
paint the other cupboard!   He did n't paint the other door,
but I believe Mrs. B. had the shawl."

And now, in continuation of the "Diary," we read:—

"*October 24th.* — Another day, exactly similar to the
previous.   Felt disinclined to work.   Walked with Hunt
to his place, returned home about eleven, and commenced
work myself, but did very little.   Read Tennyson and Patmore.   The spot very damp.   Walked to see Charlie about
four, and part of the way to meet Hunt, feeling very
depressed.   After dinner had a good nap, after which read
Coleridge — some horrible sonnets.   In his Life they speak
ironically of 'Christabel,' and highly of rubbish, calling it
Pantomime.

"*October 25th.* — Much like the preceding day.   All went
to Town after dinner; called at Rossetti's and saw Madox
Brown's picture 'Pretty Baa-lambs,' which is very beautiful.
Rossetti low-spirited; sat with him.

"*October 26th, Sunday.* — Walked out with Hunt.   Called
upon Woolner and upon Mrs. Collins to get her to come

and dine with us; unwell, so unsuccessful. Felt very cross and disputable. Charlie called in the evening; took tea, and then all three off to the country seat.

"*October 27th.* — Dry day. Rose later than the others, and had breakfast by myself. Painted on the wall, but not so well; felt uncomfortable all day. . . .

"*October 28th.* — My man, Young, brought me a rat after breakfast. Began painting it swimming, when the governor made his appearance, bringing money, and sat with me whilst at work. After four hours rat looked exactly like a drowned kitten. Felt discontented. Walked with parent out to see Collins painting on the hill, and on, afterwards, to Young's house. He had just shot another rat and brought it up to the house. Again painted upon the head, and much improved. . . . My father and myself walked on to see Hunt, whose picture looks sweet beyond mention.

"*October 29th.* — Cleaned out the rat, which looked like a lion, and enlarged picture. After breakfast began ivy on the wall; very cold, and my feet wet through; at intervals came indoors and warmed them at the kitchen fire. Worked till half-past four; brought all the traps in and read *In Memoriam.*

"*October 30th.* — Felt uneasy; could not paint out of doors, so dug up a weed in the garden path and painted it in the corner. . . . Went to bed early, leaving Hunt up reading Hooker.

"*October 31st.* — Splendid morning. . . . Painted ivy on the wall, and got on a great deal. After tea, about half-past ten, went to see powder-mill man (Young's) to commission him to fetch Hunt's picture home. Sat in their watch-house with him and his brother, who eulogised a cat, lying before the fire, for its uncommon predilection to fasten on dogs' backs, also great ratting qualities. Returned home about eleven and read *In Memoriam.* Left Hunt up reading Hooker.

"*November 4th.* — Frightfully cold morning; snowing. Determined to build up some kind of protection against the weather wherein to paint. After breakfast superintended in person the construction of my hut — made of four hurdles, like a sentry-box, covered outside with straw. Felt a 'Robinson Crusoe' inside it, and delightfully sheltered from the wind, though rather inconvenienced at first by the straw, dust, and husks flying about my picture. Landlady came down to see

1—9

me, and brought some hot wine. Hunt painting obstinate
sheep within call. . . . This evening walked out in the
orchard (beautiful moonlight night, but fearfully cold) with
a lantern for Hunt to see effect before finishing background,
which he intends doing by moonlight.

" *November* 5*th*. — Painted in my shed from ivy. Hunt
at the sheep again. My man Young, who brought another

"THE HUGUENOT." 1851
First idea

rat caught in the gin and little
disfigured, was employed by
Hunt to hold down a wretched
sheep, whose head was very
unsatisfactorily painted, after
the most tantalising exhibition
of obstinacy. Evening passed
off much as others. Read
Browning's tragedy, *Blot on the
Scutcheon*, and was astonished
at its faithfulness to Nature
and Shakespearian perfectness.
Mr. Lewis, the clergyman of
the adjoining parish, called, and
kindly gave us an invitation
to his place when we liked.
Had met him at dinner at our
parish curate's, Mr. Stapleton.

" *November* 6*th*. — Beautiful
morning; much warmer than
yesterday. Was advised by
Hunt to paint the rat, but felt
disinclined. After much inward
argument took the large box
containing Ophelia's background out beside Hunt, who
again was to paint the sheep. By lunch time had nearly
finished rat most successfully. Hunt employed small im-
pudent boy to hold down sheep. Boy not being strong
enough, required my assistance to make the animal lie down.
Imitated Young's manner of doing so, by raising it up off
the ground and dropping it suddenly down. Pulled an
awful quantity of wool out in the operation. Also painted
ivy in the other picture.

" *November* 7*th*. — After breakfast examined the rat [in the
painting]. From some doubtful feeling as to its perfect
portraiture determined to retouch it. Young made his ap-

pearance *apropos*, with another rat, and (for Hunt) a new
canvas from the carrier at Kingston. Worked very carefully at the rat, and finally succeeded to my own and
everyone's taste. Hunt was painting in a cattle-shed from
a sheep. Letters came for him about three. In opening
one we were most surprised and delighted to find the
Liverpool Academy (where his ' Two Gentlemen of Verona '
picture is) sensible enough to
award him the annual prize
of £50. He read the good
news and painted on unruffled.
The man Young, holding a
most amicable sheep, expressed
surprising pleasure at the fortunate circumstance. He said
he had seen robins in the
spring of the year fight so
fiercely that they had allowed
him to take them up in his
hands, hanging on to each
other. During the day Hunt
had a straw hut similar to
mine built, to paint a moonlight background to the fresh
canvas. Twelve o'clock. Have
this moment left him in it,
cheerfully working by a lantern
from some contorted apple
tree trunks, washed with the
phosphor light of a perfect
moon — the shadows of the

"THE HUGUENOT." 1851
Second idea

branches stained upon the sward. Steady sparks of moon-
struck dew. Went to bed at two o'clock.

" *November 8th.* — Got up before Hunt, who never went
to bed till after three. Painted in my hut, from the ivy,
all day. After dinner Collins went off to town. Hunt
again painting out of doors. Very little of moonshine for
him. . . . Advised H. to rub out part of background, which
he did.

" *November 9th, Sunday.* — Whilst dressing in the morning
saw F. M. Brown and William Rossetti coming to us in the
avenue. They spent the day with us. All disgusted with
the Royal Academy election. . . . They left us for the train,

for which they were too late, and returned to sleep here.
Further chatted and went to bed.

"*November 11th.* — Lay thinking in bed until eleven o'clock.
Painted ivy. Worked well; Hunt painting in the same
field; sheep held down by Young.

"*November 16th, Sunday.* — To church with Collins; Hunt,
having sat up all night painting out of doors, in bed. After
church found him still in his room; awoke him and had
breakfast with him, having gone without mine almost entirely,
feeling obliged to leave it for church. Hunt and self went
out to meet brother William, whom we expected to dinner.
Met him in the park. He saw Hunt's picture for the first
time, and was boundless in admiration; also equally eulogised
my ivy-covered wall. All three walked out before dinner.
. . . In what they called the Round-house saw a chicken
clogged in a small tank of oil. Young extricated it, and,
together with engine-driver's daughter, endeavoured (fruit-
lessly) to get the oil off. Left them washing fowl, and strolled
home.

"*November 17th.* — Small stray cat found by one of the
men, starved and almost frozen to death. Saw Mrs. Barnes
nursing it and a consumptive chicken; feeding the cat with
milk. Painted at the ivy. Evening same as usual."

Some further details are supplied in the following letter: —

To Mr. Combe.

"WORCESTER PARK FARM,
"*November 17th*, 1851.

" MY DEAR COMBE, — Doubtless you have been wondering
whether it is my intention ever to let you have your own
property ['The Dove' picture]. We hope to return almost
immediately, when I shall touch that which requires a little
addition, and directly send it on to you, a letter preceding it
to let you know. Hunt has gained the prize at Liverpool
for the best picture in the exhibition there. The cold has
become so intense that we fear it is impossible to further
paint in the open air. We have had little straw huts built,
which protect us somewhat from the wind, and therein till
to-day have courageously braved the weather.

"Carlo is still daily labouring at the shed, Hunt nightly
working out of doors in an orchard painting moonlight

(employed also in the daytime on another picture), and myself engaged in finishing another background (an ivy-covered wall). There is one consolation which strengthens our powers of endurance — necessary for the next week. It is to behold the array of cases, which are the barns of our summer harvest, standing in our entrance hall. . . .

"Very faithfully yours,
"JOHN EVERETT MILLAIS."

At this time Charles Collins was engaged on the background for a picture, the subject of which he had not yet settled upon. He got as far as placing upon the canvas an old shed with broken roof and sides, through which the sunlight streamed; with a peep outside at leaves glittering in the summer breeze; and at this he worked week after week with ever varying ideas as to the subject he should ultimately select. At last he found a beautiful one in the legend of a French peasant, who, with his family, outcast and starving, had taken refuge in the ruined hut and were ministered to by a saint. The picture, however, was never finished. Poor Collins gave up painting in despair and drifted into literature ; * and when the end came, Holman Hunt, who was called in to make a sketch of his friend, was much touched to find this very canvas (then taken off the strainers) lying on the bed beside the dead man. The tragedy of vanished hopes!

But I must now return to the "Diary."

"*November* 18*th*. — Little cat died in the night, also chicken. Painted ivy. In the afternoon walked to Ewell to procure writing-paper; chopped wood for our fire, and found it warming exercise.

"*November* 19*th*. — Fearfully cold. Landscape trees upon my window-panes. After breakfast chopped wood, and after that painted ivy. . . . See symptoms of a speedy finish to my background. After lunch pelted down some remaining apples in the orchard. Read Tennyson and the Thirty-nine Articles. Discoursed on religion.

"*November* 20*th*. — Worked at the wall; weather rather warmer. . . . Evening much as usual.

---

* Charles Collins was a regular contributor to *Household Words*, but is chiefly known by his *Cruise on Wheels*, a work which met with success.

"*November* 21*st.* — Change in the weather — cloudy and drizzling. All three began work after breakfast. Brother William came about one o'clock. After lunch found something for him to paint. Left him to begin, and painted till four, very satisfactorily.

"*November* 22*nd.* — All four began work early. William left at five, promising to come again on Monday. . . . After dinner Hunt and Collins left for London, the former about some inquiries respecting an appointment to draw for Layard, the Nineveh discoverer. After they were gone, I wrote a very long letter to Mrs. Combe."

The letter is perhaps worth insertion here, as showing the writer's attitude towards Romanism, which at that time he was supposed to favour, and as an indication of the general design of his picture, " The Huguenot." It ran thus : —

To Mrs. Combe.

" WORCESTER PARK FARM,
" *November* 22*nd,* 1851.

"MY DEAR MRS. COMBE, — My two friends have just gone to town, leaving me here all alone. I dine to-morrow (Sunday) with a very old friend of mine — Colonel Lemprière — resident in the neighbourhood, or else should go with them. Mr. Combe's letter reached me as mine left for Oxford. Assure him our conversation as often reverts to him as his thoughts turn to us in pacing the quad. The associates he derides have but little more capacity for painting than as many policemen taken promiscuously out of a division.

" I have no Academy news to tell him, and but little for you from home. Layard, the winged-bull discoverer, requires an artist with him (salary two hundred a year) and has applied for one at the School of Design, Somerset House. Hunt is going to-night to see about it, as, should there be intervals of time at his disposal for painting pictures, he would not dislike the notion. One inducement to him would be that there, as at Jerusalem, he could illustrate Biblical history. Should the appointment require immediate filling, he could not take it, as the work he is now about cannot be finished till March.

" My brother was with us to-day, and told me that Dr.

Hesse of Leyton College, understood that I was a Roman
Catholic (having been told so), and that my picture of
'The Return of the Dove to the Ark' was emblematical of
the return of all of us to that religion — a very convenient
construction to put upon it! I have no doubt that likewise
they will turn the subject I am at present about to their
advantage. It is a scene supposed to take place (as doubtless it did) on the eve of the massacre of St. Bartholomew's
Day. I shall have two lovers in the act of parting, the
woman a Papist and the man a Protestant. The badge worn
to distinguish the former from the latter was a white scarf on
the left arm. Many were base enough to escape murder by
wearing it. The girl will be endeavouring to tie the hand-
kerchief round the man's arm, so to save him; but he, holding his faith above his greatest worldly love, will be softly
preventing her. I am in high spirits about the subject, *as it
is entirely my own*, and I think contains the highest moral.
It will be very quiet, and but slightly suggest the horror of a
massacre. The figures will be talking against a secret-looking
garden wall, which I have painted here.

   "Hunt's moonlight design is from the Revelation of St.
John, chapter iii., 20th verse, 'Behold I stand at the door and
knock: if any man hear My voice, and open the door, I will
come in to him, and will sup with him, and he with Me.' It
is entirely typical, as the above. A figure of our Saviour in
an orchard abundant in fruit, holding in one hand a light
(further to illustrate the passage 'I am the Light of the
world'), and the other hand knocking at a door all over-
grown by vine branches and briars, which will show how
rarely it has been opened. I intend painting a pendant from
the latter part of the same, 'And will sup with him, and he
with Me.' It is quite impossible to describe the treatment I
purpose, so will leave you to surmise.

   "Now to other topics. We are occasionally visited by the
clergyman of the adjoining parish, a Mr. Lewis. He was at
Oriel, and knows Mr. Church, Marriot, and others that I
have met. He is a most delightful man and a really sound
preacher, and a great admirer and deplorer of Newman.

   "I cannot accompany 'The Dove' to the 'Clarendon,' as
I have un-get-off-ably promised to spend Xmas with the
family I feast with to-morrow, Captain Lemprière's. He is
from Jersey, and knew me when living there, and I would
not offend him.

"Our avenue trees snow down leaves all day long, and begin to show plainly the branches. Collins still fags at the shed, Hunt at the orchard, and I at the wall. Right glad we shall all be when we are having our harvest home at Hanover Terrace, which we hope to do next Tuesday week.

"Yours most faithfully

"(at twelve o'clock),

"JOHN EVERETT MILLAIS.

"Please send me a letter, or else I shall be jealous."

"THE HUGUENOT." 1852
Third idea

Millais having in this letter stated his conception of "The Huguenot," it may be as well, perhaps, to describe here its actual genesis.

After finishing the background for "Ophelia," he began making sketches of a pair of lovers whispering by a wall, and having announced his intention of utilising them in a picture, he at once commenced painting the background, merely leaving spaces for the figures. As may be gathered from what has been already said, both he and Hunt discussed together every picture which either of them had in contemplation; and, discoursing on the new subject one evening in September, Millais showed his pencil-drawings to Hunt, who strongly objected to his choice, saying that a simple pair of lovers without any powerful story, dramatic or historical, attaching to the meeting was not sufficiently important. It was hackneyed and wanting in general interest. "Besides," he quietly added, "it has always struck me as being the lovers' own private affair, and I feel as if we were intruding on so delicate an occasion by even looking at the picture. I protest against that kind of Art." Millais, however, was unconvinced, and stuck to his point, saying the subject would do quite well; at any rate, he should go on working at "his wall."

In the evening, when the three friends were gathered together, poor Charlie Collins came in for more "chaff" than his sensitive nature could stand. He had refused some blackberry tart which had been served at dinner, and Millais, knowing that he was very fond of this dish, ridiculed his "mortifying the flesh" and becoming so much of an ascetic. It was bad for him, he said, and his health was suffering in consequence; to which he humorously added, that he thought Collins kept a whip upstairs and indulged in private flagellations. At last Collins retreated to his room, and Millais, turning to Hunt, who had been quietly sketching the while, said, "Why didn't you back me up? You know these unhealthy views of religion are very bad for him. We must try and get him out of them." "I intend to leave them alone," replied the peaceful Hunt; "there's no necessity for us to copy him." A pause.

"Well," said Millais, "what have you been doing all this time while I have been pitching into Charlie?"

Hunt showed him some rough sketches he had been making — some of them being the first ideas for his famous picture, "The Light of the World."

"THE HUGUENOT." 1852
Fourth idea

Millais was delighted with the subject, and looking at some other loose sheets on which sketches had been made, asked what they were for.

"Well," replied Hunt, producing a drawing, "you will see now what I mean with regard to the lack of interest in a picture that tells only of the meeting or parting of two lovers. This incident is supposed to have taken place during the Wars of the Roses. The lady, belonging to the Red Roses, is within her castle; the lover, from the opposite camp, has scaled the walls, and is persuading her to fly with him. She is to be represented as hesitating between love and duty.

You have then got an interesting subject, and I would paint it with an evening sky as a background."

"Oh," exclaimed Millais, delighted, "that's the very thing for me! I have got the wall already painted, and need only put in the figures."

"But," said Hunt, "this is a castle wall. Your background won't do."

"That does n't matter," replied Millais, "I shall make one of the lovers belonging to the Red and the other to the White Rose faction; or one must be a supporter of King Charles and the other a Puritan."

After much discussion Millais suddenly remembered the opera of *The Hugenots*, and bethought him that a most dramatic scene could be made from the parting of the two lovers. He immediately began to make small sketches for the grouping of the figures, and wrote to his mother to go at once to the British Museum to look up the costumes.

Probably more sketches were made for this picture and for the "Black Brunswicker" than for any others of his works. I have now a number of them in my possession, and there must have been many more. They show that his first idea was to place other figures in the picture — two priests holding up the crucifix to the Huguenot, whose sweetheart likewise adds her persuasions. Again, other drawings show a priest on either side of the lovers, holding up one of the great candles of the Roman Catholic Church, and the Protestant waving them back with a gesture of disapproval. These ideas, however, were happily discarded — probably as savouring too much of the wholly obvious — and the artist wisely trusted to the simplicity of the pathos which marked the character of his final decision.

"THE HUGUENOT." 1852
Fifth and final composition for the picture

THE HUGUENOT. 1852

By permission of H. Graves and Son

It will be seen then that the picture was not (as has been publicly stated) the outcome of a visit to Meyerbeer's opera of *The Huguenots;* though some time after Millais' decision he and Hunt went to the opera to study the pose and costumes of the figures.

And now for some final extracts from the " Diary."

" *November 23rd, Sunday.* — Went to morning church; felt disgusted with the world, and all longing for worldly glory going fast out of me. Walked, miserable, to Ewell to spend the day with my old friends the Lemprières, who were at Sir John Reid's, opposite. Called there, and was received most kindly. From there went on to afternoon church. On our way met Mr. and Mrs. B——, my old flame. Wished myself anywhere but there; all seemed so horribly changed; the girl I knew so well calling me ' Mr. Millais ' instead of ' John,' and I addressing ' Fanny ' as ' Mrs. B——.' She married a man old enough to be her father; he, trying to look the young man, with a light cane in his hand. Walked over his grounds (which are very beautiful) and on to the new church, wherein the captain joined us, and shook hands most cordially with me. A most melancholy service over, all walked home. Mrs. B—— distant, and with her mother. Mr. B—— did not accompany us; found him at the captain's house — an apparently stupid man, plain and bald. Was perfectly stupefied by surprise at Mrs. B—— asking me to make a little sketch of her ugly old husband. They left, she making, at parting, a bungling expression of gladness at having met me. Walked over the house and gardens (Ewell), where I had spent so many happy months. . . . Had a quiet dinner — the captain, Mrs., Miss and Harry. In the evening drew Lifeguard on horseback ['Shaw, the Lifeguardsman,' shown at the 1898 Exhibition] for little Herbert, and something for Emily. Left them with a lantern (the night being dark) to meet my companions at the station. Got there too early, and paced the platform, ruminating sorrowfully on the changes since I was there last. . . . Reached home wet through. Good fire, dry shoes, and bed.

" *November 24th.* — Painted on brick wall. Mr. Taylor and his son (an old acquaintance of mine at Ewell), in the army, and six feet, came to see me. Both he and his father got double barrels; pheasant in son's pocket. They saw my pictures, expressed pleasure, and in leaving presented me with cock bird. Lemprières came. The parents and Miss

thought my pictures beautiful. I walked with them to the
gate at the bottom of the park, and there met Emma and
Mrs. B—— out of breath. They had driven after the
captain, also to see my landscape. Offered to show them
again, but the father would not permit the trouble. Parted,
promising to spend Christmas with them. Tried to resume
painting. All then took usual walk. Hunt, during day, had
a letter containing offer for his picture of ' Proteus.' He
wrote accepting it. . . .

" *November* 28*th.* — William came and worked at his
sketch, and Sir John Reid called to see my pictures. Were
both highly pleased. Took them to see Hunt's and Collins'.
Mr. B—— officious and revelling in snobbiness at having
such distinguished persons at the farm.

" *November* 29*th.* — All painted after breakfast — Hunt at
grass; myself, having nearly finished the wall, went on to
complete stalk and lower leaves of Canterbury-bell in the
corner. Young, who was with Hunt, said he heard the stag-
hounds out ; went to discover, and came running in in a state
of frenzied excitement for us to see the hunt. Saw about
fifty riders after the hounds, but missed seeing the stag, it
having got some distance ahead. Moralised afterwards,
thinking it a savage and uncivilised sport.

" *November* 30*th*, *Sunday.* — All rose early to get in time
for train at Ewell, to spend the day at Waddon. Were too
late, so walked into Epsom, expecting there to meet a train.
Found nothing before past one. Walked towards the downs.
and to church at eleven, where heard very good sermon.
Collins so pious in actions that he was watched by kind-
looking man opposite. Very wealthy congregation. . . .
Walked afterwards to Mrs. Hodgkinson's, but found she was
too unwell to sit with us, so dined with her husband; capital
dinner. Sat with Mrs. H—— in her bedroom, leaving them
smoking downstairs, and took leave about half-past nine, Mr.
Hodgkinson walking with us to station.

" *December* 1*st.* — All worked; bitter cold. William left us
after dinner. Hunt read a letter from purchaser of his
picture ; some money in advance enclosed in the same, and
an abusive fragment of a note upon our abilities. Felt
stupidly ruffled and bad-tempered. . . .

" *December* 3*rd.* — Hunt . . . painted indoors, and from
the window worked at some sheep driven opposite ; I still
at dandelions and groundsel. Kitten most playful about me ;

lay in my lap whilst painting, but was aroused by a little
field-mouse rustling near the box.   Made a pounce upon, but
failed in catching it.   A drizzling rain part of the day.   Cut
a great deal of wood, to get warm. . . . Returned, and
found a clerk from Chancery Lane lawyers in waiting upon
me, who came to induce me to attend chambers and swear
to my own signature upon Mr. Drury's will.   Told him I
could not attend earlier than next week.

   "*December 4th.* — Painted the ground.   Hunt expected Sir
George Glynn (to see the pictures), who came, accompanied
by his curate and another gentleman, about the middle of
the day, and admired them much.   Suggested curious alterations to both Collins' and Hunt's ; that C. should make
the 'Two Women Grinding at the Mill' in an Arabian tent,
evidently supposing that the subject was biblical instead of
in futurity.   After they were gone Hunt's uncle and aunt
came, both of whom understood most gratifyingly every
object except my water-rat, which the male relation (when
invited to guess at it) eagerly pronounced to be a hare.
Perceiving by our smile that he had made a mistake, a rabbit
was next hazarded, after which I have a faint recollection of
a dog or cat being mentioned by the spouse, who had brought
with her a sponge-cake and bottle of sherry, of which we
partook at luncheon.   Mutual success and unblemished
happiness was whispered over the wine, soon after which
they departed in a pony-chaise.   Laughed greatly over the
day, H. and self. . . .

   "*December 5th.* — This day hope to entirely finish my ivy
background.   Went down to the wall to give a last look.
The day mild as summer ; raining began about twelve.
Young came with a present of a bottle of catsup.   William
made his appearance about the same time, and told us of the
brutal murdering going on again in Paris.   He did not paint.
Young brought a dead mole that was ploughed up in the
field I paint in.   Though somewhat acquainted with the form
of the animal, was much surprised at the size and strength
of its fore-hands.   Finished, and chopped wood. . . . In
the evening Will slept, H. wrote letters, C. read the
Bible, and self Shakespeare ; and, later, walked out with
H. in the garden, it being such a calm, warm night.
Requested landlady to send in bill, intending to leave to-
morrow.   Had much consultation about the amount necessary for her, in consideration of the many friends entertained

by us. Felt, with Collins, a desire to sink into the earth and come up with pictures in our respective London studios."

On the following day Millais returned to Gower Street, his backgrounds being now completed ; set to work at once on the figures in the two pictures, Miss Siddal (afterwards Mrs. D. G. Rossetti) posing as the model for "Ophelia." Mr. Arthur Hughes has an interesting note about this lady in *The Letters of D. G. Rossetti to William Allingham.* He says :—

"Deverell accompanied his mother one day to a milliner's. Through an open door he saw a girl working with her needle : he got his mother to ask her to sit to him. She was the future Mrs. Rossetti. Millais painted her for his 'Ophelia' — wonderfully like her. She was tall and slender, with red, coppery hair and bright consumptive complexion, though in these early years she had no striking signs of ill-health. She had read Tennyson, having first come to know something about him by finding one or two of his poems on a piece of paper which she brought home to her mother wrapped round a pat of butter. Rossetti taught her to draw ; she used to be drawing while sitting to him. Her drawings were beautiful, but without force. They were feminine likenesses of his own."

Miss Siddal had a trying experience whilst acting as a model for "Ophelia." In order that the artist might get the proper set of the garments in water and the right atmosphere and aqueous effects, she had to lie in a large bath filled with water, which was kept at an even temperature by lamps placed beneath. One day, just as the picture was nearly finished, the lamps went out unnoticed by the artist, who was so intensely absorbed in his work that he thought of nothing else, and the poor lady was kept floating in the cold water till she was quite benumbed. She herself never complained of this, but the result was that she contracted a severe cold, and her father (an auctioneer at Oxford) wrote to Millais, threatening him with an action for £50 damages for his carelessness. Eventually the matter was satisfactorily compromised. Millais paid the doctor's bill ; and Miss Siddal, quickly recovering, was none the worse for her cold bath.

D. G. Rossetti had already fallen in love with her, struck with her "unworldly simplicity and purity of aspect" — qualities which, as those who knew her bear witness, Millais succeeded in conveying to the canvas — but it was not until 1860 that they married.

About the year 1873 "Ophelia" was exhibited at South Kensington; and Millais, going one day to have a look at it, noticed at once that several of the colours he had used in 1851 had gone wrong — notably the vivid green in the water-weed and the colouring of the face of the figure. He therefore had the picture back in his studio, and in a short time made it bloom again, as we see it to-day, as brilliant and fresh as when first painted. This is one of the great triumphs of his Pre-Raphaelite days. The colour, substance, and surface of his pictures have remained as perfect as the day they were put on. Nothing in recent Art I venture to say, exceeds the richness, yet perfect harmony, of the colours of Nature in "Ophelia" and "The Blind Girl"; and the same thing may be said of "The Proscribed Royalist," "The Black Brunswicker," and the women's skirts in "The Order of Release"; whilst the man's doublet in "The Huguenot" and the woman's dress in "Mariana" are perhaps the most daring things of the kind ever attempted.

Perhaps the greatest compliment ever paid to "Ophelia," as regards its truthfulness to Nature, is the fact that a certain Professor of Botany, being unable to take his class into the country and lecture from the objects before him, took them to the Guildhall, where this work was being exhibited, and discoursed to them upon the flowers and plants before them, which were, he said, as instructive as Nature herself.

Mr. Spielmann is enthusiastic in his praise of the picture. He speaks of it as "one of the greatest of Millais' conceptions, as well as one of the most marvellously and completely accurate and elaborate studies of Nature ever made by the hand of man. . . . The robin whistles on the branch, while the distraught Ophelia sings her own death-dirge, just as she sinks beneath the water with eyes wide open, unconscious of the danger and all else. It is one of the proofs of the greatness of this picture that, despite all elaboration, less worthy though still superb of execution, the brilliancy of colour, diligence of microscopic research, and masterly handling, it is Ophelia's face that holds the spectator, rivets his attention, and stirs his emotion."

The picture passed successively through the hands of Mr. Farrer, Mr. B. Windus, and Mr. Fuller Maitland, before it came into the possession of Mr. Henry Tate, to whose generosity the public are indebted for its addition to the

I — 10

National Gallery of British Art. It was exceedingly well engraved by Mr. I. Stevenson in 1866.

In the 1852 Exhibition, when both the "Ophelia" and "The Huguenot" were exhibited, there was another beautiful "Ophelia" by Millais' friend, Arthur Hughes, who is good enough to send me the following note about the two pictures : —

"One of the nicest things that I remember is connected with an 'Ophelia' I painted, that was exhibited in the Academy at the same time as his [Millais'] own most beautiful and wonderful picture of that subject. Mine met its fate high up in the little octagon room;* but on the morning of the varnishing, as I was going through the first room, before I knew where I was, Millais met me, saying, 'Are n't you he they call Cherry?' (my name in the school). I said I was. Then he said he had just been up a ladder looking at my picture, and that it gave him more pleasure than any picture there, but adding also very truly that I had not painted the right kind of stream. He had just passed out of the Schools when I began in them, and I had a most enormous admiration for him, and he always looked so beautiful — tall, slender, but strong, crowned with an ideal head, and (as Rossetti said) 'with the face of an angel.' He could not have done a kinder thing, for he knew I should be disappointed at the place my picture had."

"The Huguenot" was exhibited with the following title and quotation in the catalogue: "A Huguenot, on St. Bartholomew's Day refusing to shield himself from danger by wearing the Roman Catholic badge. (See *The Protestant Reformation in France*, vol. ii., p. 352.) When the clock of the Palais de Justice shall sound upon the great bell at daybreak, then each good Catholic must bind a strip of white linen round his arm and place a fair white cross in his cap." (The Order of the Duc de Guise.)

Mr. Stephens says : — "When 'A Huguenot' was exhibited at the Royal Academy, crowds stood before it all day long. Men lingered there for hours, and went away but to return. It had clothed the old feelings of men in a new garment, and its pathos found almost universal acceptance. This was the picture that brought Millais to the height of his reputation. Nevertheless, even 'A Huguenot' did not silence all challengers. There were critics who said that

---

* Commonly known to artists of the period as "The Condemned Cell."

the man's arm could not reach so far round the lady's neck,
and there were others, knowing little of the South, who
carped at the presence of nasturtiums in August. It was
on the whole, however, admitted that the artist had at
last conquered his public, and must henceforth educate
them."

The picture is said to have been painted under a commission from a Mr. White (a dealer) for £150; but, as a
fact, Millais received £250 for it, which was paid to him
in instalments, and in course of time the buyer gave him
£50 more, because he had profited much by the sale of
the engraving. The dealers no doubt made immense sums
out of the copyrights alone of "The Huguenot," "The
Black Brunswicker," and "The Order of Release"; while —
as to "The Huguenot" at least — the poor artist had to wait
many months for his money and to listen meanwhile to a
chorus of fault-finding from the pens of carping scribblers,
whose criticism, as is now patent to all the world, proved
only their ignorance of the subject on which they were
writing. In turn, every detail of the picture was objected
to on one score or another, even the lady herself being
remarked upon as "very plain." No paper, except *Punch*
and the *Spectator* [William Rossetti], showed the slightest
glimmering of comprehension as to its pathos and beauty,
or foresaw the hold that it eventually obtained on the heart
of the people. But Tom Taylor, the Art critic of *Punch*
at that time, had something more than an inkling of this, as
may be seen in his boldly-expressed critique in *Punch*, vol. i.
of 1852, pp. 216, 217. The women in "Ophelia" and "The
Huguenot" were essentially characteristic of Millais' Art,
showing his ideal of womankind as gentle, lovable creatures;
and, whatever Art critics may say to the contrary, this aim —
the portrayal of woman at her best — is one distinctly of our
own national school. As Millais himself once said, "It is
only since Watteau and Gainsborough that woman has won
her right place in Art. The Dutch had no love for women,
and the Italians were as bad. The women's pictures by
Titian, Raphael, Rembrandt, Van Dyck, and Velasquez are
magnificent as works of Art; but who would care to kiss
such women? Watteau, Gainsborough, and Reynolds were
needed to show us how to do justice to woman and to
reflect her sweetness."

A sweeping statement like this is, of course, open to

exceptions — there are many notable examples in both French and Italian Art in which woman receives her due — but in the main it is undoubtedly true.

"The Huguenot" was the first of a series of four pictures embracing "The Proscribed Royalist," "The Order of Release," and "The Black Brunswicker," each of which represents a more or less unfinished story of unselfish love, in which the sweetness of woman shines conspicuous.

The figure of the Huguenot (as I have said before) was painted for the most part from Mr. Arthur (now General) Lemprière — an old friend of the family — and afterwards completed with the aid of a model.

Of his sittings to Millais during 1853, Major-General Lemprière kindly sends me the following : — " It was a short time before I got my commission in the Royal Engineers in the year 1853 (when I was about eighteen years old) that I had the honour of sitting for his famous picture of ' The Huguenot.' If I remember right, he was then living with his father and mother in Bloomsbury Square. I used to go up there pretty often and occasionally stopped there. His father and mother were always most kind.

" After several sittings I remember he was not satisfied with what he had put on the canvas, and he took a knife and scraped my head out of the picture, and did it all again. He always talked in the most cheery way all the time he was painting, and made it impossible for one to feel dull or tired. I little thought what an honour was being conferred on me, and at the time did not appreciate it, as I have always since.

" I remember, however, so well his kindness in giving me, for having sat, a canary-bird and cage, and also a water-colour drawing from his portfolio (' Attack on Kenilworth Castle '), which, with several others of his early sketches which I have, were exhibited at the Royal Academy of Arts after his death.

" I was abroad, off and on, for some thirty years after I got my commission, and almost lost sight of my dear old friend. He, in the meantime, had risen so high in his profession that I felt almost afraid of calling on him. One morning, however, being near Palace Gate, I plucked up courage, and went to the house and gave my card to the butler, and asked him to take it in to Sir John, which he did ; and you can imagine my delight when Sir John almost immediately came out of his studio in his shirt-sleeves, straight to the front door, and greeted me most heartily.

"I was most deeply touched, about a fortnight before he died, at his asking to see me, and when I went to his bed-side at his putting his arms round my neck and kissing me."

A lovely woman (Miss Ryan) sat for the lady in "The Huguenot," Mrs. George Hodgkinson, the artist's cousin, taking her place upon occasion as a model for the left arm of the figure. Alas for Miss Ryan! her beauty proved a fatal gift: she married an ostler, and her later history is a sad one. My father was always reluctant to speak of it, feeling perhaps that the publicity he had given to her beauty might in some small measure have helped (as the saying is) to turn her head.

The picture was the first of many engraved by his old friend, Mr. T. O. Barlow, R. A., and exceedingly well it was done. It eventually became the property of Mr. Miller, of Preston, and now belongs to his son. As this gentleman bought several of my father's works, and is so frequently mentioned hereafter, the description of him by Madox Brown in D. G. Rossetti's Letters may be of interest:—
"This Miller is a jolly, kind old man, with streaming white hair, fine features, and a beautiful keen eye like Mulready's. A rich brogue (he was Scotch, not Irish), a pipe of Cavendish, and a smart rejoinder, with a pleasant word for every man, woman, and child he met, are characteristic of him. His house is full of pictures, even to the kitchen. Many pictures he has at all his friends' houses, and his house at Bute is also filled with his inferior ones. His hospitality is some-what peculiar of its kind. His dinner, which is at six, is of one joint and vegetables, without pudding. Bottled beer for drink. I never saw any wine. After dinner he instantly hurries you off to tea, and then back again to smoke. He calls it meat-tea, and boasts that few people who have ever dined with him come back again." Mr. W. M. Rossetti describes him as "one of the most cordial, large-hearted, and lovable men I ever knew. He was so strong in belief as to be a sceptic as regards the absence of belief. I once heard him say, in his strong Scotch accent, 'An atheist, if such an animal ever really existed.' What the supposititious animal would do, I forget."

Amongst other work of Millais this year was the retouching of "Cymon and Iphigenia," a picture done by him in his seventeenth year, and now vastly improved by a fresh impression of colour and a further Pre-Raphaelite finish of the flowers in the foreground.

"Memory," a little head of the Marchioness of Ripon, was also painted this winter. A more important work, however, is "The Bridesmaid," for the head of which Mrs. Nassau Senior sat. "The Return of the Dove" was also finished and sent to its owner along with the following letter : —

To Mr. Combe.

"83 Gower Street, Bedford Square,
"*December 9th,* 1851.

"My dear Mr. Combe, — I have touched your picture, 'The Return of the Dove,' at last; and hope it will arrive safely.

"We came home on Saturday night. My brother brought the pictures on Monday evening, one of them not having dried completely. We have all fortunately escaped colds, which (considering the great exposure we have undergone) is something to be thankful for. My first two days of London have again occasioned that hatred for the place I had upon returning to it last year. I had a headache yesterday, and another about to come now.

"You will perceive in some lights a little dulness on the surface of 'The Dove's' background. It will all disappear when it is varnished, which must not be for some little time. It is almost impossible to paint a picture without some bloom coming on the face of it.

"You recollect it was arranged between Charley and myself that it should hang nearest the window, beside Hunt's. Please let it be a little leaned forward.

"My mother is talking with Hunt approvingly of the works I have just had home, and I cannot write more without jumbling what they are saying in this.

"In great haste,
"Most sincerely yours,
"John Everett Millais.

"'The Dove' will be sent off to you to-morrow (Wednesday) by rail. The reason for hanging the picture nearer the light is that it is much darker than Collins' 'Nun.'"

Another letter addressed to Mrs. Combe, and referring to the sale of " Ophelia," carries us to the end of this year.

To Mrs. Combe.

"83 GOWER STREET,
"*December* 12*th*, 1851.

" MY DEAR MRS. COMBE, — I enclose a little book written by Miss Rossetti. I promised to send it to you a long while ago, but have only recollected it now. I think you will greatly admire it. My remembrance of it is but slight, not having read it for several years. I was glad to hear that 'The Dove' arrived safely, and that it gains upon acquaintance.

" Mr. Farrar bought the 'Ophelia' the day before yesterday for three hundred guineas. The day previous, a Mr. White, a purchaser, was so delighted with it that he half closed with me. I expect he will call to-morrow to say that he will have it, when he will be much disappointed to hear of its sale.

" Wilkie Collins is writing a Christmas book for which I have undertaken to make a small etching.

" Hunt's prize picture of 'Proteus' is sold to a gentleman at Belfast — which sets him (H.) up in opulence for the winter. I saw Charley last night. He is just the same as ever — so provokingly quiet. I fancy you have rather mistaken my feelings towards him; not a whit of our friendship has diminished. I was with him last night, but little or nothing he said. I played backgammon with the matron.

" Let me know what you think of the 'Rivulets.' . . .

" In haste, yours sincerely,
" JOHN EVERETT MILLAIS."

CHAPTER V

1852—1853

FROM the first day of 1852 down to the opening of the Royal Academy Millais continued to work away at the figures in "The Huguenot" and "Ophelia," devoting all his spare time to pictures of smaller importance. His life at this period may be gathered from the following letters, in which some reference to historical events invites a word of explanation.

A series of revolutions in France, commencing in 1848, culminated in the famous *coup d'état* of December, 1851, when for the first time universal suffrage was established, and as the result, Prince Louis Napoleon was re-elected President of the Republic for ten years certain. He soon let them know what that meant. No sooner was he installed in office than he banished into exile the distinguished general officers who were opposed to him, disbanded the National Guard and appointed others in their place, dismissed eighty-three members of the late legislative assembly, and finally put an end to the liberty of the Press. These high-handed proceedings threw all England into a ferment. The newspapers raised a howl of execration against the tyrant; and the government, taking alarm, established the Channel Fleet and called into existence a number of volunteer rifle corps to aid in the national defence. A glimpse at what followed will be found in the correspondence.

"THE RACE MEETING." 1853

To Mr. Combe.

"83 GOWER STREET,
"*January 9th,* 1852.

"DEAR MR. COMBE, — Believe me, I have made many struggles to write to you, but somehow or other I have felt stupid and incompetent directly my hand clenched the pen. I fear it is my normal state now, but feel something must be written.

"I have been working most determinedly since Christmas, but (curiously) with little effect. I have given up all visiting, so I cannot be accused on that score of giving little evidence of progress.

"Next week I hope to sail into a kind of artistic trade-wind, which will carry me on to the Exhibition. . . . The whole of this day I have been drawing from two living creatures embracing each other.

"In looking over this, I see so many 'I haves' that I feel inclined to throw it into the fire and cab off to the Great Western rail and on to Oxford, to show you that I have not forgotten you. My Christmas was a very leisurely time. I went into the country the day before, and returned the day after in a state of great depression. Both Hunt and Charley have been, I fancy, much in the same condition as myself in regard to working. The latter has not even yet determined upon his composition. I doubt whether he will have time to complete it for the Academy. Hunt came back from Oxford most elaborately delighted. I was astonished at the quantity of visiting he managed in the time.

"They say that Turner has left £200,000 — some estimate it at double that amount — which I very much doubt. I hear from good authority that a great portion of this money is going towards some houses for decayed limners, which is very creditable to Mr. T. Probably some of the worst living daubers are looking forward to the time when they are incapable of spoiling more canvases, and are lodged in the Turner Almshouses. C—— has no chance, for they must be oil-painters.

"I hope my garrulous capacity will return to me soon, when I intend writing to Mrs. Pat. Remember me to her, and believe me

"Most sincerely yours,
"JOHN E. MILLAIS."

My father had but a slight acquaintance with Turner, though my mother was among the few of her sex who were ever permitted to enter the great landscape painter's house. She knew him well, and from her I obtained some interesting notes, which I give in her own words: " I used frequently to go and see Turner and his pictures, and though very few *ladies* were ever allowed to enter his doors, he was very kind to young artists. He lived like a hermit in a great lonely house in Queen Anne Street; his walls hung with many of his own pictures, which he refused to part with. He would not sell these on any account whatever, and one day he showed me a blank cheque which had been sent to him to fill in to any amount he chose if he would sell one of his pictures, but he laughed at the idea and sent back the cheque immediately.

" The glass over many of his works was broken, and large pieces of brown paper were pasted over the cracks, for he would not be at the expense of new ones. Mr. Frith rightly described the studio when he said ' the walls were almost paperless, the roof far from weatherproof, and the whole place desolate in the extreme '; whilst Munro * used to say that the very look of the place was enough to give a man a cold.

" Withal he had a great sense of humour, and when telling a story would put his finger to the side of his nose, and look exactly like ' Punch.'

" Apropos of his physiognomy, he always resisted any attempt to make a likeness of him; but one day after dinner

STUDIES FOR "THE ROYALIST." 1853

---

* Munro of Novar, who lived in Hamilton Place, possessed several of Turner's best works, for which he had paid sums not exceeding £200. Amongst them was one of the artist's masterpieces, "The Grand Canal at Venice," which, after Mr. Munro's death, was purchased by Lord Dudley for nearly £8000.

at the house of a friend, Count d'Orsay, a clever artist made an excellent drawing of him drinking his coffee ; but this was done without Turner's knowledge, and is, I believe, one of the few portraits of him now extant.

" He disliked society, and was intimate with very few people, his principal friends being Mr. Bicknell, of Denmark Hill, and Munro, of Novar, though at times he frequented the Athenæum Club.

" After a while he took an intense dislike to his home in Queen Anne Street, and only Munro knew where he removed

MILLAIS ON THE WAY TO PAINT "THE ROYALIST"
Sketch by William Millais

to. Before this, however, he spent much time with Mr. Fawkes, of Farnley Hall, near Leeds, for whom he painted many pictures. I have stayed there, and examined the ex-quisite water-colour landscapes he did there, as well as a large portfolio of birds' eggs and feathers, also in water-colours, most beautifully finished.

" Turner had a fancy for architecture, but the lodges which he planned at Farnley are of a sort of heavy Greek design, and not quite a success.

" His one pleasure in the days when I knew him was driving himself about the country ; but he was evidently not accustomed to horses, as he paid no attention to them, being too much engrossed in admiring the landscape, and in conse-quence, one day Mr. Fawkes' family, who were committed to

his tender mercies, found themselves sitting in the middle
of the road with the trap on the top of them.

"Turner told me that the way in which he studied clouds
was by taking a boat, which he anchored in some stream, and
then lay on his back in it, gazing at the heavens for hours,
and even days, till he had grasped some effect of light which
he desired to transpose to canvas.

"No one was admitted to his house in Queen Anne Street
unless specially invited. There was a sort of little iron grille
in the centre of the front door, through which the old house-
keeper used to look and see who was there.

"As an example of the rarity of visitors, the late Lord

MILLAIS AT DINNER. 1853
By William Millais

Lansdowne, who was a great
lover of Art and a friend of
Turner's, told me that after
receiving no answers to his
letters he resolved to beard the
lion in his den. He therefore
went and knocked at the door,
when a shock-head appeared
at the iron grating, and its
owner called out, 'Cats'-meat,
I suppose?' 'Yes, cats'-meat,'
answered his lordship, and
squeezed himself in.*

"After leaving Queen Anne
Street, Turner seems to have
taken a fancy to a little old-fashioned inn near Cheyne
Walk, Chelsea. It was kept by a widow, and he asked
if he might be allowed to live there. On her inquiring
as to who he was, he said to her, 'What is *your* name?'
to which she replied, 'Mrs. Brown.' 'Well,' said Turner,
'I'm Mr. Brown.' In this house he remained for some
years, visiting only his friend Munro and the Athenæum
Club.

"At last, one day he became seriously ill, and it was only
by his constantly calling out for Lady Eastlake (the wife of
the President of the Royal Academy), and on her being sent
for, that his identity became known."

---

* The Marquis of Lansdowne was a man of great benevolence and culture.
At his table Millais and his wife constantly dined, and there they met all the
literary and artistic celebrities of the day. He gave exquisite entertainments, and
after dessert always called in the Italian cook to compliment him on the feast.

Returning now to the correspondence, I find the following letter: —

To Mr. Combe.

"83 GOWER STREET,
"*February 5th,* 1852.

" MY DEAR MR. COMBE, — Don't be alarmed at this mighty circular, and think that the French have already landed. They have not come here yet; but, to guard against such an awful event, the gentlemen of London are arming themselves and forming rifle clubs; and those who cannot give their personal assistance are aiding us by subscriptions for the purpose of furnishing rifles to those who cannot afford them, yet are willing to join in the service of their country — clerks and the like. My governor is on the Committee, and my brother and self have joined. Several very influential men are at the head of it. A number of ladies are getting up subscriptions, and 'the smallest contributions will be most thankfully received.' In the City there are a thousand double-barrelled riflemen, composed of the gentlemen of the Stock Exchange. I am sure you will see that such measures are stringent upon all Englishmen, and excuse my troubling you on such a subject.

" Faithfully yours,
" JOHN MILLAIS.

" P. S. — The advertisement of our club has appeared three times in *The Times,* and we already muster upwards of two hundred gentlemen."

Amongst those whom he saw much of at this period, and to whom he was greatly attached, were his cousins George Hodgkinson and his wife Emily. He frequently paid them Saturday-to-Monday visits, when he was working in London. during the years 1851–54. He also corresponded pretty regularly with Mrs. Hodgkinson, who has most kindly placed her letters at my disposal.

To Mrs. Combe.

"83 GOWER STREET,
"*March 6th,* 1852.

" MY DEAR MRS. COMBE, — I promised some time back to write you a letter. Pardon me, for I am a wretched corres-

pondent. I am just now working so hard that I am glad
to escape anything like painting, but I confess, writing is
almost as difficult a thing with me.

" I have very lately made the acquaintance of Mr.
Thackeray, the author of *Vanity Fair*. He called un-
expectedly upon me — not to see my picture, he said, but
to know me. I have returned his call, and find him a
most agreeable man. Mr. Pollen and his brother also
have paid me a visit, accompanied by Mr. Dean. Pollen's

SKETCH OF MILLAIS PAINTING THE BACKGROUND OF "THE ROYALIST"
By William Millais

brother is a good judge of painting, which is a rare thing
in our days.

" I am getting on slowly, but I hope surely. Ophelia's
head is finished, and the Huguenot is very nearly complete;
the Roman Catholic girl is but sketched in. I am waiting
for a young lady who has promised me to sit for the face, but
is going to undergo an operation on her throat, which will
prevent her doing so for a fortnight or more. . . . I rarely
see Hunt or Carlo, as they, like myself, stay at home in
the evenings and go to rest early, so that they may rise
likewise. I believe they are progressing with their work,
but I daresay you know more of them than I do.

" Yours most truly,
" JOHN EVERETT MILLAIS."

To Mr. Combe.

"83 GOWER STREET,
"*March*, 1852.

"MY DEAR MR. COMBE, — Recklessly I commence this letter, without the least knowledge of what is to follow. This night I promised Hunt to spend the evening with him, but am restrained by the immensity of the distance, feeling rather tired from a long walk we took together on Sunday, to Mr. Windus, the owner of all the celebrated pictures of the late William Turner, R.A. He has some

DINNER AT THE "GEORGE INN," HAYES. 1853
Sketched by William Millais

of the most valuable works in the world — upwards of fifty of Turner's most excellent paintings, some of which are valued at fifteen hundred pounds, and amongst his collection he has several of mine — one large and some small — besides drawings. Some day, when you are in town, I must take you there. It is really a treat to see the house alone. The furniture is of the most magnificent kind, and the rooms are open to the public, I think, twice a week. It is at Tottenham, about seven miles from London.

"Farrer has sent the picture of 'Mariana' to Edinburgh, to gratify the Caledonian curiosity, those people having expressed a wish to see some of the Pre-Raphaelite pictures. I am continually receiving Scotch papers with frightfully long criticisms, a vast quantity of praise and, of course,

I — 11

advice. To-day I have purchased a really splendid lady's ancient dress — all flowered over in silver embroidery — and I am going to paint it for 'Ophelia.' You may imagine it is something rather good when I tell you it cost me, old and dirty as it is, four pounds.

"'The Huguenot' I have been working at to-day, but not very satisfactorily, having been disturbed all the afternoon.

"The Rifle Club is getting on splendidly. They have taken rooms in the Strand, and are increasing rapidly in numbers. All the country clubs are joining; so ultimately it will become a very prodigious assembly. At present the rooms they have are but offices in which they have the proposed uniform — grey turned up with green. The costume will be drawn in the *Illustrated News* of next week. When the corps is regularly formed, it is likely (as most of the members are private gentlemen and well-off) that there will be some place for members from the country to meet and dine, and reading-rooms for the accommodation of the whole body.

I begin to feel tired at the sight of paints, having worked without intermission for ten months. This year I hope to enjoy the summer without a millstone of a picture hanging about my neck. The subject I intend doing will not require much out-of-door painting — nothing but a sheet of water and a few trees — a bit of flooded country, such as I have seen near you at Whitham.

"Yours most sincerely,

"JOHN EVERETT MILLAIS."

To the same.

"83 GOWER STREET,
"*March 31st*, 1852.

"MY DEAR MR. COMBE, — Many thanks for your kind wish for my visiting you after Easter. I am partly under an engagement to accompany a friend to Paris should the weather be favourable. With regard to 'The Huguenot' picture, I am happy to say I sold it to a gentleman, the very morning after you and Mrs. Pat called, for two hundred and fifty pounds. I have finished another picture, and have only to paint the skirt of Ophelia's dress, which will not, I think, take me more than Saturday. I have every hope of their being placed in very good positions, the principal hanger, Mr. Leslie, having called twice to see them, each time expressing great admiration.

"In great haste, most sincerely yours,

"JOHN E. MILLAIS."

To the same.

"83 GOWER STREET,
"*Sunday, April 18th,* 1852.

"MY DEAR MR. COMBE, — Forgive my not having answered your letter sooner. Ever since the sending in of the pictures I have been running about London, calling, and taking walks into the country. You ask me to describe the dance of Mrs. Collins. I truly wish that you had been there. It was a delightful evening. Charlie [Collins] never got beyond a very solemn quadrille, though he is an excellent waltzer and polka dancer. Poor Mrs. C. was totally dumb from a violent influenza she unfortunately caught that very afternoon. She received all her guests in a whisper and a round face of welcome. There were many lions — amongst others the famous Dickens, who came for about half an hour and officiated as principal carver at supper. Altogether there were about seventy people. I heard many very cheering remarks about my pictures from Academicians, one of whom went so far as to say that they were the best paintings in the Exhibition. I am in great hope of finding them in capital positions after these compliments.

"I have just returned from the Foundling Church. The service is exceptionally good, and the children look very pretty. During the Litany one of the smallest fidgeted one of her shoes off, which fell through the palisades and on to the head of some person below. With all the evident care that is bestowed upon their education, I am astonished that the masters do not forbid the use of thumbs and saliva in turning over leaves.

"Next week, or rather this, I mean to commence painting again, for I cannot stand entire laziness. 'Romeo and Juliet' is to be my next subject — not so large as either of this year's. It is an order from a Mr. Pocock, one of the secretaries of the Art Union. 'The Huguenot,' which

was sold to Mr. White, a dealer, has since been sold by
him to Mr. Windus, the man who has all the celebrated
Turners, and has already one of my paintings — 'Isabella,'
from Keats' poem.   I am glad that it is in so good a collection, but cannot understand a man paying perhaps double
the money I should have asked him.

   " With love to Mrs. Pat, believe me,
                    " Most truly yours,
                          " JOHN EVERETT MILLAIS."

Note. — Nothing was done towards the painting of " Romeo
and Juliet" beyond the sketch which the artist made for it in
1848, and which was shown by Mr. John Clayton at the
Millais Exhibition in 1898, and an additional design of the
balcony scene [1852].   After discussing various subjects with
Mr. Pocock, Millais' suggestion of the " The Proscribed
Royalist" was approved, and shortly afterwards the picture
was painted, and passed into the possession of Mr. Pocock.

Mr. G. D. Leslie, R.A., tells me that at this date Millais
sat to his father for the head of Lord Petre, in a picture of
" The Rape of the Lock."   " My father," he said, " painted
Sir John on a small panel, just as he was, in a black frock
coat, and a black cravat, with a little golden goose for a pin.
The portrait was a very good likeness of him at that time,
and was sold at the sale of my father's pictures in 1860.   I
don't know who purchased it."

   " The Rape of the Lock " was bought by the late John
Gibbons, of Hanover Terrace, who had a fine collection of
pictures, and it is now in the possession of his son.

                  To Mrs. Combe.

                          " 83 GOWER STREET,
                            "*June 9th*, 1852.

" MY DEAR MRS. COMBE, — With this I send you the lace
which you were kind enough to procure for me.   [It was
used in ' The Huguenot,' and afterwards in ' The Proscribed Royalist.']   In returning it to the lady, I hope you
will express my acknowledgments for her great kindness.

   " I have a subject that I am mad to commence [' The
Proscribed Royalist'], and yesterday took lodgings at a
delightful little inn near a spot exactly suited for the

background. I hope to begin painting on Tuesday morning,
and intend working without coming to town at all till it is
done. The village is so very far from any railway station
that I have no chance of getting to London in rainy weather.
My brother is going to live with me part of the time, so I
shall not be entirely a hermit. . . .

"The immense success I have met with this year has
given me a new sensation of pleasure in painting. I have
letters almost every day for one or other of the pictures, and
only wish your guest was as lucky, that he might go off to
the Holy Land as soon as possible with me. I shall never go
by myself. When I get to my country residence, I will keep
up a proper correspondence with both of you. Lately I have
hated the sight of a pen, and have scarcely answered letters
requiring an immediate reply. . . . I have been paying a
long-standing visit at a relation's near Croydon, and have
become acquainted with the clergyman of the adjoining
parish — a Mr. Hamilton, rector of Beddington — one of the
most delightful men I ever met. He is a great friend of
Mr. Marriott and others whose names I have heard you
mention. His church and village are quite *beaux idéals* . . .

"Yours very sincerely,

"JOHN EVERETT MILLAIS."

This is the first letter in which Millais mentions "The
Proscribed Royalist" and his intention to paint the subject.
Having found a suitable background in a little wood near
Hayes, in Kent, he commenced the picture in June, 1852,
and from this date till the end of the year his home seems
to have been alternately at Waddon, Gower Street, and
the little "George Inn" at Bromley, kept by a Mr. Vidler.
Most of this time seems to have been spent at the inn, which
was within easy reach of the scene he had selected; near
also to the big trees on Coney Hall Hill, where still stands
the giant oak that he painted in the foreground of the
picture, and is now known as the "Millais Oak."

Touching this painting William Millais writes : — "An
amusing incident occurred whilst we were at the 'George
Inn,' Bromley, my brother being engaged on the background
for 'The Proscribed Royalist' in the old oak wood, and
I (close by) on a large oil landscape.

"Old Mr. Vidler, the landlord, was very proud of his

signboard, representing St. George killing the Dragon, and was mortally offended at our turning it into ridicule.   One day during our stay a violent storm carried the signboard

off its hinges and smashed it to bits.   The owner was only partly consoled on our offering to paint him a new one, and added ungraciously, ' But there, now, it will never be the same thing.'

" However, he thought differently when he saw the gorgeous thing we produced. My brother painted one side and I the other.   Many people at this time came to picnic in the neighbourhood, and it soon got abroad that the new signboard was painted by a great artist.   The old innkeeper was flattered by the

THE "MILLAIS OAK," HAYES, KENT. 1898   numbers who came to see it, and made a practice of taking the sign in at night and in rough weather."

To Mrs. Hodgkinson.

"GEORGE INN, HAYES, NEAR BROMLEY,
" Tuesday Night, June, 1852.

" MY DEAR EMILY, — According to promise, I give you immediate information about our arrival.   Upon arriving at Croydon we first drove to your mansion at Waddon, where we took in the remaining luggage and trotted on here.   We ordered a repast, and in the interim of preparation walked to the oak trees and down to the farm, where I again encountered Mrs. Rutley, and expounded my views to her upon the necessity of having cover close at hand for my paintings, and how her farm exactly suited me for that purpose.   She very graciously undertook to afford shelter for my box or myself in case of rain, storm, etc., and after the colloquy was ended I joined Will (who was too timid to make a request to a stranger) and walked on here home, where we found the tea waiting us.

" The clock of the church which adjoins our premises has just struck eleven, and signals me to bed. Another bell within me foretells an animal considerably larger than the nightmare visiting me — perhaps an evening mammoth. I am writing this by the light of composition candles, supposed not to require snuffing. The wick of one hangs gracefully over like a hairpin, and the other has an astonishing resemblance to a juvenile cedar-tree, the latter prognosticating I believe the reception of letters, which will be particularly acceptable in the gloominess of our present retreat, more especially from our blessed little coz, E. P. H.

" Our landlady (Mrs. Vidler) has just called into action a spark of animation from the heir apparent of Gower Street. She broke in upon us to wish us a very good-night, and is gone with Vidler into the innermost recesses of the conjugal boudoir, probably to dilate upon the magnitude of our appetites.

" Yesterday I harpooned a most extensive whale [a patron] off the coast of Portland Place, having no less than ten footmen in attendance at dinner. The leviathan made most honourable

TOURISTS AT THE INN. 1853

overtures for an increase of acquaintance with the limner sprat [himself], who conducted himself with appropriate condescension and becoming self-denial, in defiance of the strawberries and cream. Somehow or other, I believe my evil spirit takes his residence more particularly in that all-surpassing luxury, cream. It was my ruin at Worcester Park, and directly I came here it invitingly stands within my reach. I wish I had courage enough to dash away that beverage, as Macbeth throws the goblet from him on the appearance of Banquo.

" During the journey to this place we diverted ourselves with the cup and ball, catching it upon the point during the progress of cab, train, and Croydon fly. William is snoring so loudly that you must excuse my writing more at present. I am sure he would send affectionate greetings to you had he recovered from his lethargy.

" Now to bed, to bed. 'Out d——d spot!' (a blot of ink on my finger).

" Affectionately your coz,

" JACK.

" P.S. — Wednesday morning. I have had a bad night's rest. Awoke by the maid at six, up at nine; breakfast off eggs and bacon. Very stormy aspect in the weather, the glass falling to much rain. If it comes, you will probably hear of all those magnificent oaks on Coney Hall Hill slipping down into the road, burying therein the most celebrated of artists! The landlady, unnaturally bland for a female, has already exhibited signs of maternal affection for William. . . . The rain has commenced in torrents, so no painting to-day; we must put up with profound meditations and cup and ball. The wind is so high that all the trees look as if they were making backs for a game of leap-frog."

To the same.

" GEORGE INN, HAYES, BROMLEY, KENT,

" *Wednesday Afternoon, June,* 1852.

" MY DEAR EMILY, — I am come in from an attempt to paint, but the weather is too cold and unsettled for any Christian to be out in, so I mean to console myself as best I may with writing this, and afterwards reading *Uncle Tom's Cabin*, which is certainly interesting. . . .

" Lynn has made me a regular artist's shooting-stool, shutting up and portable. The sun is positively shining, now that it is too late to begin again. Do you know I shall not recover in a hurry from those two insults — ' Ten-ston'-six,' and being taken for the newspaper stall-keeper! That comes of assisting a lady to cut books. The governor has sent me a Liverpool paper with a long criticism on my picture, ' The Hug-or-not.' . . .

" Next Sunday I am going to spend at A. Mrs. Doyle has desired her husband * to bring me forcibly. I had such a capital letter from him, with an illustration of your convicted servant painting out-of-doors, and a bull looking over a hedge with a significant expression, foreboding his intention of elevating me to the height of my profession. . . .

* Richard Doyle, the famous caricaturist.

" Take my advice, don't go out at Hastings with that new parasol, otherwise you will come back with it like this — [Here follows a sketch of Mrs. Hodgkinson being blown off a cliff out to sea, still clinging to the new parasol.]
" I remain, your affectionate
" J. E. MILLAIS."

A reminiscence of this period will be found in the following note, kindly sent to me by Mrs. Pitt : —

" Perhaps you may like to know the following story in connection with your father's life. When he was painting the picture ' A Proscribed Royalist,' near Hayes Common, I was paying a visit to my mother, and was walking with my sisters one day, when we stopped for a minute behind an artist to look at his picture.

SKETCH FOR "THE ORDER OF RELEASE."
1852

" ' How beautiful it is,' I said, half to myself, ' and how much our mother would like to see it.'

" We had not the slightest notion who the artist was, but he courteously turned round to us, and said :

" ' If your mother lives near enough, I shall be pleased to take the picture and show it to her.'

" We thanked him, and invited him to luncheon. He came, and our mother — a real lover of Art — of course admired the picture immensely, though we never knew who the artist was until the picture became public.

" It might have been a year or two afterwards that I was much struck with ' The Huguenot,' and when visiting my husband's brother-in-law (Mr. Miller) at Preston, I discussed it with him. At that time he deprecated what was termed the Pre-Raphaelite style ; nevertheless, he went and bought it."

Millais had been working steadily for more than a month

at Hayes, and was getting on well, when, to his great chagrin, he was called away from his work to attend at Oxford as witness in a lawsuit with regard to the will of Mr. Drury, of Shotover, the testator's sanity at the date of the will being questioned, and he being one of the attesting witnesses. He happened to be with Mr. Drury in 1849, when the will was made, and, having spent two or three months under his roof, he could speak with the utmost confidence as to the state of his mind.

SKETCH FOR "THE ORDER OF RELEASE," 1852

On the conclusion of Millais' evidence, Mr. Justice Williams, before whom the case was tried, complimented him in the following terms:

"Well, Mr. Millais, if you can paint as well as you can give your evidence, you will be a very successful man some day." In the end the validity of the will was established.

To Mrs. Hodgkinson.

" HAYES,
    "*August 4th,* 1852.

"MY DEAR COZ,— We have just concluded our customary game of skittles, and I hasten, with a shaky hand, to fulfil my promise of writing you a letter. To-day we were both obliged to leave off painting early, as every two minutes a shower of rain came down, so since one o'clock we have had strong exercise in archery and the knock-'em-downs. Yesterday we also took a holiday, as it was wet; so we are not getting on precisely as we could wish. . . .

"Poor Mrs. Vidler has been bedridden for some time, owing, I am told, to an encounter with some drunken fellow who insulted her. They say she doubled her mawleys in the true pugilistic style, and knocked over the inebriate vagabond, to his infinite astonishment and discomfort, so injuring his leg in the fall that he has since been at the hospital. . . .

"I wish I was in a vein for describing a club feast that came off here a day or two ago. Upwards of eighty agricultural labourers sat down to table, the stewards wearing blue and white rosettes in their buttonholes. Of course almost all of them were drunk in the evening, and some of the drollest scenes took place outside the house. About one a.m. a fight was raging, which kept me awake for some time ; and last night I never slept till four in the morning — I suppose from having drunk some rather strong tea at the Hasseys' — so to-day I feel sleepy and stupid.

"The Royal Academy conversazione I attended alone, William being upset with rheumatics. The first people I met were, of course, the Leslies, with whom I kept the greater part of the evening. The Duke of Wellington made his appearance about ten, and walked through the rooms with the President, Sir Charles Eastlake. All went off as those and most things do. I saw Mrs. Leslie (not Miss) down to her carriage, and walked home with Hunt.

"With a gentle smoothing down of George's ambrosian locks, believe me,
                    "Most sincerely yours,
                         "JOHN EVERETT MILLAIS."

                    To Mr. Combe.

                    "GEORGE INN, HAYES, BROMLEY,
                         "*Tuesday Night, October*, 1852.

"MY DEAR COMBE, — Do not be astonished, or imagine me forgetful, in allowing so long a time to elapse without writing.

"I have but just returned to this place, after spending a week (bedridden) at Gower Street, where I went to be nursed in a tremendous rheumatic cold I caught painting out of doors. I am well again now, and worked away to-day as usual at my background, which I hope to finish in two or three days at most, when I shall return to Town for good. . . . I am waiting here for one more sunny day, to give a finishing touch to the trunk of a tree which is in broad sunlight. Both yesterday and to-day I have suffered from headache, without in the least knowing the cause. I have taken medicine enough to supply a parish, and am particularly careful in my diet, drinking nothing but water — not even tea.

" This year I am going to paint a small picture of a single figure, the subject of which you will like ; and you shall, if you like, have the first refusal of it. The one I am now about is the property of Mr. Pocock, and the other (of the same size) is for Mr. Wilkinson, M.P. for Lambeth, or Mr. Ellison, the gentleman who purchased ' Ferdinand.' You recollect seeing it at Oxford. It is quite a ' lark ' now to see the amiable letters I have from Liverpool and Birmingham merchants, requesting me to paint them pictures, any size, subject, and amount I like — leaving it all to me. I am not likely to let them have anything, as they would probably hawk it about until they obtained their profit.

" I hear from Mrs. Collins that they may, perhaps, spend some part of the autumn at Hanover Terrace. I hope it will be so, as I would arrange for a tour together in the spring if all goes right — to Switzerland or Spain. Next year I hope to paint the ' Deluge,' which will not require any out-of-door painting, so I should be at liberty to take a holiday abroad. Write and let me know what you think of this ; it is a project I really intend. Remember me most affectionately to Mrs. Pat, to whom I shall write in a day or two.

" Most sincerely yours,

" JOHN EVERETT MILLAIS."

" The Proscribed Royalist " is one of the pictures referred to in the above letter, and this being the last mention of it in the correspondence, it may be well to introduce here the subsequent history of this painting.

The background was not completed until November; and to get the effect of sunshine on the brilliant satin petticoat of the female figure, Millais took the dress down to Hayes with him and rigged it up on the lay figure. The actual figure and face of the woman were finally taken from the beautiful Miss Ryan, the model for " The Huguenot," and when that portion of the work was finished he commenced (in March) to paint the cavalier hidden in the trees. For this figure his friend Mr. Arthur Hughes (himself virtually one of the Pre-Raphaelite Brothers) sat, and to him I am indebted for the following interesting note : —

" I was in the Royal Academy Library," he says, " one evening, looking at books of etchings, and had some by

"THE ROYALIST." 1853

By permission of H. Graves and Son

Tiepolo before me, when Millais came in and sat down beside me. Having asked for McIan's 'Highland Clans' (presumably for the 'Order of Release'), in his leisure he looked at the Tiepolos and criticised them at once as 'florid, artificial. I hate that kind of thing.' Then he asked me to sit to him for a head in his picture, 'The Proscribed Royalist.' I went, and sat five or six times. He painted me in a small back-room on the second floor of the Gower Street house, using it instead of the regular studio on the ground floor because he could get sunshine there to fall

HEAD OF A GIRL. GLENFINLASS, 1853

on his lay figure attired as the Puritan Girl. In the studio below he had taken the picture out of a wooden case with the lid sliding in grooves — to keep all dust from it, he said — and after my sitting he used to slip it in again. When I saw the picture I ventured to remark that I thought the dress of the lady was quite strong enough in colour ; but he said it was the fault of the sun ; that the dress itself was rather Quakery, but the sunshine on it made it like gold. His studio was exquisitely tidy. I had been admitted by a very curly-headed Buttons (' Mr. Pritchard, my butler,' as Millais used to call him), who received at the same time a tremen-

dous wigging for some slight *débris* left on the floor.   After
he had retired, Millais made it up to him by declaring he
would undertake to make that boy paint better than a Royal
Academician in a twelvemonth!   Apart from my admiration
of Millais, it was a very interesting episode to me, from the
revelation of character in the few inhabitants of the house,
and the way he ruled all, and all was ruled for him.   The
gentleness of the father and the vigorous character of the
mother, the picturesque but somewhat restless individuality
of William Millais, were all interesting.   Commissions were

Robert Bruce and the Spider

then beginning to pour in upon John, and in less degree on
William, whose forte was water-colour landscapes, exquisitely
drawn.
    "The latter came in one day, saying, 'I don't care, I'm
all right for a year.'   'And your brother for twenty,' said his
mother — a little sharply, I thought.
    "William used to work in the front room, while John
painted me in the back one.   There was but a thin wall
between the two, and we could hear William all the time, as
he was very restless, singing by snatches, whistling, calling
to John to know the time repeatedly, coaxingly, then im-
ploringly, noisily, but getting no reply, John working hard
and serious as grim death the while.   But at last his patience

gave out and he stopped work, and for the space of a minute he levelled such language at William as up to that time I had not heard used by one brother to another. But he did not tell him the time!

"During the sittings we talked once of the objection (among many others) the critics made to the amount of detail the Pre-Raphaelites gave in their pictures, and Millais said, 'If you do not begin by doing too much you will end by doing too little; if you want to stop a ball which has been thrown along the ground you must get a little beyond it.'"

Black Pines during Dunbar castle

"The Proscribed Royalist" now belongs to Mr. James Opton, having been successively in the possession of Mr. Pocock, Mr. Plint, and Sir John Pender.

The headaches of which Millais complained in several of his letters are not, I believe, uncommon among men of his craft, long confinement in the studio unfitting them for work in the open, where they must perforce sit still for hours together, exposed to every wind that blows. In early life my father suffered a good deal in this way; and it was not until his friends, John Leech and "Mike" Halliday, persuaded him to follow the hounds that he found relief from this complaint. In his next two letters he writes enthusiastically on the sport, as a source of health and strength.

To Mr. George Wyatt.

"83 GOWER STREET,
"1852.

" MY DEAR WYATT, — Many thanks for your kind attention to my wishes. The fleet must have been a wonderful sight. I was very nearly going with Leech, the *Punch* draughtsman, to see its departure, but found even greater attraction in hunting, which I have lately taken to. Every Saturday I accompany him into Hertfordshire, where good horses await us, and we stay overnight at a friend's, and set off in the morning. I have been four times out, and have only had one spill, which did not hurt me in the least.

" I should not follow the chase but that I enjoy it above all other recreation, and find myself quite fitted for such exercise. The first time I ever rode over a fence gave me confidence from the comparatively easy way in which I kept my seat. Since then I have ridden over pretty nearly every kind of hedge and ditch. Leech is a good rider, and we go together.

" With kind regards from my family, believe me,
" Yours very truly,
" JOHN EVERETT MILLAIS."

To Mr. Combe.

"83 GOWER STREET, BEDFORD SQUARE,
"*Saturday, October 23rd,* 1852.

" MY DEAR MR. COMBE, — I cannot promise to pay you a visit, as I am now going to look for another background, which I must immediately commence.

" I returned the day before yesterday with my picture finished, all but the figures. To-day I am going to the Tower of London, to look after a gateway or prison door [for ' The Order of Release ']. I am undecided between two subjects, one of which requires the above locality, and the other the interior of a church. [The artist's first idea of the background for ' L'Enfant du Regiment,' painted in 1855.]

" With regard to our proposed journey, I shall be ready, directly after my pictures are sent to the Royal Academy, to go with you to Norway or the North Pole. I look

forward to this travelling-trip, as I have had so little recreation within these last four years, and I hope you will pay
the Collins's a visit this autumn, as we could then discuss the
merits of the different countries.   I have a curious partiality
for Spain, from reading *Don Quixote* and *Gil Blas;* but,
as you say, the distance is an obstacle.   I know nothing
about Norway, but I hope it is not colder in the summer
than here.

  " Do you intend coming to town to see the funeral of

IMITATIONS OF VELASQUEZ. 1853

the Duke? I do not generally care about such things,
but I shall make a little struggle for that.   It will be worth
seeing.

  " Have you seen anything of Pollen* lately, and has
Jenkins gone yet?   Last Thursday evening I met Tennyson
and his brother Charles, a clergyman.   Politics were the
principal topic of conversation, the Laureate believing it
Louis Napoleon's secret intention to make war with and
invade England.   In this Tennyson thinks he would be

  * Mr. Pollen, a fellow of Merton College, and an authority on Art matters,
was a frequent visitor to the Combes, and met there Millais and Hunt, whose
works he admired.

successful, holding us in subjection for some little time, when
he would be kicked over to fair France to resist the attack
of almost all Europe.   I can see you smiling at this like a
true Britisher.

"Ever yours most truly,

"JOHN EVERETT MILLAIS."

"The Order of Release" (referred to for the first time
in the foregoing letter) is well described by Mr. Walter
Armstrong, who begins by quoting Mr. Andrew Lang in the
following notice : — "'In 1853 Millais painted a picture in
which both his dramatic power and his eye for the lovable
in woman are superbly shown, and shown under some
difficulties.   This is "The Order of Release," now the
property of Mr. James Renton.   It was originally painted
for Mr. Joseph Arden, who gave the commission for it
through Thackeray.   As a piece of realistic painting, it
may challenge comparison with anything else in the world.
The scene takes place not outside a prison, as more than
once has been absurdly supposed, but in a bare waiting-
room, into which the young clansman has been ushered
to his wife, while his gaoler takes "The Order of Release,"
which will have to be verified by his superior before it can
result in final liberty.   The stamp of actual truth is on it; and
if ever such an event happened, if ever a Highlander's wife
brought a pardon for her husband to a reluctant turnkey,
things must have occurred thus.   The work is saved by
expression and colour from the realism of a photograph.
The woman's shrewd, triumphant air is wonderfully caught,
though the face of the pardoned man is concealed, like that
of Agamemnon in the Greek picture, but by a subtle artifice.
The colour of the plaid and the gaoler's scarlet jacket re-
inforce each other, but do not obliterate the black-and-tan
of the collie.   The good dog seems actually alive.   The
child in the woman's arms is uncompromisingly "Hieland."
The flesh painting, as of the child's bare legs, is wonderfully
real; the man's legs are less tanned than usually are those
of the wearers of the kilt.   Perhaps he is grown pale in
prison, as a clansman might do whose head seemed likely
soon to be set on Carlisle wall.   As a matter of truthful
detail, observe the keys in the gaoler's hand, the clear steel
shining through a touch of rust.   The subject and the

sentiment, no less than the treatment, made this picture a
complete success.'

"Every word of this may be endorsed, but Mr. Lang *
has hardly, I think, laid sufficient stress on the mastery of
expression in the woman's face. In it we can see the
subtlest mingling of emotions ever achieved by the artist.
There is not only shrewdness and triumph, there is love for
the husband, contempt mixed with fear for the power symbolised by the turnkey's scarlet, pride in her own achievement,

Lord James of Douglas provides for the Royal household

From Millais' Comic Sketch Book

and the curious northern satisfaction at the safety of one's
own property — a Jeanie Deans, in fact, with meekness
ousted by a spice of pugnacity."

Spielmann has also an interesting note on this picture in
his recently-published *Millais and his Works.* He says: —
"So great was Millais' passion for accuracy, that he obtained
a genuine order of release, signed by Sir Hildegrave Turner,
when, during the war, he was Governor of Elizabeth Castle
in Jersey, and so faithfully did he copy it that the late
Colonel Turner, the Governor's son, who knew nothing
of the matter, recognised with surprise his father's signature

* Mr. Andrew Lang wrote a very excellent series of notes on the little
exhibition of Millais' work exhibited by the Fine Art Society in 1881.

in the picture, as he walked through the gallery in which
it was exhibited."

The head of the woman (painted from my mother) was
a perfect likeness of her in 1853, except only as to the
colour of her hair, a golden auburn, which was changed
to black, in order to contrast with that of the child.

Mr. F. B. Barwell tells me that Westall, the famous
model, posed for the Highlander.   He had been in a
dragoon regiment, from which he deserted.   Nemesis, however, overtook him one day in the studio of Mr. Cope, R.A.,
and he was taken back to his old regiment and tried by
court-martial.   Some time after this his absence was so

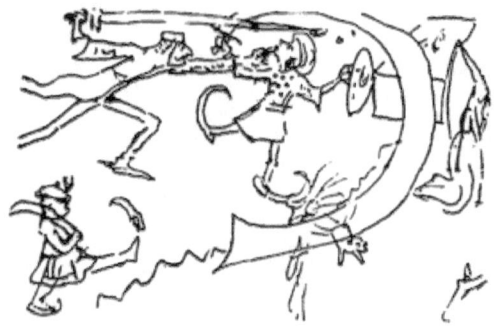

BRUCE AT THE SIEGE OF ACRE. 1853

lamented in the London studios that a subscription was
raised by artists, and he was bought out of the service.

" Unlike ' The Huguenot,'" adds Mr. Barwell, "the background of which had been severely criticised, ' The Order
of Release ' made an immense sensation.   No fault could
be found with the background, even by the old-fashioned
school, whilst the extraordinary realism and brilliant colouring added to the dramatic interest of the story, and the
novelty of execution astonished all."

The picture is said to have been the first ever hung on the
walls of the Academy which required the services of a
policeman to move on the crowd.   "Afterwards," says Mr.
Barwell, "when exhibited in Paris at the Great Exhibition
of 1855, it arrested a great deal of attention, and in an article
in *Le Temps*, by Théophile Gautier, that gentleman expressed
himself completely puzzled as to how it had been produced —
what the vehicle was, whether oil, wax, or tempered varnish

— and bestowed a considerable amount of space in discussing its merits. The article was favourable on the whole, but implied that it was another instance of those curious eccentricities only to be found in Albion."

In assessing the value of this picture it is interesting to note that it was sold by Millais to Mr. Arden, of Rickmansworth Park, for £400; that in 1878 Mr. James Renton bought it for £2853; and that at the sale of Mr. Renton's collection, on his death, it fell to Sir Henry Tate as the purchaser, at the price of 5000 guineas. In a sympathetic letter Sir Henry says : — " The last time I saw Sir John, before illness had deprived him of speech, he told me that Mr. Renton had just died, and ' The Order of Release ' was likely to come into the market. He spoke with much interest and enthusiasm of the picture. He had too much good feeling

1851

to even suggest that I should buy the picture; but we gathered that he would like it to belong to the nation, so it was a double pleasure to me to obtain it last month for my gallery, as I felt I was carrying out the wish of a greatly-valued and much-missed friend."

It was beautifully engraved in 1856 by the late Samuel Cousins, the finest engraver of this century, or probably of any other; and this, his first work on Millais' pictures, was followed by a long series of similar interpretations, all of the same high standard of merit. He was more or less engaged upon them right up to 1884, when, after beginning "Little Miss Muffet," he was obliged to surrender his tools to T. Atkinson, who finished the plate. Cousins was a quiet, plodding, and honest worker of the very best type, and his eventual election to the honour of Royal Academician was applauded by everybody as a compliment he well deserved.

The sufferings of an artist while painting, or rather trying to paint, a tiresome child, are amusingly described in the following letter : —

To Mr. Combe.

"83 GOWER STREET,
"*December 16th,* 1852.

" MY DEAR MR. COMBE, — Instead of going to a musical party with my father and brother, I will write you something of my doings. I have a headache, and feel as tired as if I had walked twenty miles, from the anxiety I have undergone this last fortnight [over ' The Order of Release ']. All the morning I have been drawing a dog, which in unquietness is only to be surpassed by a child. Both of these animals I am trying to paint daily, and certainly nothing can exceed the trial of patience they occasion. The child screams upon entering the room, and when forcibly held in its mother's arms struggles with such successful obstinacy that I cannot begin my work until exhaustion comes on, which generally appears when daylight disappears. A minute's quiet is out of the question. The only opportunity I have had was one evening, when it fell asleep just in the position I desired. Imagine looking forward to the day when next one of these two provoking models shall come ! This is my only thought at night and upon waking in the morning. When I suggest corporal punishment in times of extreme passion, the mother, after reminding me that I am not a father, breaks out into such reproofs as these : ' Poor dear ! Was he bothered to sit to the gentleman ? Precious darling ! Is he to be tormented ? No, my own one ; no, my popsy, my flower, cherub,' etc., etc., dying away into kisses, when he (the baby) is placed upon his legs to run about my room and displace everything. Immediately he leaves off crying, remarking that he sees a 'gee-gee' (pointing to a stag's head and antlers I have hung up), and would like to have one of my brushes.

Accepted

John Everett Millais
1853

"ACCEPTED" (Pen Drawing).   1853

This infant I could almost murder; but the dog I feel for, because he is not expected to understand. A strong man comes with it and bends him to my will, and all the while it looks as calm as a suffering martyr. I do more from this creature in a day than from the other in a week.

"This year I hope you will come and see the produce of all this labour before the pictures go to the exhibition — I mean a day or two previous, so that they may be quite finished. . . . Wednesday evening I went to a public dinner at Hampstead, and escaped in time to avoid returning thanks for the honour they intended doing me. I expect soon to have an invitation to a banquet at Birmingham in honour of the success of their exhibition, to which I sent 'Ophelia.' There I am afraid I must say something, as I lost only by some few votes the prize given to Ward's 'Charlotte Corday going to Execution,' and it is customary to propose the health of the unsuccessful candidate. My brother will accompany Hunt in time to attend the Magdalen evening festival, and although I shall not be with you on Christmas-day, you may depend upon it that I shall drink your and Mrs. Pat's health. Wishing her and yourself a happy Christmas, believe me,

"Ever yours most sincerely,
"JOHN EVERETT MILLAIS."

To the same.

"83 GOWER STREET,
"*December*, 1852.

"MY DEAR MR. COMBE, — You might have called fifty times and never have found all our family out, as you did the other day. If you had given me an idea that you intended calling, I should have been at home to meet you. As it was I was at the Tower of London in search of a background, in which I was unsuccessful. All the stonework is too filthy with the soot of Town to make any good colour in a background. Let me know if you are coming up to see the lying-in-state or the funeral of the Duke [of Wellington]. I have been very lucky, having got a most excellent position from the *Punch* office windows, through the kindness of one of the principal writers, Tom Taylor, the man who wrote that flattering notice of my last year's pictures.

" This day I have commenced the figure in my summer's work ('The Royalist'), and to-night will be drawing the group of my other subject ('The Order of Release'), so I have begun my winter's work. I saw, last night, a friend's * pictures, painted this year in Spain, which would make you alter your opinion about that country. The people and place must be magnificent. I never saw such costumes and natural taste in the manner of putting their dresses on. I think we must go to Spain. . . .   Yours most truly,

"JOHN EVERETT MILLAIS."

To Mrs. Combe.

"83 GOWER STREET,
"*December*, 1852.

" MY DEAR MRS. COMBE, — How did you like the funeral procession? I expected to have heard Mr. Combe's opinion. In the *Illustrated London News* there is a drawing of the Royal carriages passing the *Punch* offices, and a likeness of me sitting in the front row between some ladies. You will see by that how good a position I had. I hear from Collins that you are not coming to visit them until after Christmas. Do not make it long after, as I shall then be beginning hard work and unable to join you in walks, etc. Of course you have heard from Hunt since his return. Now that he has come home we have our old friendly meetings again, such as we used to have in former years. Charlie has so far altered as to join our evenings, which he used to look upon as almost profane.   The evenings are so continually wet that I seldom take my usual walk to Hanover Terrace. Mrs. Collins is getting quite gloomy at the infrequency of my visits.

" Wilkie's new novel, *Basil*, has come out. I have just finished reading it, and think it very clever. The papers, I understand, abuse it very much, but I think them inconsistent in crying it down and praising *Antonina*, which is not nearly so good. Have you read *Esmond*, Thackeray's last book? I hear from Hunt that it is splendid, but it is in so much request at the library that I cannot get it.

" My private opinion of the Wellington car is that it looked like a palsied locomotive. All the dignity of size was lost in the little trembling motion it had over the stones of the streets. It suggested bruises on the hero's nose from shaking

* John Phillip, R.A.

of the body in the coffin. I say 'private opinion,' because a
Royal Academician was mixed up in the design. Altogether
the sight was a most imposing one, but there is so much
talk about it that I am sick of the very name of the Duke's
funeral. It has taken the place of the weather in conversation.
The first thing one is asked in Town, upon entering a room,
is, 'Did you see it? Where from? And what think you of
it?' Young ladies, generally dumb on the first introduction,
venture upon this topic as courageously as an accustomed
orator. Believe me,　　　Most truly yours,

"JOHN EVERETT MILLAIS."

To Mr. Combe.

"83 GOWER STREET,
"*February* 15*th*, 1853.

"MY DEAR MR. COMBE,—All my family are gone out to
a musical party, excepting my mother, who is ill in her
room, suffering from a cold. I have but just returned from
Hanover Terrace. Poor Mrs. Collins (also afflicted with
cold) has entirely lost her voice. Charlie is rather desponding about the quantity of work he has got before him,
doubting the possibility of finishing for the Exhibition.

"I am progressing with my picture slowly, but of course
will finish in time. . . . Hunt is so hard at work that I
never see him. He is painting a modern subject, which
you probably know more about than I do. I have lately
become acquainted with a very busy Roman Catholic, a
most mysterious-looking individual, a friend of Pollen's.
His name is De Bammerville. I dined with him last week,
and he called to ask me to accompany him to Cardinal
Wiseman's this evening, but I excused myself. I believe
him to be a Jesuit. He has a most extraordinary appearance — an excessively dark beard and complexion, and wearing
wolf's fur round his neck and wrists, with braid — altogether
looking very like a stage Polish Count, who murders everyone and then goes down a trap-door with blue light upon
him. I expect he looks upon me as a promising convert.
He smiles at the notion of my attending Wells Street
Church, and, no doubt, pictures in his imagination my sitting
on a three-legged stool, painting a Holy Family for the only
church.　　　Yours most truly,

"JOHN E. MILLAIS."

About this time Millais presented to his cousin, Mrs. George Hodgkinson, a little picture of a female figure, for which she herself had sat. It was sent to her in June, as soon as it was done; but the husband, objecting to the position of one of the arms, wrote to the artist and begged him to take a certain portion of the arm away. To this request he received the following amusing reply: —

To Mr. Hodgkinson.

"LONDON,
"*June 10th.*

"SIR, — You desire that in your absence the young woman should have an operation performed on her left arm. I have consulted her pleasure upon the subject, and have explained that her 'frame' shall not be shaken, as we intend taking her out of it. Mr. Robinson will be in attendance, to administer chloroform, upon which I intend making an incision with my palette knife just below the elbow. Laying open the wound, we shall then have exposed the two punctured bones, the 'radius' and the 'ulna,' upon which an immediate solution of turps shall be plentifully applied. By this latter expedient we hope to eradicate the deformity and to make a *bonâ fide* restoration.

"The only companion the patient has had during her incarceration has been her trusty Dandy, 'Shy,' who has put on a very long face since he has been with her, gloomy in sympathy with his serene parent, who has been pupping and given birth to feline juveniles. . . . William has been playing one or two tricks with his mawleys upon the piano, accompanying the quartette with such good effect that the governor has thrown up the sponge in token of the total defeat of that instrument. Time was frequently called, but none but Bill came to the scratch. The Lord and Master of this house is at this moment endeavouring to bring the unfortunate piano (who is upwards of forty) back to its original tone. My female parent is in the adjoining room, making preparations for an early dinner, which principally consist in the entire subjugation of the curly-headed Pritchard, and a discovery of bottles, the contents of which are unknown to her; hence a continual application of the necks of the aforesaid bottles to the aforesaid lady's nose, accompanied by an observation, 'That's gin,' 'That's vinegar,' or 'What's

"THE BLIND MAN." 1853

Pen Drawing

that, Pritchard?' (the boy's nose takes kindly to the odour of wines.) 'Sherry, mum.' I believe that boy would be worth a publican's while to purchase.   Get him an order to taste the wines at the docks, and he would bring himself out as full as a bottle.   He has come in with the tablecloth for dinner, and mother calls for a general clearance for that meal ; so no more at present from your

" Limner,
" JACK MILLAIS."

CROSSING THE BORDER   1853
Sketch by William Millais

At the end of June, 1853, Millais, in company with his brother William, journeyed North for the first time, intending to take a good holiday after prolonged work at his easel. The expedition was at first suggested by the Ruskins, who had agreed to meet the brothers and introduce them to some of the beauties of the Northern hills.   After spending a delightful week with Sir Walter Trevelyan in Northumberland, which the railway had then penetrated as far as Morpeth, the two brothers met the Ruskins there and travelled with them by private coaches to the Trossachs, taking *en route* the picturesque old towns of Melrose and Stirling.

To the former place their host insisted on accompanying them, taking Mrs. Ruskin and her friend, Miss McKenzie, in his dog-cart. There then they parted, the visitors betaking themselves to a carriage and pair under the guidance of a postillion. This gentleman, however, proved himself hardly equal to the occasion. After a brief halt at a hostelry in the hill country, where the whisky was supremely tempting, he was taken so seriously ill that he could no longer control his horses. There was

nothing for it, therefore, but to dispense with his services and tool the animals along as best they could. William Millais gallantly undertook this task, and after depositing the unhappy Jehu amidst the luggage on the top of the coach he evolved from his own inner consciousness something that served for reins, and managed to land the party safely at Callander, where rooms had been engaged for them.

Mrs. George Hodgkinson sends me a sketch of his, made at the time, showing the

CLOSE QUARTERS. 1853

post-boy hanging on to the collar of one of his horses, as he piteously moans, " Aw'm verrarr baad — aw canna ride — oh dearr, oh dearrr ! "

At Callander the two brothers found apartments in the " New Trossachs Hotel," microscopic in size, but clean and comfortable, and took most of their meals with their friends, who were more luxuriously accommodated at the manse, at Brig o' Turk, some five hundred yards away. But, " hey, oh, the wind and the rain ! " — especially the rain. For nearly five long weeks it came steadily down, regardless of Mrs. Ruskin and her brave championship of the climate of this, her native land. Except at rare intervals, sketching was out of the

question. There was nothing to see ; but health and strength
were to be had by braving the elements. Mackintoshes had
not then been invented, but the plaid of the country afforded
some protection, and, thus habited, the whole party turned
out day by day, spending their lives in the pure air. It

The Tourists Highland reel

was soon found, however, that the plaid was insufficient
without the kilt, and as in those days sojourners in the
Highlands were expected to adopt the costume of the
country, not only for their own comfort, but as a compliment
to the natives, whose judgment in the matter of dress was
thus endorsed, it needed no great persuasion on the part

of their friends to make the two brothers array themselves
accordingly. John Millais, however, did not take kindly to
the kilt. Unlike his brother, who continued to wear it to
the end of the season, he discarded it after one day's wear,
finding perhaps more trouble with it than he did with the
plaid, until after many attempts he learnt the art of adjusting
it in the proper fashion. His first attempt — in a big storm —
was about as futile as Dame Partington's struggle with her
mop against the Atlantic waves when they invaded her house.

FISHING IN LOCH ACHRAY. 1853

He came out of the combat beaten and wet to the skin; but
alive, as he always was, to the humorous side of things, he
made, the same evening, a sketch of the event; and shortly
afterwards there appeared in *Punch* a more finished drawing
of his, entitled " How to wear a Highland plaid."

Every day the united parties went on some expedition
together, climbing perchance Ben Ledi, or fishing in Loch
Achray, famous in local tradition for salmon that never were
there, and, whenever it was possible to do so, making
sketches of the scenery around. As to Millais, his only
thought was of a pleasant holiday and rest from his usual
occupations; yet even he was caught at last by the fascina-

"THE ROMANS LEAVING BRITAIN." 1853

Line and Sepia Drawing

tion of a turn in the lovely little river Finlass. It suddenly occurred to him that it would make a capital background for a single figure if all the other parts of the landscape were subdued in deep shadow; and on Mr. Ruskin consenting to stand, he began at once a portrait of the critic, which is now known as one of the best works he ever did.

The picture was afterwards purchased by Dr. (afterwards Sir Thomas) Acland, whose recent visit to Callander had added greatly to the pleasure of the party. Millais refers to it in the following letter : —

To Mr. Combe.

" NEW TROSSACHS HOTEL, CALLANDER,
"STIRLING, *August 4th*, 1853.

" MY DEAR MR. COMBE, — Finding all my friends writing letters, I have just crossed the bog that separates us from them to send you a bulletin of our health and doings. Our patience has been most sorely tried, and has stood proof tolerably well. Cannot you see us, one by one and hour by hour, with anxious faces, trying to read the sun through Scotch mist and rain? Cannot you hear us singly giving our decided opinion of the day, hope buoying us up to tell other than our real sentiments about the state of the weather? ' It 's a varry saaft dee ' has greeted me every morning for the last five weeks, uttered by a buxom landlady, who is truly the only person I have seen unclouded about the physiognomy.

" Dr. Acland has been staying here a few days. What an amiable man he is ! He left us on Monday, and I have taken his room, because of the fine view its window affords. I was determined to bring back something, so on the very afternoon of his departure I began a new picture. Oh that I had tried this bait before with the sun, for I had barely sketched-in my work before the sun, with British effulgence, burst out upon the rocky hills. The wet birch leaves gave back tiny images of him, and all the distant mountains changed suddenly from David Cox to the Pre-Raphaelites.

" What was a purple wash became now a network of grays and lilacs, with no inconsiderable amount of drawing about their rugged peaks ; in fact, such drawing as Nature always rejoices in. This post-meridian burst of light augured well for the morrow, and, indeed, Tuesday was a prince of days, and we worked well. Wednesday and Thursday likewise, though cold latterly went far towards cramping us. Ruskin comes and works with us, and we dine on the rocks all together, but only on fine days; so this course of living has been very much the exception. Only imagine a paper being sent here — 'that all stray dogs (during the dog-days) be shot!' The mention of a mad dog suggests only heat and drought. Do dogs ever become mad in Scotland?

"Ever yours sincerely,

"JOHN EVERETT MILLAIS."

To the same.

"c/o MR. STEWART, BRIDGE OF TURK,

"CALLANDER, PERTHSHIRE,

"*August*, 1853.

"MY DEAR MR. COMBE, — My brother William has just received your letter, and as you kindly express a wish to hear from me, I take the present opportunity of sending you a few lines.

"This day (Sunday, August 14th) we have been to church, and taken a delightful walk to a waterfall, following the stream till we came to a fall of seventy feet, where we had a bath (my brother and self), he standing under the torrent of water, which must have punished his back as severely as a soldier's cat - o' - nine - tails whipping. These mountain rivers afford the most delightful baths, perfectly safe, and clear as crystal. They are so tempting, that it is quite impossible to walk by them without undressing and jumping in. I am immensely surprised to hear that Hunt is going to Syria so soon. I confess I had begun to think that his intended voyage there was a myth, for he has not

SIR THOMAS ACLAND 1853

spoken to me about leaving England, although I receive letters continually from him. I suppose he thinks it would only meet with incredulity. I am painting a portrait of Ruskin, with a background of rocks and a waterfall, which is close here, so I get at it easily in the morning.

"This year I am giving myself a holiday, as I have worked five years hard. If you have leisure to read, get Ruskin's two last volumes of *The Stones of Venice*, which surpass all he has written. He is an indefatigable writer.

William Millais   Sir Thomas Acland   Millais

We have, in fine weather, immense enjoyment, painting out on the rocks, and having our dinner brought to us there, and in the evening climbing up the steep mountains for exercise, Mrs. Ruskin accompanying us. Last Sunday we all walked up Ben Ledi, which was quite an achievement. I am only just getting the mountaineer's certainty of step, after experiencing some rather severe falls, having nearly broken my nose, and bruised my thumb-nail so severely that I shall lose it. My shins are prismatic with blows against the rocks. . . .

"Very truly yours,
"JOHN EVERETT MILLAIS."

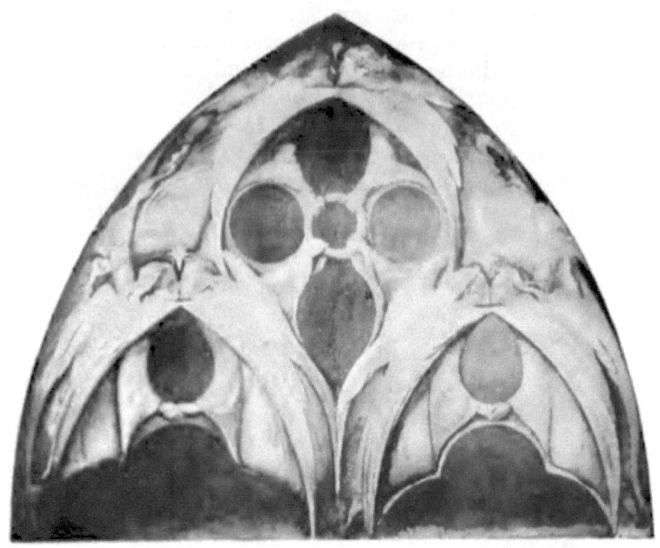

DESIGN FOR A GOTHIC WINDOW. 1853
Water-colour

To the same.

"*c/o* Mr. Stewart, Brig o' Turk,
"Callander,
"*August,* 1853.

"My dear Mr. Combe, — . . . Ruskin and myself are
pitching into architecture; you will hear shortly to what
purpose. I think now I was intended for a Master Mason.
All this day I have been working at a window, which I hope
you will see carried out very shortly in stone. In my evening
hours I mean to make many designs for church and other
architecture, as I find myself quite familiar with constructions,
Ruskin having given me lessons regarding foundations and
the building of cathedrals, etc., etc. This is no loss of time
— rather a real relaxation from everyday painting — and it is
immensely necessary that something new and good should
be done in the place of the old ornamentations.

"Surely now that there seems more likelihood of a Russian
war you will not persist in travelling eastward. Assuredly
you will all lose your heads. You in particular will verify
your cognomen of 'Early Christian' in such an event, for

that was generally their fate. Is there any chance of your coming to Edinburgh in October? Do, if you can, and hear Ruskin's lectures, and we will have a stroll over the city. Does your fountain still play? Have the gold-fish been boiled again? Is Emma still alive? And have you finished your shields? All these things I am anxious to know.   Yours very faithfully,

"JOHN EVERETT MILLAIS."

WILLIAM MILLAIS AT WORK. 1853

Both Ruskin and Millais felt that in modern architecture, no less than in modern painting, the lack of original composition and design was painfully evident. They had many talks on the subject, and as Mr. Ruskin intended to refer to this in a lecture in Edinburgh, Millais exercised himself in the evening by sketching designs of all sorts in a book which now lies before me. Figures, flowers, and animals are all grouped in every conceivable way, principally to be used in the decoration of church windows, the chief design being done on large sheets of grocery paper bought at a neighbouring shop, and pasted on strips of canvas fixed together by himself. This design (a water-colour drawing for the window referred to in the foregoing letter) represented angels saluting one another, the light being admitted through ovals, round which the arms of each figure clasped and met. It had a base line of 109 inches, and was shortly afterwards exhibited by Ruskin at his Edinburgh lecture.   Many years after that it was seen by a noted cleric, who wished to have it carried out for a new window in one of our cathedrals.   The expense, however, was found to be too great, so the idea was abandoned.   Millais was especially keen to show his ability in this particular line, for, to his mind, a true artist should be able to design or draw anything, and he had recently been somewhat piqued by the observation of a newspaper, that " though Millais might be successful in painting, he was incapable of making an architectural design."

To Mrs. Combe.

" NEW TROSSACHS HOTEL, BRIG O' TURK,
" *September 6th,* 1853.

" MY DEAR MRS. COMBE, — I am almost ashamed to write to you, after permitting so long a time to elapse without a letter. I am enjoying myself so much here that I can scarcely find time to hold a pen ; it is as much as I can do to paint occasionally. To-day I have had a sick headache, which has prevented me from painting the background of a portrait of Ruskin. When the weather permits, we all dine out upon the rocks, Mrs. Ruskin working, her

husband drawing, and myself painting. There is only one drawback to this almost perfect happiness — the midges. They bite so dreadfully that it is beyond human endurance to sit quiet, therefore many a splendid day passes without being able to work. This does not grieve me much, as I am taking a holiday this season, and when I return I mean (if you will receive me) to pay you a visit. Dr. Acland was staying with us a little while

THE IDLE AND THE INDUSTRIOUS PAINTER. 1853

"THE DYING MAN." 1853

back, and I think greatly enjoyed himself. He is a delightful companion, and joined us in games of battledore and shuttle-cock, which we play for exercise between hours.

"Mr. Ruskin is going to lecture in Edinburgh next month, and we are busy making drawings for illustration. You will probably hear of me as an architect some day! Are you going with Hunt and the Early Christian to Syria? Have you heard much of Jenkins, and how is the parson? The service here is as unlike that at Oxford as an oyster is unlike a crow. The church is a beautiful little house built on the border of a lake, and the minister is a good, hard-working, sensible fellow, who lives in the same house as we do. . . . The service, I confess, I do not like, but I am pleased with the people, who seem all earnestly desirous of doing their duty. The church is supported by the visitors to the hotels, there being no rich lairds about here, nobody but poor old bodies wrapped up in plaids. . . .

"Yours most truly,
"JOHN EVERETT MILLAIS."

In 1853 manners and modes of life of the Scotch peasantry were somewhat different from what they are now. The doggies came to church, as they still do in one or two remote districts, and the music was conducted by the pre-centor, whose comic personality is admirably hit off in one of Millais' sketches.

William Millais says of this visit to the North:—"How well I remember our going to the little Free Kirk, arrayed as well-turned-out Highland men. The service was to us somewhat comical, and we could hardly stay it out. The precentor was a little very bow-legged old man, with the wheeziest of voices, and sang the first line of the 'para-phrase' alone, whilst his little shaggy terrier, the image of his master, joined in a piteous howl. The other lines were sung by the congregation, assisted by a few collies. I afterwards tackled the little precentor, and asked him why he didn't have an organ. 'Ah, man, would you have us take to the devil's band?' was his answer.

"When the sermon came, it was most amusing to us to watch the old men passing their rams' horn snuff-mulls to one another, and putting little bone spades full of the pungent material up their noses to keep them awake.

"In front of us were two well-dressed young girls, in all

the newest fashion, and when the shallow offertory-box was
poked towards them, they put in a farthing. We afterwards
saw them take off their shoes and stockings and walk home
barefooted.

"As the whole congregation passed out, my brother
allowed that they one and all riveted their eyes on his legs,
and he made up his mind then to get rid of the beastly
kilt, and left me to carry out his purpose. Just then I

saw a carriage passing along the high-road, with a man
gesticulating towards me. I at once recognised him as
Gambart, the well-known picture-dealer. He stopped the
vehicle, and got out and asked after my brother, and then
introduced me to the lady inside — ' Mdlle. Rosa Bonheur '—
who expressed herself enthusiastically upon my appearance.
' Ah, my dear Millais,' said Gambart, ' Mademoiselle Rosa
Bonheur has been eagerly on the look-out for the Highland
garb ever since we left Edinburgh, and yours is the first
kilt she has seen. You are immortalised.' I told them that
if they had been a little sooner they would have seen my
brother in a similar garb. ' How beautiful he must look

in it,' said Gambart. It was a pity they had not seen him!
We lunched with them at Trossachs Hotel, but nothing
would induce my brother to don the kilt again."

Among the most interesting records of this period is a
large sketch-book of Millais'. The first part is filled with
highly-finished drawings, illustrating the various " ploys " of
the party — salmon-fishing, sketching, and expeditions in the
hills — the latter half containing comical caricatures of the
people who came and went.

In the evenings, after dinner, Art was frequently discussed, and Millais would occasionally make fun of the old
masters, showing in a few lines the chief materials of their
stock-in-trade. Some of these sketches (given here) are
interesting as showing how a very few bare lines can be
made to indicate unmistakably the characteristic styles of
individual masters, such as Vandyck, Poussin, Greuze, or a
Turner.

Mrs. Ruskin, being exceedingly learned in Scottish history,
used to hold forth occasionally on the doughty deeds of the
early champions of liberty and Christianity, and delighted
to narrate the thrilling adventures of Robert Bruce, of the

Crusaders, and of all the heroes of Highland chivalry.
One evening Millais pretending, I regret to say, to have
been much impressed by the woes and afflictions suffered
by Robert the Bruce in prison, and his subsequent adventures with a fine specimen of *Arachne vulgaris*, took the
sketch-book, saying that so important a subject required
to be instantly fixed on paper, and he must at once make
a design for future development. If the reader will turn

to page 176, he will see how it was that this touching subject
never found its way to the walls of the Academy. The
drawing, however, was much appreciated, and led to many
similar illustrations of Scottish history, such as the siege
of Dunbar Castle by the English the adventures of Lord
James Douglas in the Holy Land, the siege of Acre, etc.
And these from the same hand that painted "The Vale
of Rest" and "The North-West Passage!" To my mind,
they are as characteristic of Millais as any serious work of
his. There is force and reason in the broadest and simplest
lines, to say nothing of the genuine humour they exhibit.*

* Millais showed these comic sketches to Leech, who was doubtless somewhat
influenced by them in his subsequent and admirable illustrations for *The Comic
History of England* and *The Comic History of Rome*.

"VIRTUE AND VICE." 1853
Line and Sepia drawing

Before parting with the Ruskin portrait, he repainted the whole of the background. He also finished at the same time a little picture called "The Highland Lass," now in the possession of Mr. Henry Willett.

One of the keenest disappointments of his early life occurred in 1850, when, after being elected to the honour of an Associate of the Royal Academy, the appointment was quashed on the ground of his extreme youth. Since

WAYSIDE REFRESHMENT

that time, as he could not but know, his works had risen year by year in the estimation of the public, but as yet no official recognition of their merit had been accorded him by the Academy, and he began to feel somewhat sore at this neglect. He was, therefore, more than usually interested in the coming election, which was to take place on November 7th, 1853. Several influential Academicians had promised to vote for him, and, though himself an earnest supporter of authority when fairly exercised, he was not disposed to have his claim overlooked much longer. Gambart and other dealers, knowing that his pictures were always in request, had already made him tempting offers to exhibit solely with them, and from the commercial point of view it might have been to his advantage to do so; but he steadily refused to entertain the idea so long as any doubt remained as to the attitude of the Academy.

Another reason for this decision was that, having taken upon himself the championship of Pre-Raphaelite principles, he was determined to make the Academy acknowledge his power as the chief, if not the only, exponent of their principles, now that Hunt was off to the East, and Rossetti had wandered away on his own exclusive line; and if he ceased to exhibit there, some of those whose opinion he valued might perhaps think that he was afraid to continue the struggle.

SIR THOMAS ACLAND ASSISTING A CERTAIN LADY
TO PAINT ONE OF HER PICTURES. 1853

And now the eventful day approached. But let William Millais tell the tale in his own words:—"On the day when the result of the election of Associates at the Royal Academy of Arts was to be made known, my brother, self, Wilkie and Charlie Collins all started off to spend a whole day in the country to alleviate our excitement. Hendon was the chosen locality. My brother wore a large gold goose scarf-pin. He had designed a goose for himself and a wild duck for me, which were made by Messrs. Hunt and Roskell — exquisite works of Art. We had spent a very jolly day, the principal topic of conversation being the coming election, Wilkie Collins being confident that Jack's usual luck would attend him and that he would certainly be returned an Associate of the Royal Academy.

"We had been walking along a narrow, sandy lane, and, meeting a large three-horse waggon, had stepped aside to

let it pass, when we resumed our way, and shortly afterwards
Jack's pin was gone ! ' Now, Wilkie,' said my brother, ' how
about my luck ? This is an ominous sign that I shall not
get in.' ' Wait a bit, let 's go back,' said Wilkie. We were
all quite sure that he had it on on leaving Hendon. Now,
the fact of a huge waggon having gone over the ground
we had travelled by gave us very little hope of seeing the
golden goose again. A stipulated distance was agreed upon,
and black we all trudged, scanning the ground minutely.
I undertook the pacing. The waggon had ploughed deep
furrows in the sand, and just as we had reached the end
of our tether, Jack screamed out, ' There it is, by Jove ! '
And, in truth, the great gold goose was standing perched
on a ridge of sand, glistening like the Koh-i-noor itself. We
went straight to the Royal Academy, and Charles Landseer,
coming out, greeted my brother with, ' Well, Millais, you
are in this time *in earnest*,' punning on his name, which they
had entered as ' John Ernest Millais ' instead of John Everett
Millais."

It was on the day following the election that D. G.
Rossetti wrote to his sister Christina (*Letters of D. G.
Rossetti to William Allingham*) : — " Millais, I just hear, was
last night elected an Associate ;
so now the whole Round Table
is dissolved "—meaning, no doubt
that Millais, having been received
into the fold of the recognised
authority, would cease to support
the heterodox principles he had
till then so strongly upheld. But
nothing could be further from his
thoughts.

He quietly continued his work
on the same lines till 1860,
when his painting of minute
detail became gradually merged
in greater breath of treatment.
Look at the landscape in " Chill
October " (1875) and " The Woodman's Daughter " (1849). The
effect is the same ; only the mode
of expression is different. He
gained the technique used in the

A CERTAIN LADY PAINTING ONE OF HER
RELIGIOUS PICTURES. 1853

first-named picture through the scholastic and self-imposed labour of the second.

Millais' next letter is in reply to one from Mr. Combe, inviting him to stay again at Oxford, and announcing the joyful fact that he had purchased Hunt's great picture, "The Light of the World," a picture which Millais greatly admired.

BATHING. A SUPERFLUOUS NECESSITY. 1853

To Mr. Combe.

"83 GOWER STREET,
"*Thursday Evening, December,* 1853.

" MY DEAR MR. COMBE, — I am sorry that I cannot possibly leave town next week, as I find I shall be required by the Royal Academy to receive my diploma. After that, I must really set about working, for I must get something done for the Exhibition. . . .

" I called to-day upon Sir Charles Eastlake, the President, and he told me I must stay in London for the Committee-meeting next week, which is not fixed. I congratulate you on having bought 'The Light of the World.' You are a sensible man. . . .

EUPHEMIA CHALMERS GRAY (Afterwards Lady Millais). 1853

A pencil drawing made by herself from an oil painting by Millais

" I have just returned from dining with Ruskin's father, and am a little tired and sleepy, so I must finish this; for, as a true friend, you must wish me to go to bed. Good-night. My love to Mrs. Pat.

" Yours very faithfully,
" JOHN EVERETT MILLAIS."

To the same.

" FIELDING CLUB,
" HENRIETTA STREET, COVENT GARDEN,
" Monday, December 26th, 1853.

" MY DEAR MR. COMBE, — I am ashamed of myself for not having written to you before this to explain about Hunt's likeness [drawn by himself]. I am so pleased with it that, as I have no other, I must keep it for myself, but will copy it for you and send it in the course of a week or two. . . . I thought you were going to accompany Hunt to Syria. What do you mean by neglecting your promise? . . . Now that Hunt is going I don't know what will become of me.

" I hope you have all spent a happy Xmas, a more cheerful one than I spent; for I had no dinner, and was strolling about London between church services. In the morning I attended Wells Street, and in the evening Dr. Cumming's — the north and south poles of religious ceremony. Cumming is a wonderful man, sincere and eloquent. The Scotch are very manly and honest. I heard a great man named Guthrie in Edinburgh — the finest preacher I ever heard. . . .

" Ever yours,
" JOHN EVERETT MILLAIS."

CHAPTER VI

1853-1855

MILLAIS, as we have seen, was now one of the elect of the Royal Academy, and his picture, "The Huguenot," had added much to his reputation as an artist; but it is quite a mistake to assume, as so many writers have done, that after this date the current of his life ran smoothly on without any serious obstruction or impediment. His great fight — perhaps the greatest fight of all — was yet to come; and as 1853 drew to a close, the elation he might otherwise have felt was restrained by circumstances and considerations of no small moment to a man of his sensitive nature. Leading members of the Academy were, as he well knew, prejudiced against him; the Press continued to jeer at him as an enthusiast in a false style of Art; D. G. Rossetti, wounded by their carping and insulting criticism of his "Annunciation," had retired from the contest; Walter Deverell, a devoted friend of Millais and an ardent supporter of the Pre-Raphaelite movement, was seriously ill; and now that Hunt, his greatest and strongest ally, was about to leave for the East, he knew that upon him alone would devolve the duty of maintaining the cause to which he had devoted his life as an artist. Charlie Collins, it is true, was still with him, and in "Mike" Halliday and Leech he had found other firm and faithful friends; but, highly

skilled as these three men were, both as artists and connoisseurs, they could hardly be expected to share the
enthusiasm of himself and Hunt for a cause which they had
made so peculiarly their own. Individual Pre-Raphaelites,
such as Collinson, Hughes, and others, were doing good

"WAITING"

work, and the Academy did not exclude their paintings
at the annual exhibitions; but the Brotherhood itself no
longer existed in its old form as a body of associated
workers. It had become, indeed, as Hunt says in one of
his letters, "a solemn mockery, and died of itself."

A few words about Walter Deverell may not be out of
place here; for, apart from Millais' affection for him, as

evidenced by the following letters, he was a youth of rare character and great gifts, who yet, like poor Chatterton, ended his life in the deepest depths of poverty. On the death of his father in 1853 he struggled hard to maintain not only himself, but his brothers and sisters by the sale of his pictures; but, some two years before his own death, his health began to give way, and at last failed altogether under the distress of finding it impossible to keep the home together. Consumption set in, and early in 1854 he passed away. It was only a few weeks before this that Millais discovered the dire necessity of his friend, when he hastened at once to his relief. Without saying a word to him, he took steps to secure the sale of his last picture. Two of the Pre-Raphaelite Brothers sent a stranger to buy it, and in ignorance of this little ruse, poor Deverell rejoiced in being able to provision his household and stave off the reaper for at least a short time longer. Referring to this incident, Holman Hunt says:—"Millais came to me one day and said, 'Deverell is in great straits. Let us buy his picture. Will you give half, if I do?' So the picture was bought, and Deverell for the while tided over his financial difficulties."

As to the man himself, Mr. Arthur Hughes has given us an account in *The Letters of D. G. Rossetti to William Allingham.* He describes him as "a manly young fellow, with a feminine beauty added to his manliness; exquisite manners and a most affectionate disposition. He died early, after painting two or three pictures. Had he lived he would have been a poetic painter, but not a strong one. Millais, hardworking and ambitious though he was, used to sit hour after hour by his bedside, reading to him."

The following letters tell their own tale. Millais appealed to the Combes for help for his friend, and they responded with characteristic kindness of heart:—

To Mrs. Combe.

"83 GOWER STREET,
" *December* 30th, 1853.

"MY DEAR MRS. PAT,—I have a young friend, an artist of the name of Deverell (maybe Hunt has spoken to you about him). He is very clever, but unfortunately will never have strength again sufficient to follow his profession. He is given up for lost by three doctors, but may last through the winter with great care. He has no mother alive, and his father died about four months ago, leaving him in destitution, with a family of little brothers and sisters to support. The efforts he made to this end, I expect, hastened on internal disease, and now he is confined to his bed.

"Besides his own melancholy illness, a poor little girl, about eight years of age, was, soon after the father's death, struck with paralysis in the right arm, the use of which she has lost for life. Indeed, there seems to be a curse upon the family. The father was a very learned man, but a determined atheist, and died without altering his opinions. His behaviour was frightfully cruel to his now dying son. He would never permit his children to attend church, turning religion into ridicule upon all occasions. My poor friend is so careless of himself, and his eldest sister is so unfit to nurse him, that I write to ask you whether you can assist me in any way by recommending a good, kind person who could read to him, and see to his taking his meals punctually — only bread and milk. Last night I was with him, and was grieved to see the apathy of the servant and his sister, who had been out that night to a dance, and was now gone to bed! There was no fire in the room, and the invalid was hanging partly out of his bed, with his hands as cold as ice. . . . I am going there again to-night, to amuse him. It is almost cruel to tell him of his danger, as he is so alive to the distress that will come upon his family in the event of his dying; therefore, I have not spoken upon the subject, neither have the medical men, who seem to think he should be kept as cheerful as possible. Until now he has declined having a nurse, because of the expense, but I have persuaded him, as I would rather pay for the woman myself than let him continue to be neglected. . . . I spoke to Ruskin about him, and he has been extremely kind, his father sending him chicken and jellies, but these he cannot touch himself, as he is obliged to live upon milk and toast. . . . Next spring I purpose leaving England for the Continent, as I am sick of this rain and freezing climate.

"I shall take it as a favour if you will inquire quietly for me about a nurse for D——, as he is gradually wasting away and I should like him to be more comfortable.

"Ever yours,

"JOHN EVERETT MILLAIS."

1 — 15

To Mr. Combe.

"83 GOWER STREET,
"*January*, 1854.

"MY DEAR MR. COMBE, — I have made a drawing of Hunt, which I think you will find very like. It is not a copy of the one I have, but another I drew on Sunday evening. I will get it framed for you (as it would rub, sent as it is), and forward it as soon as it is out of the frame-makers' hands. . . . I shall see Deverell this evening. He would not see Mr. Stuart, when I mentioned it to him. He has some relations, clergymen, whom he says he can see whenever he wishes.

"To-day I was expecting Ruskin to sit to me for his portrait, which I was painting in the Highlands.

"Hunt goes now either to-night or to-morrow. I shall not believe he is gone until Mrs. Bradshaw, his landlady, says he is not at home. I never knew such a fellow; his room looks as though it had been given over to the tender care of a dozen monkeys in his absence. Ever yours,

"JOHN EVERETT MILLAIS."

To Mrs. Combe.

"83 GOWER STREET,
"*February* 3rd, 1854.

"MY DEAR MRS. PAT, — I have just come from inquiring after Deverell, who died whilst I was in the house. I sent (for I could not see him) a message urging him to see a clergyman, but when the cousin who had been with him got to the door of his room she found it locked, and ascertained from the nurse within that all was over.

"This same lady had often desired him to permit the visit of a clergyman, but without obtaining his consent. Latterly he would not, or rather could not, listen to what was said to him. . . . I did my best to prevail, but he always declined. He was quite sensible, and received most calmly the news of his coming death.

"I have had a most amusing letter from Hunt. He seems to have really reached Marseilles, but of course not without disasters, one of which was the breaking of a bottle of varnish in his portmanteau, which obliged him to unpack everything, and to wash the compartment before replacing the things. Ever yours most truly,

"JOHN EVERETT MILLAIS."

"RETRIBUTION." 1854

Line and Sepia drawing

After this came a long series of letters from Holman
Hunt, dated from various parts of Egypt and Palestine,
where in 1854 and 1856 he was engaged in collecting
materials for his pictures, and produced, amongst other
works, that magnificent painting, " The Scapegoat." These
letters, Pre-Raphaelite in detail and often admirably illustrated, are full of interest, not only as a record of his
wanderings in the East and the adventures he met with,

PRINCE CHARLIE IN A HIGHLAND FARMHOUSE
Pencil design.   Circ. 1851

but as a reflex of his observant mind and his constant
solicitude for his friends at home. For Millais more particularly they betray a warmth of interest that could only
exist between such congenial and affectionate friends. But
I must necessarily limit myself here to such of them as
refer more especially to the subject of this memoir, or to
matters in which they were mutually interested.

Writing from Cairo in 1854, he says : — " I hope you will
come out in the autumn. Seddon (an artist friend) will have
gone back by then, and I will have made some way into
the language, if possible. I am very likely to remain abroad
for a year or two, for it is impossible to do any good in

merely passing through a country, particularly when one
has so many prejudices to overcome as exist here. I wish
we could meet abroad to work and travel together for a
good while, with occasionally another or two for companions
— Halliday for one. The advantage of being away from
London is that riddance from bores, personal and impersonal,
one meets with there, and (with one or two intimates at
hand) the possibility of keeping all wandering ones at bay
might be attained. I don't feel certain as to the best
place to remain in. This may be the most convenient and
practicable, but my inclination points to Beirout, or some
other quarter where God's works are more prominent than
those of man.

"Certainly cultivate a beard. I am persuaded to overcome my Anglican prejudice in favour of a clean chin.
I should not do so, however, if I found it disguised my
nationality, for that is worth every other protection one
travels with. It compels cringing obedience and fear
from every native, even a dog. With this, indeed, and a
stick, or, in fact, with only a fist, I would undertake to
knock down any two Arabs in the Esbekir and walk away
unmolested, and even with the hope that they should be
well bastinadoed for having given me so much voluntary
trouble."

There would be very few artists in London if they had
such difficulties in procuring models as poor Hunt had to
face in 1854. Writing from Cairo, in March of that year,
he says: — "I wish my attempts to get models had been
encouraging in the result. Bedouins may be hired in twenties
and thirties, merely by paying them a little more than their
usually low rate of wages, and these are undoubtedly the
finest men in the place; but when one requires the men of
the city, or the women, the patience of an omnibus-man
going up Piccadilly with two jibbing horses on an Exhibi-
tion-day is required. I have made the attempt to get a
woman to sit, until, at the end of a fortnight or three weeks,
I have realised nothing but despair, although I have spared
no pains and have prejudiced my moral reputation to achieve
my purpose. The first chance my servant discovered, I
knew it would not do to inquire too narrowly into the
character of the people; so I followed him without question
into a house where at every door there was a fresh investiga-
tion of myself, in such sort as to make it appear a matter

of the greatest good fortune when I found myself at the
top of the house entering the guest-room.   This was a small
chamber without much furniture, but surrounded with divan
seats in front of a lattice-work mushrabee, where people sit
for the cool air in the heat of the day.   No one was present,
so I had leisure to examine the objects in the room and
speculate upon the beauty of the houris of the establish-
ment, and to make some study of the manner in which I

THE PRISONER'S WIFE

would arrange the sketch which I should have to do that
same day.   And here I heard women's voices outside.
Several entered veiled.   With but only about twenty words
of Arabic and a great deal of impatience, I could not afford
much ceremony, so after I had fired off the nineteen I
thought it time to walk up to the most graceful figure, utter the
remaining word, ' yea bint,' and lift up her veil — a proceeding
for which they were scarcely prepared.   The shy ' daughter
of the full moon ' squinted; and on turning to others, I

discovered that Nature had blessed each with some such invaluable departure from the monotony of ideal perfection.

" ' The evening star ' had lost her front teeth, ' the sister of the sun ' had several gashes in her cheek, while ' the mother of the morning ' had a face in pyramid shape. I told my man to express my regret that heaven had not bestowed on me enough talent to do justice to that order of beauty, by shying some backsheesh to the old woman, while I took one by the neck and gently hurled her on to the floor for having attempted to intercept my passage by the door. A fight with a man or two in going downstairs and an encounter with several dogs in the yard, and I found myself in the street, with my man behind me in a state of utter bewilderment at the turn affairs had taken. The next day I applied to the wife of the English missionary, who replied that it was a matter of the greatest difficulty. She had once induced a girl to sit, but then it was to a clergyman. Perhaps it might be possible to get her again for me, but not at present, for it was a great fast, which was observed at home indoors, and, moreover, she herself was just setting out for Mount Sinai for two or three months, and without her presence in the room nothing could be done. The day after this I persuaded my landlord to exert himself, which ended in his procuring me a lady as ugly as a daguerrotype, whom I dismissed after I had blunted my pencil in my sketch-book. In the afternoon I had another woman seized, who turned out to be uglier than any I had seen. All the public women seem to be chosen to show the repulsiveness of vice at first glance — a wise system that deserves more success than it would seem to meet. There are beautiful women here. In the country the fellah girls wear no veils and but very little dress, and these in their prime are perhaps the most graceful creatures you could see anywhere. In prowling about the village one day I came face to face with one of them, and could not but stop and stare at her. She could not pass, and when I saw this I thought some apology was necessary. Seddon's Hippopotamus* was with me, but I only explained my desire to him without further satisfaction than could be got by his going through his complete lesson with all its variations of ' Varé kood, ser; yes, ser, varé kood, ser; tiab contere quies varé kood, ser.'

* A fat dragoman.

"THE GHOST." 1853
Pen drawing

" Good-bye, old fellow. Commend my memory most kindly to your mother and father and brother, and all other friends. I am afraid I cannot write to the Collins's at once, for I want to settle to work first. Remember me to them affectionately. I will enclose a note to jolly old Halliday. I have a good excuse for not writing many letters, for, besides the engagements which one finds abroad, I have the plea of great difficulty in getting them posted. One cannot pay postage here, and I have to get them conveyed by hand to Alexandria for that purpose. God defend you always!— Yours, W. HOLMAN HUNT."

All through the summer, autumn, and winter of 1854 Hunt remained in Jerusalem, encountering many difficulties and not a little personal danger. Writing from there on November 10th, he expresses his delight at hearing from Millais, adding: — " It may be interesting to you to know that my tent was pitched on the plain of Mamre, under a tree still called ' Abraham's Tree,' where he entertained the three angels. (The tree, however, though an immense and ancient one, has no just claim to the dignity.) Here I lay down in the middle of the day, and took out your letters — Halliday's and your own — which I had brought with me, and re-read them again with a delight which made every word like pure water to a thirsty soul. I could remember Winchelsea so clearly, all our walks there together, and our meal at the inn, and I could imagine you and jolly Halliday working there within sight and sound of the sea. And how I could have joyed to be with you, to talk together for a few hours! Some day again I hope to see you, and not long hence. A few months, and I shall look for spring and England together. I am often sorry that you are no longer in Gower Street, for I cannot picture you returned to town, in a strange studio, and merry Halliday away from Robert Street. The idea is almost like losing you, for the picture of a pretty cottage at Kingston is not drawn from Nature, and may be all wrong.

" After all, your letter was full of sad incidents, notably the horrible death of the landlord of the inn. Such things make one despair of the world. Six thousand years, and so much evil! I think people look on and moralise too much. Sometimes I have an idea of an active future, in the fall of everything decent and respectable. I hope we may devise some means of serving God together. I am

in gloom sometimes as to the capacity of Art; but I
have no permanent despondency on the subject. It must
be equally strong as an instrument of either good or evil,
and of the latter one cannot doubt its power.

" Halliday told me your subject (' The Blind Girl '), which
I think a very beautiful one. It is an incident such as makes
people think and love more. It is wrong to doubt of the
good, after one has become convinced enough to take a
subject in hand. I went over all your news and your
reflections ; and, to realise the idea of our being together,
I used Halliday's envelope to make cigarettes with, and
fancied you through the fumes. . . .

" For the next week or two I shall be stationed about
sixty miles from Jerusalem, and with no means of des-
patching letters thence or communicating with any human
being above a wild Arab. The prospect is sufficiently
dreary, to say the least of it, but I am tempted to it for
the sake of a serious subject that has come into my head,
for the next exhibition of the Academy. . . . In Leviticus
xvi. 20 you will read an account of the scapegoat sent away
into the wilderness, bearing all the sins of the children of
Israel, which, of course, was instituted as a type of Christ.
My notion is to represent this accursed animal with the
mark of the priest's hands on his head, and a scarlet ribbon
which was tied to him, escaped in horror and alarm to
the plain of the Dead Sea, and in a death-thirst turning
away from the bitterness of this sea of sin. If I can contend
with the difficulties and finish the picture at Usdoom, it
cannot fail to be interesting, if only as a representation of
one of the most remarkable spots in the world; and I
am sanguine that it may be further a means of leading any
reflecting Jews to see a reference to the Messiah as He was,
and not (as they understand) a temporal king.

" My last journey was to discover an appropriate place
for the scene, and this I found only at the southern extremity
of the lake where the beach is thickly encrusted with salt,
and notwithstanding a remarkable beauty, there is an air
of desolation . . . exclusively belonging to it. Usdoom is
a name applied to a mountain standing in the plain, which
from the resemblance in sound is thought to be part of
Sodom. Its greater part is pure salt, which drips through
into long pendants whenever the water descends."

After referring to the victories of the allied troops at

Balaclava and Alma, he continues: — "I am beyond every-thing gratified at seeing that God has not taken away the lion hearts and the strong arms from English and Scotch. War is horrible, but not less justifiable, to my mind, than the slaying of animals for food, which is also revolting, when considered independent of the necessity."

Writing again on January 24th, 1855, Hunt says: — "I wonder how you all go on in London. No Pre-Raphaelite Brotherhood meetings, of course. The thing was a solemn mockery two or three years past, and died of itself. . . . I shall be glad to leave this unholy land, beautiful and in-teresting as it is. Never did people deserve to lose their empire so thoroughly as these Arabs. If they were left alone for a few years, they would com-plete the work themselves."

The concluding words of this letter are so quaintly redolent of the scriptural air he was then breathing, that it would be quite a sin to omit them: — " Remember me most kindly to your mother and father and brother of happy memory, and greet all my other friends of an inquiring turn of mind, of whom I regard Mrs. Collins as president. Remember me to the secretary, also Wilkie, and salute Charley brotherly (tell him I hope to bring him an Arab scalp even yet), also Stephens, to whom I cannot write this time. Thank him for the newspaper he sends me. I hope you get on well with your pictures. I am working like a baby in the Art."

In the spring the traveller was back in England again, and then their delightful meetings were once more resumed.

I must now hark back to the beginning of 1854, when Millais had in mind two pictures — "The Blind Girl" and "L'Enfant du Régiment" (or, as it is more commonly called, "The Random Shot") — both of which he was anxious to commence at once, and to paint concurrently. The latter demanded as a background the interior of a

church, and for some time during the autumn he roved about
in search of one suitable to his purpose. At last, on the
recommendation of a friend, he started for Winchelsea,
accompanied by Mike Halliday, and there he was fortunate
enough to find what he wanted in the old Priory Church
of Icklesham, about a mile away, and in the same neighbourhood the landscape he required for " The Blind Girl."

But first he must settle the point of view from which
to paint the interior; to which end he visited the church
on several consecutive days. At length the sexton's curiosity
was excited as to the object of this mysterious visitor, and

he asked him what he wanted.
" Oh," said Millais, " I want to
paint the church." " Well, then,
young man," replied the sexton,
" you need not hang about here
any longer, for the church was
all done up fresh last year." It
is an old-told tale, this, for
Thackeray got hold of it, and
told it at the clubs; but it is
none the less true. I have
heard my father tell it himself.

Another tale about this Winchelsea expedition is also worth
repeating. About a month after
Millais' arrival Thackeray appeared on the scene, and the
two worked together, Millais

painting while Thackeray went on with *Denis Duval*, that
fragment of a fine novel, unhappily left unfinished, in which
the principal character was drawn from Millais himself. While
thus engaged they were not altogether unobserved. To
borrow a line from one of Thackeray's most amusing ballads,
" A gent had got his i on 'em," the " gent " being an eccentric
old clergyman of the neighbourhood who looked in now and
then, and one Sunday morning appeared in the pulpit when
they were in church. They were sitting right in front of him,
and this dear old divine, catching sight of Millais, directed
his discourse to the comparative beauties of Nature and Art.
There was no mistaking what he meant, for, warming up as
he went along, he punctuated his remarks by personal appeals
to the artist as to the inferiority of man's work to God's.

Leaning over the pulpit with outstretched hands, and eyes fixed on Millais, he cried aloud, " Can you paint that? Can you paint that? " And then, turning to the congregation as he slowly drew himself upright, he added in solemn tones, " No, my brethren, *he cannot paint that.*" Again and again this embarrassing scene was repeated, until at last Millais and his friend became almost hysterical in the effort to suppress their laughter.

Coming now to the painting which led to these sensational incidents, " The Random Shot,"
I am glad to avail myself of
Mr. F. C. Stephens' description
of it in the following words : —
" This small picture represents
an incident in the French
Revolution, where some of the
populace, attacking a church
which is defended by the military, have accidentally wounded
a soldier's child who had been
taken there for safety. The
little one, wrapped in his father's
coat, has just sobbed itself to
sleep on the tomb of a knight,
where the child had been laid
out of further danger; the tears
of pain have ceased to trickle
down its face, and its sobbings
have found rest in sleep. The
tomb is of alabaster, mostly of

pure white, but dashed and streaked with pearly fawn and grey tints, according to the nature of the material, which acquires from time an inner tint of saffron and pale gold. The tale of ' The Random Shot ' is explained by showing some soldiers firing out of a window of the church."

The tomb on which the child is lying is that of Gervaise Allard, knight, one of the many beautiful works of art still to be seen in the old church at Icklesham. Dante Rossetti was probably right in saying that the artist's first idea was to depict the scene as taking place in a church besieged by Cromwell, for several of the sketches in my possession suggest more forcible and warlike movement than is to be found in the picture itself. The child, too, was originally painted in several attitudes before that of repose was selected.

" The Blind Girl," a still more pathetic subject, is described by Spielmann as " the most luminous with bright golden light of all Millais' works, and for that reason the more deeply pathetic in relation to the subject. Madox Brown was right when he called it a 'religious picture, and a glorious one,' for God's bow is in the sky, doubly — a sign of Divine promise specially significant to the blind. Rossetti called it ' one of the most touching and perfect things I know,' and the Liverpool Academy endorsed his opinion by awarding to it their annual prize, although the public generally favoured Abraham Solomon's ' Waiting for the Verdict.' Sunlight seems to issue from the picture, and bathes the blind girl — blind alike to its glow, to the beauties of the symbolic butterfly that has settled upon her, and to the token in the sky. The main rainbow is doubtless too strong and solid. Millais himself told the story of how, not knowing that the second rainbow is not really a 'double' one, but only a reflection of the first, he did not reverse the order of its colours as he should have done, and how, when it was pointed out to him, he put the matter right, and was duly feed for so doing. But the error is a common one. I have seen it in pictures by Troyon and others, students of Nature all their lives, who yet had never accurately observed. The precision of handling is as remarkable as ever, and the surrounding collection of birds and beasts evinces extraordinary draughtsmanship."

Catastrophe... ... ...

In 1898, when the picture was seen again in the midst of Millais' other Pre-Raphaelite works, nearly all the critics agreed that, for a general balance of qualities, it should take the first place in the collection; the *Spectator* remarking that: " Nowhere else in the whole range of his works did the painter produce such a beautiful piece of landscape. The picture is full of truth and full of beauty, and the grass glows

and sparkles in the sunlight after the storm. The colour throughout is as brilliant as paint can make it, but perfectly harmonious at the same time. Of quite equal beauty are the two figures, the blind musician and her child companion, and the pathos is so admirably kept in its proper place that it is really touching. There is a true humanity about this picture as well as great artistic qualities."

But best of all is Mr. Ruskin's refined and accurate description of the picture. He says: — " The background is an open English common, skirted by the tidy houses of a well-to-do village in the cockney rural districts. I have no doubt the scene is a real one within some twenty miles from London,

Nº1
How unstately the Artist outrivalled his companions even the conveyance ...

and painted mostly on the spot. A pretty little church has its window-traceries freshly whitewashed by order of the careful warden. The common is a fairly spacious bit of ragged pasture, and at the side of the public road passing over it the blind girl has sat down to rest awhile. She is a simple beggar, not a poetical or vicious one — a girl of eighteen or twenty, extremely plain-featured, but healthy, and just now resting, not because she is much tired, but because the sun has but this moment come out after a shower, and the smell of the grass is pleasant. The shower has been heavy, and is so still in the distance, where an intensely bright double rainbow is relieved against the departing thunder-cloud. The freshly wet grass is all radiant through and through with the new sunshine; the weeds at the girl's side as bright as a

1 — 16

Byzantine enamel, and inlaid with blue veronica; her up-turned face all aglow with the light which seeks its way through her wet eyelashes. Very quiet she is, so quiet that a radiant butterfly has settled on her shoulder, and basks there in the warm sun. Against her knee, on which her poor instrument of beggary rests, leans another child, half her age — her guide. Indifferent this one to sun or rain, only a little tired of waiting."

Neither the background nor the figures in this work were finished at Icklesham, the middle distance being, I think, painted in a hayfield near the railway bridge at Barnhill, just outside of Perth. Perth, too, supplied the models from

How the Representation of John R.A. was embarrassed with Sheep and further by the bland introduction of a certain master of an adjoining Hotel who moreover expected as in the life of conversation upon business that he had a mind to walk 1½ miles.

which the figures were finished. The rooks and domestic animals were all painted from Nature, as was also the tortoise-shell butterfly (not a Death's-head, as Mr. Spielmann has it), which was captured for the purpose. Both here and in "The Random Shot" the backgrounds were painted with extra-ordinary energy and rapidity, and the work, as in most of the artist's best productions, went on without a hitch.

I find, amongst my father's letters, one from Professor Herkomer, dated April 5th, 1893, in which he says: — "I cannot refrain from writing to you, to tell you of the effect your picture, 'The Blind Girl' (1856), had upon me when I saw it in Birmingham lately. I am no longer a youngster, but I assure you that that work so fired me, so enchanted, and so altogether astonished me, that I am prepared to begin Art all over again. The world of Art is your deep debtor for that work, and so am I.   P.S. — Do tell me the yellow you used for the grass."

The first owner of " The Blind Girl " was Mr. T. Miller, of Preston ; the second, Mr. W. Graham ; and, after passing through other hands, it became the property of Mr. Albert Wood, of Conway.   For its subsequent history I am in-debted to Mr. Whitworth Wallis, Curator of the City of Birmingham Art Gallery, who says : — " I borrowed ' The Blind Girl ' from Mr. Albert Wood in 1891, and induced him to part with it to Mr. William Kenrick, who presented it to the Art Gallery here as a permanent record of the success

How we took a dog cart

of the Pre-Raphaelite Brotherhood Exhibition held in this city."

In the autumn of 1854 Millais betook himself again to Scotland, in search of health and amusement, accompanied on this occasion by his friends Charlie Collins, Mike Halliday, and John Luard, of whom I must now say a few words.   John Dalbiac Luard (to give him his full name) began life as an officer in the 82nd Foot, but so devoted was he to Art, that in 1853 he left the service and took up painting as a profession.   Sharing with Millais a studio in Langham Chambers, which they occupied together for some years — in fact nearly down to the time of poor Luard's death in 1860 — he gave himself up to military subjects, of which " The Welcome Arrival " and " Nearing Home " were

exhibited in the Royal Academy and subsequently engraved.
His brother, Colonel Luard, kindly sends me a number of
sketches that Millais made of himself and his companions
during this tour, and assures me that the likeness of his
brother is wonderfully good. In the first of the series reproduced here we see the three men together. They have
just arrived in Scotland, and, having made no plans beforehand, are at a loss to know what to do. Millais, in his
impulsive way, suggests, "Oh, we'll go over and see ——
at Aytoun. He'll be simply delighted to see us and give
us some shooting. . . . Oh, no! There's not the slightest
need to give notice. We'll start early and get there in time

for breakfast." And so they did; they started very early
next morning — with the consequences depicted. However,
they got their day's shooting, marred only by a trifling
accident on the part of little Mike, who bagged Luard and
the footman instead of the rabbit he was aiming at.

Later on, when Halliday and Luard left, Charlie Collins
suggested a walking tour with Millais, and they started out
together, eventually finding themselves at Banavie, near
Fort William, where they seem to have come across " Long
John," of whiskey fame, who entertained them with samples
of his wares. Most of the second series of sketches were
made here, and in these the peculiarities of Collins' garments
are not forgotten. In the kindness of his heart Collins
looked rather to the necessities of his tailor than to his
skill, with results quite appalling to worshippers of fashion.

For similar reasons, too, he abjured fishing, a pastime he delighted in above all others. An indication of this is seen in the sketch, No. 9, where the artist and his companion appear at a critical moment. The fisherman playing the salmon is Captain Heywood, of the 82nd, a quondam brother-officer of Luard's.

The Paris Exhibition was now coming on. It was to be opened early in 1855, and Millais, being anxious that English Art should be well represented, addressed the following letter

To Mr. Combe.

"LANGHAM CHAMBERS, LANGHAM PLACE,
"*30th January*, 1855.

"MY DEAR MR. COMBE, — I was dining last Saturday at a friend's — Mr. Arden's — and met Redgrave, one of the managers of the Art department for the Paris Exhibition. He mentioned that you had kindly promised them 'The Light of the World,' and asked whether it was possible to get another of Hunt's and another of mine. I promised to write and ask whether you would send also either 'The Return of the Dove' or Hunt's picture. I know this is asking a great deal, as you would be for some little time without seeing your property; but if you can spare them, for the sake of showing the Frenchmen that we have a school of painters in this country (which they doubt), you would be doing something towards correcting that mistake. Of course the pictures are fully insured by Government, so you would be risking no loss; but you understand this, I daresay. Just let me know how you look upon this request, and I will write to Redgrave. . . .

"I still half reside with Mrs. C., that strong-minded old lady. I dined there yesterday, and met Dickens, and afterwards all went to the theatre. I am hard at work, and never have time for anything but painting, eating, and sleeping. I suppose you hear as much from Hunt as I do. There is a letter from him to a mutual friend, but none for me this post. He returns soon now, I think. Give my best greeting to Mrs. Pat. I wish you could both see my new rooms. Come up to town soon and see

"Ever yours sincerely,
"JOHN E. MILLAIS."

It was an important occasion this, for in the eyes of France England, as "a nation of shopkeepers," had nothing to show in the way of pictorial art; nothing, at least, that would compare for a moment with the works of her own artists; and now, for the first time in the history of the two nations, English painters were invited to show what they could do in open competition with their neighbours. Millais sent, amongst other pictures, "The Order of Release," "Ophelia," and "The Return of the Dove to the Ark"; and other eminent artists contributed freely, sending out specimens of their finest works. The result was a veritable triumph for British Art, and was freely and handsomely acknowledged

as such by the French Press. Théophile Gautier, the great French critic of the period, betrayed some bias not altogether unnatural in favour of his own countrymen, yet even he acknowledged the sterling merits of the English exhibits as far beyond what he had anticipated; and M. Duranty, a later and almost equally well-known critic, was still more complimentary. But perhaps the following critique, translated from one of the French papers, reflects most nearly the general opinion of the Press.

"The English contribution of paintings in 1855 was second in numbers only to the French, and came upon the Continental visitors to the Exhibition as a surprise. It was even more than a surprise, it was a revelation — a revelation of a school whose existence was not even suspected; and English painters, but little esteemed till then, obtained a very great success. The distribution of awards is in most

cases an unsatisfactory thing, and does not necessarily prove
or disprove merit; but, of whatever value they may be
thought, thirty-four were obtained by British artists in that
year."

The reasons for this success are very lucidly explained
by each of these critics.   Novelty, the contrast with, and
even the opposition to, Continental methods and ideals,
the complete emancipation from tradition, the influence
of the Pre-Raphaelites, the exceedingly strong local colour,
the conscientious endeavour to reflect Nature, and the
renunciation of self on the part of the artists: these, amongst

other circumstances, created a very strong impression upon
the European public interested in Art, and were undoubtedly
the chief features in the success achieved.   The paintings of
Messrs. Ansdell, Martin, Mulready, Millais, Hunt, Frith,
Paton, Landseer, Danby, and Corbould were especially
singled out for notice, Messrs. Nöel Paton, Mulready, and
Millais receiving the greater share.   The school of water-
colours was new, not only to Europe, but to Art, and the
French were quick to see of what the new method was
capable.

" The Rescue " (or " The Fireman," as the artist himself
used to call it) was painted in 1855, and is certainly one
of his finest works.

Its origin is thus accounted for by his brother: — " Early
one morning, as we were returning from a ball in Porchester

Terrace, we noticed the bright reflection of fire in the sky.
Accordingly we told the cabby to drive in that direction,
and a fire-engine dashing by at that moment increased our
excitement. The fire was close to Meux's brewery, and
we were in time to see the whole terrible show. On gazing
upwards we noticed two firemen plying the hose as they
stood on a rafter — themselves two black silhouettes against
the mass of heaving flame — and I shall never forget the
shout of horror that rent the air when the roof suddenly
collapsed, carrying with it the rafter and the two brave
men.

" We went home much impressed with what we had seen,
and my brother said, ' Soldiers and sailors have been praised
on canvas a thousand times. My next picture shall be of the
fireman.' "

Mr. Arthur Hughes is also good enough to send me a
note on the subject. He says : — " One day in 1855, the
moment I saw him [Millais], he began to describe the next
subject he proposed to paint — ' to honour a set of men
quietly doing a noble work — firemen ' ; and he poured out,
and painted in words of vividness and reality, the scene
he put on canvas later. I never see it or think of it without
seeing also the picture of himself glorified with enthusiasm
as he was describing it."

It was at a dinner party at the Collins's on January 29th,
1855, that Millais and Charles Dickens met (I think) for
the first time. After dinner they talked till a late hour
on pictures, and particularly on the subject of " The Rescue,"

on which Millais was then engaged. Dickens, it will be remembered, objected strongly to Millais' treatment of " Christ in the House of His Parents," and had made no attempt to disguise his feeling in speaking of the picture in *Good Words*. He refers to this in the following letter to Millais: —

From Charles Dickens.

" Tavistock House,

" *Tuesday, January 13th*, 1855.

" My dear Sir, — I send you the account of the fire brigade, which we spoke of last night.

" If you have in your mind any previous association with the pages in which it appears (very likely you have none) it may be a rather disagreeable one. In that case I hope a word frankly said may make it pleasanter.

" Objecting very strongly to what I believe to be an unworthy use of your great powers, I once expressed the objection in this same journal. My opinion on that point is not in the least changed, but it has never dashed my admiration of your progress in what I suppose are higher and better things. In short, you have given me such great reasons (in your works) to separate you from uncongenial associations, that I wish to give you in return one little reason for doing the like by me. And hence this note.

" Faithfully yours,

" Charles Dickens."

When " The Rescue" was nearly completed, Millais wrote and asked Dickens to come and see how the work had progressed, and received the following reply: —

" Tavistock House,

" *April 10th*, 1855.

" My dear Mr. Millais, — I am very sorry that I cannot have the great pleasure of seeing your picture to-day, as I am obliged to go a little way out of town.

" I asked Wilkie Collins to let you know that there is a curious appositeness in some lines in Gay's *Trivia*. You will find them overleaf here, to the number of four. The whole passage about a fire and firemen is some four-and-twenty lines long.   Very faithfully yours,

" Charles Dickens."

Mr. F. B. Barwell, a friend of the artist, has kindly furnished me with the following notes on the subject of " The Rescue " : — " This picture was produced in my studio, and presents many interesting facts within my own knowledge. After several rough pencil sketches had been made, and the composition determined upon, a full-sized cartoon was drawn from nature. Baker, a stalwart model, was the fireman, and he had to hold three children in the proper attitudes and bear their weight as long as he could, whilst the children were encouraged and constrained to do their part to their utmost. The strain could never be kept up

Nº VIII

for long, and the acrobatic feat had to be repeated over and over again for more than one sitting, till Millais had secured the action and proportion of the various figures. When sufficiently satisfied with the cartoon, it was traced on to a perfectly white canvas, and the painting commenced. It was now no longer necessary to have the whole group posed at one time ; but Baker had to repeat his task more or less all through. The effect of the glare was managed by the interposition of a sheet of coloured glass of proper hue between the group (or part of it at a time) and the window. The processes employed in painting were most careful, and indeed slow, so that what Millais would have done in his later years in a week, took months in those earlier days. It was his practice then to paint piecemeal, and finish parts of his pictures as he went on. White, mixed with copal, was generally laid on where he intended to work for the day, and was painted into and finished whilst wet, the whole drying together. The night-dresses of the children were executed in this manner. Strontian yellow was mixed with the white, and then rose-madder mingled with copal, floated, as it were, over the solid but wet paint — a difficult process, and so ticklish that as soon as a part was finished the canvas had to be laid on its back till the colour had dried sufficiently to render the usual position on the easel a safe one.

" By degrees the work was finished, but not till near midnight of the last day for sending into the Royal Academy.

In those days Millais was generally behindhand with his principal picture, and so much so with this one, that he greatly curtailed his sleep during the last week; and on the last day but one began to work as soon as it was daylight, and worked on all through the night and following day till the van arrived for the picture. (Mr. Ruskin defended the appearance of haste, which to him seemed to betray itself in the execution of this picture, contending that it was well suited to the excitement and action of the subject.) His friend Charles Collins sat up with him and painted the fire-hose, whilst Millais worked at other parts; and in the end a large piece of sheet-iron was placed on the floor, upon which a flaming brand was put and worked from, amidst suffocating smoke. For the head of the mother, Mrs. Nassau Senior, sister of Judge Hughes of *Tom Brown* fame, was good enough to sit.

"The methods here described were gradually abandoned as Millais progressed in his career."

On the whole, this picture met with a fair degree of approbation, but, as Mr. Spielmann says, "its artificiality, and still more the chromatic untruth, were savagely attacked. It was pointed out that the flames of burning wood emit yellow and green rays in abundance. Blazing timber, even incandescent bricks, would not cast such a colour, except in a modified tint upon the clouds above; that a fire such as this throws an orange light at most, and that therefore the children's night-dresses should have been yellow, with grey in the shadows, and the fireman's green cloth uniform yellow-

How on top of Coach the weather was very uncomfortable comfort

grey. The latter part of the contention Ruskin demolished, for nearly-black is always quite-black in full juxtaposition with violet colour. But he could not meet the argument that, to accept as true the ruddy glow, one must agree that it is a houseful of Bengal-fire and nitrate of strontian that is alight. Seen by artificial light, the picture almost succeeds in concealing this error of fact."

The following interesting note on "The Rescue" is taken from the *Table Talk of Shirley*, as quoted in *Good Words* of October, 1894: — "I knew Thomas Spencer Baynes intimately for nearly forty years. For ten years thereafter Baynes was my constant correspondent. From London he wrote to me as follows on May 25th, 1855: — 'I went in for half an hour to the Royal Academy yesterday,

but as I was almost too tired to stand, and did not stay
any time, I shall say nothing about it, only this, that the face
and form of that woman on the stairs of the burning house
[" The Rescue "] are, if not, as I am disposed to think, beyond
all, quite equal to the best that Millais has ever done, not
forgetting the look of unutterable love and life's deep yearn-
ing in " The Huguenot." And those children! Ah me! I can
hardly bear to think of it; yet the agony is too near, too
intense, too awful, for present rejoicing even at the deliver-
ance.   And that smile on the young mother's face has
struggled up from such depths of speechless pain, and expresses such a sudden ecstasy of utter gratitude and over-

How we warmed ourselves by
the Steamer Stove

mastering joy, that it quite unmans me to look at it.   It is
the most intense and pathetic utterance of poor human love
I have ever met.' "

Millais himself knew this to be his best work.   When,
therefore, he went to the Academy on varnishing-day, 1855,
and found that it had been deliberately skied, his indignation
knew no bounds.   He told the Hanging Committee to their
faces what he thought of this insult, and of them as the
authors of it.   But perhaps that scene is best described in
the words of Dante Rossetti, who, writing to his friend
W. Allingham, said : " How is Millais' design [' The Fireside
Story '], which I have not yet seen ?   I hope it is only as
good as his picture at the Royal Academy — the most wonderful thing he has done, except, perhaps, ' The Huguenot.'

He had an awful row with the Hanging Committee, who had put it above the level of the eye; but J. E. Millais yelled for several hours, and threatened to resign till they put it right."

Mention is also made of this incident in the *Life of W. B. Scott*, to whom Woolner, writing in May, 1855, said : — " The Academy Committee hung Millais — even Millais, their crack student — in a bad place, he being too attractive now ; but that celebrity made such an uproar, the old fellows were glad to give him a better place."

Millais' amusement, when Woolner wrote, was to go about and rehearse the scene that took place at the Academy between him and the ancient magnates.

Seddon also wrote on May 3rd, 1855 : — " The Academy opens on Monday. The hangers were of the old school, and they have kicked out everything tainted with Pre-Raphaelitism. My ' Pyramids ' and a head in chalk of Hunt's, and all our friends, are stuck out of sight or rejected. Millais' picture was put where it could not be seen. . . . He carried his point by threatening to take away his picture and resign at once unless they rehung him, which they did. He told them his mind very freely, and said they were jealous of all rising men, and turned out or hung their pictures where they could not be seen."

The latest note on the picture appeared in the *Daily News* of January 1st, 1898, in which it is said : — " ' The Rescue ' has a vigour and a courage that rivets attention. The immortal element (as Ruskin said at the time) is in it to the full. It was studied from the very life. Millais and a trusty friend of those early days hurried off one night to where a great fire was raging, plunged into the thick of the scene, and saw the effects which his memory could retain and his hand record. What a grappling it is with a difficulty which no other painter had so treated before. It is a situation which is dramatic ; the rest is Nature. In the pose of the mother, as she reaches out those long arms of hers, straight and rigid and parallel, there is an intensity of expression that recalls his Pre-Raphaelite days. The figure of the child escaping towards her from the fireman's grasp shows what mastery of his art he had gained in the interval."

The secret of this " mastery " is that Millais always went to life and Nature for his inspiration. Touching this particular picture, I heard him say that before he commenced the work he went to several big fires in London to study the

ST. AGNES. 1854

true light effects. The captain of the fire brigade was a friend of his, and one evening, when Millais and Mike Halliday were dining with him, he said, after several alarms had been communicated, " Now, Millais, if you want to see a first-class blaze, come along." Rushing downstairs, the guests were speedily habited in firemen's overalls and helmets, and, jumping into a cab, were soon on the scene of action.

Years afterwards Millais was dining one night with Captain Shaw, the then chief of the brigade, and renewed his experience at a big fire; but this time he travelled on one of the engines — a position which he found much less to his taste than the inside of a cab.

" The Fireside Story," to which Rossetti alludes, was intended to illustrate the following stanza of " Frost in the Highlands," in the second series of *Day and Night Songs*, by William Allingham : —

> " At home are we by the merry fire,
> Ranged in a ring to our heart's desire.
> And who is to tell some wondrous tale,
> Almost to turn the warm cheeks pale,
> Set chin on hands, make grave eyes stare,
> Draw slowly nearer each stool and chair ? "

Of this drawing the *Athenæum* of August 18th, 1855, wrote : — " ' The Fireside Story,' by the last-named gentleman [Millais], is a proof that he can be in earnest without being absurd, and reproduce Nature without administering on the occasion a dose of ugliness as a tonic " — a piece of criticism which called forth the following from D. G. Rossetti in one of his letters to W. Allingham : — " That is a stupid enough notice in the *Athenæum* in all conscience. I wonder who did it ? Some fearful ass evidently, from the way he speaks of Millais as well as of you."

William Allingham also refers to this drawing in a letter to Millais of November 10th, 1855, concluding with the following words : — " As I am not good at praising people to their faces, and as it is a comfort, too, to express something of what one feels, pray let me assure you here of the deep respect I have for your powers. The originality and truthfulness of your genius fill me with delight and wonder. I wish you would master the art of etching, and make public half a dozen designs now and again. Surely one picture in a year, shown in London and then shut up, is not result

I — 17

enough for such a mine of invention and miraculous power
of reproduction as you possess. This is the age of printing
and a countless public, and the pictorial artist may and ought
to aim at exercising a wider immediate influence. Be our
better Hogarth. Don't leave us remote and wretched to the
Illustrated London News and the *Art Journal.*"*

Acting on this advice, Millais set to work and studied

REJECTED. 1853

etching. By my mother's account-book I see he did etchings
on copper, though what has become of them I do not know.

The year after its exhibition in London "The Rescue"
was sent to the Liverpool Academy, where it is said to have
lost the annual prize by a single vote. Thackeray, who was
now a great admirer of Millais' works, was quite fascinated
with it, and it was due to his recommendation that the picture
passed into the hands of Mr. Arden. Some years afterwards,

* The wood-cutting of this period was so bad that even the best examples which
appeared in these journals were far from satisfactory.

when it was put up for auction at the Arden sale, at Christie's rooms, it was noticed that the canvas was covered with spots, due to its having been kept in an uncongenial temperature. The artist saw this, and offered to put things right; but, strange to say, the executors declined the offer, and it was sold, spots and all. The spots remained on the canvas for many years, and after seeing the picture in the Glasgow Exhibition in 1887, I spoke to my father about it, and, with the consent of the owners, he had it back in his studio and successfully removed the blemish.

It was in this year (1855) that Leighton (afterwards an intimate friend of Millais) made his first appearance in the Academy with an important work — a big picture of " Cimabue," which was bought by her majesty the Queen. Millais referred to him in the following words at the Academy banquet on May 6th, 1895 : — " In the early part of the evening I spoke of my first meeting with Fred. Leighton. Let me tell you where and from whom I first heard of him. It was in the smoking-room of the old Garrick Club, and the man who first mentioned the name to me was William Make-peace Thackeray. He had just returned from travelling abroad, and, amongst other places, had visited Italy. When he saw me enter the room he came straight up to me, and addressed me in these memorable words: — 'Millais, my boy, you must look to your laurels. I have met a wonderfully gifted young artist in Rome, about your own age, who some day will be the President of the Royal Academy before you.' How that prophecy has come to pass is now an old, old story. We are, as we may well be, proud of our dear President, our admirable Leighton — painter, sculptor, orator, linguist, musician, soldier, and, above all, a dear good fellow. That he may long continue to be our chief is not only the fervent prayer of the Academy; it is, unless I am much mistaken, the sincere and hearty wish of every member of the profession."

His first meeting with the future President is also a matter of some interest. Speaking of this, he said : — " The first time I met Frederick Leighton was on the war-path. It was at a meeting of four or five of the original Artist Volunteers, held in my studio in Langham Place, and, if my memory serves me, it was to consider the advisability of adopting the grey cloth which the corps now wears."

Then was cemented a life-long friendship between the

President of the day and the man who eventually succeeded him in his office.

That the advent of Leighton was received with joy by the Royal Academicians will be seen by the following passage in one of D. G. Rossetti's letters in 1855 : — " There is a big picture of 'Cimabue,' one of the works in procession by a new man, living abroad, named Leighton — a huge thing, which the Queen has bought, and which everyone talks of. The Royal Academicians have been gasping for years for someone to back against Hunt and Millais, and here they have him — a fact which makes some people do the picture injustice in return."

CHAPTER VII

Millais' affection for Leech — His first top-boots — "Mr. Tom Noddy" — Millais
introduces "Mr. Briggs" to the delight of salmon fishing — The Duke of
Athol and Leech — Letters from Leech — The ghost of Cowdray Hall — Death
of Leech — His funeral — The pension for Leech's family — Letter from Charles
Dickens — Thackeray — The littleness of earthly fame — Wilkie Collins — True
origin of *The Woman in White* — Anthony Trollope — Letters from him.

LEECH, Thackeray, Wilkie Collins, and Anthony
Trollope: what memories these names conjure up!
They were amongst the oldest and most intimate friends of
Millais, and were so closely associated with him at various
periods of his life that no biography of any of them would
be complete without some record of the others. It may be
interesting, then, to those who know them only by their
works to recall here some of the many personal qualities
that endeared them to all who enjoyed the privilege of their
friendship.

And first of Leech, the famous caricaturist of *Punch*.
Here was a man of whom, if of anybody, one might say,
" I shall not look upon his like again." "The truest gentleman I ever met," was what was said of him by those who knew
him best — by such judges of men as Thackeray, Trollope,
Frith, Du Maurier, Dean Hole, and others — and no words
could better convey the sentiments of Millais himself. To
speak of him after his death was always more or less painful
to my father, though now and then, when sport was upper-
most in his mind, he would talk enthusiastically of the happy
days when they shot or rode together or rollicked about
town as gay young bachelors bent on all the amusement
they could find.

Hear what Du Maurier says of him in *Harper's Magazine:* — " He was the most sympathetic and attractive person
I ever met; not funny at all in conversation, or ever wishing

261

to be, except now or then for a capital story, which he told
to perfection.

"The keynote of his character, socially, seemed to be
self-effacement, high-bred courtesy, never-failing consideration for others. He was the most charming companion
conceivable, having intimately known so many important
and celebrated people, and liking to speak of them; but

one would never have guessed from
anything he ever looked or said
that he had made a whole nation,
male and female, gentle and simple,
old and young, laugh as it had
never laughed before or since, for
a quarter of a century.

"He was tall, thin, and graceful,
extremely handsome, of the higher
Irish type, with dark hair and
whiskers and complexion, and very
light greyish-blue eyes; but the
expression of his face was habitually
sad, even when he smiled. In
dress, bearing, manner, and aspect
he was the very type of the well-
bred English gentleman and man
of the world and good society. . . .
Thackeray and Sir John Millais —
not bad judges, and men with
many friends — have both said that
they personally loved John Leech
better than any man they ever
knew."

This, I think, fairly sums up the
character of the man whose name,
as will presently be seen, figures so
often and so prominently in my father's correspondence. It
was in 1851 that they first met, and one of the first results
of the intimacy that then sprang up between them was Millais'
conversion to his friend's view of fox-hunting as one of the
finest sports in the world both for man and beast. Hitherto
he had insisted that, unlike shooting or fishing, at both of
which he was already an expert, hunting was "a barbarous
and uncivilised sport," and as such he would have nothing
to do with it. But Leech would not listen to this. As the

JOHN LEECH. *Circ.* 1856

JOHN LEECH. 1857
From the water-colour in the National Portrait Gallery

old ostler in *Punch* remarked, "The 'orses like it, the 'ounds like it, the men like it, and even the fox likes it"; and as to health, urged Leech, it was only at the tail of the hounds that an artist could do justice to himself after the enervating influence of the studio.

That was enough. If only for the sake of health Millais would hunt; and the following season saw him at the cover-side, booted and spurred, and bent on going with the best if only his horse would let him.

With a view to this Leech had introduced him to a boot-maker in Oxford Street for his first "tops": and according to his own account (for he never hesitated to tell a tale against himself), the interview was not lacking in amuse-ment. Being but a stripling of twenty-one or thereabouts, his calves were in the embryo state so mortifying to young manhood. He was delighted therefore when, on measuring him, the shopman said with an air of admiration, "Ah, sir, what a fine leg for a boot!" But the conclusion of the sentence was not quite so satisfactory — "Same size all the way up." Leech was so amused with this that he immor-talised the scene in *Punch*, and on more than one occasion afterwards my father sat as a model for some of his clever drawings in that periodical. From this time, indeed, till the day of his death John Leech was one of his closest friends. They hunted together in the shires, shot, fished, and stalked together; and all those amusing sketches in *Punch*, to which Leech owed his fame — all the deer-stalking, grouse-shooting, and salmon-fishing adventures depicted there as incidents in the life of "Mr. Briggs" — were but burlesque representations of Leech's own experience as a tyro on his first visit to Scotland, principally as my father's guest.

By the end of the first hunting season Millais had acquired a firm seat on horseback, and was known as a bold rider across country; and except when in later years Scotland claimed his presence, he followed the hounds with ardour year by year, visiting alternately, Hertfordshire, Bedfordshire, and Leicester, where he and Leech and Mike Halliday kept their hunters — hired by them for the season. A clever little sketch of Leech's is given here, showing Millais putting on the steam to clear a fence.

Leech, though not quite so keen a rider, was a far better horseman than his modesty would ever allow him to acknow-ledge; but little Mike, though plucky enough, was always

coming to grief, to the great amusement of Leech, who duly
chronicled his mishaps in *Punch*, under the title of " The
Adventures of Mr. Tom Noddy."

It was at Stobhall, near Perth, in 1855, that Millais introduced his friend Leech to the wild delights of salmon-fishing,
and as the friend of " Mr. Briggs " he, too, appears in *Punch*.
Leech was charmed with the prospective sport, but as a

MILLAIS HUNTING. 1854
By John Leech

novice in the art of casting he tried in vain to effect a
capture. The fish were there, plenty of them, and flies of
the most seductive character floated before their eyes; but
either the business-end of these flies was too apparent, or
their movements were suspicious, or—— But who shall say
by what process of reasoning a fish learns to distinguish
between friend and foe? Anyhow, they could not be persuaded to rise.

Harling was then resorted to. For some days Leech sat
patiently in a boat, hoping that some feeble-minded fish
would be tempted to come and hook itself as the fly dangled

carelessly from his rod, and at last he had his reward. Just below the dyke at Stanley the line suddenly straightened; Leech snatched up the rod, and away went a clean-run 25-pounder with the hook in his gills! Then the struggle began, and great excitement for the fisherman, as this bit of Stanley water is a rough place, full of rushing streams and deep holes, in which are sharp, shelving rocks, from which the quarry must be got away at once, or he would certainly cut the line.

After allowing him one good run, Leech scrambled out amongst the rocks and stones of the Stobhall shore, and the fish making straight down stream, dragged him helter-skelter over boulders and through bushes, till he was nearly at his last gasp. Then, luckily for him, the salmon retreated into " The Devil's Hole," and sulked there for half an hour. The angler then recovered breath, and ultimately, at the bottom of Stanley water, my father gaffed the fish, to the great delight of " Mr. Briggs," as subsequently portrayed in *Punch*.

MILLAIS FISHING AT STOBHALL
Sketch by John Leech 1855

Another anecdote of Leech must be related here in connection with this visit of his to Perth. During the previous year he made the acquaintance of the Duke of Athol in a way he did not like. Walking in the hills near Blair, he unfortunately got into the forest when a deer-drive was going on, and to his dismay found himself face to face with the duke. Now Leech was a very nervous man, and the duke, who in his own territory was looked upon as a king, waxed exceedingly wroth at the sight of this trespasser, and without more ado gave him what they call in Yorkshire "a bit of his mind," interlarding his speech with such terrible terms as " Roderick Dhu " and " Vile Sassenach." Leech, needless to say, beat a retreat, only too glad to escape with a whole skin; but he had his revenge a few months later when the whole world was laughing at his clever skit on the situation in the pages of *Punch*.

On a second visit in 1856, he was surprised by an invitation to come with my father to Blair and take part in the big deer-drives then going on; but with that sketch in his mind, and fearing that the duke might have recognised it as connected with himself, he could not be prevailed upon to go until my father dragged him by main force into the coach. The duke *had* seen it, and knew what it meant, and being very good-natured, had enjoyed the joke immensely; and now he went out of his way to put Leech at his ease and show him the best sport he could.

Leech had now two opportunities for caricaturing himself, and was not slow in availing himself of them. After a drive in which he failed to kill, he was so overcome by the heat of the day that he fell asleep in his shelter just as a splendid herd of stags was passing by. That is another incident in the life of " Mr. Briggs "; and again another was found in a failure to kill a noble hart which had been stalked all day.

Though the duke was in no way annoyed by Leech's skit, he could not refrain from having a little joke at his expense. The two were in a "butt" together, waiting for the deer, when, as a humorous reminder of their first meeting, the duke suddenly produced a pistol, and, presenting it at Leech's head, exclaimed in theatrical tones, " Now I am ' Roderick Dhu ' on my native heath, and you, vile Sassenach, are in my power ! " The suddenness of the attack so upset poor Leech's nerves that he let the deer go by without a shot. Eventually, however, he killed two stags by stalking, the recollection of which was a source of happiness to him for years afterwards.

In this same year another shock brought another picture from the hand of the famous caricaturist. My father took him to shoot with his friend, James Condy, at Rohallion, and on their way to the house led him through a corner of the home park, in which herds of bison, recently brought

from Western America by Sir William Stuart, were confined. The furious aspect of the animals, and its effect
upon the untrained nerves of the novice, shortly afterwards
found expression in print in the usual quarter.

Leech used to say he could never quite understand a
Scotchman. They were a curious, uncongenial people, with
queer ways and customs very perplexing to a stranger, who,
in his ignorance, might readily give offence where he least
intended to do so. An instance of this occurred one day
when he and Millais by chance came across a man in a red
shirt who was cutting down a tree in a way that suggested
at least a passing acquaintance with the whiskey bottle.
Recognising him as a local laird whom they had met before,
Leech shyly addressed him as " Mr. McR——." "Who
the devil are you calling Mr. McR——? I am THE
McR——," roared the fiery Scot, upon which Leech apologised and made off at once.

And here may be fitly introduced, I think, two characteristic letters from Leech, with the sketches enclosed.

From John Leech.

" 32 BRUNSWICK SQUARE,
"*June 14th*, 1855.

" MY DEAR MILLAIS, — I return the insurance paper filled
up, to the best of my belief, properly — though perhaps with
regard to the question, ' Is there any peculiarity in his con-
figuration?' I ought to have been more explicit. However,
when you go before the ' Board ' they will be able to judge
of your tendency to corpulence and what may be called your
general ' stumpy ' (if I may use a vulgar but expressive
word) appearance. I might, too, have attended to your
strikingly socratic profile ; but the answer I have returned
will, I daresay, answer the purpose.

" I came to town the very day you left for the North,
and called at your chambers, missing you by a few hours
only. How much I should have liked to give you a
shake of the hand, and to wish *vivâ voce* health and
happiness to you ! I do most cordially wish you may have
both for many years. . . . Last week I went out pike-
fishing at a most beautiful place called Fillgate, with one
Jolliffe, of whom you have, I think, heard me speak. He

was in the 4th Light Dragoons and was in the ever-memorable Balaclava Charge. He gave me a vivid description of the dreadful business. Altogether I have rarely had a more pleasant day. We behaved, I am afraid, in a most unsportsmanlike manner, for he was anxious to thin the pond of fish, and determined to set trimmers. About four-and-twenty of these devices were put in all over the water, and it was exciting enough to paddle after them as the bait on each was carried off by Mr. Jack. You would have enjoyed it immensely, only you would have jumped out of the boat. And we caught a 'bold biting Perch,' sir !— such a one as I have only seen stuffed in the fishing-tackle shops, and which I always believed to be manufactured by the carpenter or umbrella maker. He weighed three pounds, and *not* fisherman's weight. Let me hear from you sometimes. This, I know, is asking a good deal under the circumstances, for cannot your time be much more agreeably employed than in writing to   Yours always, my dear fellow,

" JOHN LEECH ? "

From the same.

" 32 BRUNSWICK SQUARE,
" *October* 23*rd*, 1855.

" MY DEAR MILLAIS, — I said I would write to you from Folkestone, and I did n't write to you from Folkestone — and will you forgive me ? My conscience has been pricking me so much for my neglect that I can bear it no longer, and although I have nothing of much interest to communicate, 'I send you these few lines, hoping they will find you well, as they leave me at present.' Luard wrote to me the other day from his ship, on his way to the Crimea. I trust nothing will happen to the good little fellow. I shall miss his cheery, pert face this winter. Am I to miss you too, or are you coming south ? Why not ? Let us have some fine, healthful exercise with old P——,* always very careful, of course — Old Gentleman style.

" You should come to town, if only to see a collection of photographs taken in the Crimea. They are surprisingly good ; I don't think anything ever affected me more. You

* Millais and Leech both studied " the noble art " under this gentleman.

hardly miss the colour, the truth in other respects is so
wonderful.

"When I was in Paris I saw your pictures.   Believe me,
out of some thousands of pictures, large, very large, small,
and very small, they stood out, as your works always do,

THE DUKE OF WELLINGTON
Sketched from life by John Leech at the opening of the Great Exhibition, May 1st, 1851
and enclosed in a letter to Millais

most conspicuously good.   Apropos of pictures, I want to
ask you a question.   I was with Mowbray Morris some time
since, and he told me that he and his colleagues of the *Times*
wished very much to have a portrait painted of one of their
most valued contributors and friends to be hung up in their
'Sanctum.'   They wish, of course, that it should be done by
the best man.   Both Morris and myself agreed that there

was only one best man, and that 'party' J. Everett What's-
his-name, A.R.A. Well, he asked me whether you would do
it, and I said I would ask you. What do you say? It
would, I think, be considered by them quite as much a
kindness on your part as a matter of business, although the
business part of it would be according to your own views,
supposing it came to anything. . . .

" *The Newcomes* is a wonderful book, particularly the latter
part of it — the old colonel's 'Adsum'! What genuine
pathos! I dined with Thackeray the day before he started
for America. I don't think he liked leaving England.
Would that he were back working away at another book.
You will be glad to hear that our little ones are thriving
famously. Your little friend runs about, and begins to talk.
She already has a strong inclination to draw, which develops
itself in the making of what she calls dow-dows (dogs) over
every sketch of mine that comes in her way; and, I am sorry
to add, remonstrance is of no avail, for on the slightest
attempt to interfere with any project she has, she dashes
herself on the ground and screams awfully. This must be
altered; Paterfamilias must be stern. The boy begins 'to
take notice'; that is, he screws his mouth up to all sorts of
ridiculous shapes, and, squinting, makes a little grunt, which
is supposed to be indicative of strong filial attachment.

" Always yours,

" JOHN LEECH."

And now we come to a little ghost story that my father
used to tell, and, as related by William Millais, runs thus: —
" A very singular thing happened to my brother and John
Leech when they were on a fishing tour, walking with knap-
sacks and staying at wayside inns. Happening to be passing
near Cowdray Hall, they met the squire, whom they knew
well, and he pressed them to return with him to dine and
sleep, and being some distance from their next halting-place,
and tired, they accepted the kind invitation.

" There was a terrible ghost story attached to the old
house, and after dinner everyone seemed possessed with the
determination to relate his or her experience of these weird
goblins. It turned out that the hall was so full of visitors
that only the quarters occupied by the local ghost were available, and they were situated in an unused wing of the hall.

These were offered to the two fishermen, who of course laughed and scoffed at the idea of the ghost.

"The rooms were covered with fine old tapestry and kept in beautiful order, with grand old-fashioned beds in them. When they retired to rest they were looked upon by the assembled company as heroes of the first magnitude. They were tired, however, and soon dropped into the arms of Morpheus.

"In the middle of the night my brother jumped out of bed in a cold shiver, and trembling in every limb. He told

Part of a letter from Leech to Millais, who has expressed his intention to cultivate a moustache. 1856

me that he felt as if he had been violently shaken by an invisible giant. They had been told that the ghost served its victims in such a manner. My brother went off to see Leech, whom he found sitting in the corridor, when he declared that nothing would induce him to go into his room again; and thus they passed the night in the corridor.

"Everyone was out cub-hunting when they reached the breakfast-table, and it was only late in the day that some of the visitors began to show themselves, and of course they were asked how they had slept. They laughed over the matter, and confessed that they had not seen the ghost.

Later in the afternoon the squire came in in great excitement, holding in his hand the local evening paper, first edition, and said that there had been a severe earthquake in the night, that a village quite near had suffered serious damage, and that it was a most extraordinary thing that no one in the house had felt it. And then the fishermen told him how they had passed the night. The earthquake was the ghost's understudy on this occasion, and played his part admirably."

As Leech advanced in years his melancholy and sensitiveness, due in a great measure to overwork, increased. He became so nervous that the very slightest noise disturbed him ; and living in London, as he did, he could hardly escape from barrel-organs, bands, whistling boys, and shrieking milkmen. At last that dread disease " angina pectoris " came upon him, and one evening, when Millais was painting, a terrified domestic, whom he at once recognised as Leech's housemaid, rushed in, saying that her master had another bad attack, and was crying aloud, " Millais! Millais!" The next moment Millais was off, and running through the streets of Kensington he mounted the stairs of his old friend's room, and found him lying across the bed, quite still and warm, but to all appearance dead, the belief in the house being that he expired at the moment of his friend's arrival.

A few days later he was laid to rest, and, says Du Maurier, * " I was invited by Messrs. Bradbury and Evans, the publishers of *Punch*, to the funeral, which took place at Kensal Green. It was the most touching sight imaginable. The grave was near Thackeray's, who had died the year before. There were crowds of people, Charles Dickens among them. Canon Hole, a great friend of Leech's, and who has written most affectionately about him, read the service; and when the coffin was lowered into the grave, John Millais burst into tears and loud sobs, setting an example that was followed all round. We all forgot our manhood, and cried like women! I can recall no funeral in my time where simple grief and affection had been so openly and spontaneously displayed by so many strangers as well as friends — not even in France, where people are more demonstrative than here. No burial in Westminster Abbey that I have ever seen ever gave such an expression of universal honour, love and regret. ' Whom the gods love die young.' He was only forty-six."

Finding then that little or no provision was left for his

* *Harper's Magazine*, February, 1896.

family, my father took up the case, and with the aid of a few friends (notably "Dicky" Doyle), organised an exhibition of Leech's drawings, which brought in a considerable sum, but not sufficient to provide for the children's education. A pension from the Civil List was then thought of; but it was no easy matter to obtain this, as at that time (1864) these pensions were limited almost exclusively to the families of men whose lives were devoted to literary work alone. An attempt, however, must be made; and on an appeal, kindly supported by the Prince and Princess of Wales, Lord Palmerston, Lord Shaftesbury, and other influential admirers of Leech's works, a pension of £50 a year was granted to each of the children.

Numerous letters on this subject from His Royal Highness and other notabilities lie before me; but perhaps the most interesting is that

From Charles Dickens.

"GAD'S HILL PLACE, HIGHAM-BY-ROCHESTER,
"*Sunday, December 18th, 1864.*

"MY DEAR MILLAIS,— There are certain personal private circumstances which would render my writing to Lord Palmerston, *separately and from myself alone*, in the matter of the pension, a proceeding in more than questionable taste. Besides which I feel perfectly certain that a reminder from me would not help the powerful case. I should have been glad to sign the memorial, but I have not the least doubt that the letter from myself singly is best avoided. If I had any, I would disregard the other considerations and send it; but I have none, and I am quite convinced that I am right.

"You are a generous and true friend to Mrs. Leech.
"Faithfully yours ever,
"CHARLES DICKENS."

Mrs. Leech soon followed her husband. Leech's only son was drowned many years ago in Australian waters, and his daughter Ada, who married a clergyman, has also joined the great majority.

The following letter to her is characteristic of the writer, who was always keenly alive to the claims of friendship.

To Miss Ada Leech.

"*January* 10th, 1877.

"Dear Ada, — I am much grieved to hear of the death of your good uncle, and that you should be left without his counsel and advice.

"I shall be very happy at all times to help you to the best of my ability, and hope you will send me the name and address of his solicitor, as we were joint trustees in the Government's grant settled on you, and I shall have to now act until some other gentleman is appointed with me. Moreover, any confidence you may place in me, from my affection towards your father, I will do my best to use for your benefit. I am sure your aunt, Mrs. Hayward, will be most kind to you, but I am aware there are some positions in which a man alone can act on your behalf. . . . You have, indeed, been unfortunate, but at your age you may look for a happy career yet. Just at this moment we are moving into our new house, and in mourning ourselves, otherwise I would have you with us, if you would come. Tell Mrs. Hayward how truly I sympathise with her, and believe me always

"Yours truly,

"J. E. Millais."

As to Thackeray, my father and mother always regarded him as one of the most delightful characters they ever met. Though in dealing with the infirmities of human nature his works now and then show traces of cynicism, the man himself was no cynic — was rather, indeed, to those who knew him best, a most sympathetic friend, and tender-hearted almost to a fault. For some years he entertained and brought up as one of his family the daughter of a deceased friend; and so grieved was he at the thought of parting from her that on her wedding-day he came for consolation to my father's studio, and spent most of the afternoon in tears. They met so frequently — he and Millais — that but little correspondence of any interest appears to have passed between them. The genial nature of the man, however, peeps out in the following reply to my father's invitation to stay with him at Annat Lodge, near Perth, when on his lecturing tour in 1857.

From Thackeray.

"QUEEN'S HOTEL, GLASGOW,
"*March 3rd.*

"MY DEAR MILLAIS,— I got the sad news at Edinburgh yesterday — that there is to be no lecture at Perth, my manager not having been able to make arrangements there. So I shall lose the pleasure I had promised myself of seeing you and Mrs. Millais, and the pictures on the easel, and the little miniature Millais by Millais, which I hope and am sure is a charming little work by that painter. I am off in a minute to Edinburgh for Kirkaldy, and have only time to say that I am

"Very truly yours always,

"W. M. THACKERAY."

Of Thackeray, Millais and Carlyle, William Millais tells an interesting story illustrative of the littleness of earthly fame, however highly we may regard it. He says: — "I was sitting with my brother in the Cromwell Place studio when Thackeray suddenly came in all aglow with enthusiasm at my brother's fame. Every window in every shop that had the least pretension to Art-display, he said, was full of the engravings of his popular works. On his way he had seen innumerable 'Orders of Release,' 'Black Brunswickers,' and 'Huguenots'; in fact, he had no hesitation in affirming that John Millais was the most famous man of the day. He then alluded to his own miserable failure at first, and told us how he had taken some of his works which have since been acknowledged to be the finest specimens of English literature, to the leading publishers, and how they had one and all sneeringly hinted that no one would read his works after Dickens.

"My brother told him that, curiously enough, on the day before, an incident had occurred that proved that *his* fame, even amongst his own profession, was not all that Thackeray had painted it. He had met, near Shepherd's Bush, an old fellow-student of the Royal Academy (Mr. Frith calls him 'Potherd'), who had taken the second prize to his first, at the age of twelve. The man was full-grown then, and had strongly-marked features; moreover, he wore the same old military cloak, with lion clasp, that he used to wear in

the old days, so my brother had no difficulty in recognising
him; and, addressing him at once, he said, 'Well, P——,
and what are you doing? and how are you? It is a long
time since we met.' He said he was grubbing away at
teaching — 'slow work and worse pay' — or something to that
effect. 'But who are *you*, pray?' On being told the name,
he replied, 'What! little Johnny Millais! And now may
I ask what you have done all this time? Have you pursued
the Arts?'

"Thackeray immediately put this down to satire, but it was
not, as we found out afterwards. The simple fellow either
could not believe that the famous man was his old school-
fellow, or was completely ignorant of his success.

"Before this, Thackeray told an amusing story of Carlyle,
how that he had spent a day in the reading-room of the
British Museum and had given a great deal of trouble to
one of the officials, sending him up and down ladders in
search of books to satisfy his literary tastes, and how, upon
leaving the room, he had gone up to the man and told him
that it might be some satisfaction to him to know that he
had obliged Thomas Carlyle, and that the official had
answered him, with a bland smile and the usual washing
of hands in the air, that the gentleman had the advantage
of him, but that probably they might have met at some
mutual friend's house. He had never heard of Thomas
Carlyle."

Of Wilkie Collins there is little to be said in connection
with the subject of the present work, though both he and
his brother Charles were for many years amongst Millais'
most intimate friends, and no one more admired his brilliant
talent as a novelist. Since his famous novel, *The Woman
in White*, appeared, many have been the tales set on foot
to account for its origin, but for the most part quite inaccurate.
The real facts, so far as I am at liberty to disclose them, were
these : —

One night in the fifties Millais was returning home to
Gower Street from one of the many parties held under
Mrs. Collins' hospitable roof in Hanover Terrace, and, in
accordance with the usual practice of the two brothers,
Wilkie and Charles, they accompanied him on his homeward
walk through the dimly-lit, and in those days semi-rural,
roads and lanes of North London.

It was a beautiful moonlight night in the summer time,

WILKIE COLLINS

National Portrait Gallery.   *Circ.* 1855

and as the three friends walked along chatting gaily together, they were suddenly arrested by a piercing scream coming from the garden of a villa close at hand. It was evidently the cry of a woman in distress; and while pausing to consider what they should do, the iron gate leading to the garden was dashed open, and from it came the figure of a young and very beautiful woman dressed in flowing white robes that shone in the moonlight. She seemed to float rather than to run in their direction, and, on coming up to the three young men, she paused for a moment in an attitude of supplication and terror. Then, seeming to recollect herself, she suddenly moved on and vanished in the shadows cast upon the road.

"What a lovely woman!" was all Millais could say. "I must see who she is and what's the matter," said Wilkie Collins as, without another word, he dashed off after her. His two companions waited in vain for his return, and next day, when they met again, he seemed indisposed to talk of his adventure. They gathered from him, however, that he had come up with the lovely fugitive and had heard from her own lips the history of her life and the cause of her sudden flight. She was a young lady of good birth and position, who had accidentally fallen into the hands of a man living in a villa in Regent's Park. There for many months he kept her prisoner under threats and mesmeric influence of so alarming a character that she dared not attempt to escape, until, in sheer desperation, she fled from the brute, who, with a poker in his hand, threatened to dash her brains out. Her subsequent history, interesting as it is, is not for these pages.

Wilkie Collins, of whom there is an excellent likeness by Millais in the National Portrait Gallery, died in 1870. His last letter to my father ran thus: —

From Wilkie Collins.

"12 Harley Street,
"*April 6th*, 1863.

"My dear Jack, — I have been miserably ill with rheumatic gout ever since that pleasant dinner at your house, and I am only now getting strong enough to leave England in a few days and try the German baths. . . .

" I hear great things of a certain picture of yours ['The Eve of St. Agnes'], but there is no chance of my getting to see it. If I am alive, I hope to be back in June and see it at the Academy. All the little strength I have got is now wanted for preparations for the start.

" Poor dear Egg!* No such heavy distress as that has tried me for many and many a year past. And I know you must have felt it too. Pray give my kindest remembrances to Mrs. Millais. and believe me,

" Ever yours,
"WILKIE COLLINS."

Anthony Trollope, the famous novelist, is the last of Millais' *amis du cœur* whom I need mention here. They met for the first time at a dinner given by Mr. George Smith to the contributors to the *Cornhill Magazine* and the *Pall Mall Gazette*, both of which papers owed their birth to Mr. Smith ; and the friendship there formed ended only with Trollope's death in 1882. The lovable character of the man is seen in the autobiography published after his death, in which also is a most touching record of his affection for Millais. He writes : —

" It was at that table [Mr. George Smith's] and on that day that I first saw Thackeray, [Sir] Charles Taylor — than whom in later life I have loved no man better — Robert Bell, G. H. Lewes, and John Everett Millais. With all these men I afterwards lived on affectionate terms. But I will here speak specially of the last, because from that time he was joined with me in so much of the work that I did.

" Mr. Millais was engaged to illustrate ' Framley Parsonage,' but this was not the first work he did for the magazine. In the second number there is a picture of his, accompanying Monckton Milnes' 'Unspoken Dialogue.' The first drawing he did for 'Framley Parsonage' did not appear till after the dinner of which I have spoken, and I do not think that I knew at the time that he was engaged on my novel. When I did know it, it made me very proud. He afterwards illustrated 'Orley Farm,' 'The Small House at Allington,' 'Rachel Ray,' and 'Phineas Finn.' Altogether he drew from my tales eighty-seven drawings, and I do not think that more conscientious work was ever done by man.

---

* Augustus Egg, R. A., a brilliant artist and a great friend of Millais and Collins, died in this year.

Writers of novels know well, and so ought readers of novels to have learned, that there are two modes of illustrating, either of which may be adopted equally by a bad and by a good artist. To which class Mr. Millais belongs I need not say, but, as a good artist, it was open to him simply to make a pretty picture, or to study the work of the author from whose writing he was bound to take his subject. I have too often found that the former alternative has been thought to be the better, as it certainly is the easier, method. An artist will frequently dislike to subordinate his ideas to those of an author, and will sometimes be too idle to find out what those ideas are. But this artist was neither proud nor idle. In every figure that he drew it was his object to promote the views of the writer whose work he had undertaken to illustrate, and he never spared himself any pains in studying the work so as to enable him to do so. I have carried on some of those characters from book to book, and have had my own ideas impressed indelibly on my memory by the excellence of his delineations. Those illustrations were commenced fifteen years ago, and from that time up to this day my affection for the man has increased. To see him has always been a pleasure. His voice has been a sweet sound in my ears. Behind his back I have never heard him praised without joining the eulogist; I have never heard a word spoken against him without opposing the censurer. These words, should he ever see them, will come to him from the grave, and will tell him of my regard as one living man never tells another."

The following letters also serve to illustrate Trollope's appreciation of Millais' drawings, and the profound contempt he entertained for anything in the shape of cant :—

From Anthony Trollope.

"WALTHAM HOUSE, WALTHAM CROSS,
"*June 4th*, 1863.

" MY DEAR MILLAIS, — Ten thousand thanks to you, and twenty to your wife, as touching Ian. And now for business first and pleasure afterwards.

" X. (a Sunday magazine) has thrown me over. They write me word that I am too wicked. I tell you at once because of the projected, and now not-to-be-accomplished drawings. They have tried to serve God and the devil together, and

finding that goodness pays best, have thrown over me and
the devil. I won't try to set you against them, because you
can do Parables and other fish fit for their net; but I am
altogether unsuited to the regenerated! It is a pity they
did not find it out before, but I think they are right now.
I *am* unfit for the regenerated, and trust I may remain so,
wishing to preserve a character for honest intentions.

"And now for pleasure. I get home the middle of next
week, and we are full up to the consumption of all our cream
and strawberries till the Monday—I believe I may say
Tuesday, *i.e.*, Tuesday, June 16th. Do, then, settle a day
with the Thackerays and Collinses, and especially with
Admiral Fitzroy, to come off in that week. I shall be in
town on Wednesday night. Look in at about 11.30.

"Yours always,

"ANTHONY TROLLOPE.

"Why have you not put down Leighton, as you promised?"

From the same.

"WALTHAM HOUSE, WALTHAM CROSS,

"*August 6th*, 1866.

"MY DEAR MILLAIS,— I have written (nearly finished) a
story in thirty-two numbers, which is to come out weekly.
The first number is to appear some time in October.
Smith publishes it, and proposes that there shall be one
illustration to every number, with small vignettes to the
chapter headings. Will you do them? You said a word
to me the other day, which was to the effect that you would
perhaps lend your hand to another story of mine. Many of
the characters (indeed most of them) are people you already
know well— Mr. Crawley, Mr. Harding, Lily Dale, Crosbie,
John Eams, and Lady Lufton. George Smith is very
anxious that you should consent, and you may imagine that
I am equally so. If you can do it, the sheets shall be sent
to you as soon as they are printed, and copies of your own
illustrations should be sent to refresh your memory. . . .
Let me have a line.

"Yours always,

"ANTHONY TROLLOPE."

EUPHEMIA CHALMERS GRAY   1853
Water-colour

CHAPTER VIII

O N July 3rd, 1855, John Everett Millais was married to
Euphemia Chalmers Gray, eldest daughter of Mr.
George Gray, of Bowerswell, Perth.* In accordance with
the Scottish custom, the wedding took place in the drawing-
room at Bowerswell, and immediately afterwards came the
baptism of the bride's youngest brother, between whom and
his eldest sister there was a difference in age of nearly
twenty-six years.

And here let me say at once how much of my father's
happiness in after years was due to the chief event of this
day. During the forty-one years of their married life my
mother took the keenest interest in his work, and did all in
her power to contribute to his success, taking upon herself
not only the care of the household and the management of
the family affairs, but the great bulk of his correspondence,
and saving him an infinity of trouble by personally ascertain-
ing the objects of his callers (an ever increasing multitude)
before admitting them into his presence. A great relief this,
for business affairs and letter-writing were equally hateful in

---

* Miss Gray had been previously married, but that marriage had been annulled
in 1854, on grounds sanctioned equally by Church and State. Both good taste
and feeling seem to require that no detailed reference should be made to the
circumstances attending that annulment. But, on behalf of those who loved their
mother well, it may surely be said that during the course of the judicial proceedings instituted by her, and throughout the period of the void marriage and the
whole of her after years, not one word could be, or ever was, uttered impugning the
correctness and purity of her life.

his eyes; and in spite of himself, his correspondence increased day by day.

Possessed in a considerable degree of the artistic sense, she was happily free from the artistic temperament, whilst her knowledge of history proved also a valuable acquisition. When an historical picture was in contemplation, she delighted to study anew the circumstances and the characters to be depicted, and to gather for her husband's use all particulars as to the scene and the costumes of the period.

Study of the bell in Winterton Church made by John Luard. Used by Millais for Tennyson illustrations. 1857

Her musical accomplishments (for she was an excellent pianist) were also turned to good account in hours of leisure, and not infrequently as a soothing antidote to the worries that too often beset the artist in the exercise of his craft.

The newly-married couple set out for their honeymoon to the west of Scotland; and after a lovely fortnight in Argyleshire, Bute, and Arran, where deep-sea fishing formed their principal amusement, they returned to Perth and took possession of Annat Lodge, a typical old house with a cedared garden near Bowerswell.

Among their first visitors was Charles Collins. He, however, was not bent on amusing himself; he wanted to paint, and at his request my mother sat for him every day for a fortnight. Then, seeing that the picture made very slow progress, and that she was presented as looking out of the window of a railway carriage — a setting that would have vulgarised Venus herself — she refused to sit any longer, and the picture was never finished.

After this came a visit to Sir William Stirling Maxwell, of Keir, among whose guests was the handsome and accomplished Spaniard Guyanyos Riano, who afterwards became a firm friend of my parents. Sir William was devoted to literature, and was then at work on his *Life of Don John of Austria.*

Their next visitors at Annat Lodge were John Leech and Henry Wells (now Royal Academician), both intimate friends, and when Mr. Wells left, Leech and Millais amused themselves with fishing and shooting in various parts of Perthshire, enjoying especially a week at Blair, where they were entertained by the Duke of Athol. It was here that "Mr. Briggs," of *Punch*, originated in the fertile brain of Leech.

In the late autumn of 1855 Millais took a small shooting on the south bank of the Tay called Tarsappie — handy of itself as being near the town, and, as he presently found, equally handy for other people who liked to poach there. After some experience of their depredations it occurred to him that his keeper might possibly be in league with these gentry. So one day, on the eve of a shooting party for which he had arranged, he made a little surprise visit to the ground, when Mr. Keeper was discovered reclining under

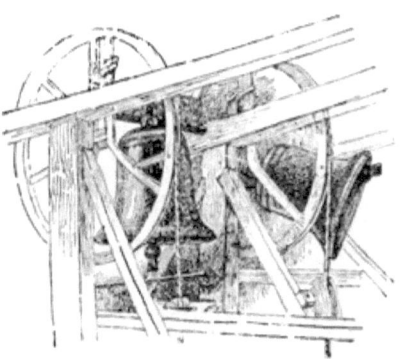

WINTERTON CHURCH BELLS
By John Luard

a tree with a goodly array of hares and partridges tastefully arranged within reach. These Millais promptly made him gather up and carry in front of him to Annat Lodge, growling and groaning all the way under the heavy load. There was a vacancy for a keeper at Tarsappie next morning.

But it was time now to get to work again in earnest. Nothing could be done during the honeymoon, and not much while guests were about; and with pictures in hand and publishers pressing for drawings any further holiday was impossible. So limiting his amusements to a day now and then at his shooting, Millais settled down to work for the winter, taking up, first, the special edition of Tennyson published by Moxon, for which he made twelve drawings, and afterwards eighteen illustrations for the edition published by Macmillan. At these he worked mainly in the evenings, with the aid of a reflector lamp, commencing immediately after dinner and seldom leaving off before midnight. And this after painting most of the day!

Mr. Wells tells me that while he and Leech were there the evenings were generally spent in this way, Millais working away in the dining-room, in company with themselves and my mother; and nothing surprised them so much as the energy and persistence with which their host worked while carrying on at the same time a lively conversation with his wife and guests.

The picture called " Peace Concluded, 1856," but better known as " The Return from the Crimea," was painted this year, the subject being a wounded officer lying on a couch, at the head of which is seated his wife. An Irish wolf-hound is also lying curled up on the sofa. Of this picture Ruskin in his " Notes " wrote in terms which have seemed somewhat extravagant to other critics: — " Titian himself could hardly head him now. This picture is as brilliant in invention as consummate in executive power. Both this and ' Autumn Leaves ' will rank in future among the world's best masterpieces."

Colonel " Bob " Malcolm sat for the man, and my mother for the lady; the portrait of her at this period being, I am told, singularly life-like. The Irish wolf-hound, " Roswell," bred in the Queen's kennels, was given to my mother by a Mr. Debas, and was the only pet animal she and my father ever possessed. They were both much attached to him, but he became such a terrible poacher that, to save him from being shot, they sent him out to Australia, to my uncle, George Gray, who found him most useful in hunting big kangaroos, until he came to an untimely end by eating some poisoned meat that had been put out for the dingoes.

The picture was purchased by Mr. James Miller, of Preston. It is not, however, a good example of his art, though there are beautiful passages in the work.

" Autumn Leaves " is too well known to need any description here. It was painted this year in the garden at Annat Lodge, and probably in none of Millais' works is the charm of the northern afterglow more strikingly presented. That it was highly appreciated by Mr. Ruskin may be gathered from the *Academy Notes*, 1856, in which he refers to it as " by much the most poetical work the painter has yet conceived; and also, so far as I know, the first instance of a

perfectly painted twilight. It is easy, as it is common, to
give obscurity to twilight, but to give the glow within its
darkness is another matter; and though Giorgione might
have come nearer the glow, he never gave the valley mist.
Note also the subtle difference between the purple of the
long nearer range of hills and the blue of the distant peak."

The picture (lately the property of Mr. James Leathart)
was originally sold to Mr. Eden, of Lytham, from whom
it passed to Mr. Miller, the purchaser of "Peace Concluded."
How he came by it is amusingly told by a writer in the
Magazine of Art of November, 1896, who says: — " I
should like to relate to you a circumstance connected with
'Autumn Leaves,' which I heard from Mr. Eden at Lytham.
When the picture reached him he did not like it, and he
asked the great painter to take it back; but this, Mrs.
Millais said, was impossible.   He was then told to sit
opposite it when at dinner for some months, and he would
learn to like it.   He tried this, but alas! disliked it more
and more.   One day a friend — I think Mr. Miller of
Preston — called, saw the picture, was enchanted, and said,
'Eden, I will give you any three of my pictures for
'Autumn Leaves.' 'As you are a great friend,' said Eden,
'you shall have it'; and so the picture changed hands.
This is what Mr. Eden told me, and it is on its way to
be amongst the world's masterpieces."

Besides these works Millais found time to paint, in the
spring of 1856, a small picture of a soldier in the 42nd
Highlanders ("News from Home"), which he sold to Mr.
Arthur Lewis, and also a little portrait of Mrs. John Leech,
which he presented to her out of affection for her husband.
And in the Academy he exhibited, in addition to "Peace
Concluded" and "Autumn Leaves," a "Portrait of a Gentle-
man," "L'Enfant du Régiment," and "The Blind Girl."

To arrange for this exhibition while continuing his work
in town, he left Annat Lodge at the beginning of April,
and took rooms in Langham Chambers along with his
friend Captain John Luard; and here, while working with a
will, they enjoyed themselves right heartily, after the free-
and-easy fashion dear to the heart of youth.   The two
painters kept open house to their friends, but generally
spent their evenings at the Garrick, where many of the
literary and artistic celebrities of the day delighted to
congregate when their work was over.

As to Millais, he was in no wise cowed by the combined forces of the Press and the Academy, who now put forth their strength to crush him as the leader of the new school of artists. Knowing that he stood on the vantage-ground of truth, he faced his foes in full assurance of victory in the end, whatever he might suffer in gaining it. And that he did suffer — in person, if not in purse — is evident from some of his letters to his wife, in which, as will presently be seen, he complains bitterly of his treatment.

ORIGINAL STUDIES FOR "EDWARD GRAY"
Tennyson illustrations. 1857

In reading these letters it must be borne in mind that in those days a great London newspaper had far more influence in the formation of public opinion than it has to-day, especially in country places, where the utterances of the great "We" were too often regarded as "confirmation strong as proof of Holy Writ." Allowance, too, must be made for the fact that the letters were written in the hot youth of a man keenly alive to praise or blame, and whose whole future depended on the issue of the struggle in which he was engaged. Not only were the leading newspapers against him, but some of the most influential members of the Academy joined in the crusade with an animosity hardly conceivable in these liberal and more enlightened times; and but for the audacity he displayed in his dealings with them, they would have given him no chance of showing his pictures to advantage.

Happily all this sort of thing has long gone by. With a magnanimity worthy of our greatest paper, the *Times* has made full amends for the mistakes of former years; and much the same thing may be said of other papers; while as to the Academy, it is to-day about as pure and fair a tribunal as any on earth.

But now to the letters themselves, from which, as a picture of my father's life at this period, I quote somewhat fully.

ALICE GRAY, 1853
Pencil study

Writing to his wife, he says : —

"*April 7th*, 1856. — We have just had breakfast. Luard is smoking a first pipe, and has prepared a palette for me to paint the little child's white dress. I found everything so nicely packed, my darling, that Luard has been noticing it and envying me.

"I cannot express the success of the pictures. It is far beyond our most sanguine expectations. I have increased the price of all three ['Peace Concluded,' 'Autumn Leaves,' and 'The Blind Girl'], which I shall get without any difficulty; and my studio has been already filled with eager purchasers begging me to remember them next year.

"All other years pass into absolute insignificance compared with this. I shall make a struggle to get the little soldier finished; but I am to go and help a brother artist, poor Martineau, who is in a fix with a picture.

"The artists here imagine that my pictures are the work of years, instead of a few months. There has been a report that I have taken to the most unfinished style, which, like many evil reports, have their good effect on me, for the pictures seem to astonish people more than ever by their finish. I know how pleased you will be to hear this; but you must not be too much elated; for this great mercy from God is very awful, and I cannot help feeling a little nervous about it, fearing a possible turn in my fortune. This, however, may be unnecessary and wrong in me; but seeing how differently He deals with many others about us, I am surprised at the steps I have made in advance."

After observing how different his and his friend Holman Hunt's styles are becoming, after running so long together, he continues: "What Ruskin and the critics are to do, I don't know; but it will be great fun for us."

In another letter at this period he says: "I am ashamed of myself for not having been to church to-day. I slept so sound that the bells were ringing before I was out of bed. Luard and Robert Malcolm get on admirably together. They are at this moment talking about the Crimea, and we have just been looking at L.'s sketches from Sebastopol. Halliday has just appeared, so I am writing this in a howl of conversation and much smoke. I dine with Leech at six."

And on *April 18th*. — "Yesterday I went with Luard to the Garrick, and afterwards to the Olympic Theatre, to see *Still Waters Run Deep*, a most admirable play, and delight-

fully acted.   This afternoon I go with Leech and his madam
to choose the bonnets.   He says there is but one really good
place — not a shop — so I daresay I shall be able to get
something pretty for you. . . ."

After sending in his pictures to the Academy he went
home to Perth for a few days, and then returning to town he
hastened to the Academy, to see how his works had been
hung.   What he found there is related in the following
letter: —

" DEAREST COUNTESS, [a nonsensical term he often applied
to my mother] — Yesterday I went to the Royal Academy, and
made Luard write to you, as you would be anxious to hear
how my pictures were placed.   Nothing could be better.   The
largest ('The Return from the Crimea') is next to Edwin
Landseer's, in the large room.   'Autumn Leaves' is in the
middle room, beautifully seen ; and, I think, the best appreciated.   'The Blind Girl' is in the third room (the first
going into the exhibition) on the line, but rather higher than
I like, as its finish is out of the reach of short people.   The
child on the tomb ['L'Enfant du Régiment'] is also in this
room, and perfectly hung.

" I saw Landseer there, and Grant, who was most civil ;
and both expressed great admiration for my work.   There is
a great movement just now in the matter of copyright, and
I enclose a paper distributed to the members on the subject.
There must soon be a better understanding between artists
and dealers.

"Last night I went to the theatre with Egg and Luard,
and afterwards to the Garrick, where I met Leech, who wants
me to dine at Richmond with him next Sunday. . . . I long
to be back for good, and begin the trees in blossom."

My father was very fond of going out in the evening,
either to the Garrick or to a theatre, with some of his
particular friends.   On May 1st, 1856, he writes: "Last
night Martineau, Halliday, and I dined with Luard at the
Garrick, after which we adjourned to the Victoria Theatre,
for the fun of the thing, to see a regular out-and-out melo-
drama, and were not disappointed.   We got a box for 5s.,
and laughed so immoderately at the pathetic parts that we
were nearly turned out.   I dine with Leech on Sunday, at

the ' Star and Garter ' at Richmond, and with Hunt to-night ; so I have plenty of occupation."

It will be seen from the following letters how the world, the critics, and the purchasers of his pictures were disposed towards him : —

" *May 2nd*, 1856. — The private view is going on, but I don't go near the Royal Academy, of course. I went for amusement to Christie's auction-rooms, to see Rogers' pictures sold, and there met Mr. Miller, who had just come from the exhibition, mightily pleased with his ' Peace Concluded.' Everything is going on splendidly, and I now wait for the verdict of the public, *who are the only really disinterested critics.* Every day I meet with the Academicians I perceive new horrors. So determined are they to insult every man who chooses to purchase my works, that this year they have done the same with Miller as they did with Arden, when he bought ' The Order of Release.' For the first time they have not sent him an invitation to the dinner, at which he smiles, knowing the reason. Anyhow, it is rather a triumph for us, as these wretched, ungentlemanly dealings only tend to reveal the truth."

" *May 1st,* 1856. — I have just come from the Academy, which is open to the public this morning. I saw Eden (the owner of ' Autumn Leaves '), which was my reason for going, but I didn't go into the rooms, as I did not wish to be seen near my pictures. The impression of all the best men is most flattering to me, in spite of the same unjust and determined opposition. On the whole, the critics are rather worse than ever, but it really does not seem to matter much, beyond leading ignorant people to say very foolish things.

" I have found out the name of the *Times* critic. It is F——, an artist. I don't, indeed, expect any better treatment from the Press in my lifetime, as the critics are too intimately mixed up with the profession. Of course, there are many criticisms as much in favour as some are against. I would not see them, however, had not Leech made me look at some, to see how absurdly contradictory they are ; but the result is the same as in other years — there is no getting near the pictures at the opening — so I am perfectly satisfied with the reception of them this year.

" The only reason for being annoyed at the continued bullying from the Press is on your account and that of your family and friends, who think more of the matter than people in London, who only laugh at it. . . ."

" *May 3rd*, 1856. — Luard is smoking benignly, and asking me about the Royal Academy, and I have some difficulty to write this and answer his questions about the exhibition. I cannot tell you of the incivility of certain of the members and their cantankerous and jealous criticisms and un-generosity. It is nothing new to me, however, for I have seen it for some years now. I dined at the Garrick yester-day, and saw David Roberts, R.A., and exchanged civilities. In the exhibition there is a very striking portrait of Miss Guyanjos, by John Phillip; but Landseer and others say it is only a libel on her. . . . Gambart [the dealer] has been

here, but I cannot get him to sign the paper. No one will, under the present state of the copyright law. If he signed it he would be responsible for the actions of others, which no man would do. Besides, there would always be such a drag in the sale of the picture, for men will not purchase anything with a claim still on it. There is a great stir in the matter of copyright, and I think some-thing will be done. As it stands, I hear it is impossible to obtain any legal hold in the matter. But enough of ' shop.' I must be off to the Royal Academy again, to make a sketch of the heads in ' Autumn Leaves ' for the *Illustrated London News*. . . ."

The plot continued to thicken. Next day Millais writes : — " I hope this will come to hand before you see the *Times*, which is more wickedly against me this year than ever. It is well understood here that the criticism is not above board, and that there is more than mere ignorance in the man. Beyond a sudden surprise on seeing the criticism, I was not much disturbed, as it has been my fate from the first, and probably will be to the last, to meet with ungenerous treat-ment from newspapers. A very young man doesn't get 900 guineas for his pictures without some attempt at de-traction. I am of course greatly astonished, as it is settled that I am to paint the principal man of the paper. This makes it a riddle, and will doubtless cause strange observations. All I beg of you and your family is to wait and see how *one* young man will oblige the great British organ to alter their views. There is some underhand trickery which must sooner or later come to light. I am not at all sure that it does not spring from the Academy itself; indeed, there is every reason to suppose it does. The envy and this determined cabal against me make me long to return home. In one word, I have the whole of the Royal Academy (with one or two exceptions) dead against me, which makes all intercourse with them unpleasant. The ' Peace Concluded ' has sold for a great deal more than any other picture in the Royal Academy excepting Landseer's, and I shall obtain a still better price next year. With this knowledge, I think we may rest very well satisfied, as such solid success is never achieved against such powerful opposition without its having unmistakable deserts. This the world will see, in spite of all these shameful attempts to ruin me.

STUDY FOR TENNYSON ILLUSTRATIONS
Circ. 1857

" I hope you will not care a straw for the *Times'* criticism. Our fathers will feel it much more than we, as they know less of the humbug of the British Press. People here in London soon perceive the injustice of such articles, so they go for nothing; but of course it retards my position in the country, where people regard as gospel what they read in the newspapers. Now let me assure you that I am ' quite calm ' (as the French say), and you must not disturb yourself by picturing me in the act of tearing my hair for mortification. Nothing of the kind, my love; I am quite merry."

When the Academy was opened to the public an extraordinary amount of interest was shown in his work. There was always a big crowd round his pictures, but he was too shy to go near them himself.

On May 8th, 1856, he writes in the following strain : — " I

never expected such complete success as the pictures are
making. People cannot get near the two largest. I saw
Marochetti [the great Italian sculptor who worked in Eng-
land] yesterday, and he made several attempts, but could see
nothing. What the Baron said is sufficiently cheering. His
coloured marble busts are magnificent beyond everything. I
was so delighted with the surpassing beauty of a soft-coloured
head (in marble, of course) of some relation of the Princess,
that I expressed a hope that some day I should be rich
enough to afford having *you* done in the same way; when he
jumped at the thought, and said he would consider it an
understood thing that he should make a bust of you in return
for any sketch I should give him, adding that he would beg
my acceptance of it if I hesitated. He has seen you, and
admires you immensely. Indeed, as he is very desirous of
getting portraits of all the most beautiful persons he can get
to sit, this kindness has something to do with your looks. . . .

" I never saw anything more shameless than the treatment
by the R.A. of my work. Every year it is the same. The
surest sign of a young man's work being worthless is
generosity and applause from the Academy! . . . I have
seen other papers all absurdly contradicting their former
selves. Most of them are better than any I have ever before
received; and some that have tremendously abused me for
years have changed their critics, and now as immoderately
praise me. The *Athenæum, Spectator, Chronicle, Press,
Advertiser*, and many others praise me up to the skies, and
papers that used hitherto to applaud now hiss me! It is
simply ridiculous, but (as I am happy to think) you all understand this, so I won't say any more about it. I don't think
there have ever been such endeavours to swamp a man as in
my case, or ever such a complete failure."

In these days, as will be seen, he felt keenly the shameless
attacks of the critics, although personally so successful; for
the artistic temperament is not prone to bear patiently
the pin-pricks of constant and malignant opposition. His
letter to my mother, dated May 8th, 1856, shows this.
He says: — " I thought of you yesterday. You may imagine
how heartily I wish you ' many happy returns of the day.' I
have a very nice letter from your father this morning, and
think that his version may be the right one. Certainly there
never were such cunningly devised machinations against my
character and fortune. It makes me hate ' London's fine

"THE RESCUE." 1855
By permission of Mr. Holbrook Gaskell

city,' and feel less dependence on the things of this world.
Poor Hunt, though well praised in the Press, has not found a
purchaser for his 'Scapegoat,' in spite of the lowness of the
price he asks.   A very highly finished picture, too, and twice
the size of my largest.

"The newspaper criticisms are by no means all against
me, and I have more confidence in the weekly and monthly
periodicals; but with *all* against me I could still hold my
place.   It is only a matter of time — perhaps beyond our lives
— but ultimately right and truth must prevail.   I confess it is
a lesson to me — all this determined opposition.   The best
art does not at first meet with general comprehension, and I
believe sincerely that the chief reason why my works are so
picked to pieces is *their being out of the scale of received
conventionalities.*   One thing you will notice is that no
criticism or reports go to say that any of the faces in the
pictures are ugly, and hundreds are daily exclaiming about
the beauty of the heads of the children.   I cease to feel any
more upon the subject, as nearly every notice goes only to
contradict the preceding one.   I see, too, everybody more or
less inclined to lean favourably to Hunt, after abusing him.
Human nature all over!   It has been gradually coming to
this, and I have now lost all hope of gaining just appreciation
in the Press; but, thank goodness, 'the proof of the pudding
is in the eating,' for in that way they cannot harm me, except
(as your father shrewdly remarks) in the copyright.   *Nothing
could have been more adverse than the criticism on ' The
Huguenot,'* yet the engraving is now selling more rapidly than
any other of recent times.   I have great faith in the mass of
the public, although one hears now and then such grossly
ignorant remarks. . . . It is just the same with music and
literature.   At Gambart's last night, a man made a complete
buffoon of himself with wretched 'comic' songs, and the
audience screamed with enjoyment.   Also at the Haymarket
Theatre the comedy there — a farrago of old, worn-out jokes,
badly acted — was received with enthusiasm, and parts meant
for pathos were mistaken for fun and laughed at accordingly."

After giving some details of the ways of the two largest
dealers in London, one of whom always dealt fairly with him,
whilst the other invariably "made a poor mouth" and
"crabbed" his pictures, but always re-sold greatly to his
own advantage, as well as making a small fortune out of the
copyrights, he continues : —

" I have been to Gambart's this morning to settle how he is to pay for ' The Blind Girl.' All men have different ways of dealing, and his way is to pay me the moment the picture is in his possession. This is understood ; and directly the R.A. closes (three months from now) he settles. . . . Now I have to see X—— (another dealer), with whom I have had no conversation since the opening. I have purposely kept away, so that he might learn the feeling of the intelligent public about the picture he has bought. If I had been before, I know he would have quoted (as he did last year) the newspaper criticisms, and their prejudicial influence,

etc., etc. But, curiously enough, *whenever an engraving comes out from his firm there is always a favourable article in the papers.* . . .

" Since there is such a demand for my works, I can afford not to be humbugged by these people, as other poor fellows are ; and I think one great reason for the opposition this year is the sudden great increase in my prices.

SKETCH FOR TENNYSON ILLUSTRATION. 1856

The dealers, of course, like to get pictures for £200 and sell them for £2000. . . . I am continually the object of unpleasant remarks from women as well as men, but beyond working out conscientiously a means of support for us both, I do not care ; and this, please God, I shall accomplish in time."

As a further insight into the rotten criticisms of the period, a day or two later he tells of the treatment meted out to Charles Reade, whom he mentions for the first time, and who afterwards became a great friend of his.

" *May,* 1856. — I have just come from the Crimean lecture of the *Times* correspondent, Russell [Sir William Howard Russell, afterwards a devoted friend], on the war. It was odd to see the man who at the time of the war was dreaded by both the army and the navy brought before the public. to receive in his turn their criticism. . . ."

Here follows an account of the lecture, which took place before empty seats, in spite of the eulogistic prelude of the *Times ;* for only the famous correspondent's personal friends mustered in force : — " I dined at the Garrick with Reade, the author of *It is Never too Late to Mend.* He is delighted with my pictures, and regards all criticism as worthless. *He has never been reviewed at all in the Times,* although his book has passed through more editions than most of the first-class novels.

White [the dealer] brought a finished proof of ' The Huguenot ' this morning, and the few slight corrections Barlow [the engraver] has to make will not take him more than a week ; so you may look for it very soon."

On May 30th Annat Lodge was enlivened by the birth of Millais' first child (Everett), news of which he conveyed to his cousin, Mrs. George Hodgkinson, in the following terms : — " Just a line to say that I am the distinguished owner of a little gentleman. The nurse, of course, says it is like me, adding that it is an extremely handsome production ! But what nurse does not say the same thing ? However, it has blue eyes and a little downy brown on the top of its head."

SKETCH FOR ST. AGNES. 1856

For the holiday season Millais took the manse of Brig-o'-Turk in Glenfinlas, and in August he and my mother went there, accompanied by her sisters, Alice and Sophie Gray. Here, after an interval of shooting and fishing, he painted a small portrait of the minister — a hard-featured and by no means prepossessing Celt — and then, returning to Annat Lodge, he set to work on " Pot-pourri " and " Sir Isumbras at the Ford."

Foreseeing that an account of her husband's pictures —

how, when, and where they were painted, and what became
of them — would some day be of interest, my mother determined to keep a record of all that he painted after their
marriage, and forthwith started a book for that purpose.
But, alas! the work was never completed. My father made
such fun of it that in 1868 she unwillingly gave it up. It
contains, however, explicit information about several of his
works. Of "Pot-pourri" she says :— "This little picture
was painted for a Mr. Burnett, but when completed he was
unable to purchase it. It was painted from my sister Alice
and little Smythe of Methven Castle, Alice's dress of green
satin and point flounces forming a happy contrast to the
rich velvet and gold trimmings in little Smythe's dress.
The background is principally crimson, and the whole effect
very rich and brilliant.

"Mr. Millais sold this picture to Mr. White, the dealer
in Madox Street, for £150, and he in turn sold it, a week or
two afterwards, for £200 to Mr. G. Windus, junior.

"When Mr. Burnett saw it he was most anxious to get it,
and White promised it to him if he came on a certain day
not later than four p.m. Mr. Windus, however, was equally
determined to have it; and, arriving early on the appointed
day, he waited till the clock struck four, and then carried
off the picture in a cab, to the great disgust of Mr. Burnett,
who arrived a quarter of an hour late." Moral — Even
in business it is well to be punctual now and then.

My mother has some interesting notes on the subject of
"Sir Isumbras," which she calls "The Knight, a dream
of the past, 1857."

"This picture occupied Mr. Millais during the winter
in conjunction with 'The Heretic.' He was extremely
expeditious in finishing the background, which did not take
him more than a fortnight. During the end of October and
beginning of November, 1856, he went every day to the
Bridge of Earn and painted the old bridge and the range
of the Ochills from under the new bridge, composing the
rest by adding a medieval tower.* The gardener afterwards
brought a large quantity of flags from the river, and they
were put in a tub and painted in his studio. The horse
gave him a world of vexation from first to last. He always

* The tower was painted from old Elcho Castle, situated on the south bank of
the Tay, six miles below Perth. An additional group of trees also aided the
composition.

"THE BLIND GIRL." 1856

By permission of the Corporation of Birmingham

said he had chosen a fine animal to paint from, but most
people thought not. He painted it day after day in the
stableyard at Annat Lodge, and had made a very beautiful
horse when Gambart, the dealer, saw the picture, and offered
£800 for it, but said the horse was too small. Millais
refused this price, thinking he ought to get more, and
Gambart left. After a little while Millais began to think
the horse was too small, and most unfortunately took it out,
and finished by making his animal too large. All the critics
cried out about the huge horse, called it Roman-nosed, and
said every kind of absurd thing about it, forgetful of the
beauty of the rest of the picture. The critics would,

ROSWELL. 1856

perhaps, not have been so ill-natured had they known the
sufferings the horse cost the painter, who worked out of
doors in the dead of winter, sometimes in frost and snow,
perched on a ladder, and sometimes sitting in bitter east and
north wind with his canvas secured by ropes to prevent
it falling. The horse was never still for one instant, and
like the painter was greatly aggravated by the intense cold.
I had to send down warm soups and wine every now and
then and attend to things generally. After the Academy
closed without any offer being made for the picture, Millais
determined to have it back to Scotland, and once more to
entirely repaint the horse. After some months he completed
it. The same animal came and stood day after day in our
yard, the representation of the old one having been completely removed from the canvas by means of benzole,

the smell of which drove us out of the painting-room for
a day or two. The new horse now appeared, to my mind,
exactly like the first one. It was almost finished, when one
day, whilst it was still wet in places, a strong wind arose
and blew over the iron chair to which the picture had been
imperfectly fixed, one corner going like a nail right through
the head of the knight. This was a dreadful accident, and
Millais was in a terrible state of mind, vowing he would
never touch or look at it again. However, in the course
of a day or two a firm of London canvas makers mended

FIRST SKETCH FOR "PEACE CONCLUDED." 1855

it so beautifully that the rent could not be seen. I thought
this picture doomed to failure, for on the day it left us to go to
the Liverpool Exhibition, it poured in such torrents and was
so stormy, that I became superstitious. However, with the
new horse and the knight's leg lengthened, it attracted considerable attention in Liverpool, and the committee did not
know whether to give Millais the prize of £50 for it or for
his 'Blind Girl.' 'The Blind Girl,' however, carried the day
by one vote."

Colonel Campbell, an officer quartered in Perth, sat for
the figure of the knight, whilst the little boy and girl were
respectively the artist's eldest son and Miss Nellie Salmon,
now Mrs. Ziegler.

" Time and varnish," I have heard my father say, " are
the greatest Old Masters that ever lived." And, in the face
of recent experience, who will dare to say they are not? As
quaint old Tusser has it, " Time tries the troth in everything "; tries, too, our Art critics, and their right to dogmatise
as they do on works that Time has not yet touched ; and in
this matter of " Sir Isumbras " his judgment is dead against
them.

In 1857, when the picture was exhibited in the Academy,
it was greeted with howls of
execration, the lion's roar of
Mr. Ruskin being heard high
above the jackal's yelp of his
followers. The great critic
could see in it no single point
for admiration; only faults of
fact, of sentiment, and of Art;
but now that time and varnish
have done their work, we find
it as universally praised as it
was formerly condemned — a
lesson that living painters may
well take to heart for their
comfort in times of depression.

Mr. Stephens, who has
written so well on Millais'
works, says of this picture : —
"'Sir Isumbras at the Ford'
was the subject of the picture
Millais made his leading work
in the year 1857. It represented
an ancient knight, all clad in
golden armour, who had gone
through the glories of this life

SKETCH FOR "THE CRUSADERS." 1856
A picture never completed

— war honour, victory and reward, wealth and pride. Though
he is aged and worn with war, his eye is still bright
with the glory of human life, and yet he has stooped his
magnificent pride so far as to help, true knight as he was,
two little children, and carries them over a river ford upon
the saddle of his grand war-horse, woodcutter's children as
they were. The face of this warrior was one of those pictorial victories which can derive their success from nothing
less than inspiration. The sun was setting beyond the forest

that gathered about the river's margin, and, in its glorious decadence, symbolised the nearly spent life of the warrior."

In his *Notes on the Grosvenor Gallery*, 1885, he gives a vivid account of what followed on the exhibition of the picture in 1857. "The appearance of 'Sir Isumbras,'" he says, "produced a tremendous sensation. Satires, skits, jokes, deliberate analyses and criticisms—most of them applied to purposes and technical aims not within the artist's intention when the picture was in hand—crowded the

FIRST SKETCH FOR "SIR ISUMBRAS"

columns of the comic as of the more serious journals. Utter ruin and destruction were prophesied of the artist who, somewhat rashly, had followed a technical purpose, but whose success in that respect cannot now be questioned. Among the most edifying of the comments published on 'Sir Isumbras' was a large print entitled 'A Nightmare,' and believed to be the work of Mr. F. Sandys, a distinguished brother artist, who probably was not without grievances of his own against critics. It generally reproduced the work in a ludicrous manner, and showed the painter while in the act of crossing the ford on the back of a loud-braying ass. Seated on the front of the saddle, in the place of one of the wood-cutter's children, Mr. Dante G. Rossetti is supported by the mighty hands of the steel-clad knight. Clinging round the waist of the champion is a quaint mannikin, with a sheaf of painter's brushes slung at his back, instead of the original figure, meant for Mr. W. Holman Hunt. The intention of the designer of this satire was to suggest the position of the Old Masters and the modern critics at this period. On the bank of the river are three different figures of M. Angelo, Titian, and Raphael. The first stands with his face averted and his arms folded, while Titian and Raphael kneel in front of him, looking towards the animal and his freight. A small scroll proceeds from the animal's mouth, with the legend, ' Orate pro nobis.' This print was not without its good technical qualities, and, except so far as the ass and the smallest riders were concerned, did no very grave injustice to any of the figures. Instead of his sheathed sword an artist's mahl-stick was suspended to the girdle of Sir John Millais, and by the side of this hung a bunch of peacock's feathers and a large paste-pot, inscribed ' P.-R.B.' for ' Pre-Raphaelite Brotherhood.' "

The lines relating to Sir Isumbras, which appeared in the Academy Catalogue in Old English type, were written for the occasion by Tom Taylor, who also wrote the extremely humorous verses attached to Mr. Sandys' skit. The former I give here : —

> " 'The goode hors that the knyghte bestrode,
> I trow his backe it was full brode,
> And wighte and warie still he wode,
>   Noght reckinge of rivere :
> He was so muckle and so stronge,
> And thereto so wonderlich longe
>   In londe was none his peer.
> N'as hors but by him seemed smalle.
> The knyghte him yeleped Launcival ;
> But lords at borde and grooms in stalle
>   Yelept him Graund Destrere."

About the sale of this work my mother had a good tale to tell. One evening in 1858, when they were living in London, she was standing outside the house, waiting for the door to be opened, when she was accosted by a grey-haired man in shabby garments, who said he, too, wished to come in. The observation startled her, for she had never seen the man before ; and, mistaking him in the darkness for a

tramp, she told him to go away. "But," pleaded the
stranger, with a merry twinkle in his eye, " I want ' The
Knight Crossing the Ford,' *and I must have it !*"   The idea
now dawned upon her that he was a harmless lunatic, to
be got rid of by a little quiet persuasion.   This, therefore,
she tried, but in vain.   The only reply she got was, "Oh,
beautiful dragon!   I am Charles Reade, who wrote *Never
Too Late to Mend*, and I simply must have that picture,
though I am but a poor man.   I would write a whole
three-volume novel on it, and then have sentiment enough
to spare.   I only wish I had someone like you to guard my
house !"

And he got the picture!   For, though a stranger to my
mother, my father knew him well, and was pleased to find
on his return home that it had fallen into his hands.   Reade
was, in fact, an intimate friend of Millais, and when in town
they met together almost daily at the Garrick Club.

That he was proud of his purchase the following letter to
Millais attests : —

From Charles Reade.

"GARRICK CLUB.

" IL MAESTRO, — The picture is come, and shall be hung
in the drawing-room.   I cannot pretend to point out exactly
what you have done to it, but this I know — it looks admirably well.   I hope you will call on me and talk it over.   I am
very proud to possess it.   Either I am an idiot, or it is an
immortal work.   Yours sincerely,
                                                "CHARLES READE."

In another letter he says : — " It is the only picture admitted
into the room, and has every justice I can tender it.   As
I have bought *to keep*, and have no sordid interest in crying
it up, you must allow me to write it up a little.   It is infamous that a great work of Art should be libelled as this
was some time ago."

In a letter to Millais, asking for a ticket for the " private
view" day at the Academy, he says: — " The private view,
early in the morning, before I can be bored with cackle of
critics and entangled in the tails of women, is one of the
things worth living for, and I shall be truly grateful if you
will remember your kind promise and secure me this
pleasure."

"SIR ISUMBRAS." 1857

By permission of Mr. R. H. Benson

On Charles Reade's death, "Sir Isumbras" became the property of Mr. John Graham, and on his death Mr. Robert Benson bought it for a large sum.

Touching the alterations and additions it received in 1892, Mr. Benson kindly sends me the following note:—"As to 'The Knight' I bought it at Christie's, at the sale of the pictures of Mr. John Graham of Skelmorlie, in (I think) 1886.

It was framed in an abominable stucco frame, of about 1857, with rounded top corners. I had a carved frame made from one of the fine models in the South Kensington Museum.

MOTHER AND CHILD. *Circ. 1860*

"I think he (Millais) was glad that we got it, and Lady Millais too. One day I asked him what he thought of putting some trappings on the horse, and he jumped at the idea, saying that he should like to have the chance of improving the outline — the silhouette, as you may still see it in Hollyer's photo — and relieve and break the blackness of the beast.

"Thenceforward we went about, my wife and I, taking notes and studies of horse-trappings and armour wherever we met with them. Our most promising finds were in the Escurial, in the armoury at Madrid. One day in 1892 (it was July 11th) he wrote asking us to let him have it, and to send him our notes. There was to be an exhibition at the Guildhall, and he wanted it to be seen again. So I sent it with the notes and a photo, on which I roughly pencilled what we thought it needed, viz., a fuller throat, a crest, a dilated nostril, a twisted tail, a deeper girth (to give the horse strength to carry the man in armour, not to speak of the children), a broad bridle, instead of the thin green

and yellow rein, and lastly the trappings. We also wanted
the green and yellow bridle abolished, and a certain garish
flower by the horse's ear. We particularly begged him to
leave the exceptionally large, open eyes of the girl, as being
characteristic of 1857 and of the effect he then sought. He
kept it a month. I confess we were nervous, knowing the
difficulty he was sure to feel in matching the work of 1857,
and feeling our own audacity in having ventured to suggest
by the pencilling on the
photo just what we wanted
done and no more. I tried
more than once to see him,
and once Mrs. Holford
came with me, but whether
he was there or not, we
could not get into the
studio. But on August
11th the picture came back
finished.

STUDY OF A CHILD. Circ. 1858

"We were (and are still)
delighted with what he
did. He just removed the
blot, and the picture re-
mained all that we loved
most in his work — a
splendid portrait of an
old man, an adorable little boy, and a glorious landscape, a
strong but balanced scheme of colour, and a composition
which, by selecting the pictorial moment, tells a simple story
— a romance if you will — that makes us all akin.

"Here is the letter he wrote me (copy enclosed) : — "

To Mr. Benson.

" 2 PALACE GATE, KENSINGTON,
"*August 11th*, 1892.

"DEAR BENSON, — Send for the Knight on Saturday
morning, as I have done all I can for the picture, and very
glad I am to have had the opportunity of making it so
complete. I have seen many old and useful drawings at the
Heralds' College, where they have the whole pageant of the
Field of the Cloth of Gold meeting of Henry VIII. and
Francis I., and some of the harness is covered with bells,

which adds a pleasant suggestion of jingle to the Knight's progress. I have also been studying horses daily, and the stud is good enough now. It was most incorrect, and has necessitated a great deal of work.

" Faulty as it undoubtedly was, the poetry in the picture ought to have saved it from the savage onslaught of all the critics, notably John Ruskin, who wrote of it, ' This is not a fiasco, but a catastrophe.'

" On the other hand, Thackeray embraced me — put his arms round my neck and said, ' Never mind, my boy, go on painting more such pictures.' . . . I am very proud of having painted it, and delighted to know it is in the hands of one who appreciates its merits.

" Sincerely yours,

" J. E. MILLAIS."

As a matter of fact the alterations took the artist a very short time to complete, when he had once decided what they should be. After lunch he would stroll up Kensington Gardens to the " Row," where he leaned over the rails, making a few notes and rough outlines of horses as they passed along, until he got the particular movement of the animal that he wanted to express. But, as will be gathered from his letter, the preliminary work involved a good deal of trouble.

In the spring of 1857 Millais and his wife took rooms in Savile Row, London, where he chiefly occupied himself with his picture " The Escape of a Heretic, 1559." Of this work, which was intended as a pendant to " The Huguenot," my mother writes : —

" The idea of making a pendant to ' The Huguenot ' occurred to him whilst we were visiting Mr. W. Stirling at Keir, in the autumn after our marriage. That gentleman possesses a book of fine old woodcuts of the time of the Inquisition, when persecutions in the Netherlands were carried on under the Duke of Alva. He also possesses a series of Spanish pictures which had been used to illustrate his own work on *The Cloister Life of the Emperor Charles V.* Amongst these woodcuts were several representing burnings in Spain, the women and men being habited in the hideous dress of the ' San Benito.' The victims were generally attended by priests exhorting them to penitence as they pursued their way to the martyrs' pile. The 'San Benito' dress consists of an upper shirt, without sleeves, of coarse sacking painted yellow, with designs of devils roasting souls in flames. With the aid of some engravings of monks of the different orders, sent by Mr. Rawdon Brown, and the habit of a Carthusian from the Papal States, lent by Mr. Dickenson, we easily made up the dresses for the models, whilst Millais drew the staircase of Balhousie Castle for the prison from whence the girl is escaping by aid of her lover. Millais worked on this picture and 'The Knight' at the same time. The expression of the lover's face gave him immense trouble. The model was a young gamekeeper in the service of Mr. Condie. He was handsome, very lazy, continually getting tired, and not coming when sent for. Millais took the face, and mouth particularly, many times completely out. The girl's expression was very troublesome also, and he was long in pleasing himself with it."

Whilst Millais waited the hanging of his pictures at the Royal Academy his wife travelled again to their home in the North. His letters to her at this time are particularly interesting, as showing what he thought of the artistic outlook.

SKETCH FOR TENNYSON ILLUSTRATION. 1855

In the first, dated May 13th, 1857, he says : — " My friends Bartle Frere and Colonel Turner dined with me at the Garrick yesterday. They are both old friends of mine, and we had a very pleasant party. I met Thackeray there, and he spread out his great arms and embraced me in stage fashion, in evidence of his delight at my pictures. He never before expressed such extreme satisfaction, and said they were magnificent."

The *Times'* review of the Royal Academy then came out with a stinging critique on his pictures, and all the other

SKIT ON "SIR ISUMBRAS" AND THE P.R.B.

By Fred Sandys

papers joined in chorus. On this he wrote to his wife, on
May 15th : — "Doubtless you have seen the *Times* and its
criticism. When I heard it was written in the same spirit
as usual I did not read it. I therefore only know of its
import through my friends. The general feeling is that it
is not of the slightest importance. Criticism has been so
tampered with that what is said carries little or no weight.
Ruskin, I hear, has a pamphlet in the press which takes a
pitying tone at my failure. The wickedness and envy at
the bottom of all this are so apparent to me that I disregard
all the reviews (I have not read *one*), but I shall certainly
have this kind of treatment all my life. The public crowd
round my pictures more than ever, and this, I think, must
be the main cause of animosity. . . . . I should tell you
that although my friend Tom Taylor is said to have written
the first two reviews in the *Times*, this last is not attributed
to him.

"The only good that I can see in the criticism is its
unusual length (from what I hear it is nearly a column). I
confess I am disgusted at the tone of the thing ; indeed
with everything connected with Art.

"Combe, of Oxford, came yesterday. He wants me to
paint him a picture about the size of the 'Heretic' (*anything larger than that size is objected to*). There is no encouragement for anything but *cabinet pictures*. I should
never have a small picture on my hands for ten minutes,
which is a great temptation to do nothing else. I saw
Tennyson again at the Prinseps', and was most entertained at
the 'petting' that went on. Miss B. [a famous beauty] was
there, and asked after you. She has fallen off, but is still
beautiful."

In May, 1858, they went as usual to Bowerswell, where in
due time the artist applied himself to "Apple Blossoms," or
"Spring" as it was latterly called, painting it in neighbouring
orchards.

Here I must again avail myself of my mother's notebook,
and her remarks on "Spring Flowers," as she calls it.

"This picture, whatever its future may be, I consider the
most unfortunate of Millais' pictures. It was begun at Annat
Lodge, Perth, in the autumn of 1856, and took nearly four
years to complete. The first idea was to be a study of an
apple tree in full blossom, and the picture was begun with
a lady sitting under the tree, whilst a knight in the back-

ground looked from the shade at her. This was to have
been named 'Faint Heart Never Won Fair Ladye.' The
idea was, however, abandoned, and Millais, in the following
spring, had to leave the tree from which he had made such
a careful painting, because the tenant at Annat Lodge would
not let him return to paint, for she said if he came to paint
in the garden it would disturb her friends walking there.
This was ridiculous, but Millais, looking about for some
other suitable trees, soon found them in the orchard of our
kind neighbour Mrs. Seton (Potterhill), who paid him the
greatest attention. Every day she sent her maid with
luncheon, and had tablecloths pinned up on the trees so as
to form a tent to shade him from the sun, and he painted
there in great comfort for three weeks whilst the blossoms
lasted. During that year (1857) he began to draw in the
figures, and the next year he changed to some other trees
in Mr. Gentle's orchard, next door to our home. Here he
painted in quiet comfort, and during the two springs finished
all the background and some of the figures. The centre
figure was painted from Sir Thomas Moncrieff's daughter
Georgiana (afterwards Lady Dudley); Sophie Gray, my
sister, is at the left side of the picture. Alice is there too,
in two positions, one resting on her elbow, singularly like,
and the other lying on her back with a grass stem in her
mouth. He afterwards made an etching of this figure for the
Etching Club, and called it 'A Day in the Country.' When
the picture of 'Spring Flowers' was on the easel out of
doors, and in broad sunlight, the bees used often to settle
on the bunches of blossom, thinking them real flowers from
which they might make their honey."

In July, 1858, my mother went to St. Andrews, in Fife,
and to her Millais wrote:—

"I have been working hard all day; have finished Alice's
top-knot, and had that little humbug Agnes Stewart again,
but I am not sure with what success. I had capital trips
with the MacLarens [neighbours living at Kinfauns Castle]
to Loch Flukey [Loch Freuchie, near Amulree, formerly an
excellent trout loch]. We caught eleven dozen trout, and
had great fun about settling where to sleep. I slept on the
dining-room table, in preference to a sofa, as the horse-hair
appeared a likely harbour for fleas, etc. A great tub was
brought in for the morning bath, and towels about the size
of pocket-handkerchiefs, so I used my sheets instead. . . .

"APPLE BLOSSOMS." 1856–1859

By permission of Mr. Clarke

I was up at five in the Hielands, and fished a beautiful
little river (the Braan) before breakfast. I hope you will
get tremendously strong. All that salt water ought to do
wonders. Sophie must also come back blooming, to be
painted in my picture."

On the envelope of this letter is an amusing sketch, showing some lady bathers coming out of the sea, and men
playing golf close by.

In August Millais went South on a visit to his parents at
Kingston-on-Thames, where they had a charming little house
overlooking the river. He
went by sea, taking with
him my mother's two young
sisters, Sophie and Alice,
who had also been invited;
and in the following letter
he gives us a little insight
into the home life of the old
people : — " Here we are in
William's [his brother's]
room. The girls are sitting
with me in perfect quiet, as
they are still very unwell.
Neither of them could eat
any breakfast, and every-
thing is whirling about them,
as it is with me. Otherwise
I am perfectly comfortable,
having managed my cigar
after breakfast. We have

SKETCH FOR "RUTH." *Circ.* 1855

just been listening to my sister [Emily Millais, Mrs. Wallack]
playing on the piano — 'awfully well,' as the girls say. . . .
My father has most gorgeous peaches and nectarines ripe
against the wall, and much finer than the glass-house ones at
Perth, which shows the climate to be warmer.

" Now to tell you about my sister. Although I had nearly
forgotten her, I think I would have known her again, she is
so like William, and not at all American, as I had expected.
She is still pretty, and her little boy is here — very like her,
with a good profile, and very excitable. She is very strong,
though not so to look at, and has the un-put-down-able 'go'
of William, for since breakfast she has played to me more
than you could play in a month, and is not the least tired.

. . . It is rather a loss William not being here, as he would complete the group so thoroughly.

" The place is covered with pretty flowers, and really looks lovely. My father has just come down and shown me two most beautiful water-colour drawings of William's, both of which are sold, and I have this minute come from looking after Alice, who is recovering quickly. She is in the arm-chair, and my father is playing the guitar to her. I can't tell you how very odd it seems to me, being amongst them here again. There is certainly a dash of the French about them all, for they are all so extraordinarily happy and satisfied with themselves."

After this visit he went off shooting and fishing, as usual, for a couple of months, and on his return to Bowerswell he nearly finished the " Apple Blossoms," and commenced (in October) " The Vale of Rest."

Here my mother's note-book again proves helpful as an illustration of his life and work at this period; interesting, too, as a reflection of her own views on the only subject on which they were at variance. As a strict Presbyterian she greatly disliked his working on Sundays, as he often did when the painting fever was strong upon him; and her entries on this subject are at once quaint and characteristic. She writes : — " Mr. Millais exhibited no pictures in 1858. He began a last picture of a Crusader's return, and stuck, after five months' hard labour. I was much averse to his painting every Sunday, and thought no good would come of it, as he took no rest, and hardly proper time for his meals. He made no progress, only getting into a greater mess; so when spring came we were thankful to pack up the picture and go to Scotland. Here he occupied himself on his 'Spring' apple blossoms picture, but did not set vigorously to work till the autumn. This winter [1858] he has achieved an immensity of work, and I attribute his success greatly to his never working on Sunday all this year. I will describe his pictures of this year in order, and begin with the Nuns ('The Vale of Rest'), which, like all his best works, was executed in a surprisingly short space of time.

" It had long been Millais' intention to paint a picture with nuns in it, the idea first occurring to him on our wedding tour in 1855. On descending the hill by Loch Awe, from Inverary, he was extremely struck with its beauty, and the coachman told us that on one of the islands there were the

ruins of a monastery. We imagined to ourselves the beauty
of the picturesque features of the Roman Catholic religion,
and transported ourselves, in idea, back to the times before
the Reformation had torn down, with bigoted zeal, all that
was beautiful from antiquity, or sacred from the piety or
remorse of the founders of old ecclesiastical buildings in
this country. The abbots boated and fished in the loch, the
vesper bell pealed forth the 'Ave Maria' at sundown, and
the organ notes of the Virgin's hymn were carried by the
water and transformed into a sweeter melody, caught up on
the hillside and dying away in the blue air. We pictured,
too, white-robed nuns in boats, singing on the water in the
quiet summer evenings, and chanting holy songs, inspired by
the loveliness of the world around them. . . .

" Millais said he was determined to paint nuns some day,
and one night this autumn, being greatly impressed with the
beauty of the sunset (it was the end of October) he rushed
for a large canvas, and began at once upon it, taking for
background the wall of our garden at Bowerswell, with the
tall oaks and poplar trees behind it. The sunsets were
lovely for two or three nights, and he dashed the work in,
softening it afterwards in the house, making it, I thought,
even less purple and gold than when he saw it in the sky.
The effect lasted so short a time that he had to paint like
lightning.

" It was about the end of October, and he got on very
rapidly with the trees and worked every afternoon, patiently
and faithfully, at the poplar and oak trees of the background
until November, when the leaves had nearly all fallen. He
was seated very conveniently for his work just outside our
front door, and, indeed, the principal part of the picture,
excepting where the tombstones come, is taken from the
terrace and shrubs at Bowerswell."

The background of "The Vale of Rest" remains very
much to-day what it was when Millais painted it. A few
of the old trees are gone; but there are the same green
terraces, and the same sombre hedges; there, too, is the
corner of the house which, under the artist's hands, appeared
as an ivy-covered chapel. The grave itself he painted from
one freshly made, in Kinnoull churchyard; and much amused
he was by the impression he made while working there.
Close by lived two queer old bachelors, who, in Perth, went
by the names of " Sin and Misery." They watched him

intently as he painted away day by day amongst the tombs
without even stopping for refreshment, and after the first day
they came to the conclusion that he made his living by
portraying the graves of deceased persons. So they good-
naturedly brought him a glass of wine and cake every day,
and said what they could by way of consolation for the hardships of his lot.

The rest of the tale is thus told by my mother:—"The
graveyard portion was painted some months later, in the very
cold weather, and the wind often threatened to knock the

SKETCH FOR ILLUSTRATION. 1858

frame over. The sexton kept him company, made a grave
for him, and then, for comfort's sake, kept a good fire in the
dead-house. There Millais smoked his pipe, ate his lunch,
and warmed himself."

It is always interesting to hear from artists who have
painted a successful picture, how and under what circumstances it was done. One man will tell you that his work
was the inspiration of a moment, and the whole thing was
dashed off in a few days, maybe a few hours — as was Landseer's "Sleeping Bloodhound." Another has, perhaps, spent
months or years on some great work; it has been painted,
repainted, altered a hundred times, and then not satisfied the
painter. Again, an unsatisfactory pose of a figure has often

driven a conscientious artist to the verge of insanity. And
this was the case with the figure of the woman digging
in "The Vale of Rest." I have heard my mother say she
never had such a time in her life as when my father was
painting that woman.

Everything was perfect
in the picture except this
wretched female, and no-
thing would induce her to
go right. Every day for
seven weeks he painted and
repainted her, with the result that the figure was
worse than ever, and he
was almost distracted.

My mother then pro-
ceeded to hatch a plot with
my grandmother *to steal
the picture!* This was
skilfully effected one day
when he had left his work
for a few hours. The two
arch-plotters took it be-
tween them and carried it
into a wine-cellar, where it
was securely locked up.

When the painter re-
turned to work and found
his treasure gone he was,
of course, in a dreadful state
of mind, and on discovering
the trick that had been
played him, he tried every
means to make them give
it up to him, but this they
steadfastly refused to do.

SKETCH FOR ILLUSTRATION. 1859

Here then was a predica-
ment! For some days he would settle to nothing, and the
model, who received good payment, would insist on coming
every day and sitting in the kitchen, saying that she was
engaged till the picture was finished. The situation at last
became comic — Millais furious, the conspirators placid,
smiling, but firm, and the model immovable.

At last he was persuaded to set to work on some water-colour replicas of "The Huguenot" and "The Heretic," for Mr. Gambart, and as he became interested in them he gradually calmed down. When the picture was eventually returned to him, he saw at a glance where his mistake lay, and in a few hours put everything right.

My uncle William tells an amusing story about this, which is worth repeating in his own words: — "Millais, as everyone knows, had the greatest power in the realistic rendering of all objects that came under his brush, and the veriest tyro could not fail to recognise at a glance the things that he painted. I remember, however, a case in which the power was not recognised ; in fact, the objects painted failed to convey the faintest notion of what they were intended to represent. An old Scotchman, after looking at 'The Vale of Rest' for some time, said to my brother in my hearing, 'Well, the picture 's all well enough, but there 's something I don't like.' My brother, who was always ready to listen to any criticism, said, 'What don't you like? Speak out, don't be afraid!'

"'Well,' said he, 'I don't like the idea of water in a grave.' 'Water in a grave?' said my brother. 'Well, there it is, plain enough' (pointing to a mattock), 'pouring into the grave.' He had actually mistaken the sheen of a steel mattock for a jet of water, and the handle for a bridge across the grave. This was too good a story not to be passed round, and it was told on the occasion of the picture being privately exhibited at the Langham Chambers, just before being sent to the Royal Academy. There was a good assemblage of people, and amongst them, though unrecognised, the old gentleman himself. The story was told with great gusto by John Leech (in my presence), and a roar of laughter followed, coupled with the words, 'What an old ass he must have been!' Whereupon the old gentleman sprang up from the sofa and said, 'I 'm the verra man mysel'.' It was honest of him, to say the least."

Mr. M. H. Spielmann, who has carefully studied Millais' works, says of it : — "This picture I have always felt to be one of the greatest and most impressive ever painted in England ; one in which the sentiment is not mawkish, nor the tragedy melodramatic — a picture to look at with hushed voice and bowed head ; in which the execution is not overwhelmed by the story; in which the story is emphasised by the com-

position; and in which the composition is worthy of the handling."

"This is the year Mr. Millais gave forth those terrible nuns in the graveyard": thus Mr. Punch characterised the year 1859. * Even Ruskin, denouncing the methods, and admitting (unjustly) the ugliness and "frightfulness" of the figures, was constrained to allow it nobility of horror, if horror it was, and the greatness of the touching sentiment. His charge of crudeness in the painting no longer holds good. Time — that grand Old Master to which Millais did homage in act and word — has done the work the artist intended him to do; and I venture to think that in the New Gallery of British Art there will be no more impressive, no more powerful work than that which shocked the Art world of 1859.

In 1862 Millais saw how he could improve the face of the nun that is seated at the head of the grave, so he had the picture in his studio for a week, and repainted the head from a Miss Lane.

During 1858 was also painted "The Love of James the First of Scotland." It will be remembered that this un-fortunate monarch was confined for many years in Windsor Castle. In the garden below his prison used to walk the beautiful Lady Jane Beaufort, and he fell in love with her; but his only means of communicating with her was by dropping letters through the bars of the grated window. This is the scene represented in the picture. The castle and wall were taken from the picturesque old ruin of Bal-housie Castle, which overlooks the North Inch of Perth. On p. 361 is given a photo of the exact wall, with the model's hand dropping a love-letter from the window. Millais' model for this picture was Miss Eyre, of Kingston, whose sister, Miss Mary Eyre, he also painted the following year as "The Bride" — a girl with passion flowers in her hair. †

While the work was in hand, an old woman came for three days, and stood staring alternately at the artist and the castle, evidently without any notion of what he was about. Disliking the presence of observers while he was at work, he looked up suddenly and exclaimed, "Well, what are you

---

* The *Times* was this year favourable, and acknowledged "The Vale of Rest" as a work of merit.

† This lady was singularly like the Countess de Grey, and on this account the portrait was purchased at a sale by Lord de Grey.

looking at?"   To which she replied, "Weel — that's juist
what a was gaein tae ask ye.   What are *you* glowerin at?"
Cetera desunt.

To the uninitiated I may explain that, in the Scotch tongue,
"glowerin" means staring rudely and intently.

At this time (November, 1859), though work went on
briskly, began a long period of anxiety on account of my
mother's health, ensuing on the birth of her eldest daughter.
She had imprudently gone, one cold winter's day, to Murthly,.
to make a drawing of some tapestry in the old castle, for one
of my father's pictures ; and, sitting long at her task, she
contracted a chill, which affected the optic nerves of both
her eyes.   A temporary remedy was found, but in late years
the mischief again reappeared, to the permanent detriment
of her eyesight.

SOPHIA GRAY." 1853

CHAPTER IX

W E come now to the turning-point in the life of the painter — to the period when, with the exception of a few strong men of independent judgment, all the powers of the Art world were set in array against him — the critics, the Academy, and the Press — and, under their combined influence, even the picture-dealers began to look askance at his works as things of doubtful merit. Buyers, too, held aloof, not daring to trust their own judgment in opposition to so great an authority as Mr. Ruskin; for by this time Ruskin had attained a position in the land absolutely unapproached by any other critic before or since. With a charm of diction unequalled in English prose, he had formulated certain theories of his own which every artist must accept or reject under peril of his severest condemnation; and as " Sir Isumbras " — the last of Millais' works that may be termed purely Pre-Raphaelite — was found to sin against these requirements, it fell under his ban as utterly unworthy of the applause it had gained from the public.

It has been well said that " the eye of a critic is often like a microscope, made so very fine and nice that it discovers the atoms, grains, and minutest particles without ever comprehending the whole, comparing the parts, or seeing all at once the harmony." And, as will presently be seen, that was, in Millais' view at least, the affliction from which Mr. Ruskin was suffering at this time.

It is not given to every man to withstand such a formidable attack as that to which my father was now exposed. From the financial point of view the situation was critical

in the extreme.   Ruin stared him in the face — ruin to himself, his wife, and family.   One cannot therefore wonder
that, under the strain and peril of the time, his letters
betray not only his amazement at the crass stupidity of some
of his critics, but his deep sense of injury, and a rooted
belief that envy, hatred, and malice were at the bottom of
all this uproar.

All this, together with a record of his doings during the
months of April and May, 1859, will be found in the following extracts from his letters, in reading which it must be
borne in mind that these letters were intended only for the
eye of his wife, for whose comfort at this trying time he
would naturally and rightly open his mind without any
thought of egotism or empty boast.

The letters are dated from his father's house at Kingston,
to which in joyous anticipation of success at the coming
Royal Academy Exhibition he betook himself with his
pictures early in April.

"*South Cottage, 7th April.* — There are three or four
people after my pictures, and I have no doubt of making
more than I expected by them.   William will write to you
about what was said, but I will simply tell you in a word
that nothing could possibly be more successful, ' The Nuns'
especially.   I have called it

> ' The Vale of Rest,
> Where the weary find repose —

from one of Mendelssohn's most lovely part-songs.   I heard
William singing it, and said it just went with the picture,
whereupon he mentioned the name and words, which are
equally suitable.   Marochetti said to William, before a
number of people, that ' The Nuns' should have a place
in the national collection, between Raphael and Titian ; and
Thackeray and Watts expressed nearly the same opinion.
Indeed, the praise is quite overwhelming, and I keep out
of it as much as possible, as I am not able to bear it, I feel
so weakened by it all.   While William was showing the two
large pictures, I was painting away at the single figure,
which I finished perfectly, having worked at it from five
in the morning.   I felt quite inspired, and never made a
mistake.   It is, I think, the most beautiful of all.

"Nothing could exceed the kindness of my people about
me, and only through their indefatigable assistance could

"THE BRIDE." *Circ.* 1858

By permission of Mr. A. D. Grimmond

I have finished the third. All were framed and sent in to the Royal Academy in good time."

The three pictures were "The Vale of Rest," "The Love of James I. of Scotland," and "Apple Blossoms." They had been seen and praised by hundreds of people before they were exhibited to the public, and the artist knew they were the best he had ever painted; but no sooner did they appear on the Academy walls than they were attacked as already indicated, the admiration of the public who persistently crowded in front of them, and his own knowledge of their value, being the only consolation he could lay to heart. His next letter betrays the revulsion of feeling caused by this cruel, not to say malignant, attack.

SKETCH FOR "THE BLACK BRUNSWICKER." 1860

"*April 10th.* — In the midst of success I am dreadfully low-spirited, and the profession is more hideous than ever in my eyes. Nobody seems to understand really good work, and even the best judges surprise me with their extraordinary remarks. . . . Nothing can be more irritating and perplexing than the present state of things. There seems to be a total want of confidence in the merits of the pictures, amongst even the dealers. They seem quite bewildered. Even John Phillip said that he thought it was high time I should come and live in London. As if that had anything to do with my Art!

" I would write oftener to you, but really I have nothing either pleasant or satisfactory to write about. I am far from well, and everybody says they never saw such a change in any man for the worse. I could scarcely be quieter, too, as I never stay in town or have any wish to be amongst riotous fellows; yet the reaction of leaving off work is very trying." . . .

"*April 13th,* 1859. — There seems to be but one opinion

amongst unprejudiced people as to the success of my pictures this year, but £1000 for a picture is a very rare thing. It is true that that sum has been given already this year for a picture by O——; but you must remember that my pictures are not vulgar enough for the City merchants, who seem to be the only men who give these great prices. . . . I am much better after yesterday's headache, and got up this morning early, and have been reading and playing chess with my mother ever since. . . . It is a fine day, so I shall go and see the University Boat Race. Yesterday I met in the Burlington Arcade an old friend from India, the brother of our old friend Grant who died. (I drew him in pen-and-ink, dying, surrounded by his family.) The brother has grown into an enormous man, with moustaches nearly half a yard broad — a very handsome fellow."

" *April 18th*, 1859. — Hunt and Collins dined here yesterday. The pain in my chest is nearly gone, so I am no longer uneasy. It must have been from working too hard and leaning forward so much, but I hope to begin my work again this week. . . . Ruskin was talking to young Prinsep, and said he had been looking at the ' Mariana,' which I painted years ago, and had come to the sage conclusion that I had gone to the dogs and am hopelessly fallen. So there is no doubt of what view he will take of my works this year; but (as Hunt, who has a high opinion of their excellence, says) if he abuses them he will ruin himself as a critic. Already he is almost entirely disregarded. I hear that Leighton has a picture in the Royal Academy, but nothing of its worth. This picture, whether good or bad, will be set up against mine. The enmity is almost overwhelming, *and nothing but the public good sense will carry me through*. . . . I am sanguine, in spite of every drawback, though I know there is a possibility of my not realising my anticipations regarding the sale of the pictures; but in that case I am perfectly prepared to keep them. They must not, and shall not, be thrown away."

" *April 19th*. — William was singing at his Hanover Square Rooms last night, but I could not be there. He seems to have made a real success, as he always does in public. I am wonderfully well and have quite recovered my spirits, and am now prepared to act determinedly. No persuasion will now induce me to sacrifice my work. You see, by putting a very high price on it, *the dealers are entirely shut out*,

and thereby become my most inveterate enemies, which is
no joke considering the powerful influence they have.   They,
added to the Royal Academy, which is always against me,
make the army a difficult one to combat.   When I sold my
works to the dealers they were my friends, and counteracted
this artistic detraction.   There is, without doubt, an immense
amount of underhand work, and I can scarcely regard a
single professional man as my friend.   I am quite settled,
however, in my position, to stand
a violent siege."

"*April 23rd.* — The day after
to-morrow I shall attend the Exhibition [at the Royal Academy]
privately with the members.   I
am prepared for some disappointment; it always happens.

" To-night at 12 all the parish
children sing through the village,
headed by the parson, my father,
William, Arthur Coleridge, and
others.   Leslie (the choir-man)
is here, staying with Coleridge;
he played delightfully this morning in the studio. I am sure, dear,
you would be charmed with the
society here; the people seem to
appreciate the family very much,
and are endless in their kind-
nesses, sending things to my

SKETCH FOR "THE BLACK BRUNSWICKER"
1860

mother [she was very ill at this time] and inquiring daily
after her health. William, too, is surrounded by pretty girls."

After his visit to the Royal Academy to see how his
pictures were hung, he writes : —

"*April 26th.* — It is always a melancholy thing to the
painter to see his work for the first time in an empty room ;
and yesterday was a most dreadful, dark, rainy day.   Everything looked dismal.   The single figure is not well hung,
although perfectly seen.   All three, of course, lose in my
eyes, for they are surrounded by such a perplexity of staring
colour ; for instance, an officer in size of life, in a brilliant
red coat, is hung next to ' The Nuns,' which must naturally
hurt it. ' The Orchard ' [' Apple Blossoms ']. I think. looks
better.   There are no less than three pictures of orchard

blossoms, but small, as the artist had no time to enlarge
them.   Hook's are very fine indeed, small, but lovely in
colour — quite as good as my own.   He is about the only
first-rate man they have.   Boxall has some *beautiful* portraits
— one of an old man especially so.   Stansfield and Roberts
as usual.   Landseer, of course, good; but, between ourselves, not quite so much so as of yore.   He was most
kind, and said he understood the quality of my work entirely; and when I told him they were unsold, he laughed
and said, 'Oh, you need not mind about that.   I would
sell them fast enough.'   Frank Grant, too, was most cordial,
and asked after you.   He and Landseer went backwards
and forwards many times between ' The Orchard ' and ' The
Nuns.'   I am told by all the Hanging Committee that they
have come to the conclusion that ' The Vale of Rest ' would
have been perfect had I left the digging nun alone, and that
' The Orchard ' is spoilt by Sophie's and Alice's heads to the
left of the picture."

"*April 28th.* — I got home here [at Kingston] last night
after a hard day's rubbing at the pictures, which improved
them immensely.   I see things are creeping favourably on.
Landseer this year is a most energetic admirer; he said
yesterday, before many of the members, that my pictures are
far beyond everything I have ever done.   Roberts, too, said I
am sure to sell them at the private view.   I have a few truly
good friends in the Royal Academy, *amongst the best men*,
in spite of the wicked clique who, of course, do their best to
run me down.   There is no great ' catch ' this year, except
perhaps O——'s companion picture to his last year's one.   It is
very good (well painted), but egregiously vulgar and commonplace; but there is enough in it of a certain 'jingo ' style
to make it a favourite.   This work may at first attract, but
after a while it will not stand with the public.

" Ruskin will be disgusted this year, for all the rubbish
he has been praising *before being sent into the Royal Academy*
has now bad places.   There is a wretched work like a photograph of some place in Switzerland, evidently painted under
his guidance, for he seems to have lauded it up sky-high ;
and that is *just where it is* in the miniature room!   He does
not understand my work, which is now too broad for him
to appreciate, and I think his eye is only fit to judge the
portraits of insects.   But then, I think he has lost all real
influence as a critic.

"To-morrow is the private view. I have given my
tickets to John Meech and his wife. He knows all the
Press men, *and is respected by all*, so his opinion will be taken
and carry weight. Did I tell you I rowed with my father
up to Hampton Court, and met William and a large party,
Miss Boothby [whom William Millais afterwards married],
Miss Eyre [who sat to Millais several times], Coleridge, etc.
Miss Boothby and I and William and Miss Eyre had a race
home, and we beat them. My hands suffered in consequence,
so I cannot row again just now."

"*April 29th.*— I have just come from the private view.
To tell you the truth, I think it likely I shall not sell one
of the pictures. The clique has been most successful
against me this year, and few people look at my work.
Ruskin was there, looking at 'The Nuns'; and Tom Taylor,
who said nothing. Everywhere I hear of the infamous
attempts to destroy me (the truth is these pictures are not
vulgar enough for general appreciation). However, I must
wait, for I don't know what the Press will say yet. Seeing
that there is such a strong undercurrent against me, it is
possible they may lift me up.

"Gambart was there, and several dealers, *but none spoke
to me*. They are not anxious to *look into my eyes just now*,
and no wonder! Reade is sitting beside me as I write
this.

"The fact of the matter is, I am out of fashion. There
will doubtless be a reaction, but the state of affairs in the
Art world is at present too critical to admit of a good reward
for all my labour. This is rather trying to me, I confess,
after all my slavery, but it will account to you for my want
of belief in the profession. You see, nobody knows anything about Art, so one is all at sea. The failures are most
terrible in London just now, and things look very bad.
What will become of Art, I don't know. It will not be
worth following, if I cannot sell pictures such as these. I
am sorry I have no good news for you, dear, but the look-
out is anything but refreshing."

"*May 5th.*— I returned here last night and opened three
letters from you—all so kind and nice that they quite set
me up. There have been no inquiries for any of my
pictures; but now they are once more crowded — this time
more than ever. You may, perhaps, laugh at it, but I have
heard it said that the want of purchasers is a great deal due

to Ruskin having in his last pamphlet said that I was falling off.

" Hunt and Leech, as well as the Rossettis and their clique, have expressed their admiration of my work of late, and yesterday Marochetti was kind enough to express the same sentiments. Landseer, who was with him, asked my address, in case he should have to write me, indicating his desire to sell them for me. After such opinions from such men, what is outside criticism? Yet, in spite of myself and my own convictions, I feel humiliated.

" It has become so much the fashion to abuse me in the Press, that my best friends now occasionally talk in the same way. I have lost all pleasure and hope in my profession.

" William has gone to the Exhibition, and I made arrangements to go to Aldershot with Leech ; but all this anxiety, however much I try to dispel it, destroys my peace of mind, and I have a bad headache. Everybody bothers me too about living in the *North*, and says I have cut all my original friends, and will inevitably lose their interest. I candidly confess I never had such a trying time in my life. I would not care a farthing if I were a bachelor, but for your sake I cannot take such injustice calmly. It is a strange and unexpected end to all my labour, and I can only hope it will not affect you overmuch."

" *May 10th.* — Many happy returns of the day, my darling. I have just returned from Cambridge, where I met *Mrs. Jones, of Pantglass*, the duke's enchantress. She made many inquiries about you, and sent her best love. She is most amusing, and I talked with her all the evening. She is a very handsome woman, with a fine figure, and got up most gorgeously. I was made much of by the Cambridge men. Ruskin's pamphlet is out, and White says it is favourable, although stating that the pictures are painted in my worst manner. How extraordinary the fate of these pictures has been! Never have pictures been more mobbed, but now the crowds mostly abuse them, following the mass of criticism ; yet the fuss they are making in a way makes up for the abuse. No words can express the curious envy and hatred these works have brought to light. Some of the papers, I believe, have been so violent that for two days together they have poured forth such abuse as was never equalled in the annals of criticism. My works are not understood by the men who set themselves up as judges.

Only when I am dead will they know their worth. I could not believe in such wanton cruelty as has been shown to me this year. There is no doubt that the critics have ruined the sale, for all who would have come forward now say that the nuns and grave are miserable to look at, and the apple-blossoms full of ugliness. Let me, however, assure you, that they *must* win their way to the front in time.

"The country is blooming everywhere now, and everything is happy. It is dreadful to be away from you so long. I am so glad to hear the children are well. I wish I could embrace them all; it would be delightful after all this vexation. Fate seems determined to make my profession hateful to me."

Needless to say how welcome at such a time was the hearty support of the few members of the Academy and artist friends who refused to join in the cabal against him and his works, prominent amongst whom were Hunt, Landseer, Leech, Thackeray, Reade, and the two Rossettis. Amongst outsiders, too, were many sympathising friends, whose kind words and letters helped him to take heart again even in the darkest hours when oppression had well-nigh driven him to despair.

Amongst these was his friend Mr. Lloyd, from whose letter I venture to quote a few memorable words. He says: — "I merely wish, by writing to you, to protest on behalf of myself and many friends against the injustice of the London critics, and to assure you that whenever I have discussed your picture ['The Vale of Rest'] with persons whose opinions are deservedly valued, I have found them nearly as enthusiastic admirers of it as myself. Some, too, agree with me that it is not only your greatest work, but that it by far excels in truthfulness, in rendering, and in nobleness of conception any picture exhibited within my recollection on the Royal Academy walls by any other artist. That you will live to see its merits more publicly acknowledged I have little doubt, and I sincerely hope that the ingratitude and prejudice of those who presume to dictate to the public what to admire will not induce you to disbelieve that there are thousands to whom your paintings are a great intellectual pleasure, and that the gradual liberation of the public mind from conventional rules will bring thousands more to the shrine hallowed by yourself and those of your brother artists who boldly and conscientiously pursue the path of truth."

Returning now to Millais' own letters, I find : —

"*May* 13*th.* — There is a decided improvement in the look of things. Gambart writes me a long letter, and I have a commission for a picture from New York. I am perfectly certain that there will be a reaction in my favour, sooner or later, as the abuse has been so violent. I wish I could afford to keep the pictures, as I am perfectly sure they will one day fetch very large sums. There is no chance of my selling my pictures *to gentlemen* — the dealers are too strong.

SKETCH OF MISS KATE DICKENS FOR "THE BLACK BRUNSWICKER." 1859

Picture-buyers can barter with them when they cannot with the artist, and my pictures have remained unsold so long that no one will believe that they are valuable. All the other pictures of any pretensions in the Exhibition are sold. This is, of course, fearfully dispiriting, and a matter of wonder to me, as I have a high reputation; but my detractors have really induced the public to believe that the faults in my pictures spoil all the beauties. The crowds, too, round the pictures increase, but I am too much disgusted to think more about them. If I sell them, I will wipe the memory of them for ever from my mind, they have been such torments to me."

At last the star of hope appeared on the horizon, in a quarter where it was least expected. The picture-dealers

began to come round, making timid inquiries as to prices;
and one of them actually bought "The Vale of Rest."
Commissions, too, came in, and the whole aspect of affairs
was suddenly changed. The effect of all this upon Millais
will be seen in the two following letters, written, it will be
noticed, on two con-
secutive days.

"*May* 16*th.* — Cheer
up! Things are quietly
coming round. Already
there is quite another
aspect of affairs. W. is
to give me a decided
answer whether or not
a client of his will have
'The Nuns.' There is
a demand also for the
small picture, and G.
wants to have the copy-
right, and is to let me
know to-morrow morn-
ing whether he will have
the picture. Indeed,
now I have n't a doubt
that I shall sell all three.*
So much for the brutal
criticisms! The fact is,
I shall have my own
way after all. If dealers
give my prices they
must make twenty per
cent. on them.

"Last evening I was
dining at the Prinsep's,

SKETCH OF MISS KATE DICKENS FOR
"THE BLACK BRUNSWICKER." 1859

and Watts quite cheered me. He says *they will live for ever,
and will soon find their proper place.* It will be a great triumph
in the end. The curious part of it is that 'The Orchard' is
considerably more popular than 'The Nuns,' and much more
crowded. Hunt and Rossetti are wild about the latter. One

* "The Vale of Rest." bought by Mr. Windus, of Tottenham, through W. the
dealer, for 700 guineas, was afterwards sold to Mr. Tate for £3000. It now hangs
in the Tate Gallery, and is by common consent regarded as one of the artist's
greatest pictures.

sees now how abuse can create attraction! I have just
been to G. to sign the last forty prints of 'The Order of
Release.' He tells me that 'The Royalist' had done well
for him, and you will remember how fearfully it was abused
when exhibited. X. [a dealer] begs me to paint the
'Petrarch and Laura,' and the dealers all look rather sheepish
in asking me what I want for the pictures, being evidently
afraid of one another, and yet not liking to appear too eager."

"*May 17th.* — I enclose X.'s letter, which you will understand. Whatever I do, no matter how successful, it will
always be the same story. 'Why don't you give us the
Huguenot again?' Yet I will be bound the cunning fellow
is looking forward to engraving this very picture. You see
he says at the end of his note he will 'risque' engraving it if
I like!

"I have now enough commissions to last me all next year,
so I am quite happy. I am so glad to hear you are getting
well and strong again. That is better than all the sales of
pictures."

On May 21st he went to meet his wife at Birmingham,
and brought her back with him to Kingston, where, after all
the excitement of this year, he was glad to have a quiet time
while working away at his small commissions.

Before saying good-bye to "The Vale of Rest," let me
quote the words of Frances Low, who has admirably caught
the spirit of its teaching: — "Who that has ever seen this
picture forgets the wondrous sunset light that lingers, with
a thousand evanescent hues, over the evening face of Nature,
transforming and transfiguring decay, death itself, into a radiant
golden vision? The spell of the figure is deepened by the
dramatic face of the nun, whose deep, mysterious, and in-
scrutable eyes seem to reflect the spirit of inanimate Nature,
with its unsurpassed loveliness and terror, and bid the
troubled human soul seek its answer there."

At the end of June my mother went North again, to make
ready for her husband's coming — to a house near Bowerswell,
called Potter Hill, which they had taken for the autumn; and
there he wrote to her: —

"*July 20th.* — 'The Knight' ['Sir Isumbras'] leaves by
carrier to-day, and I go up to town with a little sketch of it
for White, and 'The Bridesmaid' for Gambart. What do
you think? I have have nearly finished one of the heads from
Miss Eyre, and by staying another week I shall manage to

do the other. I shall love to see you again, and to get home.
. . . Yesterday I dined with Colonel Challoner at the mess
— a very nice old boy indeed, and rather like what poor old
Captain Lemprière was.

"I have managed everything satisfactorily. William is to
bring 'The Vale of Rest' and 'James' Love' ['The Love
of James I. of Scotland'] to Perth with him immediately
after the close of the Royal Academy on the 30th, when
'The Orchard' goes to Liverpool. In 'The Vale' I have
just to make the nun's face a little prettier; must give also a
few touches to 'James' Love.' Then William will return with
the pictures, taking one to Windus and the other to Gambart.
I could not well touch the nun's face without a look at Mrs.
Paton [the woman who sat for the figure].

"I am working very hard, considering the heat of the
weather. Miss Eyre (the younger one) is waiting for me to
paint her. She makes a most lovely picture, and it is admired more than anything I have ever done of the kind."

The autumn holiday followed, and then, greatly refreshed,
Millais returned to town, intent on finding a home there for
himself and his family. From his old quarters in Langham
Chambers, to which he now went back, he wrote to my mother:

"*November 17th*, 1859. — Yesterday I dined at the Garrick,
and was with Gambart driving about all day looking for a
house. Saw three, but all dampish and too near Mr. G——
and a lot of the artistic crew whom I do not wish to know,
so I will look in healthier localities. Napoleon's old house,
where his loves resided, is not to be let for any term under
seven years, which is of course out of the question for us.
White is delighted with the sketch, and says that 'The
Orchard' is certain to sell this winter. There was an election
of two Royal Academicians yesterday at the Academy, the
choice being the last-made Associate, Phillip, and one Smirke,
an unknown architect or sculptor, I really don't know which.

"I happened to be dining last night next to Roberts and
Stansfield, who would not be persuaded to believe my statement that I was not aware that it was election night, which
was perfectly true. Both Stansfield and Roberts voted for
Phillip, and I believe I had n't a vote at all. So you see it is
pretty well as I have always told you, but it is really a matter
of entire indifference to me, as my position is as good as any
except Landseer's; and this they too well know. All the
petty insults they can heap on me they will.

"After dining at the Garrick I went to the Cosmopolitan, and there met Morier [Sir Robert Morier, afterwards our Minister at St. Petersburg], who was just going away to Berlin. He did not know me, and took me for Leighton, so I have been taken twice for him of late. There must be a likeness between us. Charley Collins is writing a novel, which is already advertised. Gambart is making strenuous efforts to get ' The Rescue ' to engrave. He has sold both ' James' Love ' and ' The Girl on the Terrace,' so you see he does not want for immediate profit on my work."

"The Black Brunswicker," one of Millais' most successful pictures, was now in his mind. In his next letter he gives his first idea of the way in which the subject should be treated.

"*November 18th.*— Yesterday I dined with Leech, who had a small dinner-party. Mrs. Dickens was there, also Mr. and Mrs. Dallas, whom you remember, and Billy Russell (the *Times* correspondent) and his wife. Shirley Brooks and myself were the rest of the party. We had some very interesting stories and gossip from Billy Russell, which would delight you all. I will keep them for you when we meet. Oddly enough, he touched upon the subject of *the picture I am going to paint*, and I asked him to clear up for me one or two things connected with it. He is a capital fellow, and is going to write me a long letter with correct information, which he can get. I told him my project (as it was absolutely necessary), but he promised to keep it secret, knowing how things are pirated. It was very fortunate, my meeting him, as he is the very best man for military information. My subject appears to me, too, most fortunate, and Russell thinks it first-rate. It is connected with the Brunswick Cavalry at Waterloo.

"' Brunswickers ' they were called, and were composed of the best gentlemen in Germany. They wore a black uniform with death's head and cross-bones, and gave and received no quarter. They were nearly annihilated, but performed prodigies of valour. It is with respect to their having worn crape on their arms in token of mourning that I require some information; and as it will be a perfect *pendant* to ' The Huguenot,' I intend making the sweetheart of a young soldier sewing it round his arm, and vainly supplicating him to keep from the bugle-call to arms. *I have it all in my mind's eye, and feel confident that it will be a*

"THE BLACK BRUNSWICKER." 1860

By permission of H. Graves and Son

prodigious success. The costume and incident are so powerful that I am astonished it has never been touched upon
before. Russell was quite struck with it, and he is the best
man for knowing the public taste. Nothing could be kinder
than his interest, and he is to set about getting all the information that is required.

"I sat next Mrs. Dickens, who desired her best remembrances to you, and hopes you will call and bring the children
to see her.

"To-morrow I am going shooting with Lewis in Kent.
I have made up my mind not to live in town, but out in
the Kingston direction, as all the houses I have seen here
appear dirty and damp. White, too, thinks it would be
decidedly better for me to be out of the way of cliques.
I will draw in my picture ['The Black Brunswicker'] here.
White confesses to me that, with the exception of Landseer
and myself, there is not an artist whose pictures are safe
to sell. Most men get a fictitious value placed on their
works, and ruin themselves by producing too much. Their
pictures are for sale every month. I am glad to think that
when mine sell they are placed permanently.

In the spring of 1860 they took a nice house at the corner
of Bryanstone Square, where he went on with his work on
"The Black Brunswicker." And thereby hangs a tale.
Miss Kate Dickens (Charles Dickens' daughter, now Mrs.
Perugini) sat for the lady — a handsome girl, with a particularly
sweet expression and beautiful auburn hair that contrasted
well with the sheen of her white satin dress. The picture
had not long been finished before the figure was claimed
by more than one of the celebrities of the day; while, as
to the Brunswicker, no less than five or six distinguished
officers were said to have sat for it; but the fact is that my
father, wishing to obtain the handsomest model he could,
went, on the invitation of his friend the Colonel of the
1st Life Guards, to inspect the regiment on parade at
Albany Street Barracks, and there he found the very man he
wanted in a private soldier — a splendid type of masculine
beauty — and having, after great difficulty, obtained the
uniform of a Black Brunswicker, he dressed him in it and
painted his portrait. The poor fellow (I forget his name)
died of consumption in the following year.

The curious in such matters may like to know how the
figures posed. I may say, therefore, that the two models

1 — 23

never sat together. "The Black Brunswicker"* clasped a lay-figure to his breast, while the fair lady leant on the bosom of a man of wood.

The work was sold to M. Gambart for one thousand guineas. It took a long time to paint, and my father was so pleased with it that he afterwards did a replica in oils, which is now in the possession of the family.

Mrs. Perugini has kindly favoured me with the following note of her experience as a sitter for this picture: —

"I made your father's acquaintance when I was quite a young girl. Very soon after our first meeting he wrote to my father, asking him to allow me to sit to him for a head in one of the pictures he was then painting, 'The Black Brunswicker.' My father consenting, I used to go to your mother and father's house, somewhere in the North of London, accompanied by an old lady, a friend of your family. I was very shy and quiet in those days, and during the 'sittings' I was only too glad to leave the conversation to be carried on by your father and his old friend; but I soon grew to be interested in your father's extraordinary vivacity, and the keenness and delight he took in discussing books, plays, and music, and sometimes painting — but he always spoke less of pictures than of anything else — and these sittings, to which I had looked forward with a certain amount of dread and dislike, became so pleasant to me that I was heartily sorry when they came to an end and my presence was no more required in his studio.

"As I stood upon my 'throne,' listening attentively to everything that passed, I noticed one day that your father was much more silent than usual, that he was very restless, and a little sharp in his manner when he asked me to turn my head this way or that. Either my face or his brush seemed to be out of order, and he could not get on. At last, turning impatiently to his old friend, he exclaimed, 'Come and tell me what's wrong here, I can't see any more, I've got blind over it.' She laughingly excused herself, saying she was no judge, and would n't be of any use, upon which he turned to me. 'Do *you* come down, my dear, and tell me,' he said. As he was quite grave and very impatient, there was nothing

---

* "A gentleman came into his studio, and seeing his famous picture of the 'Black Brunswicker,' asked, 'What uniform is that?' Millais, who had been at great trouble and expense to procure the exact costume, replied, 'The Black Brunswicker.' 'Oh, indeed,' said the visitor; 'I knew it was one of the volunteers, but I was n't sure which regiment.'" — *The Memories of Dean Hole.*

for it but to descend from my throne and take my place
beside him. As I did so I happened to notice a slight
exaggeration in something I saw upon his canvas, and told
him of it. Instantly, and greatly to my dismay, he took
up a rag and wiped out the whole of the head, turning at the
same time triumphantly to his old friend. 'There! that's
what I always say; a fresh eye can see everything in a
moment, and an artist should ask a stranger to come in and
look at his work, every day of his life. There! get back to
your place, my dear, and we'll begin all over again!'"

As the time approached for the opening of the Royal
Academy Exhibition, 1860, great was the curiosity amongst
those who had seen "The Black Brunswicker"* as to the
view the Press would take of it, after the furious onslaught
they had made on the artist's previous works. The remarkable success of these works, in spite of all their sneers and
taunts, would hardly, it was thought, encourage them to
renew the attack; but that they would give it a word of
welcome was not to be expected, good as the picture was,
and however much it might be admired.

And now, when it appeared on the Academy walls, the
public hailed it enthusiastically as one of the greatest gems
of the Exhibition; but, with few exceptions, the Press,
apparently willing to wound, but yet afraid to strike, reviewed it in the most ungracious spirit. To Millais, however, these anonymous criticisms had ceased to be of any
moment. Confident in his own powers, and in full assurance
of success after the victory of previous years, he now found
renewed pleasure in his work, and never spared himself in
perfecting to the best of his ability whatever he had in hand,
whether oil-paintings or black-and-white drawings for the
magazines, then in great request. Of this year's letters
I have few beyond those written to his wife immediately
before and after the opening of the Academy.

"*April 27th*, 1860. — The Leslie dinner was most agreeable. The company there — Duke of Argyle, Lord and
Lady Spencer, Lady Wharncliffe, Sir E. Landseer, Mulready,
and myself. I went home afterwards with Sir Edwin, and
spent some four hours in conversation over brandy and
water. Yesterday Frere's dinner was delightful. To-morrow

* The picture occupied three months in painting. The success caused the artist
to make an exact copy of the original. This, however, was never quite finished,
and is now in the possession of the family.

I go to the Royal Academy to touch up.   Hunt's picture
seems to be doing well as an exhibition."

"*May 2nd.* — I write this from Martineau's, where I have
just seen Hunt and Val Prinsep.   All yesterday I was at
the Royal Academy, and in the evening I had such a bad
headache that I was obliged to return and go to bed early.
I am, however, all right this morning.   I found the woman
in 'The Black Brunswicker' looking much better than I had
hoped, and I very much improved her.   The whole picture is
by far the most satisfactory work I ever sent there.   Everyone has expressed the same opinion; its success is certain.
I met Tom Taylor at the Cosmopolitan with your father, and
he said he had heard nothing but '*dead good*' of it."

After commenting on some other Academy pictures, he
continues: — "The fact is, the Royal Academy is the only
place for a man to find his real level.   All the defects come
out so clearly that no private puffing is worth a farthing.
You cannot thrust pictures down people's throats."

"*May 3rd.* — You seem to see much more than we do here.
I have seen no criticism on Hunt's picture [Holman Hunt
was having a private exhibition of his work, which was very
successful], and have only heard of one in the *Illustrated
London News*.   The *Times* has n't noticed it yet.   I read
what it said of 'The Black Brunswicker,' which was flippant,
and not at all hearty in praise; moreover, it reads the story
wrong.*   The *Athenæum* is all right, but as it is written
by a friend [F. G. Stephens] it is not surprising.   That the
picture is a great success there is no doubt.

"I was at the Royal Academy this morning, but did not
go when the public were admitted.   Cooke (Royal Academy)
asked me to dine with him at the Academy Club dinner at
Greenwich, the annual feast.   Although I accepted, I was
obliged to excuse myself, for I met Dalziel yesterday, and
he said I must give him the 'Framley' illustration on Wednesday, so I have returned from the Academy to design
it.   Cooke was evidently much vexed, and some of the
Royal Academicians seem to think I wish to avoid them,
they are so suspicious of me.   I could not help it, however,
and they must think what they like.   Yesterday I went to

---

* Millais meant the incident to be taking place on the eve of Waterloo or
Quatre Bras, June, 1815, at which battle the leader of the Black Brunswickers,
the Duke of Brunswick, was killed.   The young Prussian is supposed to be saying
good-bye to an English girl.

Arden's with Gambart, who, in my presence, offered more than once to buy from him 'The Rescue' [the picture of the fireman] for £2000! Fancy that! *I received £580 for it.* Gambart appears to be in the best spirits, and anxious to have everything I am doing. He says if I will let him have my pictures to exhibit separately from the Royal Academy, he will give me as much again for them; it would be worth his while. Arden is very anxious to have 'The Black Brunswicker,' and I am to paint a duplicate the same size directly it comes from the Academy.

" I must now go and read *Framley Parsonage*, and try and get something out of it for my drawing. The dinner was very grand, and many of the blue ribbon swells were introduced to me, and asked whether the *Times* reading was correct. My picture certainly looks most satisfactory. There is nothing in the Exhibition to attract but Landseer's, Phillip's, and mine. I will try and leave this place on Thursday or Friday. This is a long letter, but I have lots to tell you when I come. So glad the children are well and your mother progressing. Keep yourself quite happy, for we have every reason to be thankful this year."

" *May 4th*, 1860. — I write this from Barwell's after having been for about two minutes at the private view. That sight is always so sickening to me that I cannot stand it. I saw Gambart, and dine with him this evening. I think I told you Windus has sold 'The Huguenot' to Miller, of Preston, for over a thousand (White told me as much). Hunt's exhibition is a *tremendous* success, and I believe Gambart is to give him £5000 for his picture. The public are much taken with the miniature-like finish and the religious character of the subject. The Royal Academy are tremendously jealous of the success of the picture, and his pocketing such a sum; but he has been seven years at it, and he says it has cost him £2000 painting it. He hasn't earned a farthing all that time. I saw Watts' fresco in Lincoln's-inn Hall this morning, and it is *magnificent* — by far the best thing of the kind in the kingdom. . . . To-morrow is the dinner at the Royal Academy, and next week I hope to get to work at the blocks for the parables and the *Cornhill.* I will come very soon, and will then get on with 'The Poacher's Wife' and other work."

" *August 14th.* — I have finished all my work except the parables, which I can do in the North. Bradbury and

Evans want to buy my woodcut services, and I see them
with Leech to-day at one. I will not bind myself in any
way. At the same time, if they make me a thoroughly
good offer, it is worth considering. Leech says he thinks
they would give me £500 a year if I could regularly supply
them; but this has to be considered, as I cannot let illustration interfere with my painting. It is pleasant to hear of
my wood drawings rising to so much value. . . ."

Down to this time his black-and-white drawings, of which
he made many, principally for contemporary literature, were
done on boxwood, and destroyed in the process of cutting-in.
Happily, however, the highly-finished illustrations, of which
he did a large number in 1853 and the three following years,
were drawn on paper in pen and ink, and finished in sepia-
wash or body colour; so most of these drawings are still left
in their original state, instead of being cut to pieces and
ruined by the barbarians of the wood-cutting art.

Truly the wood-cutters of that day had much to answer
for. Except, perhaps, Swain, Dalziel, and John Thompson
(who cut the Tennyson blocks) not one of them had the
faintest conception of how to retain the beautiful and delicate
lines of the original drawings; and even the best work of
these experts would make the hair of the engravers of
Harper's Magazine stand on end nowadays.

The black-and-white artists of to-day have their drawings
reproduced by various processes, which leave little to be
desired; but if they could see, as I have done, some of my
father's wood blocks before and after the drawings had been
cut upon, they would indeed feel how much their predecessors
had to suffer — even more, perhaps, than the old Celt of
historic fame, who exclaimed, as he held his head in church
on Sabbath morning, after "a nicht wi' Burns," "Puir auld
Scotland, ye 're sons are sair afflicted, whiles."

The choicest of my father's black-and-white drawings have
never been seen by any but the family. I am therefore all
the more glad to give some of them here, reproduced by our
best modern processes. Very few people have any idea of the
labour and care that he expended on these drawings. Each
one of them was to him a carefully thought-out picture, worthy
of the best work that he could put into it; and I think it will
be seen from the specimens here given that he did not over-
estimate the value of the art. He maintained, indeed, that the
few men quite at the top of the tree, both in line and wash,

were entitled to rank with the best exponents of oil and water-colour ; and if he had lived I feel quite sure that, with his keen desire to encourage true Art, in whatever form displayed, we should in time see workers in black-and-white admitted as freely to the honours of the Academy as are the line-engravers.

Few and far between are those who could ever hope to achieve this distinction, but I have no hesitation in saying that infinitely better Art is to be found in *Harper's Magazine*, the *Century*, *Scribner's*, our Art magazines, and the best illus-trated books of the day (and now and then in the *Graphic* and the *Illustrated London News*) than in one-half the pic-tures that hang on the walls of the Royal Academy and other Art galleries.

Look at the drawings of such men as Phil May, Caton Woodville, C. D. Gibson, E. A. Abbey, Alfred Parsons, Frederick Remington, E. Smedley, Reginald Cleaver, Archibald Thorburn, John Gulich, D. Hatherell, Frank Brangwyn, and half a dozen others of similar standing. Many of these are supremely excellent as works of Art ; and yet they are not only unrecognised by the powers that be, but go for nothing in the market by comparison with hun-dreds of old engravings that have nothing but their antiquity and their rarity to recommend them. And why? Simply because they are not in fashion. No recognised connoisseur of Art has taken up black-and-white work with a view to a collection ; and since few men dare to trust to their own judgment as buyers of Art works, fashion (too often but a passing phase of ignorance and vulgarity) controls the market. It may be said, perhaps, that as a black-and-white artist myself I am disposed to overrate the value of this class of work. My answer is that I have said here only what I have so often heard from my father — a man who touched every branch of the painter's art, who succeeded in all, and who knew the difficulties and relative values of each.

In 1860 he made a whole series of drawings for Anthony Trollope's novel *Framley Parsonage* — drawings afterwards sold to Mr. Plint, the dealer who, years before, had bought his " Christ in the House of His Parents " — besides illustra-tions for the *Cornhill Magazine*, and a considerable amount of work for Bradbury and Evans. And from this time onwards, down to 1869, he was chiefly engaged in black-and-white work and water-colour drawings, under commis-sions from various publishers and picture dealers, including

Hurst and Blackett, Chapman and Hall, Bradbury and
Evans, Smith and Elder, Dalziel Brothers, and Gambart.
He also did a little work for the *Illustrated London News*
and drawings for *Punch*, one of which is referred to in
the last chapter, the works illustrated by him during this
period including Trollope's novel, *Orley Farm*, and occasional
numbers of the *Cornhill Magazine, Good Words, London
Society*, etc.

The money he received for these drawings was but a
nominal recompense for the labour bestowed upon them ; for,
unless perfectly satisfied with the finished production, he
would tear it up at once, even if he had spent whole days
upon it, scamped work in any shape being an abomination
in his eyes. It was a constant source of lament to him that,
under the pressure of monetary needs, even first-rate men
were sometimes compelled to turn out more work than they
could possibly do with credit to themselves. He would
notice this now and then in the illustrated literature of the
day, and out would come the remark, " Another poor devil
gone wrong for the sake of a few sovereigns ! "

He himself liked the work as an occasional change from
oils ; but knowing how little the pencil could make by comparison with the brush, he refused to be drawn into regular
magazine work, which (not altogether without reason) Marie
Corelli stigmatises as " the slough of despond." His best
work of this sort, and one of the best examples of wood-
cutting, were to be seen in the series of drawings representing " The Parables of our Lord." They were engraved by
the brothers Dalziel, and he made replicas of them in water-
colour for a window that he afterwards presented to Kinnoull
parish church in memory of my late brother George — to my
mind one of the most beautiful windows in Great Britain.
All the backgrounds to the parables were drawn from
Nature at or around Bowerswell, and many of the landscapes
can be easily recognised, having altered little since 1862.

During this time, too, he seems to have done a great
number of water-colours, most of them being either copies
of, or designs for, his larger works. For these there was a
constant demand, and the dealers worried him into painting
no less than seven or eight water-colour replicas of " The
Black Brunswicker " and " The Huguenot." He also made
one or more copies of " The Ransom," " My First Sermon,"
" My Second Sermon," " The Minuet," " The Vale of Rest,"

"Sir Isumbras," and "Swallow, Swallow, Flying South,"
nearly all of which were bought by either Gambart or
Agnew. Indeed, if a complete collection of his water-
colour and black-and-white works at this period could be got
together, they would make, I venture to think, almost as
interesting an exhibition as that of 1897, in which scarcely
one of them was included.

In 1860 he took the shooting of Kincraig, Inverness-shire,

OLD WALL OF BALHOUSIE CASTLE, PERTH
Used by Millais in his background of "James' Love"

along with his friend Colonel Aitkin, and after some hesitation (as expressed in the following letter to his wife) he threw
aside his work in the month of August, and hastened to join
his friend in the North.

"*August 17th,* 1860. — I write this amongst a great gathering of men and ladies, one of whom is at this moment
singing most beautifully. Mr. Mitchell (the clergyman who
married William) is here, and Arnold and his wife. Miss
Power is also here, and sings charmingly. Mrs. Cobb, too,

and her husband, in rifle-corps uniform, fresh from drill. The ladies are all working at needlework whilst the music is going on, and as I cannot talk I employ myself in writing. Arthur Coleridge brought his wife here this afternoon, and she appears to be quite charming.

"I have just received yours, enclosing Aitkin's letter. I don't know but what I may yet come straight up to the shooting, and bring the copy I am working at, as I can finish it anywhere for the matter of that. I don't mean to say I would paint at the shooting-lodge, but would finish it afterwards at Bowerswell. I feel certain that no other man in my position would neglect his holiday; so, instead of grinding on, I shall have a fling at that place. The house appears roomy, and you could go with me. I am sick of hearing of everybody going to his shooting. No one would enjoy it more than I, instead of having to stick to this beastly copying ['The Black Brunswicker']. . . . I feel a good deal better to-day, hearing of the sport that Aitkin is having. Please send me the 'Framley' manuscript, as I want to get all these drawings done and out of my hands."

He took his holiday, and then, returning to Bowerswell, he worked hard at "The Poacher's Wife" and "The Ransom," and in the spring of 1861 he went back to town, where he had engaged rooms at 130 Piccadilly, with a studio attached. From there he wrote to my mother : —

"*May 27th*, 1861. — I am sorry to hear that your mother is so ill. . . . Monckton Milnes came just now with a friend. He was charmed with the picture ['The Ransom'], and says that Stirling, of Keir, should have it; he himself is so enchanted with it that he will probably have it himself. I had a very pleasant dinner at the Leslies', Lady Waterford, Lady Mills, and many others there. On Wednesday I go to Epsom, to see the Derby, with Joseph Jopling [an artist and intimate friend].

"On Saturday I went to Tattersall's, to see the betting-room and paddock, where I saw, among others, some friends of yours. Young S—— [a boy from Perth, who had just come into a little money], with his betting-book in his hand, was quite surprised to see me there and, I thought, disconcerted, by the way he hurried off. Poor young fool, he will certainly bring about a speedy smash in such society as I saw him — being with Lord S——, men with millions, and the sharpest rogues in the world.

"Jopling is staying with friends in the country, so I do not see much of him. I am alone here all day, and only occasionally disturbed by callers. . . . Yesterday I went to Thackeray's house at Kensington, and it is beautiful; and in the evening, after the Leslies, I went to the Cosmopolitan, and got home very, very late — or rather early. Fortunately, with all this dining out, I feel in the best of condition and spirits."

He had now bought No. 7 Cornwall Place, South Kensington, which, when remodelled under the direction of his architect, Mr. Freake, he used as the town house of himself and his family from the winter of 1862 to 1878, when they finally took possession of the large house that he built at Palace Gate.

"*May 28th,* 1861. — Sir Coutts Lindsay, Lady Somers. and Mrs. Dalrymple have just been here, and were in ecstasies about the picture. Although I ask a big price for it, which the dealers are trying to beat down, I shall not give way an inch, as they are certain to resell it immediately to some nobleman's collection, and make an immense profit by it. Last evening I dined with Lord Lansdowne. We had a delightful dinner : everything most magnificent. The beautiful Lady Waterford was there, and I had a long talk with her. She is rather handsomer than when I saw her seven years ago — a little stouter, and certainly the *noblest-looking woman I ever saw.* She is coming to see my picture, but returns to her castle in Northumberland immediately. She asked after you. General Hamilton, too, who dined with us in York Terrace, was there.

" I went afterwards to Captain Murray's, and to the Alhambra to see Leotard, a French gymnast, who flies through the air from swinging ropes — very extraordinary. To-morrow is the Derby, and to-day I have been working most successfully, having nearly finished the other illustration for Hurst and Blackett — one of the 'Orley Farm' ones — and the fourth one for Mr. Plint. My model, Miss Beale, was sitting until Sir Coutts Lindsay and his party came, and held in her arms a baby, *which I had borrowed !* I have heard nothing from Freake; but the studio is progressing.

" Dalziel was here yesterday, and very anxious to get me to finish the drawings of the parables by next year for the great exhibition, and I of course promised to do my best."

"*May* 30*th.* — Yesterday morning, before going to the
Derby, I called to see Lady Waterford and her drawings.
She was so pleased, I think, for I found her drawings
magnificent, so I could praise honestly. She was very kind
and nice, and begged particularly to be remembered to you.

"Yesterday at the Derby was the usual crowd and dust;

WATER-COLOUR DESIGN FOR "THE RANSOM." 1862

but I only got a small headache this time, and slept it
off in an hour or so, after which I got up and went to
Lewis's Club, where he gave Jopling and myself something
to eat. After that we went to Cremorne. One striking
fact which greatly astonished me was the absence of in-
toxication. I never saw one man or woman drunk the
whole day, and must have passed thousands upon thousands
of people; nor did I see a single row either at the race-

course or the gardens, to which almost the whole company came straight from the course. The gardens were beautifully lit up with thousands of lamps, and the night was warm and lovely. Then there was dancing on the greensward — of course, amongst a certain class. Two splendid bands of music, and eating and drinking in every direction ; yet not a single person drunk. I am very fresh this morning, and going on with the ' Orley Farm ' illustrations. Jopling, too, is up, and beautiful in summer array. Last night, of course, I saw everybody, from every place I know — Perth men from their regiments, Stirling of Keir, Monckton Milnes, Leech, Thackeray, William, Jue (his wife), and the Hoares. . . .

"This evening I spend quietly with Dalziel, to look over proofs and talk the parables over, and on Saturday I have promised to go to Kingston and see my people, and perhaps row up the river, as they propose a picnic."

"*June 6th*, 1861. — Plint has just been here and bought the picture of Mrs. Aitkin and John Lindsay, and I have promised to paint a small oil for him of Lucy Roberts. Plint gave X—— £1150 for ' The Black Brunswicker,' * and some time ago gave him £1000 for ' The Royalist.' *So much for X—— telling me that he had lost by me !* Now, when he comes, I will say nothing to lead him to suppose that I know all about it ; but it puts me on my guard for the future."

" The Ransom," however (his big picture), was not sold ; so he went to Bowerswell at the beginning of August, and had some pleasant days, trout-fishing at Loch Leven with Leech and John Anderson, the minister of Kinnoull.

Before closing this chapter it is necessary to say a few words about " The Ransom " and its subsequent history. Commenced with " Trust Me " in the autumn of 1860, the picture was not completed till the spring of 1862. The subject is that of the detention of two maidens who had been captured during the Middle Ages. The girls are seen in the act of returning to their father, a black-bearded knight, who in turn has to present gold and gems for their release. The costumes in this picture were most carefully studied. " Most of them," says my mother, " were made by me, and I designed them from a book on costume lent by Lady Eastlake." She

* When first sold to a dealer " The Black Brunswicker " fetched £816. In May, 1898, it was sold by the executors of the late James Renton for £2,650.

then gives a few particulars as to the background and models. " The tapestry was the last part which was painted. It was done in the unfinished portion of the South Kensington Museum, where Mr. Smith, the decorator, hung it in position for the artist. Millais had great trouble with the knight. The head was taken from his friend Major Boothby, who gave him many sittings ; but at the last moment he considered the expression unsuitable, and so called in the services of a Mr. Miller. The figure of the knight he drew from a gigantic railway guard, appropriately named ' Strong,' who was afterwards crushed to death in Perth Station. The page was a handsome youth named Reid, and Major McBean, 92nd Highlanders, and a labourer sat for the guards. Both the girls were painted from one model, Miss Helen Petrie."

THE autumn of 1861 was spent in Sutherlandshire, where, as I gather from his letters, Millais found great enjoyment, while fishing and shooting along with his friend "Mike" Halliday. In August of that year they were staying at Lairg, from which he writes to my mother:—

"We dined on Sunday at Rose Hall, and enjoyed it immensely; they were so kind. Lord and Lady Delamere were there, and he is a capital fellow. In the evening, after dinner, we drew blindfolded several subjects, and the result was absurd, as you may imagine. We dine here again next Sunday. Both Holford and his wife were most kind, and expressed great regret that they could not give us beds. Yesterday Mike and I shot all the day, but the ground is very inferior to Kincraig. Poor little man, he could n't walk the hillsides, and was done up so completely that he could n't shoot a bit. Halliday only shot three brace, which made in all seventeen brace and a half, *all of which*, by Mr. Holford's orders, is left to us. I send away a box to you, and another to Kingston."

In another letter he says:—

"I am almost sorry I sent you the grilse yesterday, for I killed a fine salmon this morning, 10 lbs. weight. I hooked

368 JOHN EVERETT MILLAIS [1862

it when far away from anyone, and had the fish on for more
than half an hour without being able to make anybody hear
my shouting. At last Mike caught sight of me waving my
bonnet, and came to my assistance with the gaff, and after
playing the fish until it was quite done, he succeeded in
securing it. It was a beautiful clean salmon (not grilse) just
up from the salt water. It struggled awfully, and took me
down the river in the most gallant way. We have just
returned from dining with the Holfords, who are indefatigable in their kindness and attention. I never experienced
such unaffected kindness, and Mike finds the same. Poor
little chap, he hasn't even risen a fish at all yet, except
trout."

The letter winds up with an injunction to practise croquet,
which was all the rage just then.

The later autumn days and the following winter were
mainly devoted to painting " The Woman Looking for the Lost
Piece of Money " — showing a female figure in the moonlight
holding a lighted candle, with which she searches the floor.
The picture unhappily came to an untimely end, but an
engraving of it (made before it left the artist's hands) gives
some idea of the striking effects of mingled moonlight and
candle-light as depicted. In 1862 Millais gave the picture to
Baron Marochetti in exchange for a marble bust of my
mother by this famous sculptor, and one day the gas meter
in the Baron's house in Onslow Square exploded, and the
picture (frame and all) was shot through the window into the
street, and completely destroyed.

During the spring of 1862 he was hard at work on a
portrait of Mr. Puxley, a hunting squire, and the little picture
of " The White Cockade," in which a Highland lady is seen
attaching the white badge of the Jacobites to her lover's
cocked hat. My mother sat for this picture, and an excellent
portrait of her at that time is preserved there. A Scotch
friend, hearing by chance of the subject of the painting, was
good enough to present her with one of the original cockades
worn in the bonnets of Prince Charlie's followers — a badge
now extremely rare.

The summer of this year was an exceedingly busy one for
the artist. He did an immense quantity of work for *London
Society*, Messrs. Smith, Elder, and Co., Macmillan, Chapman
and Hall, Sampson Low and Co., Dalziel, and Bradbury and
Evans, and something too for the *Illustrated London News.*

"SWALLOW! SWALLOW!" 1864

From the water-colour in possession of Mrs. Stibbard

By permission of Sir John Kelk

In the Academy he exhibited "The Ransom" (sometimes called "The Hostage"), "Trust Me," "The Parable of the Lost Piece of Money," and "Mrs. Charles Freeman." And, as a joyful prelude to his autumn holiday, another little olive-branch appeared on the scene in the person of my sister Carrie (now Mrs. Stuart-Wortley).

August was now at hand, and with a light heart he fled away to his beloved Scotland, where he had taken care to secure beforehand what promised to afford excellent sport. First of all he went to the Helmsdale, the fishing of which he and his friend, Colonel Cholmondeley, had taken for that month. There, however, the fates favoured the fish rather than the fishermen, and at the end of the month he moved on to Inveran Inn, near Tain, where Mike Halliday and he had part of the river Shin for the month of September. Here another disappointment awaited him as to the fishing; but his letters show that in other respects the holiday was an enjoyable one. Writing to my mother on September 2nd, he says:—

"I arrived here yesterday morning at half-past five, and travelled all night, never getting a wink of sleep. However, when I had had a tub I felt all right. There was no bed for me anyhow. Brandreth was here, and left this morning with his wife, who came up from Dunrobin. He is a most kind fellow—took me out shooting all yesterday, and the result will come to you in the shape of a box of grouse. Mike took Mr. B.'s gun in the evening, and we got ten more brace, which made it a good day. Mr. B. has given me all his part of the river to fish in, besides the right to shoot with Mike on a moor fifteen or sixteen miles away from here; also to take three days on the moor immediately adjoining this inn, where we killed the birds yesterday. It is very fortunate, as the fishing is *very bad* this year. I went out last evening, after the shooting, and only rose one fish. . . . The Cholmondeleys were very sorry at my leaving, and were most kind. You may expect to see him in Perth about the 15th. Brandreth also gave me a *magnificent* salmon-rod—*insisted* on my taking it—and supplied us with a lot of lights and tobacco. Leech is not here yet. Have you heard of him? The river is too low here now, strange to say, and last year it was too high."

Towards the end of the season he took up his quarters at

Bowerswell; and with a view to the well-known picture, "My First Sermon," my sister Effie, then a child of five years, was selected as the model.   She also sat two years later for the companion picture of "My Second Sermon," and from that time onwards all the children in turn were enlisted as models for different pictures.

Later on in the autumn of 1862 some lines in Keats' beautiful poem, "The Eve of St. Agnes," caught the fancy of the artist, inviting him to illustrate them on canvas; and this he determined to do at once.

> " Full on this casement shone the wintry moon,
> And threw warm gules on Madeline's fair breast.
>
> *   *   *   *
>
> Of all its wreathed pearls her hair she frees ;
> Unclasps her warmed jewels one by one ;
> Loosens her fragrant bodice ; by degrees
> Her rich attire creeps rustling to her knees :
> Half-hidden, like a mermaid in seaweed,
> Pensive awhile she dreams awake, and sees
> In fancy fair St. Agnes in her bed.
> But dares not look behind, or all the charm is fled."

But where was a suitable background to be found?   The picture, as conceived by the artist, demanded an interior such as was not to be seen in Scotland, so far as he knew; but in the historic mansion of Knole Park was a room well known to him, and exactly suited to his purpose.   So, coming South rather earlier than usual this year, he and my mother betook themselves to Sevenoaks, where, at a wayside hostelry, they remained throughout December.

Knole was close by — a large house tenanted by an old caretaker — and, except the floor (then covered with modern parquetry), this wonderful old room had undergone no change whatever since the time of James I.   The old furniture and fittings of solid silver were still there, the same old tapestry adorned the walls, and a death-like stillness pervaded the apartment — "a silence that might be felt" at the midnight hour when the moonlight was streaming in through the window and no fire was burning on the hearth.   And yet that was the time when the picture must be painted — that and a few hours later — otherwise the exact direction of the moonbeams falling on the figure could not be caught.   No wonder, then, that my father, though by no means a nervous man, was sensible of a high state of tension while sitting at his work for three nights in succession amidst such weird and comfortless surroundings. My mother, too — for she it was who sat for the figure — was similarly affected, while her discomfort during those weary hours may be readily imagined. Think of the slender garments in which the figure is draped, the bodice unlaced, the room unheated ; and this in the depth of winter !   No wonder that she was accustomed to speak of it afterwards as the severest task she ever undertook.   But the reward came at last, making amends for all it cost to win it.   The painter caught the spirit of the poet, and embodied it in his canvas.   The finishing touches were done at Cromwell Place,* with the aid of a professional model, Miss Ford.

SKETCH FOR "THE EVE OF ST. AGNES"

My mother says in her notes : — " This picture was marvellously quickly executed.   After three days and a half at Knole and two days more at home, the work was complete, and highly finished.   The magnificent bed represented was that in which King James I. slept. It cost £3000, and the coverlet was a mass of gold thread and silver appliqué gimp and lace ; the sheets were white silk, and the mattresses of padded cotton wool.

" Millais' fingers got numb with the cold, but there was no time to be lost, as the private view day was drawing near. When we got back from Knole the figure of Madeline had to be altered ; and when the work was exhibited the public thought the woman ugly, thin, and stiff. 'I cannot bear that woman with the gridiron,' said Frank Grant (Sir Francis Grant, P. R. A.), alluding to the vivid streams of moonlight on the floor ; and Tom Taylor said, 'Where on earth did you get that scraggy model, Millais?'"

---

* Millais lit up his canvas with a bull's-eye lantern when painting this subject in London. He found that the light from even a full moon was not strong enough to throw, through a stained glass window, perceptible colour on any object, as Keats had supposed and described in his poem.

The picture, after passing successively through the hands of Mr. Charles Lucas and Mr. Leyland, is now in the possession of Mr. Val Prinsep, R.A. It was seen by Art lovers on the walls of South Kensington, and was amongst the works in the recent " Millais Exhibition " at Burlington House.

An appreciative letter from Val Prinsep is of interest as showing what artists thought of this work. Writing to Millais he says : —

" It was a great pleasure to me, my dear old chap, to be able to purchase your picture. There is not an artist who has failed to urge me to do so. For the profession's sake I am glad your picture is in the hands of one of the craft, for it is essentially a painter's picture. After all, what do the public and the critics know about the matter? Nothing! The worst is, they think they do, and hence comes the success of many a commonplace work and the comparative neglect of what is full of genius. I 've got the genius bit, and am delighted.   Yours ever,

" VAL PRINSEP."

No sooner was it finished than, in execution of a commission from Mr. Marley, of Regent's Park, the artist set to work on a portrait of Mr. Henry Manners, now Marquis of Granby. Other pictures, too, followed in quick succession, notably " Suspense," " The Bridesmaid throwing the Lucky Slipper," and " The Wolf's Den," the last-named showing portraits of all the artist's elder children.

For the rest, the year (1863) was one of mingled joy and sorrow. In September my brother Geoffroy was born ; but a few months later the sudden death of Thackeray, the bright and genial novelist, cast a deep gloom over the household, both my father and mother being devotedly attached to him. They had noticed with distress his failing health and loss of appetite, when dining with them shortly before their annual migration to the North ; but neither of them ever dreamt that this was the last time that they and he would meet. In a letter to my mother on Christmas Day my father wrote : —

" I am sure you will be dreadfully shocked, as I was, at the loss of poor Thackeray. I imagine, and hope truly, you will have heard of it before this reaches you. He was found dead by his servant in the morning, and of course the

"THE EVE OF ST. AGNES." 1863

By permission of Mr. Valentine Prinsep, R.A

whole house is in a state of the utmost confusion and pain.
They first sent to Charlie Collins and his wife, who went
immediately, and have been almost constantly there ever
since. I sent this morning to know how the mother and
girls were, and called myself this afternoon; and they are
suffering terribly, as you might expect. He was found lying
back, with his arms over his head, as though in great pain.
I shall hear more, of course. Everyone I meet is affected
by his death. Nothing else is spoken of."

And again, three days later : ---

" I go to-morrow with Walker, Prinsep, and Theodore
Martin, to poor Thackeray's funeral — Kensal Green Ceme-
tery; half-past twelve. I send every day to ask after the
mother and girls. They are dreadfully broken by the
death.

" My model is waiting, so I must leave off now. I made
a beautiful little drawing of Lady Edwards' baby lying in the
bassinet. Of course I had to idealise somewhat, as there
was a look of pain in the face.

" I had five men dining with me last night, and the
conversation was entirely about the loss we have all sus-
tained. Cayley, Doyle, Prinsep, Martineau, and Jopling
were the party."

In another letter, on December 31st, he added : —

" I went yesterday to the funeral, in Theodore Martin's
carriage. It was a mournful scene, and badly managed. A
crowd of women were there — from curiosity, I suppose —
dressed in all colours; and round the grave scarlet and
blue feathers shone out prominently! Indeed, the true
mourners and friends could not get near, and intimate
friends who were present had to be hustled into their places
during the ceremony of interment. We all, of course,
followed from the chapel, and by that time the grave was
surrounded. There was a great lack of what is called
'high society,' which I was surprised at. None of that
class, of whom he knew so many, were present. The
painters were *nearly all* there — more even than the literary
men. The review of his life and works you sent me is
quite beautiful — just what it ought to be — I suppose by Dr.
John Brown, who was a great friend."

" My First Sermon " was exhibited this year in the
Academy, and at the Academy banquet on May 3rd, when
(according to a newspaper report now before me) the

Archbishop of Canterbury, in a graceful speech, referred to it as follows : —

"Still, Art has, and ever will have, a high and noble mission to fulfil. That man, I think, is little to be envied who can pass through these rooms and go forth without being in some sense a better and a happier man; if at least it be so (as I do believe it to be) that we feel our-selves the better and the happier when our hearts are enlarged as we sympathise with the joys and the sorrows of our fellow-men, faithfully delineated on the canvas; when our spirits are touched by the playfulness, the innocence, the purity, and may I not add (pointing to Millais' picture of 'My First Sermon') the piety of childhood."

This little picture of Effie* was extremely popular. The artist himself was so pleased with it that, before going North in August of that year, he made an oil copy of it, doing the work from start to finish in two days! A truly marvellous achievement, considering that the copy displayed almost the same high finish as the original; but in those two days he worked incessantly from morning to night, never even break-ing off for lunch in the middle of the day. Well might he say, as he did in a letter to my mother, "I never did any-thing in my life so well or so quickly." The copy was sold as soon as it was finished, and I see from an entry in my mother's book that he received £180 for it.

He was now, so far as I can judge, at the summit of his powers in point of both physical strength and technical skill, the force and rapidity of his execution being simply amazing.

Leaving my mother at Bowerswell early in January, 1864, he returned to town, where, soon after his arrival, John Leech came to see him. As an old and intimate friend of Thackeray, Leech was distressed beyond measure by his death. He should never get over it, he said; and a month or two later his words gained a painful significance by his own death from heart disease. My father was constantly with him during the last stage of this terrible complaint, and never ceased to lament the loss of his old friend and companion.

This year proved to be most prolific of all in point of work. Writing to my mother on January 13th, he said : —

"I will come and look out for a background for 'Moses.'

* "My First" and "My Second Sermon" were both painted in the old church at Kingston-on-Thames, where Millais' parents resided. The old high-backed pews had not then been removed.

I am just going to begin Effie sleeping in the pew. It is very dark, but enough light for drawing. Have done both 'Arabian Nights' drawings, and another (two since you left) illustration for *Good Words*. I missed my train to Trollope on Sunday, and had to take a hansom all the way to Waltham — two hours there, and two back, but I got there in time for dinner.

" Hablot Brown is illustrating his new serial. Chapman is publishing it, and he is not pleased with the illustrating, and proposed to me to take it off his hands, but I declined. Messrs. C. and H. gave him so much more for his novel that they wished to save in the illustrations, and now Trollope is desirous of foregoing his extra price to have it done by me."

" Effie sleeping in the pew " was, as indicated above, the subject of " My Second Sermon," in which, the novelty of the situation having worn off, the child is seen fast asleep, being overcome by the heat of the church, and probably by the soporific influence of the pulpit. The Archbishop of Canterbury referred also to this work in his speech at the Academy banquet in 1865. According to the newspapers of the period his words were : —

" I would say for myself that I always desire to derive profit as well as pleasure from my visits to these rooms. On the present occasion I have learnt a very wholesome lesson, which may be usefully studied, not by myself alone, but by those of my right reverend brethren also who surround me. I see a little lady there (pointing to Mr. Millais' picture of a child asleep in church, entitled ' My Second Sermon '), who, though all unconscious whom she has been addressing, and the homily she has been reading to us during the last three hours, has in truth, by the eloquence of her silent slumber, given us *a warning of the evil of lengthy sermons and drowsy discourses*. Sorry indeed should I be to disturb that sweet and peaceful slumber, but I beg that when she does awake she may be informed who they are who have pointed the moral of her story, have drawn the true inference from the change that has passed over her since she has heard her ' first sermon,' and have resolved to profit by the lecture she has thus delivered to them."

" Leisure hours," a picture combining the portraits of Mr. John Pender's two daughters, was next taken up. Then came " Charlie is My Darling," a picture for which Lady Pallisser sat, and to which a little romance is attached. Whilst

Millais was at work on this picture Sir William Pallisser visited the studio, where he was much struck with the face of the lady as portrayed. He begged for and obtained an

"MY SECOND SERMON." 1863
By permission of H. Graves and Son

introduction, and afterwards falling deeply in love with one another, she became Lady Pallisser. That work, too, was exhibited this year, and is now in the possession of an old friend of my father's, Mr. James Reiss. An illustration in

"LEISURE HOURS." 1864

By permission of Lady des l'œux

oils of Tennyson's charming "Swallow, Swallow, Flying South," was also in hand now, for which my mother's sister, Alice Gray (now Mrs. Stibbard) sat; but the picture, though finished in time for the Academy, was not exhibited till the following year.

A portrait of Harold, son of the Dowager Countess of Winchelsea, was also painted this year, and satisfied with the work already done, Millais went off in July to the Helmsdale to try his luck once more as a fisherman. Of his life there, and the sport he met with, I have unfortunately no record, as, my mother being with him, no letters passed between them.

It was in the late autumn of 1864 that the artist completed an excellent portrait of Wyclif Taylor, son of his friend Tom Taylor, of *Punch* fame — a portrait that seems to have given great satisfaction to the parents.

From Tom Taylor.

"8 RICHMOND TERRACE, WHITEHALL, S. W.,
"*December 27th,* 1864.

"MY DEAR MILLAIS, — I cannot allow the day to pass without thanking you for your beautiful portrait of our boy. It is an exquisite picture of a child, and a perfect likeness. Both his mother and myself feel that you have given us a quite inimitable treasure, which, long years hence, will enable us to recall what our boy was at the age when childhood is loveliest and finest. Should we lose him — which Heaven avert — the picture will be more precious still.

"It seems to us the sweetest picture of a child even *you* have painted. If you would like to have it exhibited, I need not say it is at your service for the purpose.

"With renewed thanks, and all the best wishes of the season for you and yours,

"Believe me, ever gratefully yours,
"TOM TAYLOR.

"P.S. — I send you my Christmas gift in return, however inadequate. The . . . Ballad Book, which owes so much to your pencil."

I have suggested that in point of technical skill Millais attained the zenith of his power in 1864, but the fact is too plain to be overlooked, that 1865 marked a distinct advance in the direction of larger and more important pictures, and greater breadth of treatment. His first picture this year was " The Evil One Sowing Tares"; and then came " Esther " and " The Romans Leaving Britain," both of which present a fulness of power and facility of expression such as he had never before displayed, and this too without any sacrifice of the high finish that characterised his earlier works. In these pictures he seems to have accomplished with a single dash of the brush effects that, in former years, he attained only by hours of hard work.

Miss Susan Ann Mackenzie, sister of Sir Alexander Mackenzie, sat for the principal figure in " Esther."

A lady kindly furnishes me with the following note : —

" The robe thrown over the shoulders of 'Esther' was General Gordon's 'Yellow Jacket.' * In this 'Yellow Jacket' General Gordon sat to Valentine Prinsep, R.A., for the portrait for the Royal Engineers' mess-room at Chatham. Millais so admired this splendid piece of brocade that he dressed Miss Muir Mackenzie in it, but *turning it inside out*, so as to have broader masses of colour. With her fine hair unbound, and a royal crown in her hand, she sat for ' Queen Esther.' The picture was bought from a dealer by my husband, and it has since passed to Mr. Alex. Henderson with the rest of his collection."

Millais was painting Miss Mackenzie's head when the Yellow Jacket was brought in, and, as he draped it on her, he said: " There! That is my idea of Queen Esther; you must let me paint you like that."

The subject of " The Romans leaving Britain " is one which had always had a great attraction for Millais. We see here, as Mr. Stephens says, " the parting between a Roman legionary and his British mistress. They are placed on a cliff-path overlooking the sea, where a large galley is waiting for the soldier. He kneels at the woman's feet, with his arms clasped about her body; his face, though unhelmeted, is hidden from us in her breast ; her hands are upon his shoulders, and she looks steadfastly, with a passionate, eager, savage stare upon the melancholy waste of the grey and restless sea."

---

* " At the end of the Taeping Rebellion, and when Gordon gave up the command of the 'ever-victorious army,' the Chinese Government tried to offer him rewards. He would take nothing but the rank of Ti-Tu, or Field Marshal, and the ' rare and high dignity of the *Yellow Jacket*.' " — BOULGER'S *Life of Gordon*, vol. i. p. 122.

The sentiment and pathos of this picture were much admired, and soon after the close of the Exhibition (1865) Millais received the following interesting letter from Miss Anne Thackeray, daughter of the novelist before referred to, written from the home of the Tennysons at Freshwater, Isle of Wight: —

"I thought of you one day last week when we took a walk with Tennyson and came to some cliffs, a sweep of sand, and the sea; and I almost expected to see poor Boadicea up on the cliff, with her passionate eyes. I heard Mr. Watts and Mr. Prinsep looking for her somewhere else, but I am sure mine was on the cliff. Mr. Watts has been painting Hallam and Lionel Tennyson. We hear him when we wake, playing his fiddle in the early morning. They are all so kind to us that we do not know how to be grateful enough. We have had all sorts of stray folk. Jowett and the Dean of Christchurch, and cousins without number. It has been very pleasant and sunshiny, and we feel as if we should like to live on here in lodgings all the rest of our lives. Last night 'King Alfred' read out 'Maude.' It was like beautiful harmonious thunder and lightning. . . . I cannot help longing to know the fate of 'Esther' . . . . after she went in through the curtains."

The daughter of Scott Russell (the engineer of the *Great Eastern*) sat for the British maiden " Boadicea," and the picture ultimately became the property of Sir Lowthian Bell. The background was painted down at Truro in Cornwall, where for a week Millais was the guest of Bishop Phillpotts at Porthwidden.

At this time he had some idea of painting one of the closing scenes in the life of Mary Queen of Scots, and with a view to this he exchanged several letters with Froude, the historian, who kindly gave him all the information in his power. His letters, however, went to prove that the incident the artist had in mind had no foundation in fact, so the idea was at once abandoned.

In July he commenced the picture known as "Waking"—a portrait of my sister Mary sitting up in bed—and was getting well on with it when his little model showed signs of illness that compelled him to leave off for a time. It was finished, however, later on, and is now in the collection of Mr. Philip Harter, of Leamington. A bed, with all its accessories, is not commonly a thing of beauty, but in this case the artist made it so, the high finish of the still-life adding greatly to the general effect. Writing to my mother on the 29th of this month, he says: — " I am working very hard. Have commenced the duplicates of ' Esther,' and commence the Romans to-day. ' Joan of Arc ' is gone, and I am hourly expecting Agnew to send for Alice [' Swallow, Swallow ']."

On August 12th he and his friend Reginald Cholmondeley went off to the North — this time to Argyle, where Sir William Harcourt had taken a shooting called Dalhenna, amongst the lovely hills near Inverary. The great leader of the Liberals proved a most admirable host, and many are the good stories told of the jovial times the three friends had together. How Millais enjoyed it may be gathered from the following letters to his wife, all dated in August, 1866. In the first he says : —

" Harcourt and I shot twenty-three brace yesterday in a frightful sun, and enjoyed the day very much. Cholmondeley is not well (knocked up by the heat), so he didn't accompany us. H. is sending all the birds to England, and we don't like to have birds for ourselves. The cuisine is like that of a good club. His cook is here and manservant, and the comfort is great — altogether delightful — and the grapes and peaches were thoroughly appreciated. The Duke and Duchess of Sutherland left yesterday. She looked so pretty at luncheon on Sunday. We have a great deal of laughing. To-day we are going to fish in Loch Fyne for *Lythe*, which afford good sport ; and to-morrow we shoot again. Cholmondeley has his keeper and dogs with him. H. has a kilted keeper of his own, besides the ponies for the hill with saddlebags. We are going to visit the islands in a yacht, as the rivers are too dry for fishing salmon.

" I have been unusually well since coming here, and very merry. Lord Lorne is a very nice pleasant fellow, and all the family are kindly, and as soon as the Duke returns we are to dine there. Our cottage is such a pretty spot — roses and convolvulus and honeysuckle over the porch, and a swallow feeding her young within reach of our hands."

Of these Dalhenna days Millais loved to recall an amusing incident, the hero being one of the three shooters, who shall be nameless. One evening during a casual stroll about the domain, the sportsman spied a magnificent " horned beast "

"THE ROMANS LEAVING BRITAIN." 1865

By permission of Sir Lothian Bell

grazing peacefully on their little hill. In the gloaming it loomed up as a stag of fine proportions ; and without pausing to examine it through a glass, he rushed into the house, and, seizing a rifle, advanced upon his quarry with all the stealth and cunning of an accomplished stalker. The crucial moment came at last. His finger was on the trigger, and the death of the animal a certainty, when a raucous Highland voice bellowed in his ear, " Ye 're no gaen to shute the meenister's goat, are ye ? " Tableau !

In a second letter to my mother he says : — " Harcourt is having a new grate put into his kitchen, to soften his cook. We have come in the dog-cart here for the day, taking boat at Cladich and leaving it almost immediately in terror, from the unsafeness of the boat in heavy waves. We walked on here, and H. at once let go a storm of invective against the landlady and the waiter, both being so supremely in-different about our custom, that we had great difficulty in assuaging our appetites. After long suffering we obtained only very tough chops and herrings. We return to-morrow and shoot again on Saturday. To-day we drove through what the natives call the ' Duke's policies,' and met the great man himself, who was all smiles and politeness.

" I will return directly the fortnight is out, but not before, as H. looks on me as his mainstay in shooting, Cholmon-deley not being well and avoiding the heavy work on the moor. The weather has been unendurably hot, but I thrive in it, and would be happy but for the midges, which nearly destroy all my pleasure. Harcourt is going to make out a plan for our tour abroad, as he knows all the parts we intend visiting. Outside has been a dreadful boy-German band playing for two hours, but now they have left off with ' God Save the Queen '; while just above us a duet has commenced, by two young ladies — ' Masaniello.'

" We have killed comparatively little game, but enough to make it pleasant, and I expect plenty of black game. Rabbits are abundant, and no one could be more kind and jolly than Harcourt.

" I like to hear from some of you every day, that you are all well; and after this fling I will return and work like a Trojan, before going South. I would like, if possible, to paint the firs at Kinnoull as a background, besides the copies."

In his next letter he describes his meeting with Dr. Livingstone, of whom he saw a good deal during the rest

of his stay at Dalhenna. After this he frequently dined at
the Castle, and had long and interesting talks with the
famous explorer, who used in the evening to amuse the
Duke's children with his wonderful tales of Africa, then a
terra incognita.

He writes : — " On Friday we returned to Loch Awe, and
near Inverary found Lord Archibald Campbell and another
younger brother catching salmon for the amusement of Dr.
Livingstone, who is at the Castle. We were introduced, and
I had a chat with the Doctor. They caught salmon in a
poaching way with lead and hooks attached, which sank
amongst the imprisoned fish, who are in pools from which
they cannot get out. The same afternoon the Duchess
called with a carriage full of pretty children, and asked us to
dine, which we did after killing twenty-eight brace on the
hill. There was no one staying at the Castle but Livingstone, but the party was large enough, as there are sons and
tutors in abundance. In the evening we played billiards, and
at tea drew out the African traveller, who is shy and not very
communicative. To-morrow we shoot again, and I think of
returning on Wednesday. The black game shooting commenced yesterday and I killed two, and this week we shall
beat the low hills for them. . . . I am anxious to return now
and get on with my work; but having promised to stay a
fortnight, I stay that time."

In September he rejoined his family at Bowerswell, and
after working for a month on " The Minuet " (a picture for
which my sister Effie posed as the principal figure, my Aunt
Alice sitting at the piano in the background), he and his wife
and Sir William Harcourt made a tour on the Continent,
travelling through Switzerland to Florence, where they were
fortunate enough to meet their friends Sir Henry Layard and
Lord and Lady Arthur Russell. Layard, the famous archæo-
logist, was born in Florence, and Italy was an open book to
him. He was, moreover, a most charming companion, and
under his guidance my father was enabled to see all the best
Art collections in the city, including the treasures left by the
Prince Galli, who had recently died. He was the last of his
race, and had bequeathed all his paintings and pieces of
sculpture to the hospital of Florence, including the marble
statue of Leda and the Swan, by Michael Angelo, a work
of Art which had been in the possession of the Galli family
for over 300 years. This statue Sir Henry strongly advised

Millais to buy at any price, saying that, if he did not do so,
he would buy it himself for his friend Lord Wimborne,
although he had no commission to do so. It was probably
the last occasion, he said, on which a genuine work by
Michael Angelo would be for sale, as the Italian Government
were then about to put in force an Act prohibiting the removal
from the country of great and well-known works of Art.
Millais, therefore, attended the sale and purchased the
" Leda," which was at once packed and sent off to London.
A most fortunate thing for him, for the very next day came
a missive from the Russian Government requesting the
Italian Government to buy the " Leda " for them at any
price, and the latter were not too well pleased when they
heard that it was already on its way to England.

One evening my father and mother were invited to dine
with a Mr. Spence at the Villa Spence — a house that formerly
belonged to the Medicis, and is now one of the show places
in Florence, with its exquisite gardens and wonderful under-
ground chapel. They did not know whom they were to
meet, but on arriving there they found amongst the guests
Mario, Grisi and her three daughters, as well as Adelina
and Carlotta Patti, and their brother-in-law Strakosch —
altogether a dinner-party of geniuses. But geniuses enjoy
themselves very much like other people. They told each
other all the best stories they could think of in connection
with their public lives, and after dinner Strakosch played,
and Millais danced nearly the whole evening with Adelina
Patti, who proved herself almost as good a waltzer as a
vocalist. They met again at some state function in London
about a year before his death, when she recalled the happy
time they had spent that evening at the Villa Spence.

From Florence, accompanied by their friends, they visited
Bologna and Venice, where they stayed with Mr. Rawdon
Brown in his palace on the Grand Canal. Then to Rome,
where they had to undergo the delights of fumigation by
sulphur, and were nearly suffocated ; for this was in the days
of Cardinal Antonelli, when the fear of the plague was at its
height. Here, as at Florence, Sir Henry Layard again acted
as their guide to the Art treasures of the city, and Lord Arthur
Russell took them into the Vatican to see the Pope, Pius IX.,
whom my mother used to describe as a very nice, benevolent-
looking old gentleman. He was dressed all in white, with a
black biretta, and acknowledged their salutations as he passed.

Almost immediately after he had passed out, the Abbé Liszt came into the room, and was presented by the British Ambassador to my father and mother. Liszt at once struck up a conversation with my mother, to the great mortification of her husband, who was most anxious to talk to him, but could not speak a word of any other language than his own. After bidding good-bye to their friends in Rome, Millais and his wife went on alone to Pisa, to see Sir Charles Eastlake, P. R. A., who was then on his death-bed.

Leghorn was now their aim, and after visiting several other places on their way, they arrived there at midnight in a way they did not anticipate. About ten miles from their destination the railway engine broke down, and there was nothing for it but to finish their journey as they did, in a country cart, sitting on the top of their luggage. There, however, they had the good luck to fall in with Mario again, who afterwards took ship with them for Genoa, where, with the aid of despatches, he helped them through the intricacies of the custom-house — a very real service in those red-tape days. The splendid Vandykes of Genoa were an immense pleasure to my father, but I never heard him express a wish to see any other masterpieces in the foreign galleries except the series of pictures by Velasquez in Madrid, for he already knew the Paris and Hague galleries, and loathed travelling in any form. And now their faces were set towards England, home, and duty ; and as there was no railway in those days along the Riviera, they took the " diligence " all the way to Marseilles and from there home by sea.

"Sleeping," "Waking," and "The Minuet," the three pictures which Millais exhibited in the Royal Academy of 1867, may certainly be classed amongst the specimens of his later Pre-Raphaelite manner, of which the "Vale of Rest" was the first example. It would seem, therefore, that just for this one year he returned to his old love, before the production of his broader works of " Jephtha " and " Rosalind and Celia," both commenced in 1867.

These three pictures were exact portraits of my sisters Carrie, Mary, and Effie, and (as I have often heard from those who knew them from their infancy) were not idealised in the slightest degree. The art of the painter was exercised only in seizing upon the beauty of a particular child at a certain moment, and transferring it to his canvas. That was not idealising, but simply catching the child at its very best.

"SLEEPING." 1876

By Permission of H. Graves and Son

None of the three little girls ever enjoyed sitting for their portraits. As one of them expressed herself at the time, " It was so horrid, just after breakfast, to be taken upstairs and undressed again, to be put to bed in the studio." When tired of gazing seraphically upwards she would wait till my father was not looking, and then kick all the bedclothes off, perhaps just as he was painting a particular fold — a trick which the artist never seemed to appreciate. The idea for " Sleeping " was suggested by seeing my sister Carrie, then a very little girl, fast asleep the morning after a children's party. Millais went to the nursery to look for the child, and found the French maid, Berthe, sewing beside the bed, waiting for her charge to wake up ; and when sitting for this picture the little model used often to go to sleep in real earnest.

My sister Mary tells the following story about " Waking." Being left alone for a few minutes during the painting of this picture, she slipped out of bed and crept up to the table where the palettes and brushes were left ; and then, taking a good brushful of paint and reaching as high as possible, proceeded to embellish the lower part of the work with some beautiful brown streaks. Presently she heard her father returning, and bolted back to bed. Foreseeing that in another minute he would discover the mischief, she wisely hastened to explain that she had tried to help him in his work by painting for him the brown floor that she knew he intended. Poor Millais turned in a desperate fright to his picture, and saw the harm that had been done, but with his characteristic sympathy with children he never said a word of reproach to little Mary, seeing that she had really meant to help.

During 1865 and 1866 he made water-colour copies of " Ophelia " and " The Huguenot," " The Black Brunswicker," " The Minuet," " Swallow, Swallow," and " The Evil One Sowing Tares," and copies in oil of " Esther " and " The Romans " ; also two oil pictures, one of which was a portrait of a Miss Davidson, and the other a small one of Effie as " Little Red Riding Hood."

From Sir William Cunliffe Brooks the shootings of Callander and a small part of Glen Artney were taken in 1866. This was a grouse shooting, but now and then a stag came on to the ground. Millais got three, and then a fourth made its appearance, and returned again and again to the ground — one of the grandest stags ever seen in that

neighbourhood.   My father was of course keen for a shot, but
he happened to know this stag, having spied it on several
occasions on the borders of the neighbouring forest rented
by Sir William, and being on most friendly terms with the
owner, he let it go.   Afterwards, in the course of conversation, Sir William expressed his anxiety to shoot this particular
stag, but added (as any true sportsman would), " If he is anywhere about your march you had better kill him."

Days went by, and the end of the season was approaching,
when one evening Millais espied the great stag feeding on
his ground about fifty yards from the march.   Now was his
chance — his last chance of a shot at such a monarch as this.
He was excited beyond measure, and his stalker was even
more elated, for (as unfortunately sometimes happens) there
was intense rivalry and bitterness between him, a man of
small pretence, and the head stalker at Glen Artney, who was
a tremendous swell in his own conceit.   Then the stalk began,
and just as the quarry crossed the march a shot from Millais'
rifle laid him dead.   At that moment, to the astonishment of
my father, who had seen nobody else about, up rose Sir
William and his stalker, who had been after the same game.
The stag was therefore carted off to Glen Artney, and Sir
William being satisfied with my father's explanation, the two
remained as good friends as ever.

After slaying this noble hart, he could not refrain from
exulting over his success in a wild letter to his friend Sir
William Harcourt, who replied as follows: —

From Sir W. V. Harcourt.

" STUDLEY ROYAL, RIPON,
" *October 3rd*, 1866.

" MY DEAR MILLAIS, — I received your insane letter, from
which I gather that you are under the impression that you
have killed a stag.   Poor fellow, I pity your delusion.   I
hope the time is now come when I can break to you the
painful truth.   Your wife, who (as I have always told you)
alone makes it possible for you to exist, observing how the
disappointment of your repeated failures was telling on your
health and on your intellect, arranged with the keepers for
placing in a proper position a *wooden* stag constructed like
that of . . . You were conducted unsuspectingly to the spot
and fired at the *dummy.*   In the excitement of the moment

you were carried off by the gillie, so that you did not discern the cheat, and believed you had really slain a 'hart of grease.' Poor fellow, I know better; and indeed your portrait of the stag sitting up *smiling*, with a head as big as a church door on his shoulders, tells its own tale. I give Mrs. M. great credit on this, as on all other occasions, for her management of you. I am happy to hear that the result of the pious fraud has been to restore you to equanimity and comparative sanity, and I hope by the time I see you again you may be wholly restored. . . .

" Pray remember me to Mrs. M.

" Yours ever,

" W. V. HARCOURT.

" I see that, in order to keep up the delusion, puffs of your performance have been inserted in all the papers."

There are some fortunate beings in this world who have never missed a stag, and never can or will; but Millais was not one of these. In the following letter to his friend Mr. W. W. Fenn (written during his tenancy of Callander), he describes faithfully and amusingly the hardships and disappointments of deer-stalking: —

To Mr. W. W. Fenn.

" CALLANDER, N.B.,
" *Sunday, October 7th,* 1866.

" DEAR FENN, — My wife and eldest daughter have gone to the Free Kirk; and that I may do as good a work, I send you a line, albeit I am aching in all my limbs from having crawled over stony impediments all yesterday, in pursuit of ye suspicious stag. You know the position of all-fours which fathers assume for the accommodation of their boys, in the privacy of domestic life, and you can conceive how unsuited the hands and knees are to make comfortable progress over cutting slate and knobbly flint, and will understand how my legs are like unto the pear of over-ripeness.

" I had two shots, the first of which I ought to have killed, and I shall never forget the tail-between-legs dejection of that moment when the animal, instead of biting the dust, kicked it up viciously into my face. After more pipes and whiskey than was good for me, we toiled on again, and a

second time viewed some deer, and repeated the toilsome
crawling I have referred to. Enough! I missed that too,
and rode home on our pony, which must from my soured
temper have known it too. I tooled him along, heedless of
the dangers of the road, until the gladdening lights of home
flickered through the dining-room window. Mike is not
a sympathising creature under these circumstances, being
thoroughly convinced that a cockchafer's shoulder ought to
be hit flying at a thousand yards; so, after the never-failing
pleasure of the table, I retired, to dream of more stomach
perambulations up and down precipices of burning plough-
shares, the demons of the forest laughing at my ineffectual
efforts to hit the mastodon of the prairies at fifteen yards
distance. You may depend upon it, roach-fishing in a punt
is the thing after all. When you don't excite the pity and
contempt of your keeper, what boots it if you don't strike
your roach? (probably naught but the float of porcupine is
aware of it), but when you proclaim to the mountains, yea,
even to the towns adjoining thereto, that you have fired at
the monarch of the glen, how can you face the virgins and
pipers who come up from the village to crown you with
bog-myrtle, and exalt your stag's horn through the streets
rejoicing? Every shot fired in the forest is known to be at
a stag or hind,

> 'And the shepherd listening, kens well
> That the monarch of the glen, fell,
> Howsomever, if it ends well,
> As happens rarely,
> And the highland laddie breechless,
> Hears the shot, and stands quite speechless,
>   Etc., etc., etc.'

This inspiration comes from 'The Lady of Shalott.' I
think in my old age I must betake myself to the chase of the
gaudy butterfly with net of green, gaffing with the domestic
bodkin. There 's the stag-beetle, anyhow, and the salmon-fly;
and what can exceed the danger of following the pool-loving
dragon-fly?

"All gone to Callander — to the kirk — and the wife will
return presently, seriously inclined; so will I cast off this
skin of frivolity. You must forgive me for being a boy still,
and a little wild after yesterday's excitement. Michael returns
in a day or two, and we shall very shortly leave this for a
short stay at Perth, and then home to sit under the trophy

"WAKING." 1866

By permission of H. Graves and Son

of my own antlers. On the whole, the stay here has been pleasant, in spite of a nearly perpetual rain, which (distilled through peat-bog) has dyed my poor feet a sweet cinnamon brown like the Lascar crossing-sweepers.

"You will hear from Stephen Lewis his adventures, which I believe he will narrate to his customers seated all around him in Turkish shawls, in the manner of the 'Arabian Nights.'

"How Arthur is ever to hold his own after the prowess of Stephen remains to be seen; but — I would n't be Arthur. A strong smell of roast mutton calls me away, and I think your mother will have enough work in deciphering this.

"Remember me very kindly to her, and tell her, tell her, that when I return, I come to thee!

"Very sincerely yours,

"J. EVERETT MILLAIS.

"I have n't uncorked a tube or moistened a brush, but I hope the hand has n't lost its cunning."

At the end of the season my father and mother spent a week with Sir William Cunliffe Brooks at Drummond Castle, which he rented from Lady Willoughby de Eresby, a place which, in point of situation and entourage, has no superior in Great Britain; indeed, it would be impossible to imagine more lovely surroundings. The old castle stands on an eminence in a park in which all the natural beauties of wood and lake are enhanced by floral and arboreal gems from foreign lands. Wild fowl of various sorts adorn the lakes, and herds of half-wild fallow-deer roam through the park, whilst up in the great wood of Torlum may in autumn be heard the voices of the big wood stags.

The sanctuary in Glen Artney Forest had remained untouched since the visit of the Queen and Prince Consort in 1845, and now, as the deer were becoming too numerous, Sir William decided on a drive. Three rifles were posted on a high ridge above the sanctuary, and over a thousand deer came up by three separate passes. Six or seven of the best were killed, and of the survivors about seven hundred made their way into the next corrie, within ten yards of the ladies who had gathered there to see what they could of the sport. My mother used to describe this as the finest sight of the kind she had ever witnessed.

CHAPTER XI

HOLMAN HUNT

A great friendship, and a spur to noble ambition — Cairo in 1854 — The donkey and the buffalo — A human parallel — The Jewish model, a shy bird — The difficulties and dangers of life in and around Jerusalem in 1854 — Adventure at the Brook Kerith — Reflections on life — Millais must put forth all his strength — A final tribute.

FROM what has been already said, it will be seen how close and intimate was the friendship between Holman Hunt and Millais. They were friends together in early youth, and together they fought and conquered the Philistines in the days when Pre-Raphaelitism was attacked on every side; and though for many years (from 1867 to 1880) they saw but little of each other, owing to Hunt's long residence abroad, they kept up a continuous correspondence, the following portions of which (interesting from many points of view) the writer kindly allows me to embody in these pages.

It is not for me to sing the praises of this distinguished artist, whose works are reverenced of all who know what high Art means (I am sure he would not thank me if I did); but this at least I may say, that no man had ever a firmer or a truer friend than my father found in Hunt, and that his friendship was reciprocated with equal warmth of heart. The fame of the one was ever dear to the other, and as to Hunt, so far was he from any sense of jealousy, that he never lost an opportunity for urging his friend to put forth all his powers whenever any great exhibition was on foot either at home or abroad. "The usual Liberal whip," my father would playfully remark, when one of these missives came by post; and seldom, if ever, did he fail to respond to the appeal.

The letters proclaim the man — letters full of thought, of keen but kindly criticism, and enlivened here and there with touches of quaint humour; but voluminous and interesting as they are, I must restrict my selection to the narrowest limits.

Here are a few extracts from letters during his first visit to the East in 1854.

Writing from Cairo in March of that year, he says: — " The

"THE PARABLE OF THE SOWER"
By permission of J. S. Virtue and Co

country is very rich and attractive, but I am inclined to mislike it on that account, for I have no patience with the Fates when they tempt me to become a *paysagiste*. The Pyramids in themselves are extremely ugly blocks, arranged with imposing but unpicturesque taste. Being so close at hand, it is difficult to refuse making a sketch of them. With some effect and circumstance to satisfy the spectator's expectation and the charm of past history, it might be possible to gather a degree of poetical atmosphere to repay the patience one would expend; but I would rather give the time otherwise. Their only association that I value is that Joseph, Moses, and Jesus must have looked upon them. There are palm trees which attract my passing admiration. Without these, in places, one might as well sketch in Hackney Marsh. . . . I find a good deal of difficulty in living in quiet here, for there are four or five other Englishmen in the hotel, some of them very pleasant fellows; but I want solitude for my work, and it is impossible to feel secluded enough even when —— is away. When he is present, serious devotion to thought is often shattered with intolerable and exasperating practical jokes, and by his own unbounded risibility at the same. . . . I hear no news here but what hoarse-throated donkeys shout. These loquacious brutes are the only steeds one can get here without purchasing a horse, so I do not enjoy the luxury of following the hounds as you do. Appended you see an example of the ordinary load an ass has to carry in this country. They are themselves veritably one of the burdens of Cairo. One is never free for a second from their wanton braying. When you are talking with a friend in the street, or in the bazaar making a bargain, you are moved to excusable exasperation fifty times in an hour by the spasmodic trumpeting of some donkey who lifts up his voice close to the small of your back, or in front of you. In face of our hotel there are several animals tied up under the trees — fastened by the horns and legs. In a particular pen there is a small *ménage* of a domestic character, but unfortunately it is not a happy family, the poor buffalo-cow of the party being evidently exhausted with listening to her near neighbour the jackass. The cow's original disposition is of the utmost and most admirable patience, but even vaccine nature has its limits, and our cow, soft-eyed and beautiful as she is, cannot refrain from remonstrating when her neighbour's refrain has been too frequent and (apparently) too personal. You should have seen her the other morning. She had patiently listened to his complete discourse some fifty times; but when he cleared his throat to give out the text once more, she waived her politeness so far as to indicate that she had heard all that before. The donkey on his part, however, persisted. He evidently thought such an excellent homily could not be heard too often. Buffalo turned to retire, evidently with a different conviction, but her tether checked her retreat. She was infuriated at this discovery, and turned round upon the braying beast with her butting head, as if she would make him swallow his words once for all. But here the trial came. She could not reach him, and so he could not be turned from his purpose. After a moment's pause he took up his broken argument again, and in a posture better suited to the new position of the refractory member of his audience, until at last he wound up, triumphantly glorying in her defeat and complete resignation. I feel ofttimes like that poor cow, and cherish an undisguised hatred of the whole braying race."

SKETCH FOR "THE PARABLE OF THE GOOD SAMARITAN." 1857

"*Jerusalem, September 5th*, 1854. — It is evident that it will be impossible to get my present picture done for r year. I go every Friday and Saturday and on feast day days of humiliation to the synagogue, to see the Jews worship. I also take every opportunity to get introduced to them in their homes. They are polite, and I can study their characteristic gestures and aspects; but for special attendance at my house I can scarcely get them at all. When by the exercise of great interest one is brought, he looks about like a scared bird, and if he sees any piece of carpentry — a window sash, or a border of a panel — that looks in his suspicious eyes like a cross, away he flies, never to come back any more. My landlord, a converted Jew, who has journeymen-tailors under him, has brought me one or two, but even these get advised not to repeat their sittings, and thus my subject-picture is in the most unsatisfactory, higgledy-piggledy state, with many disjointed bits begun and not completed. The Rabbis keep up the bitterness by excommunicating all who come to my house, for they suspect me to be a missionary in disguise. . .

"You could not conceive the possibility of men being so

fanatical and rancorous as the Fellahs and Arabs of this
place.   The tame men in the city are in a degree polite to
Europeans (with what degree of sincerity I don't know), but

"THE PARABLE OF THE GOOD SAMARITAN"
By permission of J. S. Virtue and Co.

out of the gates, away from the shadow of our firm English
Consul, no Briton would be safe, but for the probability that
his coat has a good pistol or two in the pockets which he is
ready to use.   With the chance of escaping detection, they
would shoot anyone for the spoil they might get."

"THE EVIL ONE SOWING TARES"
By permission of Mr. E. M. Denny

He had proof enough of this at the Brook Kerith, to get
to which he had to descend a steep cliff 500 feet high: —
" When I was sketching, a shepherd, with a boy of fifteen

"THE PARABLE OF THE PRODIGAL SON"
By permission of J. S. Virtue and Co.

and three or four others a year or two younger, came and sat
down beside me. To show them I intended to have my own
way, I told the man to sit further away on one side and the

boy on the other. I could not order them away altogether,
as they greeted me civilly on first arriving, but it was difficult
to attend to my work, for they required looking after. I had
laid aside my pistol-case on account of the heat, and in two
minutes the man had got hold of it and was unfastening the
button. I clutched it away, and cautioned him that if he
touched anything of mine again I would send them all away,
at the same time buckling the weapon round my waist.
Then, turning my head, I found the younger gentleman with
his hand in my pocket, upon which I reached out, boxed his
ears, and pushed him aside, and standing up ordered them
all away. This brought on a hubbub. Seeing that I was
determined in my course, the man said they were Arab
fellaheen, who would not be put off. Would I give them
some English gunpowder? No; I would give nothing.
'Very well,' he said, 'I will bring down all the fellaheen to
kill you.' Meanwhile my friend Dr. Sim was lying asleep in
a cave at some distance, and on looking towards him I saw
another young Arab, who had crawled into the cave, engaged
at the opening in examining the articles in his hand with the
closest possible interest; so I called out lustily enough to
wake Sim, and at this point the Arab boy bolted with Sim's
boots. They all went away then, threatening dreadful things,
and I set to work again to make up for lost time. In a few
minutes I heard a furious altercation. . . . Sim was standing
high on a rock, while the man was crouching down aiming at
him over a ledge; but as my companion stood unmoved with
his gun under his arm while the Arab was dreadfully excited,
I was not alarmed. It appears that the fellow had approached him on his descent, demanding powder, that Sim
had called him majnoon (madman) and ordered him off. At
last, Sim closing upon his adversary with his gun cocked, the
latter moved off to safer quarters."

The following letter relates to Hunt's third journey to the
East: —

" JERUSALEM,
" *October* 12th, 1871.

" MY DEAR MILLAIS, — I was very glad to get yours of
August 20th, which came here about three weeks since.
I should have written since my last, notwithstanding that
I had had no answer to mine, but I was excessively occupied,

and always thinking that in another few weeks I should be
on my road home to England.

"I was truly sorry to hear of your father's death. . . .

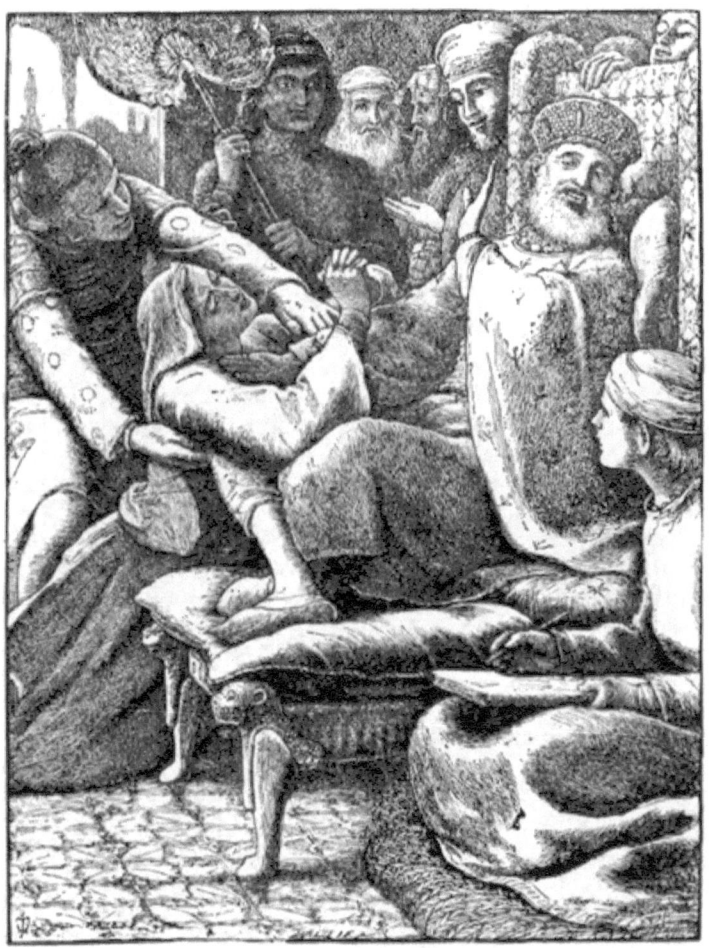

"THE PARABLE OF THE UNJUST JUDGE"
By permission of J. S. Virtue and Co.

He was a good old fellow, and associated in my mind
with all manner of kind and pleasant hospitality, and true,
generous friendship, and I had hoped to spend many other

pleasant hours with the dear old boy — for he was always a boy, and all the better for this. Well, our next chat must be in the Elysian Fields, where we shall have lots of things to talk about, and where (however soon it may be) he will enact the part of old stager, as he did when I first knew him in Gower Street! And what a lot of old chums there will be whom, when I left England last, I counted upon smoking many mundane pipes with again — Halliday, Martineau, Phillips, my good brother-in-law George, an old chum and fellow-traveller of old here, Beaumont, as well as the boring, good-natured ——. They will coach us as to the course we are to take there, and tell us where to find people we want to see and know (when it may be allowed to such new-comers to be admitted to their society), and whether and where our own most sacred ones may be overtaken.

" Life here wants something to make it bearable. Having no sort of counter-interest, my work becomes the most frightful anxiety to me, and sometimes I am sure I have lost a great deal of labour from nursing all manner of fears about it. When a notion once gets into my head it goes on worrying me until I see everything by its light, and I am tempted to change back again. When I began my work I had very ambitious hopes about it, but (like Browning's man, who in infancy cried for the moon, and in old age was grateful for the crutch on which he hobbled out of the world) I should be glad now to find it only done in any way. There are peculiar difficulties in the subject I have devoted my time to — such serious ones that, had I only foreseen them, I would have left the subject to some future painter; but I tried to console myself by thinking that other pictures I have in my mind to follow will go more easily and be a great deal better.

"I am like you in loving my Art very intensely now, the more it seems that I am denied all other love ; but I am reminded of the remark of a little child, who, talking about love to her mother, said it *pained* so. My love for Art pains me — it hurts me sleeping and waking; there is no rest from it — and I, getting old in desponding service, feel (quoting Browning again) like

> ' Only the page that carols unseen,
> Crumbling your hounds their messes.'

" If I had my life over again (which ofttimes I should crave God for some reasons to spare me) I might (if fools

"GREENWICH PENSIONERS AT THE TOMB OF NELSON." 1868

By permission of Mr. H. Roberts

could be kept from hindering), out of the raw materials I
started my days with, make a satisfactory painter; but this
life is made so that wisdom and riches come too late. The
prizes that boyhood sighs for come when toys are no longer
in request; those which youth covets are withheld till youth
is flown; and so on to the grave. One must continue one's
journey minus the means and weapons which carelessness or
over-confidence rejected at one's place of outfit — the tale
of the foolish virgins again, who, in going back, came at
last too late. One must go on now, trusting that the oil
will last to the journey's end, though the lamp may not be
so brilliant as it should be. The one fact that continually
perplexes me is how the confidence of youth carried me
through difficulties that now quite bring me to a standstill.
I had no fear then of the distant royalty of my mistress,
but bit by bit I have learnt the width of the gap between
us; and the very sense of her greatness paralyses my hand
in attempting the simplest service. It is very imprudent
to confess all this, for the world will never believe in anyone who does not have unbounded confidence in himself,
and will, on the contrary, accept any humbug who declares
himself infallible; but you are not *the world*, but an old
fellow-servant, who knows too well what sincere service is
to be prejudiced against my work because I confess the
trouble it gives me. I marvel at men who, like X——, never
see a fault in anything they do, and regard with scorn any
who venture to suggest an improvement. For the time
they are enviable, yet I believe there is a degree of self-
satisfaction which limits a man's powers woefully. . . .

"I am sorry for William's loss of his child. Give my love
to him as well as to all your family, and tell Mary I shall
come and try her at her Catechism soon.

"Yours ever,

"W. HOLMAN HUNT."

It will be seen from these letters how interesting was
Hunt's life in the Holy Land, and how pregnant with thought
are the graver incidents to which he calls attention. Some
day, perhaps, he may be tempted to give to the world a full
record of his life and adventures, which — judging from the
vast mass of correspondence it has been my privilege to read
— could not fail to find acceptance with the public.

Outside of our own family he was my father's sole con-
fidant; nothing was hidden from him, and his letter to my
brother Everett, in August, 1896, expresses only what we
all know to be the inmost sentiments of the writer. Referring to my father's death, he says: — " After fifty-two years of
unbroken friendship the earthly bond has separated. New
generations with fresh struggles to engage in ever advance
and sweep away many of the memories of individual lives,
even when these have been the most eminent. . . . It would
be a real loss to the world if your father's manly straight-
forwardness and his fearless sense of honour should ever
cease to be remembered. There are men who never
challenge criticism, because they have no sense of individual
independence. My old friend was different, and he justified
all his courses by loyalty and consistency as well as courage
— the courage of a true conscience. As a painter of subtle
perfection, while his works last they will prove the supreme
character of his genius, and this will show more conspicuously
when the mere superficial tricksters in Art have fallen to their
proper level."

A DESULTORY chapter this — a thing of shreds and patches — needful, however, as an introduction to intimate friends of Millais not yet noticed in these pages, and interesting perhaps as a reminder of some historic events in the lives of others with whom during this period he came into contact.

Three historic gatherings my mother was wont to describe as making a great impression on her mind. The first at which she and my father were present was at Stafford House, where the late Duke of Sutherland gave a grand ball in honour of General Garibaldi, who was then on a visit to this country. The great soldier, wearing as in Italy the red shirt ever since associated with his name, entered the ball-room with the Duchess of Sutherland on his arm, and was greeted by all present with the homage due to Royalty as he passed down the room, stopping here and there for a moment's talk with some of the guests. Very striking was the expression of his face, at once so earnest and so genial; and still more conspicuous was the contrast between his simple dress and the gorgeous array of all the rest of the company.

Some time after that came the reception given at the Foreign Office to the grandfather of the present Czar of Russia, whom my mother described as a very sad and dignified-looking man. They had the honour of being presented to him, and soon after his return to Russia, for which he set out on the following day, the cause of his sadness was

only too painfully manifested. At a dinner party at Mr.
Cyril Flower's (now Lord Battersea), at which they were
present, a telegram from Miss Corrie was handed to one of the
guests, Lord Rowton, announcing an attack on the life of the
Czar, whose escape uninjured was little short of miraculous.
The would-be assassin had placed an infernal machine under
the floor of the Imperial dining-room, timed to blow up
immediately after the entrance of the Czar and his suite, which
always took place at the same hour. It happened, however,

SKETCHES FOR "THE PRINCE CARRYING THE PRINCESS UP THE HILL"

that Prince Alexander of Bulgaria being late for dinner on
this particular evening, the Imperial party waited a quarter
of an hour for him, and during this time the bomb exploded, making a complete wreck of the dining-room, but
happily doing no further injury. It was a doomed life,
however, that he carried, and he knew it. A year later the
assassins returned to their ghastly work, and, sad to say,
succeeded.

The third occasion to which my mother referred was the
State ball given in honour of the Shah of Persia. The
Shah, as is well known, has a grand collection of jewels,
including some of the finest the world has ever seen; but
even he must have been astonished by the wondrous display
of diamonds that met his eyes that night. About 800 tiaras
were worn by the ladies present, who were, perhaps, not

"THE MINUET." 1866

By permission of H. Graves and Son

altogether unwilling to show him what old England could do in that way.

Strawberry Hill, Twickenham,* was one of the most interesting places at which, during the seventies, my father and mother were privileged guests, and many were the pleasant days they spent there.   It was then the seat of Frances, Countess of Waldegrave, a woman of singular beauty and great natural talent, and as the daughter of Braham, the famous singer, very proud of her Jewish descent.   She would say of Lord Beaconsfield, who was a constant visitor, "We are both children of Abraham, and he will do anything for me."

Amongst the many Art treasures there was the famous picture by Sir Joshua Reynolds of the three Ladies Waldegrave; and the Countess, who was devoted to Art, added largely to the collection.   She had a long gallery built, which she filled with life-size portraits of her most distinguished friends.

Hers was an eventful life.   She was little more than sixteen when she married the Earl of Waldegrave, and on his death she took for her second husband his half-brother, Mr. Waldegrave, who had the misfortune to be arrested by mistake for a murderer.   He was consigned to the Fleet prison, where his wife accompanied him ; but almost immediately afterwards the real murderer was discovered, and he was set at liberty.   On his death she married the Right Hon. George Vernon Harcourt, and after many years of wedlock, he too left her a widow.   Another suitor then appeared in the person of the Right Hon. Chichester Fortescue (Lord Carlingford), whom she ultimately accepted as her fourth husband.

Her Saturday-to-Monday parties were proverbially enjoyable.   Rank and talent met and mingled there on equal terms of amity and good fellowship.   Whoever might or might not be there, there would certainly be no dulness in that delightful house — none of that horrid boredom that Society is apparently so fond of inflicting upon itself.

For mere rank and fashion, however, Millais cared but little.   Talent and geniality of temperament were the "open

* Strawberry Hill, one of the most beautiful estates in the vicinity of London was for many years the residence of Horace Walpole of historic fame.   On the death of the Countess of Waldegrave it was bought by the late Baron de Stern, and is now the property of his son.

door " to his friendship, and that he found these qualities
in abundance among his personal friends may be seen from
the following names of some with whom during the period
covered by this chapter he was more or less intimately
associated.

Omitting the vast majority of his brother artists — for the
mutual affection that prevailed between him and them will
be seen later on — I note amongst eminent literary men
Whyte Melville, William Black, George Meredith, Gilbert,

Pinero, Tom Taylor, Charles
Reade, Wilkie Collins, Mark
Twain (Samuel Clemens), Bret
Harte, DuMaurier, Archdeacon
Farrar, Hamilton Aidé, Rhoda
Broughton, Henry James, John
Forster, Matthew Arnold, and
Robert Browning.

A CAT. *Circ.* 1890

Amongst the scientific men
his principal friends were Sir
Henry Thompson, Sir James Paget, Professor Blackie, and
Sir Richard Owen.

Politicians and diplomats included Lord Dufferin, Gladstone, Lord Salisbury, Lord Rosebery, Lord James, Sir
William Harcourt, and Sir Clare Ford.

Army and Navy — Viscount Wolseley, Sir George Nares,
and Captain Shaw.

Musicians — Madame Albani, Sainton Dolby, Madame
Norman Neruda, Henry Leslie, Blumenthal, Frederic Clay,
Arthur Sullivan, Corney Grain, Henschel, Duvernoy,
Essipoff, Papini, and (last but not least) John Ella, from
whom there is a pile of interesting correspondence which
of itself would fill one of these volumes.

Actors — Sir Henry Irving, Johnston, and Norman Forbes
Robertson, Wallack, Joseph Jefferson, the Bancrofts, John
Hare, and Arthur Cecil (Arthur Blunt).

Of his intimate friends more particular notice will be
found in the course of this work ; but none, I may say, were
more beloved by him than Sir John and Lady Constance
Leslie, and Mr. and Mrs. Perugini.

Nor must I pass over here the distinguished Spanish
artist Fortuny, for whom Millais had a great regard.   They
met in Paris in 1867, and during his subsequent visits to
England Fortuny was always a welcome guest at Cromwell

Place. In Rome, where he finally settled, his most intimate friend was D'Epiné, the famous sculptor, whose pathetic letter announcing his death discloses at once the character of both the sculptor and his friend.

From D'Epiné.

" ROME,

" *Sunday, November 22nd, 1874.*

" MY DEAR MILLAIS, — I write quickly two words to tell you that our poor friend and great artist Fortuny is dead! It is like a brother I have lost! Since twelve years I used to see him every day nearly.

" Last Sunday he was well. I passed all the day at his studio, where he was showing to me his lovely studies from Portia, near Naples, where he spent all the summer; and to-day he is cold!

" I write with tears in my eyes! What a loss for Art, for his friends, for his family, for his country! It is a public mourning. Send a word to Leighton to tell him this sad news. I have not the courage to tell you more.

" He died (in five days!) from a *perniciosa* fever he took, working in his garden. His doctor saw nothing, except yesterday morning, when only *quinine* was given to him.

" Yesterday, at three, he shook hands with me, saying, ' My poor D'Epiné, I feel I am lost!' He died two hours after!

" Now is gone one of the most extraordinary artists of this century — the chief of a new school, a good friend, a man full of life and hope.

" I tear like a boy, writing these lines. I have been happy enough to make his bust eighteen months ago! I send a photograph of it to you. You can send it to the *Graphic* or *Illustrated London News* if you wish. I authorise them to publish it if they think proper. It is, I think, the only portrait existing of him!

" Your friend,

" D'EPINÉ."

Among Millais' distant friends were also Luder Barnay, the famous actor in German opera, and Jan van Beers, the celebrated French painter, from whom he received the following letters. Barnay's missive being the first English letter he

ever penned, it is not surprising to find in it some reminiscence of "English as she is spoke." The letter is dated
June 17th, 1881 : —

From Herr Luder Barnay.

"DEAR FRIEND AND GREAT ARTISTE, — I have promised to
send our *répertoire.*

June 23rd	.	.	'Jules César.'
" 25th	.	.	'Wolhlm Tell.'
" 27th	.	.	" "
" 30th	.	.	'Jules César.'

"This were the first words in English language which I
read. I hope that the God of England you helpe to understand it.   Believe me,
                      "Dear friend,
                              "Your sincereli,
                                      "LUDER BARNAY."

From M. Jan van Beers.

"10 RUE DELAROCHE, PASSY, PARIS.

"MON CHER MAÎTRE, — Je n'ai pas perdu pour attendre !
The engraving is very fine and artistic, and the *dédicace* is
so kind and nice that I feel quite proud and happy to have
that sweet souvenir of you. There are plenty of painters,
but great poets in painting are extremely rare, and I consider
you as *the great poet-painter of our time.*
"So you see *why* I am so happy with that engraving of
that Shakespearian picture, which *tells* the same tale as
Hamlet's famous scene of the graveyard.
"When you come to Paris I shall be delighted to expect
you in my new house, which will only be entirely finished
in November. I hear with great pleasure your health is
much better now.
"With many thanks and best wishes for your happiness,
believe me,   Respectfully yours,
                              "JAN VAN BEERS.

"I shall send you the little smiling lady ; but as I have
only one small proof (I promised to Mr. Aird, our friend,
not to have the picture reproduced) I shall have it copied
for you."

"THE WIDOW'S MITE." 1869

By permission of Thomas Agnew and Sons

And now to friends at home who yet remain to be introduced. Amongst them was a young artist named Jopling, a man of considerable talent, whose progress in his profession was hindered only by his habitual *laissez-faire* and an inordinate love of amusement. He was extremely good-natured, and blessed with a sunny temperament that infected all with whom he came into contact. It was not long, therefore, after their first meeting in 1854 that Millais and he became firm friends, and when, in 1860 and 1861, they were both living in London, they saw a good deal of each

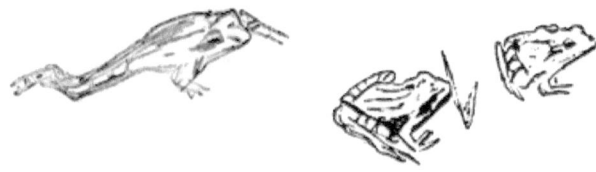

STUDIES OF FROGS. 1860

other. Anxious to encourage him in his work, Millais commended him to his friends, and frequently got commissions for him; but "Joe" (as he was always called) had other demands upon his time, and in his happy, careless way he attended to them rather than to the real business of his life. He was a first-rate rifle shot, a member of the English eight, and at Wimbledon in 1861 he won the Queen's Prize as the best marksman of the year. It was his success in this direction that Millais refers to in the following letter:—

To Mr. Joseph Jopling.

"BOWERSWELL, PERTH,
"*July 12th*, 1861.

"MY DEAR JOPLING,—I feel bound to confess myself in error when I said you would come to 'no good,' and that I have not respected your wifle * qualities as I should have done. My sincere congratulations, in which Mrs. M. begs to join. I saw your chances in the competition increasing, as I looked daily at the paper, but no more thought you would get the prize than you did yourself.

"All yesterday I was out fishing with my two sisters-in-law

* Mr. Jopling's R's were all W's.

and a party, but with no success, it was so terribly stormy.
Do you think now of coming North? If so, come soon —
before I return. I am going to work at my pictures at once,
and was very glad to see my children again.

"Do you get a cup from the Queen, and £260? What
a handsome centre-piece for Mrs. J. to smile upon during the
matrimonial dinner parties! Now you must get married to
an heiress. *Don't lose time.*

"Ever yours sincerely,
"J. E. MILLAIS.

"Don't forget Chapman and Hall in your prosperity. I
remember your hitting 'Aunt Sally' three times running at
Mike's [Michael Halliday's] long range.

"(Postscript by Mrs. Millais.) Best congratulations. I
you come North we shall be very glad to see you. Yours
truly, E. M."

In 1873 Joseph Jopling married the lady whose work
and personality are now so well known in the Art world
of London. Millais saw her for the first time in November
of that year, and wrote at once from St. Mary's Tower : —

"DEAR JOE, — I thought when I left you you were a 'gone
coon.' I think she is very charming, and some people will
say, a great deal too good for you. . . ."

For many years after that Mr. and Mrs. Jopling were
constant visitors at Cromwell Place and Palace Gate, and
many were the pleasant evenings we had when Joe and his
clever wife dined with us *en famille.*

In 1874 came another letter to Jopling, inviting him to
Scotland, where Millais was then painting "Over the Hills
and Far Away."

To the same.

" ERIGMORE, BIRNAM, PERTHSHIRE,
" *September,* 1874.

"DEAR JOE, — I am working now so hard that I am never
at home. My place of work is four miles away, and I am
working at other things outside. All the children, except
George, have gone South; but we have still plenty of
young people here, as my brother is with us, and his wife,
three children, and servants, Mr. and Mrs. Gray, etc., etc.
George, who is here, caught a beautiful clean salmon yester-

day, of 20½ lbs. He is going to prepare for Cambridge, and after that the Bar.

" It has been very hard for me to work, with everyone about me idle, but now I must buckle to in earnest.

" My wife manages all arrangements of visitors, so she appends directions. We have had Sir W. Harcourt and James here, and I dined at Lord J. Manners', and met Disraeli, who is charming. Plenty of game here, and a good billiard-table, which we squabble over. Give my regards to your wife, and kind remembrances to Sir C. and Lady Lindsay, whom I would come over and see if it was n't such a tiresome journey.

" Yours very sincerely,
" J. E. MILLAIS."

In 1879 Millais painted a portrait of Mrs. Jopling — one of the finest that ever came from his brush. It was most favourably noticed in the Press, and to that circumstance may perhaps be attributed the following letter to the artist from a stranger — one Mr. George R.: — " SIR, — May I trouble you to tell me if you could undertake to paint two likenesses from the enclosed photographs? I should like them done in oil-paint on copper, if you recommend that style. I have some others done in that way. I should be glad to know your charge for the same. The portraits would have to be painted entirely from the photographs, as it would not be convenient for us otherwise, and I may also state that having a large family to bring up, I hope the expense will not be very great."

What Millais thought of this may be gathered from his letter to Mr. Jopling, who, it must be added, was at that time laid up with an ailment affecting his legs.

To Mr. Jopling.

" 2 PALACE GATE, KENSINGTON,
"*July 22nd*, 1880.

" DEAR JOE, — I have just recommended your wife, in answer to the enclosed [the letter from Mr. George R.], so if you hear from the writer you will understand. What maniacs there are in the world!

" I hope, old boy, you will be soon about again. I shall be working on here for some time yet. Got your letter last night. Had already read poetry in *World* [some lines on Mrs. Jopling's portrait, entitled ' A portrait by Millais'], and did not quite understand. Lunch is announced, so I must go. This only to show that I am not insensible to your poor legs.

" Yours sincerely,

" J. E. MILLAIS."

In the following year Mr. Jopling's health unfortunately gave way so far as to incapacitate him from serious work as an artist. Some lighter occupation must therefore be found for him, and mainly through Millais' instrumentality this was secured in the Fine Arts Society. As soon as Jopling had obtained the post he organised a small exhibition of Millais' paintings, which was held in the Bond Street rooms in 1881. In connection with this Millais wrote : —

To Mr. Jopling.

" 2 PALACE GATE, KENSINGTON,

" *March* 4*th*, 1881.

" DEAR JOE, — I have a great objection to the introduction of other works of mine into the exhibition, unless it is positively necessary. I will write to Mr. Graham myself, rather than ' The Vale of Rest ' should leave ; and ' New-laid Eggs ' must not be put into the Gallery. Time enough if another set of my works be shown. I cannot say when I can begin Tennyson [a portrait of Tennyson that he was commissioned to paint], I am so fully occupied. I cannot scamp work, and unless I can do justice to the subject, I am not going to undertake anything new. The public would be the first to cry out against me.

" Lord Beaconsfield comes on Tuesday and Wednesday, and I have promised Sir H. Thompson to begin without loss of time. I don't want to hear what old X——— says or thinks of my work. He has got up one unsuccessful Art Exhibition after another, and I daresay is growling, albeit he has done good service at ———

" Yours sincerely,

" J. E. MILLAIS.

" I am very tired and want quiet."

"THE GAMBLER'S WIFE." 1869

By permission of Thomas Agnew and Sons

The following letters to Mrs. Jopling are characteristic. In June, 1881, she lost her eldest son, Percy Romer, and in December, 1889, her husband was also taken from her.

To Mrs. Jopling.

"2 PALACE GATE, KENSINGTON,
"*June 5th,* 1881.

"DEAR MRS. JOPLING, — Sophy tells me you would like a line from me. What to say, more than that you have been in my thoughts?

"When George [Millais' second son] died, I felt grateful for my work. Get you as soon as possible to your easel, as the surest means, not to forget, but to occupy your mind wholesomely and even happily.

"Yours affectionately,

"JOHN MILLAIS."

Another artist who was frequently at Cornwall Place was Henry O'Neil, R. A., an intimate friend of both Millais and Phillip, and a painter of pictures that seldom failed to catch the fancy of the public. He was a martyr to gout and somewhat choleric, but withal a most kind-hearted man. A philanthropist, too, in his way — one of the Old Club type — and not without some pretension as a poet. Indeed, much of his leisure time must have been spent in the writing of verses; for he was constantly sending them to Millais or his wife with a quaint little note, such as this: — " I send you my latest song — I hope not the worst. I get yearly the first primrose from a maiden aged seventy, whom for thirty years I have reverenced on account of her filial duty. Don't be angry with me for not calling. I have not put a shoe on for months." This note is dated March, 1876, and the tender sentiment of the song enclosed in it strongly appeals to me for admission. But I must limit myself to but two specimens of O' Neil's muse.

In quite another vein is the following " Reflection," with which he writes: — " I have had another note from Froude anent Mary Stuart's last words. He thinks I have not made her defiant. I never yet heard of defiance on the bed of

1 — 28

death.   In the picture I am painting of Mary at Loch Leven,
there shall be no want of defiance."

A REFLECTION.

" In Youth, I wandered over Westbourne Plain,
    And fed my eye on buttercups and daisies.
In Age, I wander on the path again :
    Daisies and buttercups are gone to blazes,
And, in their stead, I see a beastly lot
    Of stucco villas built upon the spot.

"Thus marches ' Progress ' — ever to destroy
    (From what is called ' Necessity ') all things
That from their very nature gave us joy.
    And said cursed ' Progress ' never brings
The pleasure which, once felt, can come no more.
    'T is easy to destroy.   But — how restore ? "

O'Neil was fond of cards, in which Millais occasionally
joined him at the Garrick Club.   He refers to this in an
amusing squib on sprats, from which I subjoin a few stanzas.

SPRATS.

" A wealthy man prefers a Severn Salmon ;
    The poor man is content with humble Sprats.
To one, aught but Champagne is simply gammon ;
    The other is content with Barclay's vats.
Except that one is cheap and t'other dear,
What special virtue has Champagne o'er Beer?

" In my young days two guineas I have spent
    On models — to produce a priceless gem.
To gilder's hands another guinea went.
    I looked to connoisseurs for gain.   Drat them !
For when I 'd done the utmost I could do,
I sold my priceless gem for two pounds two.

" That, as the Proverb says, may be as bad
    As baiting herring just to catch a sprat ;
But in the process there was nothing bad :
    I lost a guinea, and don't care for that.
Making a fortune has not been my forte,
And men must pay a trifle for their sport.

" Poor I have been, and poor shall ever be,
    Whilst Millais plays with me at ' Fifteen two.'
Champagne and Hock have little charm for me,
    Nor Bass, nor Barclay can my stomach woo ;
So I rely on Leotia's whiskey dairies,
And tone their potence by Apollinaris.

" St. Peter was a fisherman, 't is said,
  And no doubt fond of fish ; but yet the Sprat
  Judæa's lakes tried not, nor Sea called ' Dead.'
    I think there 's something to be made of that ;
  For when I 'm dead, with Peter I 'll be even,
  And, with a Sprat for fee, sneak into Heaven."

Fred Walker, the famous artist (now, alas, no more), was also a most intimate friend of Millais, and beloved by all the family; as well he might be, for he was the very soul of goodness and human sympathy. Unhappily for himself, he was so sensitive that an adverse word from the critics would crush him to the ground. In my father's estimation he was the finest water-colour painter of the century, a genius of the highest order, intensely alive to the poetry of Nature, and supreme in his power of expressing it; and now that he is gone the whole world seems disposed to share this sentiment. His favourite amusement was fishing, and during the seventies, when he was a frequent visitor at Perth, this was his great delight. It was at Stobhall that, under my father's guidance, he first became acquainted with the salmon; and a bad time he had of it upon one occasion. While fishing off a rock, he got hold of a real big one, and was so wildly excited that he fell head over ears into the water, and would probably have been drowned but for a timely rescue. My aunt, Mrs. Stibbard, has a delightful drawing by him, illustrating " The Temptation of St. Anthony Walker."

Again, when deep-sea fishing at St. Andrews, he had a narrow escape from drowning. He was in a boat with Millais and his family, and about two miles from the shore, when a gale suddenly sprang up and drifted them towards dangerous rocks. Having no sail, their only chance of escape was to pull for their lives through these two miles of raging sea; and they did it, though the hard work took the skin off poor Walker's hands, and he was quite exhausted when they reached the harbour. Habitually nervous as he was, on this occasion he never for a moment lost his self-possession.

Then there was Owen, simplest of men and most learned of comparative anatomists — "dear old Owen," as we used to call him, and rightly so, for he was a friend of the whole family, and his kindness to the younger members could hardly have been greater if they had been his own children.

Many a time did he take my brothers and myself to the
big museum in Bloomsbury, and discourse to us on subjects
that caught our fancy, making even dry old bones live
again under the spell of his marvellous revelations.   In
his own house, too, at Richmond, he made us heartily
welcome whenever we chose to go.   It was after one of
our visits there that this charming letter of his was sent to
my mother : —

From Professor Owen.

" SHEEN LODGE, RICHMOND PARK, S. W.,

" *December* 22*nd,* 1869.

" DEAR MRS. MILLAIS, — To whom can one open one's heart
but to the young and guileless?   At least in my den here,
where I study so many and such varieties of natures,
affected by time and the battle of life.   Ah ! it will come
quite soon enough upon them, the dear lads !

" Well, I 'm glad they felt that I wanted to make their
visit profitable.   But they *must* be *up* in their 'Seven
Wonders' when they next put in an appearance.

" We have had our share of weather damage, and
Caroline is now laid up with her cold ; but I must have
laid such a healthy layer of 'epithelial scales' on my bron-
chial tubes in Egypt that I repelled the first attack of frost
speedily.

" With every good wish to Millais and yourself and all
those about your Christmas hearth,

" I remain, always truly yours,

" RICHARD OWEN."

And finally Browning, musician and poet — " the most
unpopular poet that ever was," as he describes himself in
one of his letters, and yet a singer of so high a merit that
a special cult is now devoted to the study and dissemination
of his works.   It was early in 1862 — shortly after the death
of his wife (Elizabeth Barrett Browning), who, like himself,
was a distinguished poet — that Millais and he first came
together ; and, as might be expected of two such congenial
spirits, their acquaintance speedily ripened into a firm and
lasting friendship.

MRS. HEUGH. 1872

By permission of Mr. J Orrock

The two following letters will, I think, be read with interest now that both the writer and those whom he addressed have passed away forever. Browning's views on the art of poetry, as expressed in the first of these letters, were called forth by a letter from my mother, who submitted for his opinion and advice a poem by a young friend of hers, who had some thought of a literary career. The second letter, too, demands a word of explanation. Browning's son, Penn, having determined to follow Art as a profession, my father, who took great interest in the boy, gave him all the help in his power, and (I trust I am betraying no secret in saying this) considerably improved his first picture.

From Robert Browning.

" 19 WARWICK CRESCENT,
" UPPER WESTBOURNE TERRACE,
"*January 7th*, 1867.

" DEAR MRS. MILLAIS, — I hardly know what to advise about the poems. All depends on the state of development in which the writer's mind may be ; because, if these pieces were ultimates, so to speak, and the productions of maturity, one would have to say that in Poetry, by ancient prescript, only the best is bearable, and these are not *best* in any salient point of originality, thought, or expression. On the other hand, if they are the beginnings, really and truly, of the author, I could hope for a good deal in the end from the very imperfections of what is given here. There is a distinct conception in each piece — something the writer had in mind to say before beginning — and the working-out of the same has been a matter of less importance. There is not the usual *using up* of the effect produced by a sympathy with somebody else's poetry, which people suppose to be a spontaneous effect of their own minds, and treat accordingly. Above all, there is not the usual *singing away* till, peradventure, some thought or other turn up in the course of it ; that is, the thought suggests the tune, not the tune the thought. But there is hardly more than the impulse toward the right direction, I think — not any so positive excellence as to make one cry that the mark is hit, unless, perhaps, in some of the capital verses for children, 'The Baby House,' for instance.

" All this means only that I am certain that the writer is
too poetically-minded a person (let the worst come to the
worst) to be consigned to any rank below that of the strivers
after the best ; and those who only want to be better than
this, or no worse than that of the hundreds of rhyme-makers
' going,' might honestly be complimented on the prettiness of
such a performance. But wherever there is a chance of
getting a bird of the true sort, one finds the heart to say,
' Don't twitter, though all the sparrows do, but sing,' since
such things happen sometimes, and then we get a lark or a
nightingale, or even an owl, which last is by no means to be
despised. Moreover, you here have the opinion of the most
unpopular poet that ever was, and so will be sure not to
mind too much the sour sayings of the like of him! If the
writer continues to feel and think as earnestly as now, and
lets the feeling and thought take the words and music they
immediately suggest, just as if the experiment of expression
were being tried for the first time, not neglecting meanwhile
the mechanical helps to this in the way of proper studies both
of Nature and Art, as well as the secret of the effectiveness
of whatever poetry *does* affect the said author (not repeating
nor copying those ' effects,' but finding out, I mean, *why*
they prove to be effects, and so learning how to become
similarly effective), I don't see why success might not be
hoped for; and then it is success worth getting.

" There, my dear Mrs. Millais! Could one but help anybody never so infinitesimally! I give true good wishes to the
author, in any case.　　　Very faithfully yours,

" ROBERT BROWNING."

From the same.

" 19 WARWICK CRESCENT,
" *May 10th*, 1878.

" MY BELOVED MILLAIS, — You will be gladdened in the
kind heart of you to learn that Penn's picture has been bought
by Mr. Fielder — a perfect stranger to both of us. You
know what your share has been in his success, and it cannot
but do a world of good to a young fellow whose fault was
never that of being insensible to an obligation.

" Ever affectionately yours,

" ROBERT BROWNING."

MRS. JOPLING. 1870

By permission of Mrs. Jopling-Rowe

Browning, needless to say, was always a welcome guest at Palace Gate, and when the occasion called for it no one enjoyed more than he any bit of nonsense that might arise. One evening after dinner the guests amused themselves by trying who could get the most words into a given space with some old stumps of pens that Millais had cast aside as useless, when Browning produced the following as the result of his effort: —

> " I sprang to the stirrup, and Joris and he ;
> I galloped, Dirck galloped, we galloped all three.
> ' God-speed ! ' cried the gate as the gate-bolts undrew
> ' Speed ! ' echoed the wall to us, galloping through.
> Then the . . . . . . (*illegible*)
> As into the midnight we galloped abreast.
> " ROBERT BROWNING, *June 4th*, 1882."

And here, I think, may be fitly introduced a paper by Mrs. Jopling — now Mrs. Jopling-Rowe — which with her habitual kindness and consideration, she has sent me as a contribution to this work. It is entitled —

" RECOLLECTIONS OF SIR JOHN MILLAIS.

" The first time I saw John Everett Millais was at one of the private views of the old masters at Burlington House. I was walking with a mutual friend. ' Here comes Millais,' he said. You can imagine my excitement. I stared with all my eyes. My friend said, ' Good show of old masters ! ' ' Old masters be bothered ! I prefer looking at the young mistresses ! ' said Millais, with a humorous glance at me as he walked off. My companion roared with laughter. ' There is only Johnny Millais who would dare make a remark like that ! '

" I remember his telling me an incident that happened to himself. He was dining out, and, of course, sitting next the hostess. On his right was a charming Society woman, who evidently had not caught his name when he was introduced to her, for she presently, during a pause, started the usual subject of conversation in May — the Academy. ' Is n't Millais too dreadful this year ? ' And then, seeing the agonized contortions on her hostess's countenance, she said, ' Oh, do tell me what I 've done. Look at Mrs. ——'s face ! I must have said or done something terrible.' ' Well,' laughed Millais, ' you really have, you know.' ' Oh, please,

tell me.' 'Better nerve yourself to hear. Drink this glass
of sherry first.' 'Yes, yes; now what is it? For answer
Millais said nothing, but, looking at her, pointed solemnly
to himself. When it dawned upon her who her neighbour
was, she was spared any confusion by Millais' hearty laughter
at her *mal-à-propos* speech.

"Millais was godfather to my boy, and Sir Coutts Lindsay was the other one. We had registered the infant as
'Everett Millais Lindsay.' I was not present at the
christening, but when he and my husband came back to
the house, he said to me, 'Look here, Mrs. Joe, we have
called the boy 'Lindsay Millais.' It will be so much nicer
when he is in love, for his girl to call him Lindsay. Lindsay
is so much softer than Everett, don't you think so?' I
only thought it was like the modest delicacy of the man, who
hated, even in a trifle like this, to be prominently put before
anyone else.

"For many years he came every year to criticise the work
we were sending in to the Academy, and no man in the
world has ever given such frank, truthful, and kindly
criticism. 'Yes, yes, very good; but——' And the 'but'
was invaluable. Then it was, 'Have n't you got any more
work! I like to see lots, you know!'

"In the same way he accepted criticism on his own work
—frankly, heartily, and gratefully. 'Oh! a fresh eye is the
thing. Now, tell me, is there anything else you see?'

"Ah, what a genius — what a man! And what delightful
moments were those spent on Sunday morning in his
studio, when he welcomed any artistic friend. After talking
pictures, he would always say, 'Well, what's the news?'
He loved to hear news of his friends; and, unlike most
traffickers of news, he never said or thought an ill-natured
thing of any living soul. He always recognised the good
points of his friends as he would the beauties of Nature.

"When he made a joke one saw it coming in the humorous
twinkle his eye gave forth, as when he said to me when
he was painting my portrait, 'Ah, my godson! I never
gave him a cup at his christening, so I'll give him the
"mug" of his mother now.'

"He painted my portrait in the extraordinary short time
of five sittings. In his generous way he wished to divide
the credit. 'Ah, it takes a good sitter to make a good
portrait. If you had not sat so well, I should n't have made

such a good thing of it, but'—then he would laugh—'I
nearly killed you, you know!' For the five consecutive days'
standing had really knocked me up.

" The Princess of Wales said to him once, whilst looking
at several pictures in his studio, 'I wonder you can bear
to part with them, Mr. Millais.' 'Oh, ma'am,' answered
Millais, 'when I finish a picture, I am just like a hen having
laid an egg; I cry; "Come and take it away! come and
take it away!" And then I start upon another picture.'

" The Royal Family were most sympathetic to him in his
last illness. I remember coming away from seeing him one
day, after having had a one-sided conversation with him—I
talking and he responding on the slate he had to use when
his voice failed him. A thought struck me that it seemed a
pity to erase the last sayings of so rare a being. I was due
at a sale of work at the Royal School of Art Needlework,
and at Princess Christian's stall I looked about for an
appropriate note-book, which might in after days be held
precious to those (and there were many) who loved John
Millais. On making my want known to the Princess, she
immediately said, 'Oh! let *me* give it him. I should like to
so much!' I asked her to write her name in it, which she
immediately did, and I took it back to the dear patient.

" He was most true in his appreciation of other men's work,
and preferred that which was very highly finished. I think
he bought an example of Tito Contis simply for the reason of
its high finish. He was a great admirer of Mr. Marcus
Stone's work. I never once heard him disparage another
man's work. If he had nothing good to say about it he said
nothing. He was always delighted to come across anyone
who had a love of Art. Even young children or rank outsiders he would notice. After a visit from them, he would
say, 'Ah! I noticed So-and-so had quite intelligent views
about Art. He must be fond of pictures.'

" His power of aptly illustrating his meaning was unsurpassed. When I started my School of Art I consulted with Sir
John about it, and asked his opinion as to whether it would be
a good thing to teach by 'demonstration,' *i.e.*, to paint a
head from the model in one sitting before the pupils. 'Why,
of course,' said Millais, 'that is the best way. If I wanted
to teach a man how to play billiards, I would n't correct each
stroke he made; I would take the cue myself and show him
how to hit the ball.'   L. JOPLING-ROWE."

A little reminiscence of sport *à la Française* may fitly conclude this desultory chapter. In the early seventies Millais and his wife were staying with Baron Marochetti at his place, the Château de Vaux, near Passy — a fine old castle in admirable preservation that recalled, as my mother used to say, " Four grey walls and four grey towers overlooking a space of flowers." Knowing Millais' love of sport, the Baron got up a shooting party for him, aided by his eldest son, Maurice, now the Italian Ambassador to Russia.

Early in the morning the whole house was awakened with the tootling of horns and the barking of dogs ; and greatly amused were the guests when, on going to the windows, they discovered the meaning of this excitement. It was all in honour of " Brer Rabbit." Ferrets had already paid him a visit, and now he was to be waited on by the owner of the castle and his friends, who were at that moment assembled in the courtyard, attired in gorgeous Lincoln-green coats, high boots with tassels, slouch hats with feathers, and every man of them with a huge curly horn slung on his back, to say nothing of a cartridge belt and a gun.

At the appointed time, when everyone was down and had breakfasted, the party adjourned to the scene of action. Each sportsman was provided with a kitchen chair at the *position favorable*, and there he sat and awaited his prey. Then bang went the gun, and if successful the gunner proclaimed the fact by a performance on his horn. Such is (or was) " sport," as translated into French. *Vive la chasse!*